THE PEARL OF ANTON

THE PEARL OF
ANTON

BY GENE DEL VECCHIO

PELICAN PUBLISHING COMPANY
Gretna 2004

*The word "Pelican" and the depiction of a pelican are trademarks
of Pelican Publishing Company, Inc., and are registered
in the U.S. Patent and Trademark Office.*

Library of Congress Cataloging-in-Publication Data

Del Vecchio, Gene.
  The Pearl of Anton / by Gene Del Vecchio.
      p. cm.
   Summary: Jason Del struggles to master himself and the Pearl of
Anton in order to defend humanity in the Final Contest.
   ISBN 1-58980-172-5 (hardcover : alk. paper)
   [1. Fantasy.] I. Title.
PZ7.D3897 Pe 2004
[Fic]—dc22
                                                        2003020930

Printed in the United States of America

Published by Pelican Publishing Company, Inc.
1000 Burmaster Street, Gretna, Louisiana 70053

To Linda, Matthew, Megan, Angelo, and Madeline, for their endless support. To Rod, for illustrating the jacket. To Jenny, who came to my aid in an hour of need. To Pelican Publishing Company, for the gracious support they continue to provide. And finally, to all Dels of noble blood, particularly those few who know of their true lineage.

TRINITY

N. Pass

Valley of
Despair

W. Pass

E. Pass

Frantic
Lake

Northlands

Death Road

Fortress High

Desert of Zak

Mountain
High

Unexplored
Westlands
←

Mountain Marsh

Torsen ●

Crystal River

Unknown
→

Zol ●

Old Road

Enchanted
Forest

Charity ●

Gate's
Keep

Misty Plains

Lone Tower

Great Swamp

Meadowtown ●

Stone Forest

Swamp Lands

**Circle of
Wisdom** ●

Endur ●

Spirit Lake

Plains of
Temptation

Unexplored
South
↓

Note: Some scholars believe that Trinity was located in what became
Mesopotamia. Others believe it was in northern Italy.

CONTENTS

TRINITY

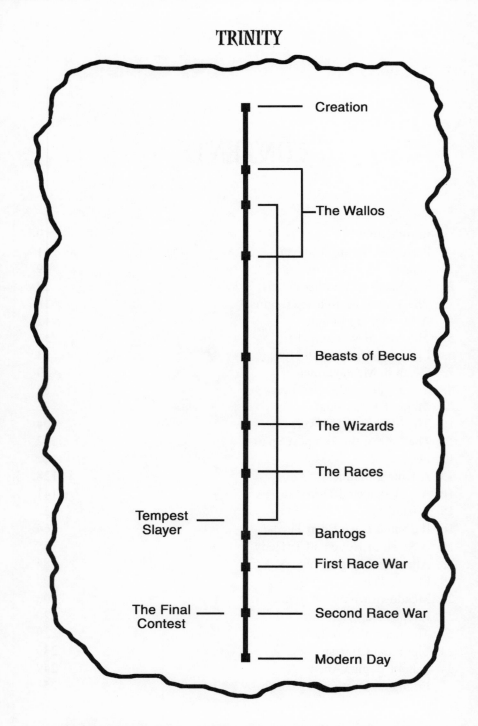

- Creation
- The Wallos
- Beasts of Becus
- The Wizards
- The Races
- Tempest Slayer
- Bantogs
- First Race War
- The Final Contest
- Second Race War
- Modern Day

Note: Timeline is not to scale. For example, the Beasts of Becus lived in Trinity for millions of years. However, fewer than one hundred thousand years separate the Final Contest from Modern Day.

INTRODUCTION

For many years, my family lived in the quiet, comforting obscurity of middle-class cottages in middle-class townships in middle-class provinces. But it wasn't always so. Before Athens surrendered to Sparta or the Etruscan civilization began, before even the Halaf settled in the upper region of Mesopotamia, my family's name was prominent among the peoples that inhabited the known lands. That was long before the *Vecchio* was added to our surname, when we were known as simply *Del,* a handle without clear ethnicity or origin. It was also a time when the Races were true Races and not merely variants of Man, when great prizes were won and lost—and then won again.

The historical accounts of my family during those ancient times were committed to the glorious Book of Endur. I herein offer one story from that collection for your consideration. It is entitled *The Pearl of Anton.* It begins with a prologue written several thousand years before the account of the Pearl and then ends with an epilogue written a few years after the account. I hope you find it intriguing.

Gene Del Vecchio

PROLOGUE: TEMPEST SLAYER

A History from the Book of Endur,
Submitted during the Watch of Tara

In the closing shadow of the Second Age, I, Tara from the race of Etha, witnessed the last of the Great Beasts of Becus devastate nearly all of Eastern Trinity. The huge creature was scaly black, with leathery wings that could lift its massive frame in a graceful but deadly flight. Its elongated skull held two narrow eyes, each crystalline red. Below these cunning slits was a gaping mouth with two rows of glistening sharp teeth that sparked its death fire: a blaze of red that charred all that stood before it. If the creature's unfortunate prey did not fall by either fangs or fire, then it was sure to succumb to either the beast's ripping talons that extended well beyond its four muscular feet, or its heavy tail that swept before it like a whip. Though dragonlike, it was not a dragon, as it was much greater in evil and strength and probing mind.

The Races called it Tempest.

Its only purpose was to destroy all that was good, all that was living, all that was made by a god other than its own. But having ravaged the east, which was now but a barren and forsaken land, the wicked beast turned its attention toward the fertile west, final refuge of the Races.

During the early years of the Tempest's new quest, a boy lived in obscurity along the western banks of the mighty Crystal River. His name was Matthew Del, last blood of the great Royal House. And within his possession, handed down since almost the Beginning, was the Wizard's Stone, brilliantly white and awesome in power. But the boy did not know the secret of its power, which troubled him greatly. Nonetheless, his heavy responsibility, also handed down through the countless ages, remained: to rid the land of evil.

At my urging, the boy carried out the plan as taught to him by his loving father, who mysteriously disappeared years before and was given up for dead. Matthew sparked the Tempest's hunger and lured it cunningly through the Ancient Forest of Oak. The strong trees would serve to constrict the beast's impatient, yearning wings. The lad was careful, his steps not so far ahead of the beast that it tired of the chase, nor so close that the creature could hurl its probing mind forth to touch the boy's thoughts and discover his plan. For Matthew was leading the Tempest purposefully to the long abandoned Circle of Wisdom, a granite slab measuring one hundred paces long and ten feet high. It was a place where a thousand Dels had perished before. But it was also at the Circle, Matthew knew, that the Wizard's *Trinket* was fabled to be at its most powerful and where he would find his only hope.

Matthew broke through the forest and sped across the great clearing, climbed upon the Circle, and gained the centermost position among the rubble. Even from the distance where I stood, I could feel Matthew's dread. The beast pushed its way through the restricting green and rose to the air, defiling the sky with its presence and gliding eagerly to the Circle to face the boy. With the closing of distance, the beast threw its probing mind forth to touch the boy's thoughts, which pained Matthew greatly. In so doing, evil discovered his plan. But the beast was not disheartened, for it uncovered a thought within the boy that was comforting to its purpose.

"I have felt your mind, foolish child!" I heard the Tempest shriek. "Now let me hear your words."

Matthew drew a steady breath, and thinking of his father, he spoke with brave words.

"I am the last descendant of the Royal House of Del. It is here that a thousand ancestors cry out in pain and death that your kind inflicted. And it is here that I will destroy thee . . . the last of the mighty Tempests."

The beast was unaffected. It meticulously surveyed the horizon until it was content with the misty, gray silence that veiled the Circle. Only then did evil shriek again.

"Your mind betrays you. You possess the Stone, but not the knowledge needed to kill my flesh. The *Trinket* you carry is therefore useless."

The words stung Matthew, for they were true. But his eyes steadied, for he still felt comforted that the Wizard's power would not forsake him.

"Today, demon, you will die. My stricken father said it would be so."

The Tempest sneered. "Foolish boy. Tomorrow I won't even remember if your flesh tasted sweet or foul."

The Tempest lurched upward. It then swooped down toward Matthew Del, the beast's cold shadow blocking the sun. A Tempest fire blasted forth. Matthew saw a blaze of red sizzle the air before him, growing closer. Trembling, he stood his ground as fear gripped his soul. He raised the gleaming, white Stone and, in his moment of need, the power rushed from it in a blinding flash. It prevented the demon's blast from scorching him. As the boy shook with power, the Tempest grew angrier but remained confident, knowing that the boy did not know the full secret of the treasure in his hand. As the beast turned and prepared for its next attack, it again examined all things upon the Circle and beyond. Again it was content. So again it struck.

Many times the Stone blasted forth to protect the boy, but Matthew trembled with worry, for the Stone rarely sought the Tempest's own flesh. Instead, it merely deflected the beast's fierce blows. After many encounters, the Stone appeared to falter, and to the boy's dismay, the Stone's strength gradually seemed to recoil under the Tempest's might. In another fearsome blast of Tempest fire, the white glistening sphere, still clenched in Matthew's hand, was suddenly engulfed in the beast's blaze. At that moment, when Wizard's white magic touched evil's flames, an intense explosion threw Matthew back in a gale of blistering heat. The beast turned and landed.

At that moment, I knew that Matthew cursed Anton, the creator, for he believed now that the Wizard's Stone was not a suitable match for the power of evil. Could legends have been wrong?

The beast stood triumphant; its red eyes sparkled with pleasure. Dark-green saliva dripped from its mouth and baked the stones beneath it. It wrapped its tail about the boy and squeezed tightly to keep Matthew fixed. The beast then inhaled a mighty wind in preparation for its final death fire.

Matthew closed his eyes, even though his charred hand stayed aloft. The remnants of Wizard's magic danced about his fist. But it was over for him, he believed. He had failed Trinity. He had failed his father. He had failed himself. And so he waited to die. A moment passed, yet nothing happened. He heard the beast suddenly pivot, stumbling amidst the debris. Strange, the boy thought, but still he waited. And still nothing happened. The Tempest moved frantically again and began to wail. It uncoiled its tail, setting Matthew free.

The boy opened his eyes and saw the creature flailing and jerking in death's grip, its head and neck twisted in an attempt to reach something behind it. It stumbled farther away, and turned this time to reveal the shadow of a Man straddling its back, holding firm. The figure suddenly brandished a brilliant Sword. The Tempest snapped wildly, but it was no use. It was unable to reach the Man upon it. The Man then turned the Sword and drove it inward to where the beast's neck met its spine. The thrashing Tempest twisted almost into itself, but it could not unseat its attacker.

Matthew, still helpless amidst the rubble, continued to look upon the sight with startled eyes. Who was this Man? Who was this savior?

The raging beast bolted upward for the safety of the sky, diving and circling. The Man held firm, plunging the Sword deeper and deeper into its lurching body. Then, when the blade was embedded up to its hilt, the rider shouted to the boy.

"Now! . . . The Stone seeks the Sword. . . . Now!"

And as those words rang out, the hand that held the Stone trembled and stretched skyward. Heat surged through Matthew's body. Then, a light, white and blinding, poured from his fist and rose to the sky, up through the belly of the Tempest to find the Sword. As the power hit, a great burst of energy rocked the Circle. The demon exploded in a rush of dazzling white power. Its rider was thrown clear. Matthew Del collapsed. As quickly as it came, the force that had come from the Wizard's Stone subsided and was gone.

I was near when the boy woke. A great calm hung in the air, though smoke and ash continued to filter a new day's light. A Man, battered and broken, knelt beside the boy, dabbing his brow with soothing water.

"You were brave, my son."

Confused, Matthew looked up into the eyes of his father. Johnna Del spoke quickly.

"The secret to killing a Tempest, my son, is to form an alliance of two. The first to lure the beast to the Circle and to be protected by the Stone. The second to gain the back of the beast, its only weakness, and to thrust the Sword of Wizards inward. And finally, the first again to bring the power of the Stone to life."

But a deep sadness gripped the boy.

"Why did you make me believe you were dead? For all those years . . . "

The words bit the father. "Remember, the evil reads the minds of those it pursues. If you knew how to kill it, or that I lived, the beast would know it also. Instead, it knew only what you knew to be true: verily, that I was dead, that you were alone, and that you knew not how to kill a Tempest. It was the perfect trap . . . the only way."

Johnna Del then lifted his son and followed me to a secret place within the Circle to heal his wounds. As Matthew groaned in his father's arms, he sought momentary comfort in the Stone, still held tight in his blackened, charred fist. But no comfort was forthcoming. The Stone no longer glowed brilliantly white. Instead, it cast a strange, lifeless gray. It appeared to be emptied of its power. Nothing in Trinity, not even Tempest fire, should have affected it as such. This was not a transformation to be taken lightly, especially by my people—the Etha.

It has been written by my mother's mother, however, that many ages will pass beyond the span of Matthew Del, Tempest Slayer. Each age will take a great toll on the Races, at times renewing their strength, and at times destroying their will. But nothing will compare to the darkest day, a day when two Great Evils—a Pure Evil and an Evil Less than Pure—will come to claim Trinity for their own. It is said that a Chosen One will spring from the Royal House to battle them both, wielding the Wizard's *Trinket,* whose riddle he will resolve. And more. The Chosen One will seek and find the long-lost Pearl of Anton, its mysterious force adding mightily to the power of the Stone.

May our Lord Anton bless and protect the Chosen One from wherever he may rise. He is our refuge, our peace, our final hope for the Race children of Trinity.

Faithfully,
Tara

THE PEARL OF
ANTON

CHAPTER 1

SCHOOL

The small stone-built schoolhouse seemed to have always been there, for no one could remember when it was not. Its longevity, so legend says, was attributed to a liquid-rock substance that was oozed between its rounded boulders until an ancient sun dried it tightly, fixing each stone smoothly and forever in place. Just outside the school sat a huge founder's rock, rising just higher than a full Man-height. And near the speckled stone's summit were deeply carved, intricate letters. While the words were now foreign to all who read them, their meaning, like the schoolhouse, had somehow survived the eons: *Children Five to Fifteen Learn Here.*

The inside of the schoolhouse proved as timeless as without. Forty small and well-worn desks were carefully aligned within, each made of the same heavy, knotted wood that comprised the school's massive double doors. The desks faced the front of the room, where a large fireplace lay comfortably embedded in the center of the stone wall. Other objects, carefully preserved, were hung about the small room in an orderly fashion: two paintings by a long-forgotten artist, a yellowing map of Trinity, strange metal etchings from foreign lands, even a few arrow points from wars long ago resolved. But the age of these items paled in comparison to the piece of furniture that rested to the right of the fireplace. It was another desk, huge in girth, that faced the small ones authoritatively. The grain of its ancient wood swirled to form haunting images of earlier times: of People remembered, of Races forgotten, of events greatly remote in geography. The desk was also unbelievably heavy, made from a single cut of wood far too large to have ever passed through the school's doors. That led some in Meadowtown to speculate that the schoolhouse was actually built around the desk. Others, however, argued the point with some vigor. Regardless, there was a certain air about the desk, and everyone agreed that it was a special piece; an ancient seat reserved for authority and respect and knowledge.

It was a place reserved for Teacher, an Etha from the fortress city of Endur. As all that Race, she was eternally stern, a person devoted only to histories. Her rigid commitment, though, was in stark contrast to her beauty, also legendary among the Etha. She had deep-blue eyes, the pupils of which were a bit larger than a human's own, making them much more penetrating. They were framed perfectly by her silky white hair, which was always drawn tightly back into a bun, highlighting her smooth alabaster skin. While she looked to be a woman of thirty, she had taught at the old schoolhouse considerably longer; in fact, she had been the teacher for nearly everyone in Meadowtown, making her years a common topic for inquisitive minds. Teacher wore the same garment daily: a forest-green robe, beautiful in design and detail. It fit her slender frame perfectly.

In the Fourth Age since the fall of the Beasts of Becus, school was in session. Some of the children were rather striking, with finely tailored clothes, well-groomed hair, and herb-scented skin. Others were less so. But in class, all were equal as they worked to complete their individual lesson plans. The younger ones practiced their alphabet. The older children were deep in mathematics: the conversion of weights, the figuring of sums, the ciphering of coins and barter. These were the calculations that would serve them well in later years as enterprising farmers or craftsmen.

Teacher knew them every bit as much as their own families did, some even better. She also knew exactly what they were doing, whether she looked up from her own studies or not. Through the corner of her exacting eyes on this particular afternoon, Teacher saw a love note pass quietly from a young boy to an older girl. The girl smiled to herself when she read it, but managed to conceal her delight with an expression of indifference, thus crushing the lad who sent it. One obnoxious boy made a hideous face at another from across the room. The expression was returned twofold. Yet another lad drew an unflattering picture of Teacher, which he promptly, but discreetly, showed his neighbors. One chuckle erupted then vanished. Teacher knew that also. As the afternoon wore on and the students were nearing their exhaustion point, a hush fell over the schoolroom.

Then, a ten-year-old boy with dusty-brown hair and eager eyes began to rigorously wave his hand.

"Yes?" Teacher asked while she continued reading.

"May I add to the fire?" a boy named Squeki Joh asked from the last row.

Teacher glanced over her shoulder at the fireplace's retreating flame. She nodded, and noticed restlessness growing.

Squeki rose quickly and sped up the aisle. He was small for his age and smart too. He was also the Mayor's son, which often compelled the boy to act as class volunteer. It was a role that he cherished. But that alone could not protect him from the trials of being smaller.

A pointed leather shoe abruptly appeared from under a desk, tripping Squeki. He fell hard to the rock floor. At the sound of his stumbling fall, laughter erupted all around. With a spiteful gleam in his eye, Ben Wateri, one of the oldest boys in the class at fifteen, eased his foot slowly back under his desk. He continued to slump in his chair, twiddling his quill as Squeki rose.

"Enough!" Teacher said in a stern voice. The time had come for more order. She studied her students. "What happened?"

Squeki glanced at Ben. This was the price he paid for being the older boy's *friend*. "Ah . . . nothing . . . just my own big feet," he answered.

Teacher's eyes flashed at Ben and then back to Squeki.

"Then continue," she commanded, returning to her book and seemingly annoyed more at Squeki's answer than his accident. Squeki put a log on the flame and returned to his seat.

After a few moments, Teacher snapped her book shut. She rose gracefully from behind her massive desk, her delicate hands clasped before her.

"History," she said coolly. "What event concluded the Second Race War?"

The room went silent. Several of the children, particularly those in the back of the classroom, slowly positioned their heads behind the students in front of them, avoiding Teacher's questioning gaze.

"Ben Wateri!" Teacher called keenly.

Caught, Ben straightened in his chair. Teacher was one of the few people in Meadowtown who still frightened him. The boy cleared his throat and attempted a reply as his black, straight hair fell downward, hiding his scheming eyes.

"The Second Race War ended when some Major got everybody to sign a treaty . . . or something." Ben looked up.

A deep silence filled the small schoolhouse. The children waited. Would Teacher be satisfied? An icy moment passed.

"Who else?" Teacher asked as she began tapping her right foot.

Ben reddened. The big boy scanned the classroom, silently warning the others not to attempt an answer. Dozens of frightened eyes retreated to desktops.

"Who else?" demanded Teacher again, her voice more compelling. The question hung uncomfortably in the air. The fire crackled and popped loudly, sending red glowing cinders up the flue. But still they waited. And just as Ben began to feel some small triumph, a solitary arm began to rise timidly in the air. The leathery hand mirrored the boy's modest clothing. He wore a thick, loosely woven, gray cotton tunic that used assorted beads as buttons. It was tied off with a rope belt cinched tight. His brown pants were wool, worn and faded. His shoes, however, were solidly made: the benefit of being a shoemaker's son. But most striking was his straight red hair that he tied back in a small tail, high-lighting his sharp, green eyes.

The boy, also fifteen, tried to keep focused on Teacher, though he could not help but see Ben through the corner of his eyes. Ben subtly shook his fist. The red-headed boy shivered and jerked his hand down. But it was too late.

"Jason Del!" called Teacher.

His love of history had gotten the best of him again, Jason thought. He rose slowly to his feet, keeping his gaze downward. Maybe if he was quick about it, he reasoned, Ben might let him get through the rest of the day unscathed. He slightly trembled.

The children waited to see if Jason's answer would be better than Ben's. But they already knew. Jason knew a lot about history, plenty more than a shoemaker's son needed to know.

Jason cleared his throat uncomfortably, glanced about, and began to speak. And although his voice was soft and fragile, his love of legend sparkled in his eyes with a vigor that rivaled even Teacher's.

"As Elf and Dwarf armies were locked in battle with each other, Major T, leader of the Mountain High Battalion, marched with his army of Men for three days straight, without rest, through a frozen wilderness. He outmaneuvered the warring Dwarf and Elf armies and intercepted their food-supply wagons, until both of the Northern Races were nearly devastated by the winter. His strategy forced the Elves and Dwarves to sign the Triad Agreement, forged by the Great Tribunal, requiring that each Race stay within its separate lands. That was thirty years ago—almost to the day."

Jason had known this story by heart since he was a small child, having learned it, and many others, from his father, one of the remaining veterans of the actual battle. Jason always felt there was something rather special about the conclusion of the Second Race War. It was an inspiring ending because brave and rugged backwoodsmen banded together to end a war between the Dwarves and Elves, a war that was not Man's own. This was a noble conclusion—if there is such a thing in war—that would allow it to live much longer than most stories—and, just perhaps, allow it to find its way into the realm of legends, along with the great Major T, who inspired Men to risk their lives to prevent the other Races from annihilating each other.

"Well done," said Teacher, almost proudly. "Well done."

Jason lowered himself back into his chair. He loved this room—the endless questions in search of answers, the paper that demanded its ink—the mysteries that sought discovery. Everything within these particular four walls had order and a sense of purpose, a feeling of eternity that could never be erased.

Teacher continued to stare at him after he settled into his seat. The room remained silent. Jason began to fidget under the unwanted gaze. He noticed a thin smile reach her lips, followed by a subtle nod of her chin. These were signs of approval, he thought. This was very strange coming from an Etha. Jason wondered what it meant. A distant bell then rang out twice, signifying the close of business within the marketplace of Meadowtown, and with it the close of the school day. The children looked up at Teacher, waiting anxiously to be officially released, knowing that while the bell governed the craftsmen and farmers, Teacher still governed them. She continued to gaze at Jason. He squirmed lower in his seat. The students' eyes darted about, but Teacher still gave no notice of the bell's receding echo. A moment passed, then another. The children were about to explode.

"No lessons tonight . . . go!" she said, and then turned around to straighten up her desk.

There was a burst of energy as the children flew out the door.

"You be careful, Jase," Squeki Joh said to Jason. "You know how Ben can be."

A moment later, the little schoolhouse seemed suddenly cavernous as only Teacher and Jason remained. But Jason was in no hurry . . . to run into Ben. And then he remembered. His mother had asked him to see if Teacher would be free to join them for dinner next week. He often looked forward to Teacher's visits and the stories she would tell. Maybe that was why he liked her so, despite the fact that, like everyone else, she always had a way of making him just a bit nervous. Jason approached her.

"Yes?" she asked.

"Mama wishes for you to have dinner with us next week," Jason said.

Teacher's eyes suddenly pierced Jason, freezing him with their intense gaze. "No," she answered, almost sadly. "I can't make it next week. Tell your mother thank you for me."

Jason swallowed hard. He wondered again if she was all right, but he was hesitant to question her on the point. It was not considered appropriate to be so nosey where an Etha was concerned . . . especially this one. So he nodded once, turned, and stepped toward the door. He peeked into the schoolyard to ensure that Ben Wateri had left the grounds. It was clear. So Jason drew a comforting breath and then dashed out the door and down the path leading toward town. Just out of sight of the school grounds, Jason was jerked about by a firm grip at his shoulder. His books flew.

"Making me look bad, eh?" Ben sneered as his best friend, David Grimm, watched with delight. Ben shook Jason soundly. His fingers ripped Jason's tunic.

"Look at you . . . the poorest kid in town," Ben said as he fingered the new hole. "So what if you know a little stupid history?" Ben growled. "Your brother is no longer around to protect you. And your crippled old father can't." Ben glanced over at David. The younger boy smiled.

Jason's mind reeled with fear, a familiar condition. He couldn't talk. His mouth went dry. He shivered. His nervous fingers cinched his rope belt even tighter than it had been, as though to protect him from a beating that he knew was near.

Ben suddenly hurled his fist at Jason's face, snapping the boy's head painfully back. Blood spurted from Jason's lip. Ben threw his fist again, pounding it into Jason's stomach. The boy coughed and doubled over, falling to the ground. He tried to suck in air, but he was still winded. He swallowed blood instead. David rushed behind Jason and pulled him up, binding his arms behind him. Ben grabbed Jason's red hair and pulled it high so that the boy's head was lifted upward and unprotected. Jason went limp, dangling, conscious of both the fear and the beating, yet unable to conquer the former to help him stop the latter.

Snarling, Ben brought his fist far back in preparation for a final, memorable strike. He let it fly. Suddenly, a handlike vise caught his fist in midflight and squeezed hard. It then twisted his arm a full turn. Ben's knees buckled from beneath him and he fell to the ground in pain.

"Let me go!" Ben cried. Nervously, David relaxed his hold on Jason. The dazed boy fell headlong into the dirt.

"What have you learned?" Teacher asked coolly as she tightened her grip even further. Ben tried to tug his aching fist away, but to no use.

"What have you learned?" she repeated calmly.

"Nothing!" he yelled.

"A pity," she said. Teacher released his throbbing hand.

Ben stumbled to his feet, holding his aching hand, and quickly ran down the path toward town. Teacher turned to David.

"Go!" she snapped.

The bully's apprentice flew.

Jason rose sluggishly to his feet and dusted off his clothes. His mind was reeling with fear, but a moment later it was replaced with shame. What begins with fear, he thought, always ends in shame. Teacher approached.

"And what did you learn?!" she asked grimly.

"It's always better not to fight," he said, a well-rehearsed response.

"Try again!" Teacher shot back.

Startled, Jason fumbled for another answer, but none was coming. The first answer always worked before. Teacher then turned his chin to inspect his cut lip. She wiped a drop of blood away. As she did so, the boy noted how frail her hand now felt, masking the grip that had brought Ben to his knees. How strange, he mused, that someone so delicate in features can have such hidden strength.

"Strength cannot always be detected by appearances alone," Jason said thoughtfully. "That is what I learned." He was surprised by the answer. For a moment, it didn't quite feel as though it was him talking, but someone else within. He suddenly blushed, feeling quite stupid. Maybe he had taken more blows from Ben than he remembered.

Teacher placed her hands on Jason's shoulders and drew him close, closer than he had ever been to her before. He dropped his eyes, but she raised his chin until there was no avoiding her gaze. She was so commanding, he thought, so commanding and strong!

"In this world of ours," Teacher began, "appearances have little to do with anything. Yet that is only the beginning of your lessons. Fear comes in many guises, Jason Del. It has many degrees. That's another lesson you must learn . . . and soon. Ben inflicts mild fears to enslave a playground. And *you* have proven unable to confront him." Her disapproving voice cut deeply.

Jason shivered as she continued.

"So what would you do if faced with an evil so great and a terror so massive that it would enslave an entire world? What would *you* do then, Jason Del?"

CHAPTER 2

THE SEEDS OF PROPHECY

Shaken and cold, his chin throbbing, Jason Del left Teacher and stepped tentatively toward his home at the southern end of town, his eyes darting about him to ensure that Ben Wateri was nowhere in sight. He hated to be so cautious, he told himself, but if it would save him from another beating in the same day it was well worth the precautions. However, his apprehension began to lessen as the people along the narrow dirt path grew in numbers, many just arriving home from the marketplace, many bidding him good day. This was a good time of year, Jason thought, a glorious time, and not one to wallow in a cold, uncomfortable fear. He approached a rock in his path and kicked it hard, punishing the stone for his own weaknesses. It was a small but comforting release. He even managed to put aside the thoughts of Teacher's strange behavior, as troubling as they had been. His step quickened.

As Jason moved deeper into Meadowtown, he passed scores of children and parents buzzing about their cottages, putting up thousands of brightly colored festival ornaments in a dazzling line. Preparations for the Twilight Festival had begun. Red and silver bows were hung above doorways. The traditional orange Poca flowers were strung together and then laced from thatched rooftop to thatched rooftop. Dried clumps of cherry-berries were tied to porch posts. But of most prominence were the Farlo branches. Though their leaves shriveled and coiled tightly during the day, they unfurled during the darkness to reveal glowing, bright-green leaves. These were reserved, as always, for the windows of Meadowtown, providing a comforting nocturnal light.

The Farlo were more than that to Jason. "Farlo" was the pet name that Jason's older brother, Theda, had given him. Theda was well aware that Jason was afraid of fights and conflicts of any sort, recoiling in the presence of threats as much as Farlo shriveled in the presence of light. And so the older brother playfully teased the younger one: Jason was "Farlo" to Theda. Jason never liked that pet name. It reminded him of his shame. It also reminded him of Theda, who died two years earlier. Jason suddenly shivered. He pulled the end of his rope belt to cinch it tighter. A memory vanished.

Jason shaded his eyes and squinted into the falling sun, but he was not able to detect the beginnings of twilight. This time tomorrow would be different, he knew, as the sun would refuse to glow fully bright all day, thus making the twilight hours arrive sooner. Then, the sun would become less bright each day for two weeks, until it was a pure gray sphere against a dark sky for a full day's count, thus marking the most important day of the season: the full-twilight day of the Twilight Festival. As always, the full-twilight day would be duly celebrated when the dull sun reached its zenith, blanketing the land with its grayness. There would be prayers to Anton, thanking the creator for his protection from the ominous dark. Families would unite and feast on wild boar and deer. A huge bonfire would dominate the marketplace in Meadowtown. Storytellers would arrive. There would be gifts to celebrate the imminent rebirth of the sun during the following two weeks, the rebirth of happiness, the rebirth of family and friends, the rebirth of nearly anything that a person wanted reborn.

There was a time when the coming of the full-twilight day was awaited with apprehension instead of glee, when stories spoke of beasts that stalked the shadows, when families gathered together to fend off evils, more real than imagined. It was in those distant times that the Farlo kept its most important vigil, glowing vibrantly about the windows to protect the people from harm. The Farlo trees had glowed for ages along the Crystal River, where they grew thick.

The street widened considerably as Jason approached the marketplace. The craftsmen were packing up what few goods they had left that day. Farmers pushed their creaky carts, once laden with wheat and maize, toward home. Across the marketplace was the old town store, owned and operated by Squeki's father, Mayor Tome Joh. The Mayor was balancing himself high on a ladder in an attempt to hang Farlo branches above his store's double doors. He was a kind, graying gentleman and Jason liked him, as did virtually everyone. Squeki was farther above, atop the roof, helping his father.

"Good Twilight to you, Jason!" the Mayor called, nearly losing his balance. "I hear you had an interesting day in class." He then winked at his son, who smiled and waved at Jason.

"I've had better," laughed Jason, a bit sheepishly, his jaw aching.

Jason passed the town hall, the only two-story building in Meadowtown. Its bell tower rose further still, casting a chilly shadow upon Jason as he walked under its gaze. About six town meetings were held in that hall every year, Jason knew. The Mayor presided over all of them. Mostly, the meetings discussed land rights and resolved small disputes that typically arose between the craftsmen of the town and the farmers who lived in the regions beyond. Mayor Joh had urged Jason's father several times to run for a seat on the Town Council, but Cyrus Del always refused. The eldest Del would reply that the town spent too much time talking and not enough time taking action, and that was that.

The road narrowed once again, and the mingling voices within the marketplace became muffled as Jason drew closer to home. His cottage was not constructed of wood as were the rest of the homes in Meadowtown. Cyrus Del had instead built the family cottage mostly of stone, even though it had taken considerable time to locate and carry the boulders. Only the roof was wood—sturdy oak, making it almost as solid as the rock beneath it. It was also a small home—the smallest in town. Ben Wateri reminded Jason of that often. But the care that went into its construction and the love that permeated its walls more than matched its size, and Jason knew it.

As he approached, Jason heard the quick tap of a skilled cobbler's hammer: metal to nail to leather. This was the same wonderful sound that had welcomed him home nearly all of his life.

Nearby homes had Farlo branches about their windows, but this one was barren. Since Theda's death, the Dels' grief smothered celebration. But Jason was suddenly captivated by a warm plume of smoke that brought a sweet and delicious smell bearing pleasant memories of festivals past. Beth Del, his mother, was baking Twilight Cakes, a buttery delicacy she had not made since Theda's death. His heart leaped.

"I'm home!" called Jason as he opened the door, his booming voice far too loud for the one-room cottage.

"Wipe your feet!" his mother snapped. She bent over an old baker's oven, perspiration lining her brow.

Jason harnessed his joy, wiped his feet, and entered quietly. The cottage was warm and cozy, illuminated by the light that entered through one modest window and by a small blaze within the fireplace. Cyrus

Del, sitting at the large oak table, brought a finger to his lips, thus signaling Jason to tread lightly. He then winked at his son with a playful nod that said all was fine. Jason closed the heavy door and left the brisk air behind him.

"I forgot how hard these things are to make," Beth Del said as she turned about to greet her only remaining child, her face and graying black hair speckled with white flour. "On the next Twilight Festival, someone else will have to do it. I'll give them the recipe!"

Jason smiled. He missed this complaint. Beth Del's Twilight Cakes were as much a part of the festival as the Farlo, enticing people to travel miles just for a bite. The recipe was known only to her, and she protected it dearly. It wasn't the spices or ingredients that were the secret, Jason knew. Instead, it was the special way she blended all of the ingredients together, followed by the great care and worry that came afterward. In the end, the cakes always came out of the oven perfect—glazed golden-brown crusts on the outside and moist and buttery inside. And after a two-year hiatus, the Twilight Cakes returned. Jason released the knot in his rope belt. Maybe things were getting back to normal for the Dels.

Cyrus scrutinized the heel of a newly crafted shoe to ensure that every nail was cleanly and stubbornly in place. His tools were lying about the table, interspersed with cooling Twilight Cakes. While his left leg was beneath the table comfortably, his right leg was locked forever straight—his *souvenir,* Cyrus Del would call it, from the Second Race War. He was dressed in a cotton shirt and a worn pair of workmen's pants. And while his hair was still a vibrant red, with only some traces of gray about his temples, the long years and difficult times were etched into his tired, leathery skin. Still, there was a modest glow—an eager glow almost—that rested deep within his green eyes. It was identical to the one that shone brightly within his son.

Beth gathered the last of the precious cakes from the oven and placed them on a damp cloth on the table, pushing her husband's tools aside to make an inch more of room.

"Come here," she beckoned to Jason, spreading her arms wide and reaching up to kiss her son.

"What happened here?" she asked abruptly, glancing at her son's torn tunic, and then examining his bruised chin and cut lip. She had the eyes of a former healer, and she had been a good one at that. "Were you in a fight?!"

"Sorry about this," Jason said, fingering the ripped threads. Habit kicked in. "But it's always better not to fight . . . so . . . so . . . I just walked away."

"Good for you," said Beth. She gave Jason another kiss. Jason glanced at his father. The large Man nodded in agreement, but Jason caught something else in his father's eyes. Theda would not have *just* walked away, Jason thought. Theda would have fought.

"Who hit you *this* time?" his mother asked.

Jason's shoulders slumped. He had been through enough already. First Teacher's probing questions, and now his mother's.

"Ben Wateri," he began, his face reddening. Shame wrapped about him like a cloak.

"Go clean up," said Cyrus, ending the familiar encounter and freeing Jason from further scrutiny. "Your mother has dinner almost ready." Cyrus gestured to an iron kettle hanging in the fireplace, a thick broth simmering slightly over the rim. He then rose to clear the table of his tools and materials. The Man's balance was awkward, with a pro-nounced limp in each step. With each movement he made, a soft jingle rose from a finely crafted thin chain that was suspended from his belt, quite worn where the chain met the leather. The chain's links hung downward and disappeared into his right pants pocket to be locked onto a Stone of value—a family heirloom—buried within. Jason knew it well. It was a part of his heritage, a link to a distant and powerful past.

Jason climbed the slim, wooden ladder that stood adjacent to the fire-place and led to his loft. He paused upon seeing a large sword that rest-ed on the mantel. The heavy blade was carefully wrapped in a thin animal skin. Only the pommel was exposed, revealing a finely crafted Tork metal, the strongest known, smoothed to a soft round. Since Jason was a small child he had been awed by the blade's beauty and intrigued by the stories that surrounded its metal edge. It was not as great as the heirloom his father carried, Jason knew, but it was still a link to a long-forgotten past: a family history that spoke of great events and greater deeds. It was the deciding factor in the war of the Wizard's tomb, the Battle of Endur, and the defeat of the last Tempest. He touched the blade, a habit for some years, hoping that the bravery of his ancestors would rub off on him: borrowed dignity. He then scrambled into his loft to change before cleaning up.

Dinner seemed to drag on as a queer silence hung in the air. His par-ents were very quiet . . . too quiet. After dinner, he found out why.

"Jason, I need you to sit with me for a moment," his father said. "There is something you need to know."

The flickering fire cast intermittent waves of light and shadow about the room, adding to the heavy mood. His father spoke in a solemn, weary voice.

"Son, as you know, our family has roots that span the ages. There was a time when our ancestors ruled the land in peace, and the name of Del had meaning to the people. While those days are gone, our family obligation continues. There's an heirloom left to us for safekeeping; one that, someday, will be called on to defend against the greatest of evils. I have told you many stories about the heirloom. But there are a couple more you need to hear now."

Jason's mind reeled. His father was talking about the Wizard's Stone! He fought to contain his excitement so as to catch every word his father was about to speak.

"First, the Wizard's Stone is not passed from father to son until the son enters the Age of Wisdom. This Age is a time when the son starts to discover his inner strengths of understanding and maturity. Though normal children develop at different rates, the children from the Royal House are different. Ages ago, our bloodline was guided so that the Age of Wisdom could be controlled . . . predicted. The Age of Wisdom for children of the Royal House occurs in the fifteenth year within reach of a new Twilight Festival. That time . . . your time, Jason . . . is now!"

Jason could feel his heartbeat in his fingertips. In all of Trinity, there was no treasure greater than the Stone. His family was the only one that truly knew—the only one that was supposed to know. He was now within reach of an inheritance handed down faithfully from father to son since Tempest Slayer. A lump formed in Jason's throat. The pounding of his heart grew stronger. It was going to be his—his! But he was still so young, he suddenly thought. He hadn't expected the heirloom for years. And what is this *Age of Wisdom?* Jason glanced at his mother and saw great pride in her eyes.

"You'll start to feel things happening deep within you," his father continued. "These are things that you never thought about before, things that will both confuse and enlighten you. In time, we'll discuss them all. But for now, I think it's fitting that we discuss the Stone; it is a great responsibility. That brings me to my second story." Cyrus Del paused for a moment before continuing, taking a deep, heavy breath.

"During a final maneuver of the Second Race War," Cyrus began, "my company was surrounded by Dwarf warriors attempting to dislodge our position. It was cold. A snowstorm had been raging since the day before. We were outnumbered. Regardless, we held firm . . . that was our job. After their seventh or eighth attack—I can't quite remember which—I became separated from my Men in the blizzard. A Dwarf ax came out of the storm and caught my leg. I lay on the snow for some time, unable to move, before a squad of some ten Dwarves descended upon me. A Dwarf officer barked orders in a language I didn't understand, but I recognized his intent . . . he ordered my death."

Jason froze. The tremble in his father's voice said it all—that war was a hideous thing, where real people fought and real people died. And his father was counted among the living and the brave. The boy leaned forward in his chair, as though trying to grab such courage for his own.

"The Dwarf officer then turned and left with half of his company, while the others remained. One of them unstrapped a lance and pointed it at my heart. He mumbled a few words . . . an apology, I think. I can still see the regret in his eyes as he raised his lance high above his head, the snow falling between us." Cyrus lowered his eyes to the table, painfully reliving the tale as he spoke.

"All I remember, son, was that I was afraid. Young and afraid. More afraid than I thought possible. Not so much for my own life but for all our ancestors, who counted on me to live, to continue the Royal House." Cyrus closed his eyes, a glistening tear squeezing through.

Jason was dumbfounded, and comforted, to think that his father felt fear, too.

"Then it happened," Cyrus whispered.

Jason stopped breathing. He wrapped his arms around his own chest and squeezed tightly, thinking momentarily of the thousands of silly fears that enslaved him. They were nothing compared to the terror his father must have felt.

"A ringing sound cut the air," Cyrus continued. "But only I heard it. It was the Stone, vibrating deep within my pocket. I then felt white heat burn in my soul, rushing upward, outward in all directions. It was completely uncontrollable . . . completely. Then, there was a flash of blinding light . . . then an explosion. A moment later, I heard only gentle snow fall. When I opened my eyes, ashes were everywhere. Trees were scorched and smoldering even as the white snow floated from the gray sky. My topcoat was burned and fell in pieces to the ground. And the

Dwarves . . . " he paused, "the Dwarves were no more. . . . Just the sickening smell of burnt flesh remained."

Cyrus leaned a bit farther back in his chair at the break in the story, taking a breath.

"Afterward, I was very weak. The ax was still embedded in my leg. I was bleeding badly. I must have passed out after that as the next thing I remembered was a healer's tent back at the camp. But since that day, Jason, I've always wondered about the power unleashed by the Stone, and to what extent I could, or should, control it. As the years crept by, the question became pointless, as that was the first and only time the power came forth while it was in my trust."

The words "in my trust" rang in Jason's ear. They were laden with responsibility.

"I'm telling you this story for two reasons. First, to let you know that the Stone will protect you . . . it lives to protect you. Second, to warn you that the power within is great. It must be handled with care . . . great care!"

Jason's expression turned grim. He hadn't realized the immense responsibility that the Stone demands. Yesterday, it represented nothing more than a fanciful story. Today, it was real, a source of life, protection, and even death. His heart soared to think that the Stone would protect him. His heart dropped to think of the evils it would have to protect him from. This was not the way he had imagined it would be: the handing down of the Stone. Then something else occurred to him. He gazed into his father's eyes.

"The Stone should have gone to Theda."

Cyrus nodded. "Yes. Theda was within a week of getting the Stone before he *fell to his death.*"

Jason's eyes turned away. He shivered. He tugged on his rope belt. An ugly memory vanished.

"It rightly goes to the firstborn," Cyrus continued. "But . . . it passes to the second should the firstborn die."

Theda was the oldest, Jason thought. The Stone should be his. Theda was the brave one. It wasn't fair. How could he benefit from gaining the Stone, Jason thought, especially when . . .

Jason tugged his belt again. The memory was banished again.

"Come here," said Cyrus, beckoning his son to rise and join him. Jason stood slowly, numbly, feeling twice as heavy as before he sat.

"Hold still," Cyrus said as he fingered his chain's old clasp, releasing it from the long duty about his belt. His worn, thick hands then moved to Jason's rope belt above his right pocket, wrapping the chain about it twice before clasping it shut. Only then did Cyrus pull at the opposite end of the links, bringing the object of power slowly from his own pocket and into the light of the fire. Cyrus grabbed his son's right hand and quickly placed the Wizard's Stone in his palm, as though afraid that it would be snatched before the transfer was consummated. It slipped smoothly and perfectly into place. Jason opened his fingers and looked deep into the gray rock. He was surprised at how lifeless it appeared, as any stone might—not the pure white of Wizards as it once had been, but the gray of emptiness. It was an age-old mystery.

Cyrus pulled his son close and kissed his forehead.

"The Stone is yours. Treat it well, my son, and it will return the favor. There are other legends beyond the Stone that I will share someday. But these are enough for now. Besides, there's plenty of time. I'm sure that your custody of the Stone will be . . . well . . . uneventful."

Jason wished for the same. He suddenly wanted his life to move quickly toward its end so that he could pass it on to a son of his own. The Stone made him anxious.

"One piece or two?" Beth asked as she grabbed a short baker's knife and held it over a large Twilight Cake.

Twilight turned to darkness and the logs in the fireplace glowed a warm, comforting red. Jason was contemplative, concerned about what might be expected of him. He pressed his father for other accounts of the Stone. He learned that with a few notable exceptions, those who held the Stone *in their trust* had led uneventful lives. Jason began to relax. An uneventful life was what he wanted most.

The wind began to blow wildly and the chill over Meadowtown deepened. A storm arrived and rain fell hard. Cyrus and Jason sat closer to the fireplace while Beth went about some chores.

"What about the Sword?" Jason asked.

"The Sword served me well during the Second Race War," Cyrus began. "But it never revealed its magic, if it has any. It never made itself known to me." Cyrus gazed up at the blade that rested just a few feet above their heads. Its exposed pommel captured the bouncing light of the fire. Cyrus grew pensive.

"For some reason, though, I've always felt as if it needs me, or that I need it." A moment passed. "Well, until the feeling passes, the Sword will stay with me. You have enough to think about already." He smiled.

"Agreed," said Jason.

Lightning suddenly struck Meadowtown hard, shaking the ground and exploding its light into the cottage. An odd glow invaded the room long after the bolt was gone. Jason shook his head, but the phantom sparks of light remained. He looked down and saw a thin light engulfing his clenched fist.

"Father . . . look!" said Jason. He raised his fist and opened his fingers wide. The Wizard's Stone was suddenly a brilliant white, its glow filling the cottage. Beth turned from her chores and stepped over anxiously to see.

"What does this mean?" Jason asked, praying that a suitable answer was forthcoming.

"I don't know," said Cyrus, perplexed. He placed a hand on Jason's shoulder.

Jason's heart pounded. He wished the Stone's light would vanish. But in defiance of his wishes, the Stone's glimmer grew more intense and started to pulsate. Jason looked at his father, terrified.

"I don't know," Cyrus whispered again. "It has never acted this way before . . . never!"

Every nerve in Jason's body screamed at him to drop the Stone and run, but he could not. He was afraid to move and afraid to stay, so he was frozen. He knew this feeling.

Bang bang bang came a sudden knock at the door. The Dels jolted. Cyrus flew out of his seat.

"Who is it?" demanded Cyrus. He grabbed the Sword down from the mantel and unleashed its blade from its leather bindings. The metal's brilliant glare stabbed the pulsating light.

No one responded to Cyrus's call. A moment passed as the storm raged on, muffling any sounds from without. Cyrus peered through the rain-streaked window and caught sight of a figure lurking in the shadows. Jason felt his mother's hands holding him tightly, nails digging in. His father seemed suddenly bigger, more threatening than he ever knew. Lightning struck again, revealing a slender frame just beyond the window's light. But darkness returned, leaving the figure unidentified. Thunder rumbled. The knock came again, louder this time.

"Who is it?!" Cyrus shouted.

A voice called out above the storm. "A messenger for the Royal House of Del!"

Cyrus's eyes flashed. No one had addressed the family as such in countless years. "Prophecy?" he breathed. "Can't be . . . not here . . . not now . . . not with . . . " He glanced at Jason.

Cyrus unbolted the door and opened it slowly, his Sword gripped firmly. The Stone flared up like a torch within Jason's hand, dominating the flames from the fire with its mad, pulsating light. Panic held him.

As the door opened a crack, a figure, cloaked in green and drenched in the massive downpour, passed over the threshold quickly, bringing a flood of water into the small cottage.

"What business do you have with us?" Cyrus demanded as he leveled the point of his blade at the intruder, blocking the path to his family.

"We shall see!" the answer came as the unexpected visitor reached for her hood and threw it back, revealing the snow-white hair of an Etha.

CHAPTER 3

THE TERRIFYING JOURNEY BEGINS

T eacher!" called Jason as he stepped forward, relieved it was someone he knew. The white glow of the Stone still squeezed through his clenched fingers. His mother's grip pulled him back. Cyrus kept his Sword leveled.

"Put that thing away, Cyrus," Teacher said in her very special, demanding tone. "Is this how you treat a guest?"

"We didn't invite you this night," Cyrus said suspiciously, pinning the Sword to her shoulder to emphasize his words. The Stone continued to cast a pulsating, almost threatening light, making even friends appear as enemies. Lightning struck, followed by crashing thunder. The cottage rumbled about them.

"Maybe you didn't invite me tonight," Teacher replied irritably, pushing the tip of the Sword downward with ease. "But apparently your ancestors did."

Cyrus gazed deeply into her Ethan blue eyes. He relaxed his blade for the moment, assured that the person standing before him was, in fact, Teacher. His stance, however, remained at the ready.

The Etha stepped quickly to Jason, grabbing his numb fist and opening it wide, seeing the Stone's radiant glow. Her blue eyes widened and she seemed to dip slightly, noted Jason, as though bowing. Teacher tenderly raised a slender finger and stroked the Stone. The lightning immediately began to diminish; the booms of thunder moved on. Jason looked about, amazed at the renewed quiet and hearing once again the beating of his own fearful heart. He wondered if Teacher heard it also. Then, slowly, the pulsating Stone began to yield. The shadows about the cottage seemed less threatening and the strange light continued to recede

38

until the Stone's wizardry was gone completely. Only a long, widening calm and the bouncing glow of the fire remained. The rain, too, ended as abruptly as it had begun. Jason waited.

"Put this away now, dear," Teacher said softly to Jason, waking him from a stupor.

Jason slipped the Stone into his right pocket, pleased to have it out of his sight.

"Care for some Twilight Cakes and hot apple cider?" Beth asked Teacher, breaking the silence and startling Jason with her calm. This was the mother he knew. No matter the event, Beth Del met it calmly. He remembered that well when Theda died. Jason knew he could never, ever live up to the courage that spilled naturally from his family.

"Love some," said Teacher, nodding slightly, her eyes sparkling with delight. The Etha glided to the family table and sat.

"Come sit down, you two," Beth said to Jason and his father as she poured steaming apple cider from a kettle, cakes in hand. "Can't you see that Teacher obviously has something on her mind?"

Jason sat slowly, reluctantly, at the table. His father did so as well but kept the Sword in his lap, his eyes bearing down on their guest. He touched neither food nor drink.

"I have known each of you all your lives. Each of you learned much at my school as children. One of you has much more to learn—and soon!"

Teacher's eyes stabbed Jason's.

"No festival will grace the land this year," she said to him solemnly. "Instead, when the full-twilight day is upon us, a Final Contest will be held between a Great Good, a Pure Evil, and an Evil Less than Pure. This Contest will decide the fate of Trinity. It will determine which among these three powers will reign supreme and eternal."

Her eyes continued to hold Jason's. What could Teacher possibly want of me? he thought. She leaned close, as though noting his every thought, even those that did not reach his lips.

"You, Jason," she continued, "will represent the Good among us."

Jason's eyes widened.

"Yes," she answered his startled gaze. "Every Man child, every Race child, and every creature that makes its abode in the friendly shade of Trinity depends on you. The battle begins in a mere two weeks' time. You will face terrors of untold proportions . . . those that would enslave a world!"

Jason's mind sparked with the memory of his conversation with Teacher earlier that day. This was the same discussion, he suddenly realized.

"We have much ground to cover," she continued. "First we travel north on an errand of some urgency. After that we travel south to the Circle of Wisdom. It is there that you will be put to the greatest of all tests. Now go pack. We have very little time. Our first stop is the township of Charity. We leave tonight!"

With that, Teacher leaned back, raised the cider serenely to her lips, and cooled the surface slowly with a breath before she drank. "Good," she whispered to herself, clearly enjoying the drink while seemingly indifferent to the echoing, tense silence about her.

"How do we know what you say is true?!" Jason's father demanded angrily, struggling to control himself. His fingers impatiently stroked the hilt of the Sword. "How do we know you are not part of the evils?" he tested further, not waiting for Teacher to answer the first question put to her.

Teacher nodded. "First, you know deep in your heart that I speak the truth," she began as she took a delicate bite of Twilight Cake. "You know of this prophecy. I made sure that your own father handed it down to you."

Jason glanced at his father, seeing recognition in his eyes.

"Second," Teacher continued, "if I were a part of the evils, the Stone never would have let me that close, never would have let me touch it. You know that to be true as well, Cyrus Del . . . Knower of Legends."

Teacher's eyes suddenly flashed, throwing away the air of indifference.

"Third, Jason and I leave tonight," she declared in a hardened voice. "You will not stand in my way!"

Cyrus bolted from his chair and sent it crashing to the floor. The Sword leaped into his hand. With one jab he pinched the blade deep into the curvature that formed Teacher's throat. He pressed the point firmly but not so much as to end her life. Gasping, Jason watched his father in terror. This was not the man who had raised him, not the one who stood by him for hours when he was sick. This was someone quite different, born of fire and duty, destined to protect the only remaining heir to the Royal House. His mother grabbed Jason tightly just as Cyrus spoke.

"It is true that we have known each other a long time," he began, his eyes on fire, his voice menacing, "but that means nothing to me where my last son is concerned. You speak the truth when you say that I am a Knower of Legends. Then tell me, Etha . . . tell me what Jason will seek on this journey of yours. There is only one answer that can pry my son from me . . . one answer that my ancestors kept among themselves through the ages. Speak truly and quick or your Ethan blood flows!"

A deep, chilling silence filled the room as Teacher considered his words. A trickle of red blood squeezed from her throat and slid onto the cold blade. Jason was amazed at Teacher's calm. There was not so much as one dot of perspiration on her brow. She glanced once at Jason, her eyes gleaming shrewdly. The look gave him the strangest feeling that Teacher knew it would come to this—that she had intentionally provoked it. Perhaps she wanted him to witness another side of Cyrus Del. Or perhaps she wanted Jason to experience real terror. The boy wanted to swallow, but he could not. It felt as though the blade was as much at his throat as it was at Teacher's.

No matter how long he would live, Jason would always remember Teacher's next words, though at the time they were meaningless to his young ears.

"We seek the Pearl of Anton," she began, his father's blade cutting deeper with each sentence, "that is buried far beneath Mountain High to the north. Such a gem, along with the Wizard's Stone, is the beginning of true power . . . the beginning of hope. The time has come, Cyrus Del, my student and my charge. The time is now!"

Cyrus's eyes widened. He shot a chilly glance at his son. Jason shivered.

"He's the One?" his father asked suddenly, incredulously. "But I thought if anyone, it would have been . . . " His words trailed off.

"Theda," Jason said, completing his father's thought.

Cyrus took a deep, shuddering breath and then relaxed his stance, withdrawing the deadly blade from Teacher's throat. Jason swallowed hard. His father cracked his fist open and let the blade fall to the table with a dull, vibrating thud. It was quite possibly the most mournful sound Jason had ever heard: Tork metal hitting solid oak. The table shook from the collision, though not as much as Jason did—right down to the pit of his terrorized soul. He suddenly felt as though all of his choices in this world were gone and that only duty remained . . . a duty unknown. There was one thing he was sure of, however. Nothing would be the same again—not Trinity, not Meadowtown, especially not him. And despite his knowledge of some ancient stories, he didn't have a clue as to why this was happening, except that it had something to do with things far more powerful than he.

Jason was terribly afraid, more so than ever. He knew, too, that it was only going to get worse.

CHAPTER 4

A MADDENING MARCH

Meadowtown was thoroughly drenched, the rain leaving the smell of wet thatch and mildew in the air. The Farlo leaves, still awaiting the Twilight Festival with vigor, continued to sparkle in the night as a few remaining raindrops slid down their shining surfaces, altering the emerald glow with each descent and sending intermittent shadow and light dancing on every cottage. Doors and windows were shut tightly, due to the rain and the long tiring day, though the flickering red and yellow light of warming fires was still visible within. Children were put to bed with stories of heroes and demons, and promises of what the Twilight Festival might bring. Their parents counted their blessings, for it had been a good year for most . . . one worth repeating.

Two shadows passed quickly north, their steps unnoticed along the storm-soaked road. Teacher took the lead, her movement fluid as she gracefully glided over dozens of mischievous puddles that lined the narrow path. Jason followed quietly. For just a moment, he considered that he was having a nightmare, until he realized that nightmares were never this cold, or this wet, or this dark, or this confusing. Why was this happening? he thought. He was leaving his family, his friends, and his life—being robbed of it all! The memory of the preceding hour was already fading—his mother's final embrace, a perplexed, but proud look in his father's eyes.

"A thousand ancestors go with you," Cyrus Del said gravely. What did that mean? Jason wondered. Which thousand ancestors? Was this another story that he did not yet know? And if a thousand ancestors did go with him, why did he feel so alone, so forsaken?

It should have been Theda.

Jason felt heavy and burdened. The Wizard's Stone was laden with an immense responsibility, weighing his pocket downward. It was in odd, stark contrast to the cheery, uplifting disposition of the dazzling green Farlo along both sides of the road. Maybe the branches knew something that he did not. Jason's spirits rose when he saw the familiar outline of the ageless schoolhouse draw near. The solid rock structure was wet to a shiny rounded gray. He suddenly thought of the beating he took that afternoon. He would gladly take another in exchange for where he was now. Jason recalled the odd questions Teacher asked after she stopped the beating.

"So what would you do if faced with a terror so great that it would enslave a world?" she had said. "What would you do then, Jason Del?"

Jason shivered.

Teacher continued quietly, keeping well ahead of Jason as she moved through a thicket of white oaks, acorns crunching under their splashing feet as the trail became a mud path cut amidst the towering trees. After an hour's march through the sludge, Jason saw a faint glow of emerald green pierce the trail ahead. The sound of rushing water pounded the air. They were now on the western bank of the Crystal River, the sound of its swollen waters almost deafening. The river rushed southward; its surface foam was sparkling, reflecting the sharp green light of Farlo trees that hugged its bank.

Teacher jumped along the slippery boulders that lined the bank. Jason followed as best he could. His mind was a jumble of thoughts and worries. He suddenly remembered his father offering him the Sword. He remembered Teacher's harsh refusal. The blade had to stay with the eldest Del, she commanded. Jason wondered about Teacher's role in all of this, about the nature of the Pearl of Anton, and about the existence of a Pure Evil. His mind spun. Questions . . . questions . . . questions . . . he had nothing but questions, an icy fear, and the damp, cold night air.

Teacher drove deeper into the northwest forest, keeping parallel with the Crystal River while attempting to find more solid ground to speed their flight. As they left the protective glow of the Farlo, the Ancient Forest of Oak became dreadfully dark, its shadows now larger and more frightening than the objects that cast them. The stars above were replaced with leaves. The fresh smell at the water's bank was replaced with the scent of forest mildew. The wind began to whistle eerily through the oak branches.

Jason became uneasy, his eyes darting about the towering foliage, whose tops were lost to the night sky. He could see perhaps twenty yards in any direction, but then it turned to a hazy greenish-gray, a mix of

brush and trees and floating mist. He had never been this far north during the fall of night, and given his already fragile state, his imagination
began to outpace his ability to control it. His footsteps seemed to echo
everywhere, sending his own startling sounds back to him. Several times
he bolted, as though to run away from his present danger. But there was
nowhere to go but to follow Teacher.

Jason managed to convince himself that he was afraid of common
dangers: large cats, boars, or perhaps even bears. But deep within, he
searched the forest for the creatures whose notoriety was largest among
the shadows, the Bantogs. Jason had never actually seen a Bantog. Few
claimed that fearful honor. Yet, tales of the demons that stalked the night
were not uncommon, particularly during the approach of the full-
twilight day. Half-man and half-beast, the creatures were said to be
twisted in their thoughts, preferring dark to light, wet to dry, fear to
calm, evil to good. And they were never predictable—never! And while
some folks thought the stories to be nothing more than old wives' tales,
others thought them real. Jason had to concur with the latter, as his own
parents had related tales of the blood-thirsty creatures of long ago, their
fabled dark-green bodies affording their virtual invisibility in the forest,
leaving only their rich orange eyes to identify their cunning. Yet, even
those who refused to believe could not deny the dreadful happenings
that would sometimes occur in the dead of night: the butchering of livestock, the barns set afire, the children that would never return from play.
Such events kept the fear and the legend alive for all.

Before long, every shadow seemed sinister, every noise an ambush,
every firefly a Bantog, until Jason's fear of the night overcame his fear
of disrupting Teacher's pace, so keenly did she keep it constant. He
trotted until he was just behind her, panting as he spoke.

"Are you sure we're safe here?" he asked submissively, careful not to
offend, his voice puffing.

Teacher jerked to a stop and turned about, startling him. A deep
silence replaced the sound of their footsteps, and the forest seemed suddenly more vast and frightening than ever before.

"Realize one thing," she whispered sternly, her eyes glancing about
the nearby grayness. "We're not safe anywhere. Eyes follow us even as
we speak."

Jason looked about wildly. Teacher put her hands on his shoulders
and squeezed them firmly to gain his attention.

"You can't see them and they won't attack us . . . yet. They're not sure of their tasks. But more importantly, they don't realize who you are. Now come." Teacher drove straight into the darkness.

He suddenly hated Teacher, hated everything about her: her cloak, her manner, her white hair, her blue eyes. Everything was all her fault, he knew. And more, she was being unreasonably harsh, more so than he ever remembered—even for an Etha. Has she no compassion for my fragile condition? he thought. But such thoughts soon faded back into fear and self-pity. Jason found familiar comfort there.

They raced relentlessly north through the Oak Forest, its trees still uninviting in the night. Through his anguish, Jason marveled at the quick and agile pace Teacher managed to maintain, now for hours. He had always thought of her as a rather fragile though headstrong person. Yet, she forged her way up and down the rugged and wet terrain, hopping gracefully over huge trunks of fallen trees that rudely obstructed her path, then plunging down muddy embankments, all but defying gravity. And she never looked back, almost sensing where he was at every step, and compensating on occasion when he lost ground against her stride.

Jason's thoughts floated now and again to the cloudy past: to the times of his youth, to a younger pupil, to a younger son, to a young brother. Somewhere that night, Jason concluded that there wasn't anything particularly special about him at all. Jason was simply the last descendant of the Royal House . . . *by default.* If he was supposed to represent Good in some contest, shouldn't he somehow feel *more* Good? Shouldn't he feel stronger? Theda was good, strong, and brave. Jason was merely "Farlo," shrinking in the light of day.

Jason staggered painfully forward. His mind was lost for hours, even as a hint of a new day's light peeked through the eastern grayness. He didn't notice even as Teacher made her way toward a huge fallen oak that rested three feet off the ground. She stopped suddenly, dropped her pack, and sat. Jason, now in a trance, continued forward, plunged over the fallen tree, and rolled to his back. His eyes jolted wide awake, and he peered upward into the widening light that squeezed through the spaces between the oak leaves high above. He glanced backward at his tutor. She had already pulled a small book from her pack and was reading it intently, ignoring his stumble.

"We'll rest here for an hour," Teacher said irritably. She raised a haughty eyebrow. "If it were only me, I could continue to Charity and be there within the hour . . . but I guess you need some rest."

Jason looked up at her through his pain and discomfort, her figure sitting erect upon the tree, framed by the green forest above. She looked as tidy and fresh as when they had departed—quite unlike his own ragged appearance.

Did Teacher hate him now? Perhaps she, too, knew that Jason was not the Del that should be following her. Something was different between them. She was prodding him more than she needed. What did she want of him? he wondered. Wasn't he due some kindness? He did not pick this fate.

The ground suddenly felt comforting, Jason thought. It was so comforting that he felt himself drifting into sleep. Before he did, he patted his right pocket to be sure the Stone was still buried within. It was. Jason sighed forlornly. Part of him secretly wished he had lost it along the way.

"How long did I sleep?" he asked as he woke.

"Four hours," Teacher replied, closing her book sharply. "Exactly three too many!"

"Then why didn't you wake me?" Jason asked suddenly, angrily, realizing that absolutely nothing had changed between them.

"Because I didn't want you complaining later," Teacher snapped as she packed her things. "And besides, I intend to make the time up today . . . any questions?"

Jason was stiff and hungry, and he wanted to go home. But he said nothing. Oddly, though, he did feel as though he had slept too much. And there was a part of him that seemed anxious to get moving, to fly toward something he couldn't quite explain. Something was definitely beginning to stir within, he realized. Maybe it was just his nerves.

"Let's go," he said. And with that Teacher rose and stalked north, with Jason running to catch up.

The township of Charity, Jason knew, was not very popular among the decent folk of Trinity. Its inhabitants were largely drifters and gamblers in search of a quick comfort . . . or worse. Most honest farmers and craftsmen from Meadowtown would bypass Charity altogether. They preferred to travel an extralong day to Torsen when in need of supplies.

Teacher slowed, becoming cautious as they approached a scattering of tents in the diminishing forest. She grabbed her hood and placed it carefully over her head to conceal her Ethan features. Just as she did, Men came into view just twenty yards away on either side of the road, huddling about smoking campfires. Some of the figures rose to their feet to get a better look at the duo. Others spoke in whispers. One called out, sneeringly, but Jason could not understand his inebriated words. Teacher's confident pace remained constant.

Jason did his best to keep his sight on the road. He was careful not to look into the eyes of others for fear that his own curiosity would draw unwanted attention. But he could not help but notice the strange assemblage of men, unshaven and filthy, some with hardly a stitch of clothing even in the brisk morning. Many were scraping the bottom of kettles in order to capture the last bit of nourishment; others were arguing or laughing in the cold morning stillness. They seemed to have no one but themselves, and nowhere to go but here. A distance up the road, four Men stood together, arguing loudly. The first Man pushed the second into the restraining arms of the other two, who held him firmly while the first knocked him unconscious. They let the large man fall into the street. Jason winced. His sore chin began to throb. He patted his pocket to calm his fear.

Teacher stopped abruptly in front of an old, two-story building where laughter fused with threatening, angry voices within. A sign was affixed, crookedly, over the structure's large double doors. *Thieves Inn,* it read.

"Our scout is waiting for us in there," Teacher said, stepping toward the door.

A scout, Jason thought. What scout? But that seemed trivial compared to the thought of entering the inhospitable establishment. Jason paused.

"Afraid, are you?" Teacher asked, turning about.

Jason could not bring himself to tell the truth, so he remained quiet.

Just as Teacher turned to approach the inn, laughter boomed from its doors and a Man was hurled out head first. He somersaulted in midair and landed with a heavy splash in the murky puddles of the street. Teacher easily pivoted out of the way. Jason was not as fortunate. The splash covered him in mud. Two burly, unkempt Men appeared at the door of the inn.

"If we ever see you again in Charity," began the largest, "bring a lot more Daca coins and a lot fewer questions."

The Man sat up and wiped the ooze from his face and neck. He was an older Man judging by his thick silver-gray hair and tough skin, though his physique appeared much younger, more muscular and trim. His face was unshaven and bore a large mustache. His clothes were in tatters and smelled of sweat and alcohol.

"Jason," Teacher said in a restrained but sarcastic voice—one he knew well. "I would like to introduce you to our scout." She pointed to the apparent vagrant now at their feet. "His name is IAM Terante. Terante is a derivative word from the ancient Latini language. It means *terrible.*"

Jason wiped the ooze from his own face and then stared down at the disgraceful sight.

"Now, Sara!" the scout blurted in a backwoodsman's accent. "Go easy on me . . . I've had sort of a tough day."

While the smell of liquor added credibility to his words, Jason was most taken by his familiarity with Teacher. Even he did not know her first name. Then again, it occurred to him that he never thought to ask. Though he was angry at Teacher, Jason was resentful of the Man's disrespect. No one was entitled to be so familiar with an Etha. It just wasn't done!

"We'll discuss your tough day later," Teacher shot back. "I can see that your friends have rattled your brain. Where can this boy clean up?" she asked harshly.

"I booked ya two rooms . . . second floor . . . at the Bestree Inn farther down the road. It's clean enough even by your standards. In fact, it might even help that Ethan disposition of yours."

Jason gasped. He expected Teacher to fly into a rage, to descend upon the no-good drifter and thrash him solid. But to the boy's amazement, she ignored his rude comments, took Jason's hand, and pulled him forward. Without turning around she shouted to the scout.

"We'll meet you downstairs in one hour. And take a bath . . . you stink!"

The scout was right about one thing, thought Jason. The Bestree Inn was quite in order: clean towels, flower-scented water, even a bar of soap—all more than he had hoped. The boy slowly peeled the tunic and trousers from his body and then washed, allowing the scented water to rid his mind and body of the night's journey. He reached into his pack and grabbed a set of fresh clothes. Beneath it were dozens of small and hearty Twilight Cakes. Jason smiled, remembering that his mother packed his bag. She included the cakes at the expense of more clothes. Jason brought one of the delicious cakes to his nose and inhaled. For a moment, he was home. But he couldn't find the will to eat. He put the cake back where he found it, dressed, and went downstairs to find Teacher.

She was sitting in a small alcove. Her features were tranquil as she read quietly and contentedly. The scout was right again, Jason thought; the Inn did suit her disposition.

"I've changed," Jason announced as he sat beside her.

"Obviously," she answered, turning immediately back to her book.

Jason remained quiet. But in truth, he was fretting. What, exactly, were the two evils he was supposed to fight? Was he supposed to be stronger than them, or maybe he was he supposed to outwit them? Several times he opened his mouth but the questions wouldn't form. He was too afraid of the answers. Out of sheer self-preservation, Jason forced his mind to drift elsewhere, to find a harbor from the fear. He thought of the scout. It was an easier memory to digest, one that he could recall without feeling as though he were going to be ill. The more Jason's mind strayed to IAM, the louder his fingers began to tap on the table, until the sound filled the small, hollow room.

"What is it?" asked Teacher, bringing Jason's mind back to the alcove.

Jason shifted nervously.

"Well?" she prodded.

"I was just wondering. How much do you really know about Mr. Terante?"

"Is that all you want to know?" she asked, seemingly annoyed by the question.

"Well . . . yes," he lied.

"All right then." She shrugged. "What do you want to know?"

"Well, he doesn't strike me as someone who can be . . . well . . . trusted," Jason said.

"Why do you say that?" Teacher asked sharply.

"His clothes, the liquor, and the smell," Jason stumbled.

"So!" Teacher began with a sharp nod. "You are still judging by appearances. I thought that lesson was behind us, *master* Del!"

Footsteps suddenly pounded through the inn's doors, moving quickly toward the alcove. A moment later, a huge Man appeared. He was dressed in rugged buckskin clothing, a jeweled Dwarf ax hanging at his belt. A sleek Elf bow and quiver draped across his back, and a broad sword was fixed at his side. Each piece had the sting of battle etched somewhere upon it. Jason instantly recognized the full battle dress of a Manwarrior as described in tales of the Second Race War. He was magnificent. The Man's proud stride seemed bigger than the alcove itself, perhaps bigger than even Charity. His gray eyes were sharp and clear, almost hawklike. Flowing silver hair framed his dark-tanned skin.

"Allow me to properly introduce myself," the Man said to Jason, a backwoodsman's accent still carrying most of his words.

"My name is IAM Terante. You can simply call me IAM, as my friends do." He grinned.

Jason accepted the big Man's grip, wincing slightly under the leathery squeeze. Before he could catch himself, Jason inadvertently put his thought into words.

"I'm sorry," he said absentmindedly.

"Sorry for what, friend?" responded IAM with a healthy smile.

"The boy was just saying that our earlier encounter with you was . . . interesting," Teacher responded.

"Oh that . . . no harm done . . . I was quite a sight," IAM said as he released Jason's hand. His voice then became deeper, apologetic, as he turned to Teacher.

"And how have you been all these years, Sarawathe?"

"I've been well, but busy," Teacher said. And to Jason's surprise, Teacher seemed to relax, as though years rolled onto the floor. But then it was gone.

"Sit and tell us what news you've brought," Teacher said.

The large Man pulled up a chair.

"Worse than we figured," he began. "Critters have been seen as far south as Torsen. They're not causin' any trouble yet, but they will," he concluded.

Jason's eyes flashed. What's a critter? he wondered.

Teacher drew close. "Eyes followed us from Meadowtown," she said in a whisper, glancing about her.

"Well then," said IAM, his pupils bouncing shrewdly, almost gleaming with excitement of a game about to begin. "That's different . . . in one hour we start for Torsen. I need to prepare." With that, the scout rose to his feet, bowed to Teacher, and gave Jason a friendly nod. He darted out the door, leaving a feeling of emptiness in the alcove.

But to Jason, the feeling was subordinate to the hopelessness that suddenly gripped him. *Critters,* he thought.

CHAPTER 5

THE AGE OF WISDOM

The terrain was hilly and overgrown along their route, but the ground was now dry near the Crystal River, giving them more solid footing along the boulder-studded bank. Still, IAM took great care in selecting their path, which he changed often, alternating from the water's swollen edge to the western foliage. The scout often knelt to feel an imprint or taste a puddle. His hawk-eyes pierced the forest and riverbank. Nothing escaped his intense gaze—not the small, brown dirt-dogs that burrowed deep beneath the moist soil of the forest, not the gray and white finches that nested high above in the towering oaks, not even the slithering green gola lizards that made their home in the inch-deep water near the bank. If the scout found something slightly out of the ordinary, Jason noted, he would alter the trio's course. Mostly, that meant only a slight change in direction, moving a tad bit east or west. On a few occasions they even backtracked, finding a longer route to avoid an area altogether. Each time, Jason feared whatever it was the scout circumvented.

Jason found comfort in the presence of their new companion. The way the scout glided about the forest was a marvel, his sword and ax and bow moving as one upon him. Twice, Jason glanced away for a moment only to discover upon looking back that the scout was gone. An instant later he would realize that the Man was only yards away, camouflaged in the forest. Yes, Jason thought, there was something about the Man. So as IAM Terante analyzed the details of his surroundings and cut a path north, Jason kept his eyes on the scout. It was far better, Jason decided, to devote his mind there than to the other more frightening thoughts.

After a day's tiring march, the travelers watched as the weakened sun began to fall into an orange twilight. It extended the twilight hours just a bit, bringing an early chill. The Farlo trees along the river began to glow vibrantly, once again creating a dazzling reflection in the flowing water below. Wispy clouds began to pass overhead, capturing the light and creating an eerie, shifting green aura above.

Jason found it difficult to match the constant and brutal strides of both Teacher and IAM. His legs hurt. A stabbing pain haunted his lower back. His toes grew numb from the hundreds of boulders that passed beneath them. He became sullen. Why is this happening to him? he thought, again and again and again.

IAM's pace suddenly slowed. Relieved, Jason stretched wearily. The evening air felt cool upon the perspiration that ran down his face and neck. A thin, lazy mist began to flow from the forest. It felt almost peaceful. But suddenly the scout knelt, shifting his eyes about, his senses alert. Teacher, too, appeared anxious, tucking her glistening white hair completely beneath her hood. The scout sniffed at the air. He cautiously lowered himself to his belly upon the rocks and brush. He waved them to a thicket of white oaks much closer to the forest. Teacher and Jason did not hesitate. They moved behind the trees.

Fifteen minutes passed but nothing happened

"What's going on?" Jason whispered to Teacher.

"Shhh!"

Jason realized he had no future other than the one others would ordain. In the company of two people, he was alone.

Ever so slowly, reaching down into his leather leggings, IAM retrieved what looked like a small club. It was made of wood and looked to be about two inches wide and a foot long. The scout pulled at opposite ends of the smooth wood, and the instrument slid into two pieces to form a cross. Using his knee as a brace, IAM stretched a cord that was affixed to both ends of the smaller piece of wood.

"A crossbow!" Jason breathed in amazement.

IAM slid an arrow out of his quiver and adjusted the tip before placing it carefully in the bow. He took aim. The Farlo trees along the bank were in his sight. Jason scanned the trees, but could see nothing.

Without warning, IAM let the arrow loose. *Twang!* The arrow arched upward, whistling, and traveled from sight. Somewhere deep in a Farlo tree one hundred yards away, it found its mark. The tree shook violently and a dark figure fell, hitting the wet gravel at the water's edge. *Thud!*

IAM rose and motioned for them to follow. At the riverbank, he turned to Jason.

"Ever see one of these, boy?" The scout rolled the body face up. Its head bobbed slightly in the shallow water. The creature was about five feet tall with an oily, green, hairless body. It had long spindly arms and thin, twisted legs. Its bony, narrow face had large pores filled with oozing green pus.

Jason froze. Though the naked creature was harmless at the moment, Jason had heard the tales of the horrid, hypnotic orange eyes that lay beneath its closed, froglike lids.

"Bantog!" Jason gasped. " . . . As in legends."

"Nothin' legendary about this one, 'cept maybe its size," IAM began, still keeping watch. He gave the creature a gentle kick. "I'd say eighty, maybe ninety pounds of flesh on this one."

In stark contrast to its appearance, the small beast had an almost sweet odor, unlike any other Jason had smelled before. The boy suddenly found himself enjoying the aroma as he tilted his nose to capture more of it. The fragrance was calming, almost inviting. But Jason caught himself, realizing that the fragrance was a trap. It entices the unsuspecting to draw near until they meet certain doom. A bow had fallen at the creature's feet. The weapon was finely carved from a green, shiny wood that Jason did not recognize. One thing was certain, he thought. It was deadly; the craftsmanship alone told him that. Bantogs are sworn, natural enemies of Mankind. And if legends are true, humans are also a Bantog's food source.

Suddenly, the creature's chest appeared to rise and fall. The body twitched.

"It's alive!" Jason shouted as he bolted. IAM slapped a hand over Jason's mouth and pulled him back.

"Slow down, son," he whispered. "He's not goin' to come around for at least an hour. That's quite a knot I put on his head."

IAM then knelt down to retrieve his arrow. The point of the scout's shaft was not a point at all, but a blunt metal end that the warrior easily removed and placed in a pouch at his side.

"Why didn't you shoot to kill it?" Jason blurted accusingly, still shaken by the creature's rekindled life. "Why didn't you use the point instead of the flat?"

"Why kill if I don't have to?" responded the scout matter-of-factly. "Besides, he didn't see us until I got him."

"But it would have killed us!" Jason seethed.

"But he didn't," IAM began with a blossoming smile. "But what is all this us stuff about? Sara and I were safe enough. It was *you* he was fixin' to kill."

Jason shook uncontrollably. He grabbed his chest to prevent it from exploding. Something was trying to kill . . . *him*. He had traveled far from home and had placed his life in their hands. He was exhausted, his entire body ached, and he was finding it harder and harder to distinguish fact from fiction. He didn't even know why he was there, other than thin legends Teacher expected him to believe. Now he had almost been killed! And everyone was so calm about it. He found himself becoming angry, and the bubbled to a boiling fury. But another part of him was struggling to come forth, too, another part he did not know all that well. It was telling him that he had to take control now, somehow, that he had to share in the responsibility of what was to come. He could no longer sit and wait and wallow in his own grief. That part within him hurled itself fully upward, shattering the self-pity that had been holding him tightly.

"Enough!" he said, quietly, but with a metal edge in his voice. He turned to Teacher.

"It's time that you tell me what's going on. You pulled me out of my home, took me on this march, and then brought me to a place where things are lying in wait to kill me."

He took a step forward, pointing a finger. "You owe me an explanation. This is my destiny. I am the *last* son of the Royal House!"

Teacher took a step toward him, and his royal blood almost froze— but it didn't. He would not allow it to. And for the first time ever, Jason realized that his mentor and he were of equal height. It was a small discovery, but an important one. Until that day, Jason had always considered her taller.

"It's about time!" Teacher seethed while jabbing her pointed finger painfully into his shoulder. "Where has this *Jason Del* been keeping himself?"

Teacher grabbed his head, held it tightly, and then tilted it backward until the light of the Farlo illuminated his pupils. She then placed her finger to Jason's left eyelid, opening it wide as a mother might do to find a dust particle or eyelash in a child's eye.

"Yes," she said, seemingly to herself. "The Age of Wisdom is finally coming upon you. I was afraid that it would never get here in time to destroy your own remorse. But it's finally here as prophecy has foretold . . . *self-pity to be the first emotion to hamper, and the first hurdle to overcome.*" She withdrew her hands. Jason noted a gleam of deep satisfaction in her eyes. "It's amazing what a little prodding can do!" she finished.

Jason was stunned. Something was beginning to burn within him. He could feel it—a think layer of maturity and strength and warmth that he couldn't explain. The Age of Wisdom? It could not erase the fear, but it greatly relieved him of the self-indulgent grief that he had carried since the journey began. And Teacher had been purposely coaxing him, even badgering him, to force him to be rid of it. She did not hate him, after all. And that knowledge filled him with comfort. He was so pleased that he no longer felt obligated to hate her, for he could never find it within himself to do that; he cared for her more than he ever thought. A glistening tear slid down his cheek, but he quickly brushed it away unnoticed as Teacher turned to IAM.

"Where can we be safe?" she asked.

IAM squinted and looked toward the forest. "There's a cave about a mile upriver—but farther west from the bank. Follow me." He pulled his ax and lifted it above the Bantog. Turning the ax about to the blunt side, he gave the creature another moderate blow to the head. Smiling at Jason, he whispered, "That should give us an extra half-hour—guaranteed!"

The cave was near the top of a gray rock mass, and the companions reached it with only a little trouble. It was ten feet deep, enough to conceal them. More importantly, it was dry and out of the cold night air. IAM sat near the opening to keep watch as Teacher escorted Jason to the back of the cave. They sat on a huge boulder.

"Our time is short so I need to speak quickly," she said. "To begin, Anton is not the creator of all things."

Amazed, Jason opened his mouth to speak. Teacher cut him short.

"The great creator is Nebus, who, with one silent breath, created much of the universe. Nebus spawned three sons. The first, Anton, was fair of features and born with a loving heart. The second, Becus, was jealous of his older brother and therefore strived to distinguish himself in all ways possible. While Becus was born fair of features, identical to those of Anton, he made his appearance to be foul and hideous instead. He chose a black heart. The third child was Cil. He admired both of his older brothers and, as such, developed characteristics of each: some good, some evil. Now, Nebus had pride in all three sons and gave them a great gift. Grabbing a piece of a star, he compressed and molded it with his very hands until a world was born for them to behold. He called a piece of it Trinity, to signify that it was for each. But, noting the disposition of each son, he gave Trinity equal hours of light, darkness, and twilight. And then on one day a year, because he felt a special fondness for his youngest, Nebus commanded twilight to reign for a full day."

"So that's why we have a full day of twilight!" Jason exclaimed as he leaned in.

"Yes. Now," resumed Teacher, "Anton delighted in the gift but was disappointed that the land was void of form. But not wanting to ask his father for more, for fear he would be perceived as ungrateful, Anton created the Wallos . . . good-natured industrious creatures capable of great accomplishments. These talented beings are responsible for much of the form we see today . . . the mountains, rivers, trees, and even the lesser animals. Theirs was truly the first art. And to help the Wallos prosper, Anton gave them a brilliantly white Pearl cut from his own being. Such a gem was said to be capable of great and mysterious powers, allowing the Wallos to construct such a world as this."

"The Pearl of Anton," Jason whispered.

"Correct again. Now, the Wallos lived in Trinity for many, many years, perfecting their craft and the land. And it was said that they could live forever, in fact, if no evil befell them. But it was not to be, for Becus became jealous of his brother's efforts, and he was anguished for a great time until he conceived of his own hideous beasts—the Terocs, the Gerlocks, and the most ferocious, the Tempests. The Tempests were capable of a great death fire and of reading the thoughts of those they pursued."

Jason shivered. He had heard stories of this beast and of its doom at the hands of his own family.

"As Anton turned his back for but a moment, which can span thousands of years for us, Becus sent his brood forth upon Trinity and they soon controlled the land. Nothing could stand before them. The beasts turned the soil and vegetation foul. They eradicated mighty rivers and even devoured the lesser animals that the Wallos had conceived. In a final blow to Anton, Becus sent the Tempests to destroy the Wallos themselves. The beasts were shrewd, first setting out to steal the Pearl of Anton, which they did, hiding it in the depths of Trinity beneath Mountain High to the north. Once the Wallos were without the power of the Pearl, they were no match for the Tempests, and the noble creations of Anton were soon destroyed. When our Lord looked back upon the land, he was crushed, and for many years Anton did not touch the realm of Trinity, for his creatures were gone forever."

Jason was completely entangled in the roots of these legends. The pain and suffering that transpired so long ago seemed to dwarf any complaints he had found in his own life. His fifteen years seemed suddenly so trivial in comparison to the vastness of what had come before.

Teacher continued.

"Ages passed and more destruction ensued as the evil creatures attempted to remove any sign of the Wallos and Anton. They even turned upon each other, and Becus took delight in all of it. Then, after many ages, Anton's heart was suddenly lifted with the promise of a wondrous thought. He conceived of a notion of a soul . . . a conscious state of existence that would live beyond the physical life, so that his children would, if evil befell them, rise above Trinity and forever dwell with him in peace. With that conceived, Anton labored long to develop new beings. But the soul took much energy to create. Thus, in order to birth such a spirit, sacrifices had to be made in the flesh, which resulted in the creation of the four Races . . . the Elves, Dwarves, Etha, and Man. Fearful that his creations would be easily consumed by his evil brother's horde, Anton created a dozen Wizards also . . . not really a Race, but entities capable of great magic."

Jason's eyes sparkled. Wizards were one legend that he had always thought false, but now even that had substance and credibility.

"Anton sent the Wizards to Trinity ahead of his Races in order to destroy the Beasts of Becus. But time was of the essence because the Wizards' stay on the land was limited. Upon their arrival, the Wizards kept to themselves, studying the land and its many wonders, hoping to find a way to best use their magic. Finally, a plan was conceived. The Wizards united their might and created a great winter upon Trinity. Ice filled the lakes and waterways, and the skies were crowded with a constant flurry of snow. The Terocs and Gerlocks went in need of food and water for a great many years. They found little and were destroyed. But several of the Tempests lived. Their might and their ability to breathe fire allowed several to escape the frozen death. Worse yet, the Wizards' power started to wear off, as it proved an immense task to control the winter for so long. Eventually, their magic broke, the seasons returned, and a few Tempests yet lived. With the Wizards' time running out, Anton sent his Races to Trinity in hopes that they could unite with the Wizards and defeat the remaining Tempests. Their forces were mighty and they won many great battles until only one last Tempest remained. But the three Wizards that still lived were weakened severely by the encounters. So, with little time left, the Wizards put most of their powers into a

Stone that they forged in a great fire at the Circle of Wisdom. With their remaining blaze, a great Sword was forged as well."

Jason's eyes flashed.

"In this way, the Wizards' power could stay with the Races even though it was time for the Wizards to leave. The Wizards then sought the noblest family of Man and instructed them on the use of the *Trinkets,* telling them no more than what they needed to know. That family became known as the Royal House of Del."

Chills passed through Jason's body as he heard his family's name. He had never before imagined that his ancestors were so much a part of the creation itself, so much a part of Anton's great plan. He stroked the pocket that contained the Stone.

"The Wizards then sought the help of my people, the Etha, and entrusted one family among them, my family, to keep watch over the descendants of the Royal House and to instruct them should a time of need arise. Otherwise, the Royal House was to know nothing of our watch. These instructions have been passed down through my ancestors from mother to daughter for ages untold."

Jason felt Teacher's arms about his shoulders, squeezing. "We are much alike in a way," Teacher began. "Both of us are fulfilling obligations that were set into motion ages ago. I can understand your feelings more than you'll ever realize."

The boy felt warmth from her that he never knew existed. It was as though a portal to her soul had opened, and he was allowed a brief look within. And to his amazement, he detected specks of pain and pride eternally mixed. Perhaps they were a lot alike, Jason thought. Perhaps they were indeed. Teacher removed her embrace, and the portal was once again shut.

"The Wizards' time had come," she began anew. "Once their plans were made, the remaining three drifted and were gone. But the last Tempest soon learned of the Wizards' plan and searched for the Royal House of Del. Upon finding them at the Circle of Wisdom, it destroyed one thousand of your ancestors. Only one survived . . . Nicoli."

A thousand ancestors! Jason thought, cringing. These were undoubtedly the same thousand ancestors that his father had referred to upon their parting. *A thousand ancestors go with you,* Cyrus Del had said. Jason now hoped it was true—more than ever.

"Nicoli took the *Trinkets* into his own possession and, with the periodic aid of my family, protected them for many years, while planning for the day when the last Tempest would be destroyed. But the day was late in coming, as the Tempest's mind probe made it all but invincible. Finally, Nicoli's great-grandson, Johnna Del, and another of my family, Tara, devised an elaborate and risky plan, which they did not make known to Johnna's son, Matthew. They allowed the son to believe that his own father was dead, killed in the northern country while trading goods. Matthew mourned a great time. Johnna himself often urged Tara to send word of hope to his son. But she would not for fear that the plan would be destroyed. Instead, Tara spoke to Matthew only about his obligation to the Royal House, filling the boy with strength and the desire to fulfill his father's will . . . to destroy the last Tempest. His desire restored, Matthew lured the Tempest to the Circle of Wisdom as his father had many times described. The creature was deceived by the boy's thoughts, thinking that he was alone. Battle ensued. The Stone proved formidable but quite uncontrollable, serving only to thwart the Tempest's own force, to protect but not attack. But when the time was at hand, Johnna rose from the chambers beneath the Circle and plunged the Sword deep into the Tempest, taking it by surprise. The power of the Stone grew and was guided to the beast, taking the offensive, concentrating its power, seeking the Sword . . . thus destroying the last Tempest."

Teacher paused. While Jason could not see her clearly through the darkness, he felt her frame relax, as though she had reached a natural break in her long tale. Once again she had mentioned the Circle. His family was so tied to its stone, he now realized. Jason decided to venture a question, one that related to a fragment of legend he did know, a puzzlement that had been in his family for eons. It was the riddle of Tempest Slayer. It was also a question that struck him with awe since he was a child.

"Why did the Wizard's Stone turn from pure white to a dull gray after the battle with the last Tempest?"

"I honestly don't know what it means," Teacher said. "While the Stone will protect the Royal House when in need, I don't know why it returns to gray as it remains even now, for it was once a constant, brilliant white. But its grayness must be of great significance, or Tara would never have mentioned it in her histories. She's been a model for all those who have followed her path."

Teacher grew rigid, and Jason was sure she would soon begin again. It was odd, he thought, that her account of legend seemed to tire her more than the actual march north. He wondered if it had something to do with the great care she took in selecting every word. No, not selecting each word, he realized, but reciting nearly each word from memory. This was one of her key tasks in life, he now knew, and it was paramount that she perfectly perform it.

"It was about this time that Cil, the third son of Nebus, brought forth his creatures into the world . . . the Bantogs. In many ways, they reflect Cil himself, in that they exhibit signs of both older brothers. Possessing both the inclination for evil and the consciousness of good, the creatures lead tortured, anguished lives. They're quite pitiful, really, and for many years they wrought nothing but mischief upon Trinity, mostly during the coming of the Twilight Festival. But they've spent the past few ages in the Land Forbidden to the north, hemmed in by both Elf and Dwarf . . . until now."

"Why do they want to kill me?" Jason interjected.

"I'm getting to that," Teacher responded. "Now, the three sons of Nebus had been arguing for quite some time. While Nebus was not aware of all the particulars, as a father in Meadowtown may be unaware of why his children quarrel in the sandbox, he was sure of one thing . . . he wanted it settled. But he did not want his children to battle each other directly. So, he intrigued his sons by staging a Contest, using Trinity itself as the prize. The terms were these . . . in five thousand years, only a brief time to the gods, each would pick a champion among its creations. Those champions would do battle to the death. The victor would win Trinity for its own. Becus immediately agreed, driven by competition. Anton agreed because it was his only chance to save all of Trinity from further destruction. Cil saw no recourse but to follow the brothers he loved. And for the past five thousand years, each of the sons has been planning. Anton has put his faith in the Royal House and in the powers of the Stone and the Pearl. Becus, on the other hand, has been silently creating and recreating Pure Evil. It is written that even Anton doesn't know what type of beast might be born from such madness. Our only hope is that, with the magic of the Stone, heightened by the mysterious force of the Pearl of Anton—whatever that power might be—goodness can defeat whatever vile beast Becus creates. Cil is confused, evil one moment and good the next. And in his confusion, he has sent his Bantogs against you in an attempt to kill you before the Contest even begins. That, perhaps, is his way of preventing the Contest altogether. But he, too, is creating a beast for the Contest. It is likely that it will be neither Purely Good nor Purely Evil. It will be somewhere in between."

Teacher relaxed and drew a slow breath while Jason stayed quiet at her side, thinking. Even if he eluded the Bantogs, he realized, he was to eventually fight anyway. It would be hideous and evil and he would probably die, but now he knew. It confirmed his worst fears, and yet, it wasn't any more frightening than the ignorance he faced an hour before. He was the last link in an enormous chain of events that began at the dawn of time, and he suddenly hoped that he would not prove to be the last link, for that would mean he was to fail. And that would be unacceptable, not so much for himself but for all the links that came before him. He understood his father a bit better now, and he prayed he would be ready for the task that awaited him in the murky, horrid future. He had half of what he would apparently need: the Wizard's Stone. The Pearl of Anton was in wait, with a power unknown.

Sadness suddenly gripped Jason. It was not the pity that held him earlier, but it nonetheless concerned him.

"It should have been Theda," he said, mindlessly cinching his rope belt tighter.

"We don't know that," Teacher snapped.

"But he was the firstborn," Jason shot back. "He was stronger. He was smarter. He was brave. If he hadn't died . . . right before my own eyes . . . this would be his quest. He was the better choice."

Teacher drew him close. "Perhaps it should have been Theda . . . and perhaps not. All we can be sure of is that you are now the last heir to the Royal House. It falls to you."

"Then I am the *Chosen One* . . . by default."

"Yes," she breathed. "But only Anton knows if it is *by default.*"

The air stood still around Jason. He trembled under the weight of responsibility. But he no longer believed that he was just in the depths of an evil dream. This was real. The daze had lifted from his eyes. A hundred questions raced about: questions of power, good and evil. He wondered about the Pearl, and the mysterious force it might possess. There were still many questions—too many. Responsibility began to weigh him down, but he calmed himself, suddenly feeling greater maturity within. Someday, he would understand better what it meant to be the Chosen One, he thought, even if it was *by default.* Today, he should try just to understand the histories that Teacher imparted. These were enough to think about. He paused for a moment to let them meander through his mind.

"It's fascinating," he started after a time, "that we can see all the manifestations of the creation, and even continue with rituals like the Twilight Festival, yet we have so little understanding of the true origin of such things." He absentmindedly caressed the Stone in his pocket, his eyes drifting off. The Age of Wisdom claimed a bit more of him.

"Where do we go from here?" Jason asked quietly, his focus restored.

Teacher leaned toward him until she could see through the dark and into his gaze. Her words were as strong as Tork.

"To find the Pearl of Anton!"

CHAPTER 6

I DIDN'T MEAN TO KILL HIM!

J ason stared for a time at the cave's jagged gray ceiling, its stone speckled with small crystalline pebbles that glistened in the dark. Teacher's account of the creation was startling, and his mind intently reexamined each and every word she had spoken, matching fragments of legends to form a whole. Though he realized that there were still several pieces of knowledge missing, he did not despair, for he knew there would be other discussions, when Teacher felt it appropriate or when he pushed the point. He felt a pang of regret at having treated Teacher so harshly, demanding that she more fully explain his role in the journey. Still, he saw the gleam in her eyes when he stood up to her, telling him that his action was part of the things he was to learn, part of his own Age of Wisdom. It told him, too, that there was another side of him buried within, a side that had strength he respected, a side that saved him from pitying himself. And he knew that, if need be, he could call that part of himself forth again and it would come.

Using the moment of silence, Teacher moved to the cave's entrance to join IAM. She sat next to their scout but said nothing to divert him from his keen watch. Teacher reached within the folds of her green cloak and produced a few yellowing sheets of paper that were barely visible in the scant light of the cave's opening. A quill was soon in her hand and she began to write, pausing on occasion, but only briefly, to find just the right word before committing a precious thought to parchment. She wrote for several minutes until her hand became curiously still for a time, drawing Jason's attention away from the ceiling, where his thoughts had gathered and mixed. He looked toward his companions and watched as they cautiously lowered themselves to the stone, their eyes locked onto something far beyond the cave's entrance. Jason dropped to his hands and knees and edged his way along the cold rock floor, snuggling in between his companions and following their eastward gaze from atop their stone perch.

The Ancient Forest of Oak was bathed in darkness. It was quiet, except for the sound of the Crystal River that lay one-half mile to the east. Stretching his sight along the tops of the mighty oaks and through a clearing, Jason beheld the Farlo trees along the bank as they sparkled to their fullest, casting a glow on the flowing river beneath it. But he noted that the water's flow was interrupted by a wave of darkness that moved steadily south along its shore. And near the crest of that wave were pairs of orange specks, bobbing up and down in unison.

"Bantogs," Jason breathed, his heart pounding heavier.

"Yep . . . and lots of them," IAM whispered. "I'd say at least two dozen along the bank. Good thing we left."

There were two loosely formed rows of the creatures with bows and quivers slung over their shoulders. Another creature, much taller and bulkier than the others, stalked alongside the rest. The larger beast suddenly raised an arm. *Crack!* It was the sound of a lashing whip. The beast had no apparent objective other than to maintain the fear that the sound engendered. It coiled the rope again and continued to hover above the marching Bantogs. This beast was considerably more dangerous, thought Jason.

"What is that?" Teacher quietly asked IAM.

"They call them Togs in the north," he said. "They started to appear about a year ago, comin' from the Land Forbidden. They're far worse than Bantogs. Ran into some myself a few months back. It wasn't pretty. They don't have fits of good in them like their smaller cousins . . . they're just plain mean. The Bantogs themselves seem to be slipping more to the darker side. We'd better get out of here before they find the critter we left on the bank."

Teacher took a breath, waiting a moment.

"Well, it looks as if Cil has become more evil yet, emulating more of Becus than of Anton. Our task will be even more difficult now."

"Where are they going?" Jason asked uneasily, as the band of darkness moved farther south along the bank and out of sight.

"Meadowtown, I'd guess," began IAM, calmly, then adding, "probably to find you."

"Meadowtown!" Jason exclaimed in a whisper. "We've got to get word to my parents . . . to Mayor Joh. . . . They've got to be warned!"

Even as his words hung in the air, another troop of Bantogs rose out of the northern darkness along the river and moved south, a Tog leading them.

"Too late to warn anybody, son," said IAM. "Besides, Meadowtown is more protected than you know." IAM motioned to Teacher as though expecting her to explain, but she remained curiously silent, allowing the scout's words to dissolve unanswered. Jason opened his mouth, a bewildered question forming, but IAM cut him short. The second band of the twisted creatures moved south and out of sight.

"Quick!" the scout ordered. "We go! Can't afford to be caught in this cave."

Without another word, Teacher and IAM picked up their packs, slid down the hard, rocky slope of the cave's entrance, then landed upon the soft forest floor before passing into the darkness. Jason hesitated a moment, gazing toward the bank. Part of him desperately wanted to turn back, to warn his parents of the beasts that drew near. But he could not. This journey—this quest—was becoming paramount in his mind, seemingly more with every passing minute. He knew that he must move on. There was no going back, for too much depended upon him. And knowing the details of his responsibility made every action seem more critical. Jason lifted his pack, glanced south toward home, and then followed his companions.

Since the Bantogs were using the glow of the Farlo trees to guide them south, IAM did what any skilled and conscientious scout would do: he stayed out of their way, leading his troupe deeper into the western forest. While the air turned dark and ominous about them, to Jason it seemed to hide their own presence rather than conceal those that would harm them. At least, he tried to keep that comforting thought.

With the routine pace restored, Jason's thoughts drifted often. He tried to keep as many pleasant thoughts as possible, and he found it easier to do than ever before. His mind even closed to the damp forest about him and went, instead, to his parents, then to legends he knew, then to his father's Sword, then to the smell of fresh Twilight Cakes baking, then to the warm comfort of his own fireplace. Jason could feel his mother's warm embrace the night he left, and the concerned but proud gleam in his father's eyes. He was grateful for his thoughts, which seemed more vivid than ever before, allowing him to so readily touch the home he loved even as his body shook with a cold sweat. In fact, the images within him had become so real, so close. They were so intriguing, indeed, that he completely lost track of time. He soon became aware of his wanderings and decided to return his concentration to the journey. He tucked the images of home carefully away in the near reaches of his mind, to be found again when needed. But as he did, Jason felt an odd sensation within, as though his mind was somehow larger this moment than last, with more pockets and folds, with the same surface but more depth. He shook his head to disperse the feeling, but it remained. This was not the Age of Wisdom, he knew. The feeling was altogether different. It was a sensation of mental expansion; for what purpose he did not know. Something within his mind had just gotten larger. As quickly as the feeling came, it left. He said nothing of it, but instead assured himself that it was merely a consequence of the fatigue. Jason refocused his thoughts on the journey and marched onward.

They pushed farther north through sparse brush and fallen trees. IAM proceeded slowly, scrutinizing the surroundings and carefully side-stepping the dried acorns that seemed to dread a heavy foot. Jason's senses felt the consuming silence of the ancient woods, vacant of the hooting owls and burrowing animals that were typically abundant in the night. The passage of the Bantogs, thought Jason, had probably made the forest animals leery, sending them deeper into the western regions. The oak trees became less dense and the terrain flatter as though the end of the forest approached. But it could not be, thought Jason. Torsen should be at least another two hours' march. Yet, a faint glow of home fires and night lights could already be seen in the sky. It should have taken many hours to come this far. Yet, he felt as though he had traveled only half that much. Then he realized that his wandering mind had taken his thoughts away from the pace. It helped greatly, he knew. His legs didn't ache half as much as they should have, nor did his lungs. Something within him was changing. Something was helping him endure the pace. He could almost feel the amenities that waited in Torsen: a hot bath, a hotter meal, and clean linens.

Just as Jason relaxed, peering through the trees to catch a first glimpse of civilization, IAM suddenly stopped, bringing the others to an unwelcome halt. The air was ominously still as IAM snapped his eyes about him, his nostrils flared. Jason saw the scout's muscles tense and flex as he searched for something in the darkness that only he could discern, something that was too close for the scout's comfort. The big Man slowly backed up a foot . . . then two. Jason and Teacher, still five yards behind him, did the same. A slight breeze brushed Jason's cheeks. Terror struck him. He detected a sweet and musky smell. It was the smell of creatures born to the night.

A patch of ground some ten paces from the scout flew upward. Two hideous creatures appeared, previously hidden in shallow, covered holes. In an instant, the companions found themselves in the sights of two deadly bows, their owners pleased with their trap. One of the beasts Jason knew instantly to be a Bantog, almost identical to the one they had left at the bank: dark-green flesh, spindly appendages, oozing pores about its face, and sharp orange, flashing eyes. But it seemed less threatening in comparison to the larger creature that stood grinning beside it: a Tog, whose thick, oily green body seemed in contrast to the honest soil that reluctantly clung to its skin. Its head was massive, its brow thick. It had pointed teeth that hung over its lower jaw, allowing saliva to drip downward. And its entire body had festering, moist welts here and there that seemed to open and close with each breath it took. But like its smaller cousin, it had orange, distrusting eyes and a contradictory sweet smell. Nearly naked, it kept its whip lashed about its thick waist as it fingered its bowstring. A huge ax draped across its back.

Jason had jumped at the sight, though intense fear kept his feet from moving further. He held his breath, believing that the creatures' odor would somehow taint his mind. He looked nervously about. Teacher was to his right. IAM was a few yards forward and to his left, looking up at the towering Tog.

"Gots yous," slurred the Tog, its jaw not meant to form human words. The Bantog anxiously watched, moving its aim from one captive to the next, keeping each frozen.

"Drops weapons slows," the Tog said, looking down upon the scout. It grinned, its tongue eagerly licking at the juices that ran out of its crooked mouth. The scout looked about, but saw no recourse. He slowly lowered his bow to the ground and then unbuckled the belt that held his sword, dropping it to the dirt, useless. His jewel-handled ax followed.

"Goods," the Tog began, very pleased with itself. "I think I kills yous first," it mocked as it raised its bow and took better aim at IAM. But before the string extended fully, the creature glanced at Jason and stopped, the sight of the boy stirring its curiosity.

"Who's yous, boy?" it demanded, vulgarly spitting the words as it shifted its deadly arrow toward Jason.

Jason couldn't speak. Even the Age of Wisdom could not extinguish the panic that was mounting.

Teacher responded quickly, attempting to divert the creature's attention.

"We're just travelers on our way to Torsen. We mean no harm."

"I kills yous second," it replied, looking at Teacher with a vile grin. "But maybe we play with yous first." The Bantog gurgled in approval.

"Yous maybe fifteens, boy?" the Tog ventured, eyeing Jason from head to toe, slowly searching with its bright-orange, inquisitive eyes. It didn't wait for Jason to reply.

"Trinkets?" it asked suddenly, its eyes now locked on the boy's chain that looped around his rope belt and led to the Wizard's Stone within his pocket. "Yous have *Trinkets* maybe?"

Jason's eyes flashed. Only legends called the Sword and Stone *Trinkets.* The boy pivoted his right hand very slowly, about one quarter turn, to help conceal the glistening chain.

"What are . . . ah . . . *Trinkets?"* he replied in a confused but unconvincing voice, his mouth dry. His heart beat wildly.

"I see chains; yous hides. Maybes it leads somewheres. But where is metal edge?"

The Tog glanced at IAM's sword, but it knew that the blade was not the one it sought.

"Nooo!" screeched the Bantog as it dropped to its knees and crawled feebly to the Tog. Jason's blood ran cold.

"No goods, no goods what we do!" it shrieked as it hugged the Tog's leg, wailing uncontrollably.

"No kill . . . no kill . . . no kill . . . " it continued to chant through its anguish, its plea echoing through the still forest.

Poor creature, Jason thought, reeling in shock himself. This was the existence as Teacher had described—beasts suspended between good and evil, tormented all of their lives by the mingling of two opposing forces that were set into motion ages ago by the youngest of gods: Cil. The Bantog continued to squirm beneath the Tog in its plea for the human lives until a great calm swept the creature. Its facial expression turned from anguish to mocking pleasure as though nothing had happened. It stumbled to its feet, bow again in hand. Yet, the beast continued to shake, ever so slightly, even as it set its sights once again on Jason. The boy was sure that a battle still raged in the depths of its being . . . a battle that eternally pitted good against a near equal measure of evil. It must be a tremendous burden, Jason thought. It was a ripping, continuous conflict. But for the moment—this moment—evil again reigned supreme.

In the surprisingly short commotion, the Tog hadn't even flinched, its arrow still leveled on Jason, its eyes still searching for the *metal edge.* Cil had reached a decision of his own, thought Jason, just as Teacher had said. The presence of the Tog confirmed it. The god was now more evil than ever, and he intended to have Trinity for himself. Jason was but one of two obstacles in his path.

"*Chosen Ones,* are you . . . yesss?" the larger one asked.

Jason's knees buckled at those words. He couldn't speak.

"Makes no differences," the Tog slurred. The creature aimed its deadly point at Jason's heart. Its horrid smile bathed Jason in terror, flooding his mind with thoughts of death: the whistling sound of the arrow, the painful jab of the point, the hard fall, the feel of warm blood upon his tunic, the arrow eternally embedded.

Suddenly, a heat flooded him, dotting his body with sweat. At first he thought it sprang from his fear. But the force was different. It was stronger and driven, and it yearned to be unleashed. It was a feeling that told him that nothing would stand in his way. It was a heat that would kill at will to save him. It was a feeling that poured hot from the Wizard's Stone!

It's happening! Jason thought wildly, his mind exploding with the memory of another story, his father's battle during the Second Race War. The boy's gaze shot to his friends. Would the power consume his companions in its blind duty to protect him? Or would the Stone not come forth in time, and they all would die? The heat continued to rise, blanketing his forehead with a pouring sweat. His ears filled with a pounding siren. The Stone was going to kill them all, he knew. Jason suddenly didn't know what to fear more: the Wizard's *Trinket* that would protect him or the Tog that would kill him. There was no way out. There was no other recourse. The fear ripped at him, shooting its way through every part of his being. As it grew, so too did the Stone grow hotter, closer to fulfilling its purpose. Jason swayed, and all of his senses seemed suddenly blurred, his mind as damp as his eyes.

"Please," Jason whispered just as the bowstring approached its greatest length, his tears flowing, the Stone burning to nearly its fullest, almost at the edge.

Jason began to bolt, to run from his fear, to leave his friends behind.

The world suddenly seemed to spin in slow motion. He saw the gleam in the beasts' eyes as their prey slightly twisted to run. He saw their fingers twitch to prepare to unleash the bowstrings. And he saw something else. The scout's arms whipped suddenly forward, his body squatting nearly to the ground to counter the force of his mighty upswing. Two Tork knives, previously hidden in the scout's sleeves, flew from IAM's hands. All of Trinity seemed suspended in time, as Jason waited for an outcome so unlikely that he was already counting himself among the dead. His mind reeled; his body trembled. He collapsed in a heap just as the knives hit their marks, embedding themselves deeply within the hearts of Cil's creatures. Two arrows went askew as the pounding blades pushed the beasts back, throwing each creature to the moist, cold ground. Each took one whimpering breath amidst the decaying leaves, then another. Then both were dead, leaving only IAM and Teacher standing in the ancient forest.

An odd silence reigned as Jason struggled to regain his mind, his body trembling in an attempt to shake the fright. While his companions stood against the creatures, he had tried to bolt. How cowardly. He could have gotten all of them killed, one way or the other.

Teacher was at his side, holding him firmly to ease his pain.

"The Stone was going to kill them," Jason sputtered, choking, "and maybe the rest of us as well." He touched his pocket and felt the residue of power unused. "I didn't know what to do."

"Well," Teacher began calmly, "we're still alive . . . so how are you?"

Jason glared at his tutor, his face contorted as he wondered if anything could move her.

"I'm fine," he lied as he rose sluggishly to his feet, trying to match her fortitude. He brushed off his tunic and then nervously watched as IAM moved to the bodies and removed his knives. Green blood spurted from the creatures' wounds as the blades slid upward, the fluid's warmth visibly rising into the cold night air. This was death, Jason thought. He had seen it once before when his brother died. Death was undignified, final, and senseless. His stomach spinning, Jason suddenly turned and heaved. Teacher held his head until his gut emptied.

"I didn't mean to kill him!" he blurted.

Teacher drew close, her eyes gleaming. "What do you mean you didn't mean to kill *him?*"

"I said *'them,'*" Jason shot back, gesturing toward the dead beasts.

"No," she corrected, her eyes pounding down on Jason. "You said you didn't mean to kill *him*. Besides, IAM killed those creatures . . . not you. So who is *'him'?''*

Jason grabbed the end of his rope belt and pulled it tight. An old, painful memory vanished. "Is that all there is to life?" he cried, ignoring her question. "There's nothing that separates life and death but a chance event and an instant of time."

"That's all there has always been," Teacher said, though her attention still appeared to be consumed by his previous comment. She let it pass.

Jason wanted to shout as loudly as he could. He wanted to scream in defiance of the master plan. How could this be? he thought. How could any of this be? In the grip of death, even the notion of a soul was cast in doubt. Maybe there was no soul, he thought. Maybe there was no life beyond. At least, Jason thought, it was the creatures that were dead. For that he could be grateful. They were hideous and evil and he knew that it was best that such beings be eradicated from all of Trinity. He suddenly hated the creatures intensely, and gladdened when he thought of their departure.

Jason sat up to find his composure. His face was pale and weary, his head a pounding ache. He gazed upward to get his bearings and saw their scout still kneeling curiously beside the warm bodies. Jason watched as IAM opened a leather pouch at his side and pulled a black dust from its bottom. IAM sprinkled it carefully upon the creatures from head to toe. Then, the scout closed the pouch and sat still, lowering his head to the ground as his lips formed words that were not carried beyond himself.

"What's he doing?" Jason asked Teacher as he turned away from the sight, his stomach still weak, his mouth filled with a dry, disagreeable taste.

"He covered the creatures with *lupas,* a burial dust used in the north. Now he prays to Anton, asking our creator to give these poor creatures a soul before their bodies grow cold and their minds fade."

"But aren't they creatures of Cil?" Jason asked, confused.

"That makes them nephews of Anton," Teacher whispered. She gazed at IAM and added, "He's a very special scout."

There was a softness in her voice, but Jason hardly noticed as he looked toward IAM. Jason was suddenly moved by the scout's code of conduct, his skill, but most of all his respect for life . . . even when it was at odds with his duty. IAM was right, he thought. Even the Bantogs are special, simply because they live in a world not of their own making and must follow dictates not of their own choosing. In a way, Jason suddenly realized, they were more deserving, because they have the least control over their actions.

Jason sank further. Nearly his entire being had wished the creatures dead—a major part was still glad. Yet the thoughts seemed hardly worthy of the champion of Anton, hardly worthy of the One who was ordained to represent all that was Good. But the thoughts still existed within him, and he continued to feel confused. How could he be good if he had such evil thoughts? Maybe he wasn't deserving of the task, he thought. After all, he got it by default. It wasn't pity he felt. Perhaps it was cold reality.

When the trio finally made their way to Torsen, through its cobblestone streets, and to a place that offered them meals and baths and bedding, Jason fell hard asleep. The events of the day had taken their toll. He dreamt of many things that restless night: of fears reborn, of destiny yet unearned, of creations and gods revealed, of immense powers he could not control. While many such dreams would be remembered, many more would not. He tossed about. Then in the depths of a most foul dream, he called out in his sleep.

"I didn't mean to kill him!"

CHAPTER 7

DEATH IN MEADOWTOWN

A red twilight morning, a bit darker this day than the last, blanketed Meadowtown as Cyrus and Beth woke in each other's arms. They shook off the residue of sleep and then exchanged soft smiles as they had done for years. But then, the prior night's events came back to them in a rush, haunting their minds and creating a painful emptiness within. Jason, their last remaining son, was gone! For them, this was day two of their Jason's journey.

They didn't speak. Beth rose and began making breakfast. Cyrus lethargically searched his clothes drawer for something to wear. His fingers dove to the bottom and touched a bundle of clothes, packed tightly, that he had not worn in years. Memories of the Second Race War flashed through his mind as he squeezed the leathers, his fingers tingling at the touch. Cyrus jerked his hand from the bundle. The memories were not always good. He grabbed an old cloth shirt and wool pants from the top of the drawer.

The table was soon set with breakfast: Twilight Cakes and a kettle of hot tea enhanced with the delicate flavor of ground Farlo leaves. The smell was as comforting as the warmth of the new fire, though both husband and wife noticed only the dreadful silence that exists when three in a home suddenly become two. It was the same silence that occurred when four became three some two years before.

After breakfast, Cyrus found himself gazing toward the Sword above the fireplace, wondering what it might bode. He wished to Anton that he knew, but prophecy did not speak to him of his role, if any, in this ominous event. And not knowing was the hardest of all circumstances for the former warrior. Cyrus's keen eyes then noticed that the point of the blade was smudged a dark red from Ethan blood, a remnant from the previous night's ordeal. He lifted the Sword off the fireplace, brought it to the table, and polished its ancient, double-edged blade.

73

As Cyrus remained lost in the Sword, Beth finished her breakfast and continued to keep busy about the cottage, straightening things that were not askew and dusting where no dust had existed for some time. Her job a short one, she finally sat at the table beside her husband and began to make a grocery list.

"I need to go to the store," she said while making notes, her eyes darting to near-empty shelves. "We're a bit short on Twilight Cakes, so I'll be baking today."

Cyrus glanced about the cottage, surprised to see it vacant of all but a few cakes. He smiled, having a good idea what became of them. "I'm not up to going to the marketplace today," he finally confessed. "I think I'll just work here." He then rose and returned the Sword to its resting place upon the mantel, leaving its metal unwrapped.

"I won't be long," Beth said as she flew out the door. She moved up the narrow street, following the trail to the marketplace. The air was brisk and clean; the smell of breakfast drifted about. The rising sun was a bit less bright than the day before, as expected during the approach of full twilight. The beginnings of the sun's retreat and the abundance of cheerful decorations created a festive mood among the people she met on the way. Beth could not return their cheer.

Mayor Joh's store was crowded. A dozen townspeople bustled about the narrow aisles, eyeing newly opened crates filled with colorfully printed cloth. Some picked through huge barrels filled with sweet apples. Others filled small bags with sugar drawn from huge burlap sacks that rested on the floor. Beth began to fill her basket with supplies. She was lost in her own grief until conversations about her cut through it.

" . . . and nobody can find her," continued one woman. "She didn't leave a note. She didn't tell anybody where she was going . . . just vanished. We didn't even find out that she was gone until our son came back home this morning and said she never showed up."

"I'm not the least surprised," began a second woman, almost snarling. "I always thought Teacher was a bit strange. She never talked much to the parents. And every time I'd try to make a little polite conversation, she would be terse with her reply and then on her way."

Beth came to attention.

"Now, ladies, let's not be so hard on Teacher," the Mayor said. "To tell you the truth, I'm a bit worried about her myself. There have been reports . . . I know this sounds crazy . . . but reports of strange creatures in the area. One fella even says he saw a Bantog. The stories are worse up north."

Heads turned.

"Ridiculous," said the women. "There are no such things as Bantogs."

"Well," began the Mayor, wiping his hands upon his apron, "the Town Council met just an hour ago to discuss the situation, and with news of Teacher's disappearance, we decided to put a guard at both ends of town just to be on the safe side."

"Cyrus!" Beth called as she blew back into their stone cottage.

"What's wrong?" he responded, a cobbler's hammer in hand as he stopped pounding a nail into a leather sole.

"Bantogs! They say there are Bantogs just north!"

"Bantogs?" Cyrus asked slowly, looking off in the distance. "If there's just a couple they can't do much harm. More than that, however, could give us some trouble."

"But even a single Bantog can kill," Beth said. "We've seen it before. Jason is in trouble."

"I know," Cyrus began. "But remember the Stone. It won't let anything hurt Jason. I'm sure he's safe. He's probably safer than the town . . . especially if those creatures think Jason is still here."

In no time at all, the news of the Bantogs raced through the village. Men searched their lodgings for long-abandoned swords and bows. Grandfathers huddled on the steps of the town store, gulped tea, and recalled their heroic exploits during the Second Race War. Their words rang with shocking clarity—a tricky task since none in the town, with the exception of Cyrus Del, actually fought in the war. Mothers stocked up supplies. Regional farmers left the marketplace early so they could reach their homes before dark.

But the children of Meadowtown reacted altogether differently. They were immensely excited by thoughts of phantoms that lurked in the night, of faraway legends that seemed closer, of heroic deeds seemingly possible. They raced through Meadowtown with sticks in hand, half of them pretending to be Bantogs while the other half pretended to be warriors until one battle was consummated. Then sides were changed and battles began anew. Over and over again they played, until many nearly dropped from exhaustion. As twilight approached, mothers tracked down their children and dragged them to dinner, assigning endless chores to prevent them from venturing outside again. The road grew quickly vacant until only three boys still played in the darkening street.

"I'm tired of this game," said Ben Wateri to David Grimm, having captured the same Bantog, Squeki Joh, for the third time in ten minutes.

Squeki was a bit tired himself, and discouraged that he had yet to play a warrior. But he knew the game was no fun with no creatures. So he volunteered again and again. After a time, it wasn't so bad to be caught. He almost looked forward to it, for it allowed him to come up from whatever dirty hole he had either found or made. But it was getting late, and he didn't particularly like playing with just Ben and David. They weren't all that sporting when it came to capturing someone. So Squeki was glad when Ben voiced his own disinterest first. The younger boy brushed himself off and prepared to leave. But Ben's mind suddenly exploded with an idea . . . an idea so enticing that he could not refuse to bend to its will.

"Hey!" he said, his eyes bouncing with delight. "Let's go looking for some real Bantogs."

"Yeah!" said David, his eyes dancing. "Then we'll bring one back and show everybody."

"How about it, Squeki?" asked Ben, prodding him with a finger.

A chill ran through the younger boy. "Ah . . . I don't think so," he said. "I should really be getting home." But he felt a responsibility to give them a warning, to tell them what his father might say if he were there. The young boy's chest puffed up proudly.

"And besides, the Town Council recommended that everyone stay in tonight. Those things might be dangerous."

"You're just chicken," taunted Ben. "They're afraid that someone else will capture a Bantog before they do. If I bring one of those things back, I bet that the town will make me Mayor or something. That's it . . . they'll make me Mayor right on the spot. Then your father can't boss people around anymore."

Ben put his arm around David and they began moving north along the street to make their plans. Squeki stepped toward home but hesitated. What if Ben did find a Bantog? he wondered. That might make his father look weak. On the other hand, if he did go with Ben, he wouldn't have to worry; a *Joh* would be there to take some of the credit. Squeki suddenly wished that Jason Del was there to give him advice. Jason always seemed so reasonable. Squeki looked about.

"Okay," Squeki yelled. "Wait up . . . I'm coming!"

The boys easily eluded the guard at the north edge of town by jumping over several fences, moving low along a few hedges, then crawling on their bellies through the tall grass of the meadow. Before long, the three boys were in the northern wood, underneath a canopy of old oaks. The sun was still above the horizon, giving them some light and making forest appear far from sinister. Faint noises arose from the town itself, providing a comfort that said, if need be, help was close.

Ben put them all to work right off. They each found a thick, fallen oak branch and then began to use their carving knives to cut off the lesser sprouts, thus shaping the three branches into suitable clubs.

"Yep," began Ben as he continued to strip his club bare. "Once I bring a Bantog back, I'll be famous." He glanced at Squeki. "Who knows, maybe I'll even see fit to keep *Joh* on as Mayor. Then he'll be working for me. Yep," he mused, "he'll be working for me."

Squeki grumbled but otherwise stayed quiet. It made him even more resolved to succeed in this endeavor. He would show Ben what Johs are made of.

As a thick twilight fell, Ben Wateri made his plan. "Squeki," he whispered. "Get in the middle of the clearing. Then make some noise to draw them in. We'll get behind them when they approach and we'll club them good. Those things won't even know what hit them."

Squeki did as he was told. He stood in the middle of the clearing and began yelling mild insults into the northern forest. David and Ben hid in nearby trees. One was to the west of the clearing and one was to the east. Fifteen minutes passed, the sun fell farther below the horizon, the dark grew wide, the chill rose, and Squeki's voice became hoarse. The glow of the Farlo trees was now visible farther east as an eerie silence fell suddenly hard. The boys continued to look excitedly about, not even realizing that the normal sounds of the forest were absent this night. Squeki continued to bait creatures unknown to him, hoping that if something was snared, he and his father could take part of the credit. The air suddenly became filled with a delightful sweet scent, one the boys had not experienced before. They sniffed the air. It was disarming. What could it be?

Twang went the hushed sound of a bowstring, a subtle sting of doom. Ben looked anxiously across the clearing just in time to see David Grimm fall, an arrow sticking through his chest. David twitched uncontrollably, his eyes blanched with terror and his hands digging at the decaying leaves upon the forest floor. He went suddenly limp—and dead! Shock held the other boys fixed.

Twang broke the silence a second time as an arrow hit Squeki in the thigh, kicking his leg out from under him and sending him crashing to the ground. The young boy held his leg and rocked, grunting and crying out in pain. Three creatures came swiftly out of the northern forest, moving toward him.

Ben turned and bolted. But he slid to a stop upon seeing a hideous, naked creature that stood ten paces away, bow leveled. The boy filled with terror as he peered into the beast's hypnotic orange eyes.

"Yous tell peoples he's dead," slurred the Bantog as it pointed its bow briefly at David Grimm. "Yous tell peoples he's hostage," it said as it pointed at Squeki, still squirming about, whimpering.

Ben glanced about to see three Bantogs around the younger boy, poking the lad gleefully with their dark, slender bows.

"Tells thems that yous gets hims back if wes gets *Chosen Ones* and *Trinkets*. Remembers . . . *Chosen Ones* and *Trinkets*. But firsts," the Bantog grinned, "theys must believes yous."

The beast released its bowstring and let the arrow fly. It pierced Ben's shoulder and knocked him backward to the ground. As the boy twisted in agony, the creature came forward, towering over him, a new arrow fitted snugly in its bowstring.

"Now theys believes you," it chuckled. "*Chosen Ones* and *Trinkets* wes wants . . . now runs or yous dies!"

"Oh no!" Beth cried as the town-hall bell rang out.

Cyrus grabbed the Sword from the mantel.

"Let's go," he said, and he and his wife flew. As they rushed out the door, a runner passed them in the twilight. He called to all the homes along the way.

"Children have been taken hostage! Bantogs! Quick! To the town hall!"

The runner jumped a short garden fence and arrived at the front door of the Grimms just down the road. Cyrus and Beth paused. Erma and John Grimm answered the door. The runner spoke quickly, but the Dels could not discern his words. Erma began to shake. John Grimm then growled at the runner, demanding verification of something as he grabbed the startled messenger and pulled him upward. The runner blurted out the message once again, and then lurched nervously away from John's grip. Erma Grimm wavered. John Grimm reached for his wife and then, having caught her, held her close as she began to cry hysterically. The runner sped up the road to Healer Kantor's cottage.

Cyrus and Beth raced to the Grimms and heard of the messenger's awful news. In just moments, the entire southern end of Meadowtown had gathered about them, stunned at the few words that the messenger had brought. The frightened crowd then moved quickly toward the town hall, the light of Farlo lining their chilly way.

Cyrus and Beth split from the masses and went to the town store so that they could check on Ben Wateri's condition. Old Healer Kantor was right behind them. They passed through the store to the Joh residence in the rear, then to Squeki's bedroom, where Ben Wateri had been placed, the flicker of candles lighting the room. Ben's parents were huddled dejectedly with their son as he lay slightly on his side, the arrow still embedded in his shoulder and sticking out his back. The boy's head rested in his mother's lap as she placed wet cloths on his forehead. He was sweating profusely and appeared to be unconscious. The Johs were not present, although Quen's shrill voice emanated from another room, interrupted now and again by the Mayor's failing attempts to comfort his wife.

"Let me see," said old Healer Kantor as he sat on the bed and placed a wrinkled, somewhat trembling hand on Ben's forehead. The Dels stood in the doorway. The Healer opened one of Ben's eyelids and peered within.

"The arrow shouldn't be causing this kind of reaction," he concluded. The Healer pulled Ben slightly to one side to get a better view of the arrow point. His finger moved toward it.

Beth's instincts flared. "Don't touch it!" she warned suddenly, freezing the Healer's hand. "Let me see it first." Beth's skill as a healer was common knowledge, though she had not practiced in years. She touched the flat side of the arrowhead, noted the edge, and then raised a drop of Ben's blood to her nose.

Her eyes shot to Ben's parents. "Has anyone been scraped by the point?"

Dazed shakes told her no.

Just then, Ben Wateri had a fit of convulsions, gasping for air. Beth stood back, knowing what would come. The boy coughed violently, his torso heaving upward in seizure, his eyes widening in terror. He looked back into his mother's frightened stare. Then he fell slowly back into the bed, his head landing limply in his mother's lap. He was dead.

His mother screamed. His father reached for her. They were quickly led to the master bedroom. Along with David Grimm's parents, they grieved.

"What was it?" the Healer asked Beth as he draped a sheet over Ben's body.

"A Bantog poison," Beth began sadly. "One of many. This variety works slower than most. It allows the victim to linger on."

"Then you've seen this before," remarked the Healer.

Beth glanced up at her husband.

"Yes," Cyrus said. "We've seen this before . . . long ago up north. But we never thought we'd see it again."

Healer Kantor left the room and returned quickly with Mayor Tome Joh. Strain was painted on his face.

"Kantor tells me you've had some experience with these things," the Mayor said, his voice drained. The Dels nodded. The Mayor trembled. "Squeki is still out there. Ben said he's a hostage until we give them something."

Beth and Cyrus glanced at each other. The Mayor moved closer.

"Now tell me the truth, Cy. Do you think my son is already dead?"

"He's alive, Tome. The poison they use is rare, so I doubt they used it on Squeki. They'll keep him alive until they get what they want."

Beth and Cyrus followed the Mayor as he made his way to the main chamber of the town hall and sat in his reserved council chair. The Dels found the last two seats, in the back. People continued to arrive until they were huddled on the floor, along the center aisle, and even at the base of the podium. When the torrent of people turned into a trickle, Tome Joh rose.

"My son, Ben Wateri, and David Grimm ventured just north of town. David was killed in the forest. Ben Wateri has died, too, after making it back. My son is still out there, being held hostage. It was Bantogs."

A murmur of shock rose from the townspeople.

"The town is secure for now!" called the Mayor. "The Bantogs told Ben that they want something they call the *Chosen One* and *Trinkets* in exchange for Squeki. Does anyone know what that means?"

A hush fell over the hall as eyes shot to one another. The Mayor repeated his question. But along with the hundreds of others in the hall, Cyrus and Beth shook their heads. The people wouldn't understand, they both instinctively knew. They wouldn't believe. Worse yet, if they did believe, they might try to surrender the Sword to the Bantogs, who, most likely, would kill Squeki once they had it anyway. They had to keep silent.

"I was afraid of that," said the Mayor when no one answered. He wiped his eyes and took a breath. "So now, how do we save my son?"

Cyrus squeezed Beth's hand.

The Mayor did the thing he knew best, the thing that kept him in office through the years: he solicited the opinions of others, listening to their thoughts before settling on a direction. He knew that he desperately needed their help, for he could not face the Bantogs alone. He needed a plan. And he needed enough people supporting the plan to get volunteers to carry it out. An hour quickly passed as the townspeople recommended various options. There were many arguments and counterarguments. Tempers flared. Old wounds festered. It was even put to a vote to do nothing, consider Squeki dead, risk no lives to save him, and devote the energy to fortify the town instead. While the plan was enticing to many, it was voted down by a large margin, mostly out of respect for Tome, who abstained during the vote.

Cyrus found the whole debate disgusting. So many people, he thought, and not one decision among them.

"I need some air, Beth," he said. "Wait for me here."

"I'll come with you."

"No. Stay here in case they reach an agreement. Then come get me. I'll be close."

Without waiting for a reply, Cyrus Del rose and limped quietly into the night air. Another hour passed until the townspeople narrowed the options to three. First the townspeople could send a fact-finding party out to question the Bantogs on their request . . . specifically about the nature of the *Chosen One* and *Trinkets*. Upon receiving a fuller description, they would obtain the items if they had them or, if not, try to barter with other goods. The risk here was to the members of the fact-finding party, who may become hostages themselves. Second, they could surround the Bantogs by first sending a party westward, then north, then east to arrive at the Bantogs' rear. Another party would then be sent directly north to gain the Bantogs' attention. Both groups would attempt to rescue the boy before the Bantogs could act. This, too, seemed risky—to both the boy and the rescuers. Third, they considered tricking the Bantogs into believing they had the *Chosen One* and *Trinkets* by exchanging a box of goods for the boy and arriving back into town before the Bantogs realize what had happened. But this idea seemed more wishful than sound.

With the options voiced, the debate grew more intense. Another hour passed, with more debate. In a way, they had decided—and the decision was to do nothing. And Beth knew it. She now saw it as clearly as Cyrus did hours before. In the town's own way, it was happier with indecision. It meant that nothing else would occur. And there was a definite comfort in stagnation.

Quen Joh burst into tears. "What should we do?!" she shrieked. Startled, sympathetic eyes shot toward her. Children woke and began to cry.

"My son, my little baby, is in the hands of murderers and we're doing nothing."

She fell to her knees and pressed her hands up against her forehead, the anguish overpowering her. Tome Joh knelt and placed his arms about his wife, holding her tightly as she continued.

"Dear Anton," she cried, her head cocked upward, her stabbing words penetrating the bell tower and rising into the cold night.

"My little boy is all alone. . . . Tell us what to do. . . . Please, dear Anton, tell us what to do."

Boom!

The heavy doors to the town hall swung inward, crashing against the walls. A cold wind entered, chilling the gathering and causing the fire to flicker wildly. Everyone, with the exception of the Johs, who were lost to themselves, turned to follow the disturbance. Their eyes opened wide as a Man stalked through the doorway and pushed through those who stood in his path. He wore rugged buckskin clothing. He had a Dwarf ax hanging from a thick leather belt. An Elf bow looped about a rigid shoulder. A quiver was tied tightly to his back. A brilliant sword was strapped loosely at his side. But he was far from immaculate. The ax and sword were stained with a fresh, seemingly green blood, as were parts of his leathers. The quiver was nearly empty of arrows. And the Man himself was scraped and dirtied. But all of this went unnoticed, for in his arms he carried a smiling young boy, a bloodstained bandage tied tightly about his thigh. People gasped.

"Mom! Dad!" the boy screamed as he was carried to his parents.

Tome Joh jerked his head upward. He shook his wife to get her attention. Quen Joh looked up, her eyes filled with tears, her head spinning just as Cyrus Del, the warrior, lowered Squeki into her arms. The parents and child fell onto each other and cried.

Cyrus turned to the podium and, for the first time ever, addressed the assembled people of Meadowtown. The hall was silent.

"The Bantogs were only a small scouting party . . . but that threat is gone," he assured everyone. "Still, we have to prepare. An army of these creatures is on its way. We have one day, maybe two. I'm not going to lie to you. It's only going to get worse . . . a lot worse. And I'll add this. We're going to need a lot more action and a lot less words. If you can't pull together . . . if you can't act . . . you are all going to die!"

CHAPTER 8

YOU FIGHT FOR THE CHILDREN

J ason's eyelids twitched slowly as his mind followed the object of his
dream. It was the Wizard's Stone. He saw the sphere from all angles,
and it proved perfectly smooth. It was spinning rapidly. It seemed so
close to him, so much a part of him. There was no chain or clasp to bind
it, which allowed it to move freely about a huge, almost boundary-less
room. And it seemed to cherish the freedom, the freedom that permitted
it to go wherever or do whatever it pleased. Yet it wasn't free at all. No
matter how huge the room became, the Stone would always be a prisoner. And rather than gray, in this cavern it was a brilliant white. As
Jason watched, the Stone's fierce rotation began to subside. It moved to
the middle of the cavern and steadied itself as if waiting, patiently, for
direction. After a time, the Stone began to shrink until it became so tiny
that it vanished, lost somewhere within the deepest reaches of whence it
came.

Jason awoke and opened his eyes slowly. His head ached. He rubbed
his temples for several minutes to rid them of the pain. The discomfort
gradually receded.

He suddenly remembered the encounter with the Bantog and the Tog
the day before, and the Wizard Stone's uncontrollable power. His mind
sparked, remembering his dream. The boy looked at his wrist and found
his chain locked and intact, leading to a clasp that held the gray Stone
tightly. He remembered anchoring the chain about his wrist when he
undressed the night before. The Stone hadn't gone anywhere, he realized. Though it was still gray, it made him anxious nonetheless.
Concentrating, he carefully put the fretful feeling away in one of the
new voids within his mind. He was suddenly surprised at how easy it
was to do—to dispense with a thought as if it were a physical object. He
had felt this before, but it was intensified now. He could almost *see* the

thought in his mind, resting upon the shelf where he had placed it. But even as he was examining the oddity, it suddenly vanished. More puzzles, he mused.

Jason opened his eyes wider, yawned, stretched his arms wide, and beheld where he dwelt. It was a small room. There were no windows. The scent of fresh air suggested that a vent was somewhere about. The light in his chamber was a dull white and came from a small, milky globe attached to the ceiling. Steam rose from a washbasin near the bed. A fresh cotton shirt and wool pants were draped over a chair, while his boots, now clean of the previous night's travels, stood alone in the corner of the room. The wooden headboard of his bed was engraved with familiar shapes: stars, circles, and triangles. All four walls were painted a light blue, filled with thousands of bright specks that appeared to form clusters of stars.

"Astar!" Jason whispered. He could be nowhere except the ancient home of the astronomers. He remembered the tall red-brick building they approached the night before with its rusty, iron gate and decaying, keystone-arched doorway. He also remembered its dome-shaped roof, the zenith starkly supported by statues of strange beasts that were inlaid into the lower brickwork. It was quite the opposite of the younger town of Torsen that nestled at its feet, with its smooth cobblestone roads and orderly rows of short, wooden cottages. This building was definitely out of its time, Jason thought. No one had built with red brick in over a hundred years. Nor did buildings these days reach beyond two stories. But Astar did, reaching for four. He then recalled the old Man who let them in the night before. He was as curious as Astar, with his long silver hair and wrinkled, rosy cheeks that seemed to clash with his blue velvet robe. Without so much as a word, the Man led them to their rooms on the second floor, which had hot dinners and warm baths waiting. His job fulfilled, the Man disappeared in silence.

Jason pulled himself out of bed and bathed. He dressed quickly and then carefully secured the Stone within his pocket, wrapping the chain back around his belt. He found his pack and extracted a Twilight Cake. He devoured the pastry instantly. He may not be home, Jason thought, but as long as the Twilight Cakes lasted, it would feel as though he carried a piece of home with him always. Though still hungry, he decided to save the rest.

Jason left his room in search of his companions. He reached the first floor, which had a rather large room containing a huge fireplace whose mantel rose above Jason's head. Though there was no fire, the air seemed warm nonetheless, circulating constantly. The walls were covered with maps of the sky: spheres of yellow, dots of blue, clumps of fiery red specks, and globs of black that swallowed up everything else. But no one was present, so Jason roamed. Each chamber looked barren compared to the first. They were all gray, void of windows and wall coverings. They did, however, contain the curious sunglobes that provided the light he needed to find his way. As Jason began to wonder if he were all alone, his nose caught the familiar scent of breakfast coming from the next chamber. He heard the sound of delicate metal scraping metal, as though a morsel of food were about to be gathered and consumed. He entered.

The small room was filled with sunlight that filtered through a skylight high above. The walls were white but empty. A table was occupied by an aging but fit warrior.

"How ya doin', my boy?" asked IAM as he lifted a forkful of breakfast into his mouth.

"Much better," responded Jason.

"Come and sit here," the big Man said between chews. "I've been waitin' for hours. Why . . . this is my third breakfast. Would you like somethin' to eat?"

"Maybe some eggs and bread," Jason said as he looked about.

"Don't worry . . . they'll find you. The walls have ears, don't you know."

Not more than a minute passed before the same gentleman who greeted them the night before pushed his way through the swinging door with cooked eggs, bread, butter, jam, and hot tea. He left as quickly as he came.

"How did he hear me?" Jason asked.

"No idea . . . eat up," IAM said as he continued to devour his own meal.

Jason attacked his food. Everything tasted fresh and vibrant, as though the meal was enhanced with a spice that heightened each food's natural flavor. Even the tea was unusually potent, complementing the meal perfectly.

"Were you in the Mountain High Battalion?" he asked of the silver-haired backwoodsman.

"Sure was," said IAM, a spark igniting in the older Man's eyes as he took another bite.

"What did you do . . . I mean, what were your responsibilities?"

"Pretty much what I'm doin' for you—a little scoutin', a little fightin'."

"Did you know Major T well?"

"Pretty much," he said with a smile, a nod emphasizing his words. He chewed.

"Did you ever meet my father, Cyrus Del?"

IAM glanced up, surprised.

"Everybody in the Battalion knew Captain Del, either by name or reputation."

"Captain Del?" Jason blurted, having never heard his father's rank before.

"Why sure. Cy was Major T's finest officer." IAM cocked an eyebrow. "You mean your father didn't tell you that?"

"No," Jason said with a faraway smile. His father never liked to discuss the war. He always used to say, *"What's done is done."*

"I hope that he at least told you how he became a hero," remarked IAM.

"A hero?" Jason asked, again revealing his ignorance.

The big Man smiled wide, his white teeth gleaming against his tan skin.

"Now, that's a history worth the tellin'," IAM said as he reclined back in his chair. In contrast, Jason leaned forward, his whole body poised and ready. These were the stories he lived for. And for the moment, there was no Contest, no fearful battle before him, no thoughts of what this particular day might bring. There was just the anticipation of a good tale.

"As you probably know . . . that's if Teacher taught you right . . . " He smiled. "The Elf and Dwarf armies were battlin' it out for some five years in the Valley of Despair. Mountain High was all around them. The Northern Dwarves were camped in the north end of the valley and the Elves to the southwest. Each was attemptin' to claim the valley for its own. Just imagine . . . thousands of Elf and Dwarf warriors, each tryin' to destroy the other, each capable of doin' it if given the chance. Now, Major T, disgusted by it all, united the Men of Trinity and trained them to fight. His only purpose was to bring the stupid war to a close. At first, he tried making peace between the northern Races, but neither side would listen. The disagreements went back ages. So then he started disruptin' each army by capturing a few Elves here and a few Dwarves there. He sent a lot of mixed signals to each camp too. That way, neither side had accurate information on the troop strength of the other."

Jason smiled. "Major T was pretty clever."

"Some might say so," IAM returned, winking. "In all, we must have prevented a few dozen battles. But in truth, we weren't really stopping the war . . . just making it more difficult for them to kill each other fast. That's when the Major developed his greatest plan. He decided to enter the Valley of Despair through the Eastern Pass and split his army of one thousand into two groups: one to rim the mountain to the north and cut off Dwarf supply wagons that came over the Northern Pass; the other to rim the mountain to the southwest and cut off Elf supply lines that came over the Western Pass. And as everybody knows . . . no supplies . . . no war . . . real simple."

"That's the part I did know," Jason declared, proudly.

"News then came that the Northern Dwarf army was being reinforced and resupplied by a thousand Dwarf warriors from the eastern lands . . . distant cousins. They planned to move through the Eastern Pass before we did in order to flank the Elf armies—not good news if you happened to be an Elf. The whole Elf Race could have been destroyed . . . an entire Race! We got to the pass first, but we couldn't stay. We had to move most of our men to the other passes to block the supply routes. Your father volunteered to stay and block the Eastern Pass, preventin' the Eastern Dwarves from entering the valley. Major T ordered him to take two hundred men but Cy refused, agreein' to take only one hundred, knowin' that the Major would need as many men as possible to block the other passes."

IAM paused and leaned closer to Jason. The big Man's gray eyes grew sharp and serious—almost biting. "Your father was the only Man who could refuse the Major's orders and get away with it, son. That's somethin' to remember!"

A chill flashed through Jason's body. There was a message in there for him, though he could not fathom what it was. The backwoodsman then leaned back, allowing a smile to once again reach his lips as he continued.

"The plan was made. Your father got one hundred volunteers and positioned them along the Eastern Pass, blocking it tight. As the Major's army started to move further up the pass, the Eastern Dwarves arrived and ran smack-dab into the Captain's Men. They threw everythin' they had against your father's company. From the ridge above we could see the first battle . . . one hundred Men against one thousand Dwarves. What a sight! But the Captain had taken superior positions. After the first assault, we counted ten of his Men dead to about fifty Dwarves. We saw one other attack, which ended about the same. Then, the Major's forces, and me with them, finally pushed beyond the ridge, split into two, and each went to secure the other passes."

IAM poked at his meal, taking a small bite.

"The Major left two scouts behind to observe the outcome of the battle and to report—one to each half of his now split army—should the Dwarves break through. I'm told that for another day your father's troops held seven assaults in all. Then, during the eighth assault, there was some kind of explosion in the pass. Most of the mountain fell in."

Jason froze. This part of the story he did know. That was the Stone. He patted his pocket to make sure the gem was in place.

"When the dust cleared, the Eastern Pass was nearly gone . . . blocked solid. The Eastern Dwarves could do nothing else but return home. The scouts found your father along with the remains of his company . . . exactly thirty-two Men. They led them to the Major, who was commandin' the push to the Northern Pass."

IAM's mind began to wander, his voice becoming soft.

"I remember that like it was yesterday. The cheers of the crowd when your father was carried back, a Dwarf ax still buried in his leg. I also remember the senior healer's decision to cut your father's leg clean off."

"His leg?" Jason asked. "They were going to cut it off?"

"Yep . . . the healer almost did it, too. He had a saw in hand and everythin'. But a young apprentice healer stopped him. She said the leg could be saved." The scout smiled. "Your father had the prettiest young healer I'd ever seen . . . jet-black hair and ruby lips. But it was her commitment that I admired the most. No one could shake her from doing what she believed to be the right thing. She was tough on the outside, but I always suspected she was soft on the inside." The scout's eyes suddenly twinkled. "I think her name was Joanna. . . . " he began teasingly. "No . . . it was Meredith. No . . . that's not quite right either. Beth! That's right . . . that's what her name was . . . it was Beth!"

Jason's jaw dropped.

"Anyway, the rest of the story you probably know. The Battalion managed to block the Elf and Dwarf supply lines for about four weeks. That is all it takes in the midst of winter to bring an army to its knees. Elf and Dwarf leaders sent peacemakers. The Major sat with them and worked out the details . . . the Triad Agreement, they called it. The Elves kept the land that was west of the valley. The Northern Dwarves kept the land to the north. Neither shared the valley itself or the mountains surrounding it. The Eastern Dwarves went back to the eastern lands. Separation, it was. It was a terrible thing, but it was the only thing that they could agree on."

IAM took another mouthful of food.

Jason was quiet. He had discovered more about his parents in the past fifteen minutes than he had in the last fifteen years. And it was an odd feeling to suddenly realize that his father and mother had both led full, daring lives long before he was ever born. There was so much they hadn't told him. And there was so much that he hadn't thought to ask about. He suddenly wished that his parents were there, in the brightened room, so that he could tell them that he knew a little bit more about each of them. And as such, he knew a little bit more about himself.

Jason heard familiar footsteps enter the room. He looked up just as Teacher approached. She was more beautiful than he had ever seen her. Her forest-green robe was gone, and she wore a blue silk gown instead. It fit her slender body well, highlighting her sharp blue eyes. Her shining white hair was not in its usual bun. Rather, it flowed loosely around her delicate shoulders. And what was more, Teacher was smiling!

"Elf cakes and tea, please," she said to no one but the room. She sat beside Jason, her eyes piercing him.

"Did you sleep well?"

Jason paused, fixed on her smile. He had never seen it before. "Yes," he finally said. "I slept very well . . . thank you."

"How do you find Astar?" she asked.

Jason looked about the room. "Is there magic here?" he asked just as Teacher's breakfast was delivered.

"No. Not really." She broke one of the Elf cakes in two and dunked half of it into her tea before popping it politely into her mouth, chewing it completely.

"In a way," she began again, "it was Man's attempt to reach magic, to gain and manipulate power that he was not given at birth. He called it *science:* a reaching for magic that he would never really obtain."

"How does it work?"

"A flowing of forces, a blending of others, and a conversion of some. It's all the same, really . . . contrived . . . coming from without instead of from within. Let me show you."

Teacher reached about her neck and pulled up a chain that held a gold locket, its surface polished to a bright shine. She opened the face of it by gently pressing a minute lever. On the inside of the locket was row after row of small white crystalline beads . . . dozens in all. The ninth bead in the first row was aglow. As they watched, its light faded but was replaced by a new glow in the tenth bead.

"When the last bead in the last row is set aglow," she said pointing, "the Final Contest will begin . . . roughly ten and a half days hence."

Reality flooded over Jason. IAM's story and Teacher's smile almost helped him forget his responsibility. He gazed at the locket. *The last bead in the last row,* he thought.

Teacher closed the locket and dropped it beneath her neckline.

"It's not magic. It's merely a mechanism, a useful device that will keep us on track and help us in our daily lives. Astar is much like that, and so is science."

Jason developed an instant dislike for the locket. It was a reminder of his pace, his accomplishments, his ending perhaps. He turned his mind elsewhere, unwilling to give into the misery. He forced out a question.

"Why are there no references to my father in regular history books?"

"Well," Teacher began, "some histories are better left buried."

Jason frowned. "How did all of this get so out of control? I mean, the Races at war, hating each other, fighting, dying, when they are all part of Anton's creations? We're supposed to be good. It just doesn't make sense."

Teacher wiped her lips gently. "When Anton created the Races, he emphasized in each Race certain strengths. The Elves received an abundance of beauty and agility and sense of duty. The Dwarves received a fair amount of skill in craftsmanship. My people, the Etha, received wisdom and endurance. Man was actually created last. It was Anton's attempt to balance as many of the Wallo traits as possible. Yet all the Races are filled with specks of greed, pride, love, hate, envy, and many other elements, both good and bad. Traces of evil, you might call them. Only Anton truly knows why he did this."

That would account for the feelings within him, Jason thought. Yet it was far from comforting. If he is to be the champion of Anton, he needed to strive for goodness; he needed to suppress the evils and embrace only the pure.

"In a way," he began in a saddened voice, "we are no different than the Bantogs."

"And in a way you are right," added Teacher. "But it's a matter of degree. We are, in the main, good with traces of evil. Bantogs are pulled from one end of the spectrum to the other. So while the comparison is right, the outcome is quite different." Teacher rose from her seat and extended her hand to Jason.

"I need to show you one more wonder of Astar. Our time here grows short."

Jason took her hand. It was so warm, so soft, so much like someone who would be named Sarawathe.

"We'll be back in a bit, IAM," Teacher said as they moved toward the door.

"No problem," the scout returned. "In fact, take your time." IAM then whispered, "Five more eggs, please."

Teacher led Jason down a musty hallway, its length filled with thick cobwebs that they pushed aside. At the end of the hall they encountered an old steel staircase that spiraled upward into a dark gray tunnel. They climbed the stairs to the top, where a landing led to a small iron door. They opened the door and entered darkness.

"It's okay," Teacher said as she stepped farther into the room, pulling the boy along, searching her way through the darkness. She stopped abruptly.

"Here they are."

Teacher guided Jason's hands to one of two chairs positioned in the middle of the room. He felt his way into its soft, leathery embrace. The Etha sat in the chair beside him, the outline of her figure completely lost in the dark.

"Now, Jason, what you are about to see is a bit . . . different! Try to ignore the strangeness of it, and concentrate instead on the things you see. The things you see are important."

Jason heard a low, vibrating hum as his chair pivoted slowly backward, stopping when it had tilted forty-five degrees. Then, he saw a pinprick of white light appear before him, perhaps no more than ten feet above his head. It began to twinkle. Then a red speck appeared—then another white, a blue, another red, another white. Again and again they came in the various colors until, finally, the ceiling was filled with a glittering radiance of twinkling white and red and blue specks. Some were alone while others formed dazzling clusters. It was the night sky. The stars began to blur and race past him, and Jason was catapulted forward.

His fingers gripped the arms of the chair and he could almost feel the force that propelled him. Then, the pace began to slow and the sky was suddenly filled with the approach of a single yellow star. The ball became larger and larger until it finally exploded onto the ceiling. Jason shielded his eyes from the sight until the brightness began to yield. When he looked again, the star was falling back, getting smaller in the heavens, but revealing more than a half-dozen spheres that rotated around it. The image then moved to one of the many spheres, plunging downward until the object filled the ceiling with greens and blues and browns, each mixing and swirling above. It looked like a huge map, its surface bearing the groove of a great blue river that flowed from a rugged mountain range in the north to an unknown destination in the south. Vast green forests laid claim to the west, and sweeping brown deserts owned the east. And although Jason could recognize only small portions of it, he knew that he gazed at Trinity.

"It's beautiful!" he gasped.

"I'm glad you think so. I thought it was important that you see what you are fighting for. But there's more."

Abruptly, all the lights went out and the image was gone.

Jason felt the Age of Wisdom tighten its grip.

"We're really a small part of the total," he said in the darkness.

"Yes."

"But an important part," he concluded.

"Yes."

The darkness seemed such a good place to ponder, so much like his mind.

"If we have souls," he began, "then why do we fight to survive? Why do we even bother with the Contest that draws near? Why can't we just die?"

His question sounded more defeatist than he had intended. But he let it be.

"Without birth, we have no chance at life. Without life, we cannot rise to Anton. That is the plan. And that, too, is why we die: to make room for the new while completing our own passage. But there is a great sadness in the plan. And it is this: an embodied soul cannot pass to Anton until it is sufficiently developed . . . matured."

"What does that mean?"

"It takes a certain amount of energy for the soul to be hurled from this world to the next. If the transference takes place at too early an age, in too young a person, the passage will be traumatic, and the soul may not reach Anton unscathed. It will, instead, be lost forever."

Jason trembled. "Then, I'm not really fighting for my own survival. I'm not fighting for the land. I'm fighting for souls that do not yet exist, and for the souls that have already been born but are still too young to survive the passage should they die."

"Exactly."

"So fighting is not always wrong. You can't always just walk away. You can't always just take a beating." He thought about Ben Wateri.

"No."

"How old must a child be to ensure that his soul survives the passage?" He thought about Theda, who was fifteen when he died. Jason unconsciously tightened his belt.

"There is little hope for those less than five years old. There is much hope for those over fifteen. But in-between is a gray area. It depends on the child's maturity and life force."

"The founder's stone at school," Jason whispered. "It's engraved with the ages of the school years . . . *Children Five to Fifteen Learn Here.* Your teachings are not just about reading and math. Your lessons are also trying to help us mature and gain inner strength."

"That is correct."

"Nearly everything has meaning. Doesn't it?"

"Yes. The trick is to discern what it is."

"Then I truly fight for the children."

"Yes . . . not for glory, or your own survival, or the land. You fight for the Race children of Trinity!"

CHAPTER 9

MAJOR T UNMASKED

Ages ago when the first snow on Mountain High melted in the warming sun, the water rushed south and etched a deep, permanent groove into the face of Trinity. And with the water's passing, the Crystal River was born in a vibrant flow that united the land from north to south. But the rocky terrain one mile south of Mountain High was strong and resisted the water's corrosive rub, thus causing the northern reaches of the river to fan out just enough to create a widening marsh. While the water in the center of the marsh passed quickly south with the river, the water at the periphery oozed slowly against green reeds that sprouted throughout. In time, the Farlo trees that grew tall along the river also rimmed the Mountain Marsh, and the smallest of creatures called this soaked land their home.

As twilight once again signaled the gradual approach of night amidst the marsh, a rugged scout stood immobile to the south. He peered toward the shallow basin of water, its depth frigid from the approach of winter, as a brisk clean wind meandered south to bite his leathery cheeks. But IAM refused to feel the cold as his gray eyes shifted shrewdly, finely reviewing the intricacies of the land that lay ahead. The Farlo had just begun their green glow in anticipation of the night, their branches blowing slowly in the breeze above the marsh they seemingly governed. The sky was an orange-gray, but alive with the comforting sound of winter crickets and the playful movement of airborne insects.

Satisfied with all he perceived, IAM waved to the bushes behind him and out came his two charges. Both were now clad in buckskin leathers—much like their scout's own—provided by the hospitality of Astar. Teacher led the way, her silky white hair once again pulled back, her demeanor appearing well rested and alert. Jason followed. Unlike his companions, he was exhausted from a hurried pace that extended far beyond his capacity to bear it gracefully. His lungs ached. His legs wobbled. His red hair was wet from perspiration that trickled down his forehead. Each day his stride was better than the day before. And each day his companions challenged him with a longer and faster run. Time was precious, he knew. So was building his physical condition. And the pace, he suspected, was meant to satisfy both objectives.

Jason's weary sight focused upon the shimmering rim of distant Farlo that rested above a water-soaked land. It was teeming with millions of insects that buzzed about, some casting a red glow of their own. He looked beyond the Farlo to a magnificent slab of rock and snow that formed an up-reaching, impenetrable gray wall. The huge edifice seemed to touch the sky and be everywhere at once, blocking out even the view of the stars that began to pierce the consuming twilight. Although the boy had never before seen the massive ridges that spanned the horizon, he knew at once that he looked upon Mountain High.

"Jason!" Teacher reprimanded. "Don't waste time . . . come!"

Teacher's disposition was back to normal, Jason thought, probably a result of the pace, which reminded all of them of the great task ahead. He blinked his eyes, wiped the sweat off his brow, and refocused on the task.

"The marsh is far too wide to circle quickly," said IAM. "We've got to wade through the shallows."

"How long is it across?" asked Teacher, her blue eyes scanning beyond.

"Directly ahead, the marsh pinches inward. I reckon it's only a few hundred yards wide."

"Let's go," Teacher said.

The soil and grass began to squish beneath their feet as insects darted and hummed about their heads. IAM and Teacher ignored the insects, but Jason swatted at the bugs in a losing attempt to shoo them away. His efforts only served to bring more in search of fun. Suddenly, a wave of pain crashed over his bewildered mind, rising up from the new voids within. The boy wavered in agony. He reached to hold his head between his hands. Teacher caught him just before he fell into the marsh.

"You all right?" she asked, her eyes piercing him.

"No!" Jason cried. He winced and knelt, massaging his temples firmly. The pain grew. "Ahhh!" he screamed out.

"Beneath the pain," asked Teacher sharply, "what do you *feel?*"

Jason winced again and closed his eyes. He looked inward. He saw his own memories more vividly than before. They appeared to be like physical objects that he could review and probe. Beneath that, he saw ripping waves of the pain pouring from the empty, evolving spaces much deeper in his mind.

"The empty spots hurt," he blurted, thinking instantly that his words were nonsense. They were not wasted on Teacher.

"Good," she said as her fingers moved to soothe the muscles that connected the boy's neck and head, driving a finger to the base. As fast as the pain arose, it vanished. Jason steadied himself, and then cautiously tilted his head from one side to the other, testing the longevity of the relief.

"When did the pain start?" Teacher asked sternly.

"A moment ago," he said, taking a deep breath.

"I mean before now."

"Oh . . . well," he began as he continued to rub his temples softly, remembering the painful dream he had at Astar.

"A day or so ago, I guess . . . but it was never this bad." Jason looked into Teacher's eyes and realized that she knew more than she was telling. "What is it?" he asked.

"A beginning," Teacher answered as she checked his pupils.

"It's not the Age of Wisdom . . . is it?"

"No. It's something else altogether. Something that . . . "

"Sara," IAM interjected, "I don't know what this is all about, but we've got to get goin'. That marsh isn't gettin' any narrower and we're losin' what little light is left."

"Okay," Teacher responded, then turned back to Jason. "If there's anymore pain . . . anything odd happening in there," she said as she tapped his forehead, "tell me immediately!" Her voice was strong. "That is where it all begins!"

Jason nodded. More riddles, he thought, as he took another cleansing breath.

The trio began their trek across the basin of water and mud, pushing the tall reeds aside with each step. Their feet quickly sank beneath the surface and vanished in the murky water. It got quickly deeper, rising to just below their knees. The reeds grew thicker. They soon crossed half the distance and found themselves encircled by a dazzling ring of Farlo that surrounded the entire marsh. Jason filled with awe.

"Listen," IAM said, stopping dead in the marsh. The scout shifted his head slightly to the right and then left, positioning his ears so as to catch the most casual of sounds. Fearful, Jason did the same. But try as he might, the boy heard nothing except the sound of water gently lapping up against his legs.

"I don't hear anything," Jason whispered. He was comforted by his assessment.

"That's the point," Teacher said, her eyes darting about. "There's nothing to hear."

The sound of all living things had vanished. The insects that fluttered and dove about were gone—all gone! Jason's heart began to pound, the adrenaline flowing wildly through his veins.

IAM jolted about. A hundred yards south, on the horizon through the Farlo trees, a dozen Bantogs were on a full sprint—and headed their way!

"Run!" IAM shouted.

They bolted north through the cold marsh, reeds still growing thicker about them. The Bantogs reached the water in an instant, their slick green skin allowing them to move through the water as though born to it. They began to howl as they caught the scent of Man-flesh. Chills grabbed Jason's spine and spurred him onward. He looked back. Some of the beasts stopped; the good in them was winning out. But they were soon prodded onward by a huge Tog that followed. It whipped the creatures into pursuit. Jason suddenly tripped and fell headfirst into the marsh, inhaling water as he fought to rise above the surface. Hands grabbed his shoulders and yanked him up. It was IAM!

The Bantogs had cut their distance by half and began to shoot arrows while on the run. The first volley of deadly points arched like a half-moon and fell. One pierced IAM's backpack, stopping short of its target. The trio flew onward. The sound of their feet pounding the water was deafening. It drowned out even the yells of the Bantogs that grew closer by the second. Jason looked toward the bank, his body numb with fear, and knew they would never reach it before the creatures descended upon them.

Without losing a step, IAM drew an arrow from his quiver and fitted his bow.

"Move beyond!" he yelled. Teacher and Jason passed him. The scout let an arrow fly. It sliced through the reeds and pounded into the skull of the lead Bantog. The creature jerked backward into the cold water. Jason thought of the Wizard's Stone, and the power that rested within his pocket. He grabbed the Stone, thinking he could summon its force in order to direct it toward the beasts. But he could not, and it stayed inert at his side. He could feel no heat burn within its lifeless sphere. Did it know that he faced no real danger? Or was it that the point of death had yet to arrive?

A sharp cry rang out from the woods in front of them. IAM burst past his companions. The scout scanned the northern rim of Farlo, checked the Bantogs' distance, and then the examined trees again. He suddenly changed directions slightly, jumping quickly through the water on a diagonal, to the east. The marsh was still just below their knees.

"When I count to three," IAM shouted, "drop to the marsh! Understand?!"

Teacher and Jason nodded. The Bantogs drew within fifty yards.

"One!"

An arrow whistled past Jason's shoulder.

"Two!"

Two arrows fell just short of Teacher. Any moment, Jason thought, the arrows would find their mark.

"Three!"

Jason plunged downward. As he fell, he felt the breeze of an arrow pass his head, but the wooden shaft of death did not come from behind him. It emanated from the Farlo that lay some fifty yards ahead. The stinger was only the first.

Twang . . . twang . . . twang . . . twang . . . twang . . . twang cut the air as Bantogs screeched, falling backward into the icy water.

Twang . . . twang . . . twang . . . twang . . . twang . . . twang. Jason heard the beasts continue to fall to arrows that were kissed with an accuracy far beyond anything he had ever seen.

Jason heard a monstrous roar close behind him. His blood froze. A volley of arrows rang out.

Twang . . . twang . . . twang . . . twang . . . twang . . . twang.

A massive body fell at Jason's side with a tremendous splash. The boy jerked about and looked right into the dead eyes of a Tog. Six arrows had pierced its head. Thick green blood poured from the wounds. Jason convulsed and rolled away through the water.

Two slender figures suddenly dashed from the trees, each gripping a bow with an arrow tightly fitted in place. The two runners bounced gracefully over Jason and his companions in pursuit of three Bantogs that had fled. IAM and Teacher rose to their feet and pulled Jason up. All three were dripping wet, and happy to be alive.

A third figure—a bit larger than the other two—exploded from the Farlo and raced toward IAM. The runner knelt before the scout in the murky water. Jason was entranced. The figure was thin, yet muscular. He was fair of skin, quite handsome in fact, with trimmed golden hair and long, pointed facial features. Though his leathers were not unlike theirs, his were more delicate and tailored, and made to blend with the forest green.

"An Elf!" Jason gasped.

"We have broken the Triad Agreement as set forth at the close of the Second Race War," began the Elf, his attention focused only on IAM, though he never raised his eyes to look at the scout directly. "It is your right to put us to death," he stated nobly.

"How came you to break the Triad?" IAM inquired with a voice equally noble, so noble that it surprised Jason.

"We traveled over the southernmost rim of the Valley of Despair . . . land forbidden to us as stipulated in the agreement with the Dwarves. Then we traveled over Man Land to reach this destination. We must therefore die to satisfy the terms of the Triad."

"But why did you break the agreement?" IAM demanded, his back-woodsman's accent all but gone, his voice cutting with an edge of steel and duty.

"Two days ago we were on our first hunt of the winter far to the north-west when we came across a pack of Bantogs commanded by a Tog. The pack split in two. They were too far south for their breed, and much more armed than we liked. So we intercepted one band in order to deter-mine what mischief they had planned. The last to die told us that they were to wait in these trees on the north end of the Mountain Marsh in hopes that their other troop would force certain travelers across the marsh and into their arms."

The Elf paused for a moment, glancing at Jason, then back to IAM.

"We had not intended to enter the valley—the quickest route—in order to take the Bantogs' place in the trees. But then, as a touch of good entered the creature's black heart, it told us the identity of the one they sought most . . . the Chosen One." The Elf shot a longer look at Jason. The Elf's eyes grew. "But I still cannot believe that the time has truly come."

"It has!" IAM exclaimed.

The Elf nodded, then peered directly into the scout's eyes.

"Then I am glad that I took such a task as this . . . and more. I would gladly give my life to save you alone, the savior of Elfkind, the great Major T."

Jason's mind reeled. Of course! Teacher shot a glance in his direction, her lips almost smiling. Who else, he suddenly realized, would Teacher select to guide them to the fabled Pearl of Anton? It all made sense:

IAM's respect for life, his quiet, understated strengths, his skill in the forest, his steel. This was the kind of scout that a thousand Men would follow into battle. He was also the kind of Man who would save the Elfin Race from extinction at the hands of the Dwarves. IAM Terante and Major T were one and the same.

"I hope," continued the Elf, "that I have helped to pay a small part of the debt greatly owed to you." He lowered his head and waited.

"On your feet, Prince Alar," IAM said strongly, knowing full well the Elf before him. "We owe you our lives."

The Elf stood proudly and the Major rested his large hand upon the Elf's slender shoulder.

"I absolve you of your transgression of entering Man Land."

The Elf nodded in appreciation. "Then my remaining duty is to reach King Tor of the Northern Dwarves and tell him of my transgression. It is still his right to put us to death for entering the valley itself."

The Major softened. "I understand."

Jason was stunned by the Elf's code of ethics. No one would know that the Elves entered the valley except for them. King Tor would certainly never know. Yet the Elves would tell him nonetheless . . . even at the risk of death. This was what it meant to be truly *good.*

IAM smiled. "Go to King Tor and tell him of your actions. And why you took them. You will receive justice at his hand. Just thank Anton it is not King Zak of the Eastern Dwarves you must face. For that you can be grateful."

"On my life," said the prince. The Elf pounded his fist against his breast as if to confirm his words.

Just then, the two Elves who pursued the fleeing Bantogs returned in a sprint, bowed low to Major T, and then faced their prince.

"The Bantogs are no more," said the tallest.

"Then we go to King Tor to have him decide our fate," the prince responded. He turned to the Major. "Can we help you in any other way before we leave?"

The Major glanced at Teacher.

"Yes," said the Etha. "Tell King Tor that we travel in search of the Pearl of Anton, and that we will return to the Circle of Wisdom when our task is complete. He will understand."

"On my life," he responded, pounding his chest. "May Anton be with you." The Elf shot one more glance at Jason.

"And with you," said IAM.

With that, the Elves dashed through the trees and were gone. A chorus of humming insects soon rose above the marsh. Without a word, IAM moved toward the dead Tog and Bantogs and began sprinkling their bodies with *lupas*. Teacher led Jason to a fallen tree that sat just where the marsh met solid ground. The boy felt his pocket to ensure that his trust was still with him. It was. He hated his inability to control the Stone's power. It should rise forth at his choosing, he thought. Jason felt like a prisoner.

Teacher reached out and touched him.

"What did you learn?" she asked.

The boy thought of the Elves. He glanced at IAM.

"Duty transcends everything," he said instantly. His heart was calm.

"Good . . . very good," Teacher said as she continued to dissect his expressions. "Now deeper. Close your eyes. Look into the new, empty portions of your mind and tell me what you *feel* about IAM."

Jason was confused by Teacher's request but shut his eyes nonetheless, concentrating on his last image of their scout. He sought the vacant reaches. He probed them carefully, hoping to avoid the pain that rose from the emptiness earlier. A tingling sensation rushed through his consciousness. For the first time, the scout was truly unveiled.

"I feel goodness, strength, caring, respect." Then, he felt a puzzling sensation. "And I feel a deep, deep sadness as well." The boy opened his eyes and his mind rose above the depths, leaving the sensation behind.

"How did I do that?" he asked, dizzy with revelation.

"It's part of your blood, and a part of what will come," Teacher answered.

"Did my father go through this?"

"Somewhat . . . but not like this . . . not this deep."

"So that's what the empty spaces in my mind are for."

"Not really. It's only a fragment of the potential, but that's the only explanation I can give for now. Close your eyes and concentrate again . . . find the blank spot."

Jason sought the emptiness and it opened to him once more. He heard Teacher's words penetrate the void.

"And the Elves?" she asked.

Jason held the last image of the fair Race as they glided into the forest. His mind tingled.

"I feel great pride, duty, skill, and nobility."

"And the Tog?"

Jason winced. Even though the creature was dead, its body reeked of its former self.

"Evil. Lust. Endless torment. A speck of good."

"Excellent . . . excellent," Teacher breathed. "Enough."

But it was not enough for Jason. The power was too new and the feel of it intriguing. His eyes sprang open and held Teacher's, feeling her very soul. He saw her stripped of the mask she painted. His mind was flooded with thoughts of the woman she was: loving and kind and immensely gentle—almost to a fault. But all of those qualities were buried by the responsible Etha she had to be: stern, calculating, and even harsh. And it was all for him . . . an unbending commitment that tied her to the Royal House for as long as she had lived. And in it all, between what she was and what she had to be, Teacher somehow remained pure, true to herself and to those about her. Jason drove deeper still. Near the pit of her soul, he found an odd sadness, one that strangely mirrored the sensation he had found within IAM. It was more than that, he suddenly realized. Their pain was identical in every respect. Jason suddenly knew that they each shared a great loss that neither could speak of, nor dare remember.

"I feel wisdom, gentleness, commitment, great love, and a great loss," Jason said.

A warm smile melted over Teacher's face, the same one that Jason remembered from Astar. She then surprised him with an embrace, and for the first time, Jason realized that he was truly important to her; not just for what he represented, but because few on Trinity, with the possible exception of IAM, knew her better than he. Teacher began to pick the grass and mud from his hair.

"Don't make a habit of probing my mind," she said.

Jason blushed.

"What's goin' on over here?" asked IAM upon returning, his backwoodsman's drawl back in place.

"So who are you now: a drunkard in the street, a scout, or a war hero?" Jason asked, smiling.

"Whoever I need to be," said the warrior with a wink. "That's what's kept me alive all these years."

The trio broke into laughter and, for the first time, they all embraced. They were now as one, Jason thought: a legendary warrior, a stoic Etha, and the youngest among the Royal House. He left one family, only to find another.

CHAPTER 10

THE MERGING OF POWERS

With Mountain Marsh having fallen into darkness and the stars sparkling above, the travelers forged north to reach Jewel Pond, a small pool of water that butted directly against the southernmost towering face of Mountain High. The land rose sharply to reach the pool, impeding the trio's progress. Despite the dense foliage, the growing cold, and their aching muscles, the companions finally stood before the crescent-shaped water hole. The wind blew strong there, whistling as it left the snow-topped mountain. Far above, near-freezing water trickled through granite and patches of snow to form small streams. Just two miles east, these transformed into Mountain Falls and then the Crystal River.

Jason crossed his arms and hugged his body tightly in an attempt to warm himself. The wind pierced his leathers, which were still wet from the trek through Mountain Marsh. Every breath he exhaled was gray and visible, immediately scattered by the frozen wind. He was drawn to the pool of water before them. Its surface produced warm, glittering wisps of silver and red vapors that gently caressed his shivering face. The pond seemed so out of place amidst the dark cold, Jason thought, like a fire amidst the ice. The boy leaned over the water to bathe in its rising heat.

Jason's mind wandered. They had seen death once again, striking the Tog and Bantogs quickly. He was surprised that, though death still troubled him greatly, it affected him less this time. The thought wasn't comforting. No one, he thought, should get used to death—no one!

"What do we do now, Sara?" asked IAM as he scrutinized their surroundings. "We're goin' to catch our death out here."

"We have one more dip to take," Teacher said as she bent to touch Jewel Pond.

"You mean we're going in that?" Jason asked. He peered into the radiant water.

"Yes," Teacher said before turning to IAM. "You did bring the Kevin Farlo?"

"Never go anyplace without one."

"Then we're ready. Each of you hold one of my hands, and tight. We're going to the other side."

"The other side of what?" asked Jason.

"The other side of the rock, of course," Teacher answered, nodding toward the base of Mountain High just beyond the pond. She grabbed Jason's hand.

Teacher led them directly into the water. Jason entered cautiously. He knew how to swim, but not all that well. The only benefit he could find in the water was its warmth, which awakened his toes from their numbness. The water rose to his knees.

"Once our heads are submerged," Teacher began, "it's about ten steps to the other side of the mountain wall."

Jason glanced nervously at IAM. The scout winked back at the boy. The silver-haired warrior trusted Teacher completely, Jason knew. And in truth, this was probably a small matter compared to all the things that the Major had done before. A moment later the water met the Jason's chest. Then it rose above his shoulders. The water rose to his chin. He took a deep breath and disappeared below the pond's surface. Jason opened his eyes to the dazzling silver and red ripples above his head. Teacher's outline, shifting and fluid, moved gracefully ahead of him. IAM was invisible on her other side. Jason took another step and sank deeper. Immediately, his lungs began to ache. He felt a tightening of his throat and chest. He filed the thought quickly away as he took another downward step, then another. The pond began to darken considerably. The sight of Teacher began to fade. He took several more steps. He felt a slight rise in the gravel bed. He was just past the midway point. While the thought was comforting, his lungs could not be so easily dismissed. He needed air! He tugged at Teacher's hand to signal that he was in trouble, but she held firm and pulled him onward.

The water went black. In the wet abyss, Jason's chest exploded in pain. He struggled to prevent himself from sucking in the deadly water. His ears pounded in sync with his racing heart. He panicked. Jason couldn't remember how many steps he had taken, or even the direction he should go. Teacher's grip dragged him through the deadly black warmth. Kicking his legs frantically, Jason pushed upward, then broke the surface. He gasped for air and then coughed and choked violently in pure darkness, spitting up water even as he sought another breath.

"Jason . . . you there? . . . You okay?" he heard IAM ask, the big Man's words oddly echoing.

"I'm here," Jason replied, spitting and still gasping. "It's so dark . . . I can't see a thing." He stepped forward, then felt the water recede. A final step brought him to solid ground. His hand was still in Teacher's grip.

In the blackness was the sound of metal scraping wood, followed by a small sliver of white light that suddenly reflected upward and bounced about the walls of a cave. As the scraping noise continued, the light grew brighter until Jason saw gray, smooth rock all about him. The pond lay behind him, but it was now as black as the hole where he found himself. A stone staircase was in front of him. It spiraled downward into more darkness. Jason turned toward the scraping sound and saw his scout carving a wooden branch, some eight inches long and an inch thick. As his Tork blade sliced the bark away, the wood beneath it glowed bright white.

"I never saw Farlo glow on the inside before . . . or white instead of green," said Jason, his breathing now deep but steady.

"This is a particular variety—Kevin Farlo, they call it. You just gotta know where to pick 'em, that's all."

In no time, the cave was filled with the soft glow of the white Farlo.

IAM stepped forward, reached the steps, and began his descent, with the Farlo held low to light the passage.

"You all right, now?" Teacher asked Jason in the receding light.

"Better," he wheezed, a bit embarrassed.

Before the light could fade further, Teacher moved to the stairwell and began to follow IAM down. Jason did the same. The air grew warmer as they descended through the stone tunnel. The heat soothed the pounding in Jason's ears. Finally, the ache left him completely. His weary attention was captured by the stairs themselves, an endless rock-spiral of superb craftsmanship. The entire banister was filled with intricate carvings of animals, plants, mountains, and rivers—some of which Jason recognized, but many he did not. The mural looked alive as the glowing Farlo cast moving shadows. The boy ran his hand along the delicate artwork to ensure that the figures were, in fact, stationary. The wall of the stairwell was in fine contrast to the banister. It was absolutely smooth, made of a gray stone. There were no rough spots, no bulges, not even a discoloration of the rock. It had been carved and polished to perfection, reflecting back the trio's own visages. Jason thought of the skill needed to accomplish such a feat, and he was in awe. He found himself wishing that his father was there with him. Cyrus Del, he knew, would appreciate such workmanship.

"We're there," said IAM after an hour's time. "Wherever *there* is."

Jason peered about the small chamber. The room was perfectly round with a narrow passage at the far end. Teacher took the lead and traveled down the corridor, which became suddenly aglow with green Farlo roots that dangled above their heads, their stringy fibers obviously connected to trees somewhere upon the surface of the mountain itself.

The three travelers went a few miles in an easterly direction—as best as Jason could tell—until they arrived in an enormous cavern of perfectly polished stone. Green light from the Farlo roots, hanging much farther above now, glared off a seemingly smooth sheet of glass that was twenty feet wide and ran the full length of the huge cavern.

"A river!" Jason breathed as his eyes followed the silent flow of the underground water. "And it's moving north!" he exclaimed. "Isn't it?"

"There will be plenty of time for answers," said Teacher. "Right now, we need to change these leathers and dry them over the fire spout." Teacher pointed to a nearby stone formation, some three feet tall with a hole down its center.

The trio changed quickly. As Teacher and the Major began to make a camp for the night, starting a fire and rummaging through their food packs, Jason brought everyone's wet leathers to the fire spout and carefully aligned them about its outer lip. He leaned over the stone's edge and peered down its long funnel. He saw a pinpoint of glistening red far below. Then, the rising heat of the fire spout seared upward to blast his face and hair. Jason pulled his head quickly back and watched as the heat pushed the air violently upward. If he had stayed a moment more, his face might have been scorched to nothingness. The waves then lessened considerably, but he was not inclined to look over the fire spout again.

Jason moved to the river and strolled along its bank until he was about a hundred yards north of camp. He was surprised to find a line of five slender boats, all made of a thinly crafted Tork. The river did flow north, Jason decided, along a narrow canal lit by Farlo roots. The riverbed was smooth granite, which allowed the water to pass silently, its depth no deeper than five feet. Beyond the chamber, the canal narrowed so much that the bank was only four feet wide on each side. Each bank curved upward to form the sides and then the ceiling of the canal itself. Jason could see other large chambers, similar to their own, farther up the river. Great care and skill had merged to form such a structure.

Instinctively, Jason's mind shot outward now with his sight, following the river north. His new power served him well. For while his eyes could see no farther than a few hundred yards into the hazy green-gray of the tunnel, his mind seemed to follow the bank indefinitely, meandering smoothly with the gentle flow of water. And to Jason's surprise, he was able to sense love, care, and harmony in every turn of the bank. It was mixed with deep pride. Those who created this magnificence were long gone, Jason knew, but their essence remained. Jason's mind soared farther north, spurred onward by the beings' touch. But somewhere in the darkness, just beyond a bend of joy, lived a chill of terror. Jason plunged unsuspecting into it. It seethed with an ancient hatred of all that existed. Its only purpose was to destroy. The thoughts oozed and flowed with utter blackness, laced with vivid desires for evil, thinking only of the joy that came from the endless agony in others. But what was worse, Jason suddenly realized that this was not an essence of something past. This creature still lived. And it was waiting for him!

Jason struggled to break loose. But he could not. It was far greater than the evil he sensed of the Tog. Pain began to rise. The evil infected every part of his being with an enduring, immobilizing hatred. Then with a desperate jerk, Jason finally pulled himself free and fell backward to the ground. After a few minutes, Jason calmed himself long enough to think. This evil would kill him if it could. It lived to do just that. He took a deep breath. It had been an exhausting day, he thought. Maybe— just maybe—he was overreacting. He convinced himself that his mind was simply tired. Jason returned to the fire spout and absentmindedly checked the leathers."

"Dinner!" Teacher called.

Plates were filled with boiled vegetables. Tea was poured. Twilight Cakes were distributed. The smell of the food was overwhelming in the cavern, as though the ancient tomb welcomed the signs of life, doing its most to enhance its arrival. The trio sat in a small triangle and began to eat.

"Remember the legend of the Wallos, Anton's first children destroyed by the Tempests?" Teacher asked.

Jason nodded.

"The Wallos were master builders," she continued as she ate. "They built the Crystal River, which allowed them to travel quickly south. But once there, they needed a quick route back, so they bore this tunnel with a slight declination to the north. It's called the Granite River."

The goodness Jason felt could only be that of the Wallos, he thought. Their kindness, craftsmanship, and love was present everywhere. He suddenly felt honored to be within the cavern, in a place where few had ever ventured.

Teacher took a sip of tea before continuing. "After both rivers were constructed, the Wallos created the glowing Farlo trees. While the trees brightened the Crystal River above during the nighttime hours, their roots continuously brighten the Granite River below. Some of the roots grow miles through solid rock to reach these caverns. This cavern, in particular, is useful for our present needs. It will save us a hike over that frozen mountain."

"Amazing," said Jason. "So that's why Farlos line the Crystal River."

"The dry wells," Teacher began again, "reach to the core of Trinity. The Wallos used the heat to forge the mountains. They also used it to warm the land at night and during the winters. That's why the soil always takes longer to cool at night, and why it never freezes over during the winter days. The Wallos experimented with creating smaller forms of life too, such as algae, moss, grass, flowers, and eventually even insects, birds, deer, and such. All of this brought immense beauty to Trinity and great happiness to the Wallos and to Anton."

"Then," Jason began, "there are many creators . . . first Nebus, then Anton, then Wallos."

Teacher glanced at him, her blue eyes delighted. "The Races always had difficulty believing that point. They always felt it easier to grasp if they could point to just one divinity that created it all. The truth is often reshaped in a ways to make it more easily digested." Teacher popped her last small morsel of Twilight Cake into her mouth. She put her plate aside and began to make a bed for the night. "We will make good time on the Granite River. Then we will enter a deep vault beneath Fortress High. It is there that the Pearl of Anton waits." She looked at Jason. "It is protected by two creatures of Becus that are called the spawn of Tempest. They are smaller than their namesake—but no less deadly!"

Jason's eyes darted north, looking up the endless canal. His fear returned.

"I felt it," he said.

"I know. I saw it in your eyes when you returned from the bank. I know everything that rages within you, just from the flare in your pupils, or the way you carry your shoulders, or the tremble in your speech."

"Then you probably know my next question."

"I do," said Teacher. "You're wondering how we take the Pearl of Anton."

Jason nodded.

"With cunning or strength . . . I don't know which," Teacher answered.

The Major threw his plate down at his feet. It fell with an empty clang. "If it must be done, then we will do it," he commanded, his voice the same as the one that welcomed the Elves.

Jason was comforted by the Major's strength. But as the Pearl of Anton loomed closer, unanswered questions created emptiness in the boy's awareness.

"What is the source of the Pearl's power?" he asked pointedly.

"I don't know," Teacher said. "That is one lesson we must learn together."

Oddly, Jason wasn't convinced that his mentor was telling the truth. And before he could draw it back, his mind reached out and touched Teacher. He felt a hint of deception. It was buried deep within his mentor. She had not told the whole truth, he confirmed. But he also felt there the same unbending commitment he had touched at Mountain Marsh. And the commitment was to him—only to him. The boy suddenly felt ashamed for intruding upon Teacher's mind. If she is hiding something, he thought, it's for his own good. He pulled his mind back.

"Are you through?" Teacher asked.

Jason shot a glance toward her, his cheeks flushing. "Sorry," he said.

"It's good that you cultivate your gift," Teacher began, "but not on me!" She leaned closer. "All will be made clear. But you must learn one lesson at a time."

She shaped her pack into a pillow, lay back upon it, and eased into sleep.

Jason lay back as well. But once again, his mind would not allow a pleasant slumber. He dreamt of the boy he used to be, the person he had become, and the one he might ultimately find at the end of the journey. It haunted him. His mind continued to pull his thoughts this way and that, into fears. And with his frantic mind went his body, jerking through the night, restless. Near the end of his sleep, the image of the white Wizard's Stone came to him once more. As before, it was independent of its chain. It began to spin wildly before his mind's eye. Jason thought it seemed closer now, though still unpredictable. Then it was joined by another image. It shone a brilliant white and had an aura that sparkled and danced. He felt as though he should know of it, but he did not. The two images began to grow in size. They came closer and closer together as though seeking each other. For a reason he could not explain, Jason did not want them to meet. If separate, the two images were safe, almost lifeless. But together, they were deadly. The images moved closer. He tried to keep them apart, but his mind could not will it. He felt useless.

The images touched. A deafening roar blew outward, followed by a ball of white, searing fire and pain. Jason's mind was consumed with the blast. He felt an endless power that was his for the taking. It beckoned him. It pulled him toward it. It begged him to command it. He once thought of controlling a force such as this, but now the idea seemed horrid . . . unthinkable. It was a power that could destroy a world. It was far too much for him to wield. He refused. Jason struggled to awaken from the dream, pushing himself up through the reaches of his mind. The merged images rushed after him. But Jason hurled himself upward, crashing through the fleeting barrier to reality. He woke in a cold sweat and looked about. His companions were preparing to leave, both dressed in leathers once more. He must have been asleep for a while.

"Time to go," Teacher said. "This is the beginning of day four."

"They can't touch," Jason stammered, looking up toward his friends.

"What?" asked the Major.

"The Wizard's Stone and the Pearl of Anton," Jason gasped. "They cannot touch." He swallowed hard.

Teacher drew close. Her voice hardened. "They must touch," she began, holding Jason's face firmly with both of her hands. "And you must learn to control them both!"

CHAPTER 11

THE LAIR OF THE TEMPEST SPAWN

The slender Tork boat glided effortlessly north upon the Granite River. Caverns appeared intermittently along the river's narrow banks. They were filled with beautiful treasures—not the kind valued by the Races who lived above, but the kind cherished by a much wiser creator who once dwelt below. Lush green and flowering vines were plentiful, their leaves basking in the warm light of the sparkling green Farlo high above. Groves of trees grew there also, their thick ageless trunks securely rooted in the stone bank, their branches bearing ripening fruit—much larger than that grown upon the surface. Other flora blossomed in a vivid spectrum of red, blue, yellow, and orange flowers that sparkled with a glow of their own. Schools of large and brightly colored fish swam alongside the boat and played with the current, at times breaching the surface in an attempt to catch a better look at the foreign creatures within the boat.

The companions watched carefully, knowing full well that they alone were privileged to behold such a sight, now lost to the ages. Teacher was in the bow of the boat, her large blue eyes capturing every sight at once. IAM was at the tiller, guiding their way. Jason sat between them, completely entranced, his eyes dancing at the wonders. The sights allowed his mind to avoid the thoughts that would eventually haunt him this day.

Within an hour of beginning their water passage, Jason felt an odd tingling within him. It felt as if someone or something were inviting his mind outward, asking him to come and taste more of the fruit of life that passed peacefully, joyfully by—the essence of Wallos.

Teacher reached within her pack and found what she needed: a quill and paper. She began to write as before, her hand moving quickly along the parchment, the flow of the water so smooth that it did not once jerk her rounded letters. After some minutes, she came to a break. The quill and paper disappeared into her pack, and she once again scrutinized the sights about her.

"What do you write about?" asked Jason from behind.

"The past . . . the present . . . our journey . . . us . . . you," she said without turning about.

Jason did not comment. Her writings were part of her duty and her heritage. His thoughts were drawn once again to the Pearl of Anton and the evil that lived to protect it.

"What can we expect there?"

"Fortress High is abandoned," Teacher began. "But it once was the center of all civilization. It predates the Circle of Wisdom. It was governed by the Council of Elders comprised of representatives of the Races. That was a glorious time, a time of peace that existed before minor squabbles among the Races, exacerbated by the antics of the Bantogs, brought it all to an end. No one now—not good, evil, or in between—dwells in the fortress itself. But far below the fortress, it is a different matter. It is said that two Tempest Spawn live in a chamber of solid granite and guard the Pearl of Anton as it sits on a pedestal between them. The beasts are believed to have risen from the ashes of the last Tempest, nurtured by Becus himself. Each beast is held by an enormous collar and chain, the end of which is embedded into the rock floor. There are no keepers in the tomb. Instead, the beasts eat their own waste and are nourished by it. Even the life force they expend into the air is said to be gathered and cycled back into the creatures. In this way, they never need care, never need to be maintained. They are the perfect guard. Their only reason for being is to protect the Pearl and destroy those who would steal it. The Wallos tried. Now it is our turn."

"How do we find the entrance?" Jason asked.

"The lair of the spawn sits one-half mile beneath the fortress. The Granite River is only a hundred yards or so beneath that. A passage, said to have been cut by Wallos ages ago, connects the two. That is what we seek. Its entrance is recognized by its rough appearance. The Wallos were in a great hurry to recover the Pearl and cared little for the skill they exhibited in the construction of the passage itself."

The Age of Wisdom could not save Jason from his fears.

"What if I fail?" he asked quietly, his greatest fear revealed.

"You will not," Teacher comforted without turning about.

"Can you be sure?" he asked, his voice falling off to a whisper.

"No! I can't. No one knows *for sure!*"

"I do," said the Major in a booming, confident voice. "You are your father's son," he continued. "I trusted Cyrus with my life. I will trust you with no less."

Jason let it drop.

The trio continued to search for another hour as they drifted north, careful not to miss an important marking that might signal the entrance to the lair of the Tempest Spawn. Jason was the first to sense the ominous passage. He felt the exuberance of the Wallos fade into melancholy. Then it plunged to fear. Finally it fell into a state of unending, unbreakable hopelessness. Jason winced, and then pulled his mind back before his own thoughts yielded to the overpowering sense of doom.

"It's ahead to the right," he said soberly.

The dark passage became visible to Teacher and IAM moments later. Only a smattering of Farlo roots dangled above. Several huge boulders, cracked and jagged, lay at the water's edge, which caused thunderous waves of white foam to rise and crash in the river just upstream near the passage. The granite all about the bank seemed discolored by an ancient fire, and a gray, dusty haze blanketed the passage itself. The Tork boat began to get pulled into the current, but IAM reacted quickly and guided the boat to the easternmost tip of the bank. Jagged steps were visible at the entrance. While a scant Farlo light was provided along the bank, there was none within the black passage itself.

Even while holding his mind within the confines of himself, Jason could feel the desperate attempts of the Wallos, digging frantically, hopelessly, to cut a path to recapture the Pearl of Anton. The struggle was evident in every rough surface and every jagged edge. His mind recoiled. With the sound of water rushing over the boulders behind him, Jason stood in aching silence next to his companions as they, too, gazed upward into the blackness of the passage.

"Whoooaaa!" came a bloodcurdling shriek from the top of the tunnel.

Chilled, Jason stepped back. Teacher stood firm. IAM drew his sword and took a confident step forward.

"Whoooaaa!" came the shriek again.

Jason shuddered. "I'm already failing," he whispered to himself. An old worry resurfaced. *It should have been Theda.* Jason cinched his belt tighter.

"They can't hurt us if they're chained up, now, can they?" IAM commented. He removed the Kevin Farlo from his boot and set the beginning of the passageway aglow with a pale white light. The scout turned and beckoned.

"What can we expect, Sara?" IAM whispered as they slowly ascended the crumbling dark steps, the air growing cold.

"The two beasts are only half the size of Tempests . . . but just as evil . . . black as night. . . . They can't breathe fire . . . "

"Whoooaaa!"

" . . . but they're quick and deadly . . . scales that can't be penetrated . . . short wings incapable of sustained flight . . . but they can glide . . . a tail as crushing as their powerful hind feet."

"Whoooaaa!"

They reached the top of the narrow passage, which turned sharply to the left. A stench filled the air as specks of dust drifted past the glow of the white Farlo and disappeared into gray darkness beyond. As IAM turned the corner, the echo of his step told him that this opening in the granite led to a larger chamber. He paused, hearing a low, rhythmic breathing coming from the larger room. He raised the Kevin Farlo high, but its brilliance would only pierce the blackness for a few hazy feet. The Major paused. Teacher was just behind him, but Jason was still a couple of paces down the tunnel.

"Whoooaaa!" Two huge shadows lunged out of the darkness.

Their blazing red eyes flashed with an age-old evil: absolute, insane, and final! The Major thrust his sword forward to meet the lunging beasts. But having reached the end of their chains, the Tempest Spawn jerked to a sudden stop within five feet of the entrance, just beyond where the Major stood. Grinding jaws snapped at the air, yearning to gain inches to sink their fangs into tender human flesh.

IAM pushed the Farlo deeper into the chamber to within a few inches of the beasts' straining reach. The glow was enough to reveal a three-foot-high granite pedestal in the center of the room. A brilliantly white gem, about an inch across, sat atop it. A pulsating aura extended beyond the surface of the jewel and appeared to flow about it, as if the gem were shaping the air. There were shattered implements spread about the corners of the chamber, bits and pieces of spears and swords, ancient by their look. Obviously, the Wallos tried what they could in what little time they had left to recover the Pearl. What a cruel trick it was, to put the jewel so close, yet have it be so far. While the Wallos struggled to take the Pearl from the Tempest Spawn within, the mightier Tempests were destroying the Wallos from without. Only Becus could think of such a thing.

IAM moved slowly about the wall of the chamber as the beasts continued to rage. He lifted his sword and thrust it sharply at the belly of one of the spawn as it reared upward, towering above the Manwarrior. His blow had no impact upon its scales. He slashed at the creature's legs as claws reached for his flesh. The blade glanced off.

Suddenly, the shrieking stopped. The Major was no longer of interest to them. Their red eyes darted to the passageway. There, amidst the floating dust, stood Jason. The animals began to pace, lashing their tails against the stone. Here was an enemy that clearly required more thought, more caution, more cunning. Jason felt a slight rush of thoughts pouring from the beasts. He first resisted them. Then he reconsidered. Perhaps if he used his mind probe, he thought, he might understand the beasts better. The knowledge could help him obtain the Pearl. An ounce of bravery touched him. Jason tentatively reached out with his thoughts and stroked the origin of evil ever so slightly. His mind suddenly filled with infinite blackness. He saw what they would do to him should they have a chance. His mind froze. His body shook. He panicked. Jason bolted down the passage, tumbling the last twenty feet as Teacher pursued him to the bottom. The beasts howled in triumph.

"I felt it!" he babbled when Teacher grabbed him, the child within now firmly in control. "I felt it as before . . . but stronger!"

She knelt, put her arms about him, and rocked him slowly.

"Fear is a difficult thing to master," she said. "Particularly this fear."

"We're up against it this time, Sara," began IAM as he appeared a moment later. "My sword just bounced off their scales." The Major scratched his forehead, thinking.

"Jason," Teacher said. "Did you notice the way the spawn reacted toward you?"

Jason didn't respond.

"They know of you . . . of your bloodline . . . of your Stone. They felt it. They're cautious of it . . . afraid of it." Her voice hardened. "Only you can get the Pearl!"

"Nooo!" he answered. He clutched her arms, the traces of evil still lingering in his mind. "You don't understand," he began. "I saw inside of them. I saw what they would do to me." He felt ashamed. This was not the way Tempest Slayer would have met the challenge, he knew, not the way Theda would have met the challenge, nor his father. Yet he couldn't turn away from the fear.

The low commanding voice of Major T suddenly pierced Jason. "There are two courses we can take. We can turn around, not obtain the Pearl, and let you face even greater evils at the height of the Twilight Festival. Or you can try to get the Pearl so that you are better prepared to face what lies ahead. Sometimes, son, you have to go through hell on your way to paradise."

Jason took a breath. He could not disgrace himself in the presence of Major T. The warrior expected him to be his father's son. He at least had to try.

"What do we do?" he asked Teacher as he fought off the fear.

"The Stone you carry has the power to destroy them. It is Wizard made, and they can sense it . . . feel it . . . just as you can them. For the first time in their existence, they are afraid and confused by it. We can use that. Our only chance is if they fear the Wizard's Stone more than they fear losing the Pearl of Anton. You must believe that the Stone will protect you."

Jason trembled slightly.

"There's no other way," she began. "And remember what your father said: *a thousand ancestors go with you.*" Teacher stroked Jason's hair. He felt the evolving reaches of his mind begin to dominate.

"One more thing," she started.

Jason's heart fell. He dreaded her next words for he knew what they must be.

"Once you have the Pearl, you must touch it to the Stone. The power of each must merge. We will need that, perhaps sooner than we wish."

"The dream," Jason said wearily.

Teacher nodded. "You must believe, and trust that the fear you have now is no less than that which consumed Matthew Del, Tempest Slayer, ages ago."

Jason was struck by the revelation. Legends spoke of heroes as though they were gods and not flesh and blood. But why shouldn't they fear? he thought. Even his father spoke of heartfelt terror.

Jason turned and followed them back to the passage. He tucked his mind deep within, beyond its ability to reach out. He moved forward at a measured pace.

The spawn began to wail savagely as the trio reentered the chamber. IAM led the way, holding the Farlo up high to illuminate the chamber to its fullest. His other hand clutched his sword. As Jason entered the room, the seed of fear began germinating within the spawn. They scurried back and forth, shaken.

"A thousand ancestors go with me," Jason whispered to himself as he took a step to reach IAM's side, keeping his eyes locked on the dazzling white Pearl. It was identical to the one in his dream.

"A thousand ancestors go with me," he whispered again as he and IAM took another step forward. The spawn backed up to a spot adjacent to the pedestal, continuing to scurry and seek a vantage point. Jason's right hand reached for the thin Tork chain that disappeared into his right pocket. The Wizard's Stone within began to rise to the opening until, with a final tug, it popped into the dull light of the chamber.

"Whoooaaa!" the creatures shrieked, edging back again into the dark, their red eyes frantic, their huge chains clanging and dragging on the granite floor.

Jason fought his terror and grabbed the Wizard's Stone, holding it high in his right hand. Heat began to grow within the sphere.

"A thousand ancestors go with me," he whispered again as he took another step. Jason stood before the pedestal now, the spawn lurking frantically in the shadows. "A thousand ancestors go with me," he whispered again, his lips trembling, his eyes still locked upon the Pearl of Anton. "A thousand ancestors go with me," he whispered again. He raised his left hand just inches from the shining sphere. He was so close that he could feel the Pearl's aura dance upon his skin. The power was already reaching out to him. This was the moment. His fingers began to close on the gem. The monolithic fear was trembling in his fingertips. He struggled to keep his hands steady, but they defied him. His concentration suddenly broke. His eyes darted from the Pearl to the beasts. His own seed of terror burst forth. The beasts saw it too.

"Whoooaaa!"

One of the black creatures lunged over the pedestal, grabbed Jason with its claws, and plunged him to the granite floor. Jason felt the beast's massive weight. Its claws ripped at him. He felt the warmth of his own blood spurt forth. Jason was paralyzed.

Then IAM was there. He slashed at the beast to make it give way. Then the intense, crippling fear exploded within Jason. As his terror rocketed forth, so did the white heat of the Wizard's Stone. Jason's body burned. The white force poured from the Stone, weaving its way about Jason's body until he was completely shielded from the beast's massive blows. Still the creature came on. A sudden flash of power blasted into the demon and hurled it back into the darkness. The blast blew the Major across the chamber. The smell of sulfur and smoke filled the cavern. But no sooner had the first creature fallen than the second one hurtled toward Jason. It was bigger, stronger. The light flared again, but the beast was quick and dodged the power, ripping at Jason's side and raking his shoulder raw. The Major jumped to his feet and raced to Jason's aid. The creature whipped its tail to undercut the warrior's step. IAM crashed to the granite floor and rolled to the entryway. But precious time was bought.

"Jason!" Teacher shrieked. "The Pearl! Grab the Pearl!"

Jason moved as in a dream. He lunged toward the pedestal and mindlessly snatched the Pearl with his left hand while still clutching the Wizard's Stone with his right. He rolled toward the entrance of the chamber and into the arms of IAM. The Major grabbed him and bolted out. The tomb fell into darkness.

Thud . . . thud came the sound of the massive beasts as they strained to give chase. Again and again they tested their prison more forcefully, the absence of the Pearl driving them completely mad.

Crack! The granite that anchored one of the beasts chains split. It was a hairline break. A flurry of hope exploded within the beast as it threw its weight once again against the Tork metal.

Crack! It gained more ground, but was not yet free.

Jason and Teacher flew down the passage first. The Major came last. Halfway down the narrow stone corridor, Jason's left hand began to burn.

"Aaah!" he screamed. He opened his fist. The flaming white sphere teetered and began to roll through his fingers.

"Now!" Teacher screamed, grabbing his hands and slamming them together.

The Stone and Pearl touched. Jason thought that hell had opened. Light pierced his hands as though they were translucent.

"I'm burning!" he screeched as his head shot backward. He fell to his knees, his teeth gritting. His face twisted in pain. A burning heat exploded within his entire body, hurling him backward in agony, the force ripping him from Teacher's grip. He tumbled again and again, landing near the bottom of the passage. The pain was suddenly gone. Jason felt only his mind, now swollen as though the blank spots were filled with an entity for which they were groomed. Teacher was suddenly there . . . then IAM as well.

"Can you move?" she asked frantically, but the pounding thrusts of the Tempest Spawn nearly doused her words. Jason tested his legs and rose wobbling to his feet.

Crack . . . bang! It was the final blow from above. One of the beasts had hurtled out of the chamber and crashed into the wall of the tunnel above. The Major turned and raised his sword.

"Whooooaaa!" The creature's red eyes glowed menacingly through the darkness. More than a thousand centuries it had labored in that prison. And it was now free—free to kill not only those beneath it, but all those that it knew lived upon the surface. An eternity of terror lived before its eyes. It was not about to let it pass.

"Hold your fists high!" Teacher commanded Jason. He obeyed, his mind too scattered to do otherwise. The spheres were still clenched within his grasp, his hands fused.

"Jason!" Teacher urged. "Close your eyes . . . find the images of the Stone and Pearl in your mind!"

Jason looked within himself, knowing exactly where to find them— in the expanding void. Buried deep within his mind, the two shapes spun wildly but apart. It was his dream!

The beast leaped once down the passageway, gliding to cover about a third of its length. Its chain dragged from behind, still latched to the creature's massive collar. Teeth glistened in the faint light.

"Merge the images within your mind!" Teacher screamed.

The creature leaped again, another third of the way down the corridor. Its eyes filled with a consuming evil and lust.

"Merge!" Teacher screamed again.

Jason hesitated. The indecision formed a wedge between the two images of power: one of Wizard, one of Wallo. But suddenly, the image of the Pearl shot closer before his confused, frozen mind. Its blinding light flared up. It took his breath away. With it, he felt oddly at peace. An unbreakable confidence forged its way deep into his soul. He knew his challenge now, and he had the will to meet it. He could do it. He suddenly possessed a confidence he never thought possible. And it all flowed out of the Pearl of Anton. That's its power, he realized. It was a confidence born of gods. It was a confidence that would allow him to use the Wizard's Stone at a time of his own choosing. Not even Tempest Slayer could do that!

The beast leaped a final time, its red eyes growing larger with its approach. IAM pivoted forward to protect his companions, giving them more distance and time. The beast was upon him, ripping at the warrior.

"Merge!" Jason commanded. The spheres crashed toward each other within his mind, overlapping half of their images. A blinding light exploded from the gems within his clenched fists. The magic blasted just above the Major's shoulders and drove hard into the head of the beast. The creature slammed back up into the darkness, screeching. Jason blinked at the sight, startled. He then pulled the images apart in his mind. The power ceased.

"Not even Tempest Slayer," he breathed with wonder.

Out of the dark passage the beast lunged again, startling the trio with renewed life. It blasted its way through the Major, sending him rolling to the river. But it got no farther. One thought from Jason brought the power to bear. But this time, Jason merged the images of the Wizard's Stone and the Pearl within his mind until they overlapped completely. The blinding white power flew from his fist and smashed into the body of the Tempest Spawn. The beast exploded, its limbs—and more—flying against the rock. Jason continued to pound the body of the beast until it was thrown up the long passage. The bloody mass spun back into its lair.

Jason then tried to end his force. But he could not! The images overlapped so completely in his mind that he could not find a piece of one to pull from the other. The force continued on, exploding deep into the granite steps and beyond. Still he could not stop it. He was devastated by the power he wielded. He could feel the mountain begin to shake. The granite walls and floors beneath Fortress High rumbled about him. He cried out in pain, not knowing how to stop the power.

Chunks of rock began to fall from the canal's ceiling.

"Jason!" Teacher screamed. "Pull them apart!"

He struggled again but could not. He had the confidence, but not the knowledge to relinquish the force. And oddly, he still had no fear. He had only confidence and power, but without the fear and knowledge that should go with it. The power continued to pound the passageway with a blinding force, exploding its way into the upper reaches of the mountain.

Boom! The mountain buckled to the sound of a devastating, rupturing force.

Then everything went black.

CHAPTER 12

FEAR

Created ages ago by a boiling underground spring, Frantic Lake is never at rest as it bubbles and churns just north of Mountain High. The steam rises continuously to form thunderous clouds that move south toward the mountain and beyond. On an early winter's day within reach of a foreboding Twilight Festival, the ominous clouds above Frantic Lake were darker than usual. The sun was nearly half-dim in anticipation of the full-twilight day. The lake's shores were typically vacant with the approach of winter—as most found this season too difficult in which to travel. Yet on this day, three companions were camped on the water's humid southern shore, so out of context to the cold that was beginning to blanket the rest of the western land.

"Father?!" Jason suddenly called, frantically, his body jerking upward in a soaking sweat.

"Father?!" he yelled again. Jason suddenly awoke and looked up into the steady blue eyes of Teacher, her silky white hair framed by thunderous clouds high above.

"It's all right . . . it's all right," she comforted. She stroked his face with a warm damp cloth.

"I heard my father call me . . . is he here?!" he asked, sitting up.

"No. It was just a dream," Teacher responded.

Jason took a huge breath and exhaled it slowly. He suddenly felt an ache in his shoulder. He found it bandaged tightly. Jason began to shudder, the thought of the Tempest Spawn stinging his mind and reigniting the fear. He jerked his hands upward, expecting them to be charred.

"I'm not burned," he said slowly, in disbelief.

"No," Teacher replied, as she once again brought the damp cloth to Jason's brow. "The gems would not damage your flesh."

"And the Tempest Spawn?" Jason asked, his voice trembling.

"One is dead. The other is still trapped in the granite chamber." Teacher paused, allowing the boy to collect his thoughts. "Do you remember what happened?"

"I remember the evil in the chamber. I remember IAM . . . my reaching for the Pearl." He began to sweat. "I remember the passage . . . and a power."

"Anything else?" Teacher asked.

"What else could there be?" he asked with a wince.

"Everything!" she said firmly. "Find the empty spaces within you."

Jason closed his eyes. "I can't see anything," he said, too exhausted to try in earnest.

"Let's go about this a different way," suggested Teacher. "Look at the Stone."

Jason pulled his chain and drew the Stone forth into the gray light. "It's different," he breathed. "It's about the same size, but heavier, though it's the same color . . . gray."

"It's now an Agate, a joining of the Wizard's Stone and the Pearl of Anton."

Jason lay back to calm his pulse. His mind unlocked a memory. His eyes shot open.

"I remember images . . . in my mind . . . the Pearl and the Stone coming together . . . and then the power . . . just like my dream . . . exactly like my dream!"

"That is correct."

"But how?" he asked, his eyes burning from the pounding within his head.

"The images in your mind—icons, they are called—are a manifestation of the joining," Teacher began. "As long as the Agate stays in your possession, the icons will stay up here." She pointed to his forehead. "The Pearl will allow you to gain access to the full power of Wizard's magic . . . through the merging of images that takes places in your mind."

Jason shook his head gently. In a way, it meant that he was no longer in control of his own mind. His fingers slipped the Agate back into his pocket. It felt good to have it out of sight. He rubbed his forehead.

"How does the Pearl do it?"

"That requires a bit of history," Teacher began anew. "As we discussed, Anton created the Wallos in order that they would, in turn, bring great form and beauty into the world. The task before them was great and required vast skill. When the Wallos came to Trinity, they began to mold the world as they felt best, yet such perfection requires a great deal of work and patience. After a few centuries of craftsmanship, the Wallos began to falter under the strain. The task began to look too great and they too small. Some gave up altogether for fear that they would never accomplish their perfectionist plan. Anton knew they were capable of the task, but he had never realized that capability wasn't enough. What they lacked was a complete and consuming confidence, the ultimate ability to see an endeavor through to its completion, regardless of how hopeless the situation appeared."

Jason stared at the lake, steam ever-rising above its waters.

"So Anton," he began, "created the Pearl and empowered it with great confidence. And when it was needed, the Wallos could tap into its power in order to renew their own inner strength." He looked up at Teacher and caught a brief smile as she continued.

"Correct. When the Tempests captured the Pearl they tried to destroy it—but could not. Yet they didn't need to. Without a great confidence, the Wallos were no match for evil. Their efforts to retrieve the Pearl failed. Not because of their abilities, but because of their consuming hopelessness."

Jason was amazed at how cleverly Teacher had previously concealed these facts. He smiled. If Teacher had told him that the Pearl would give him only confidence, he would never have believed it—nor would he have understood what a great confidence could accomplish lest he saw it with his own eyes.

"Confidence is a great power," he concluded.

"Yes."

"Then it was the Pearl's confidence that I felt when the creature rushed toward us."

"Yes."

"It was the confidence that allowed me to bring forth the Wizard's magic at my choosing."

"Yes."

"And it was the confidence that almost brought the mountain down on top of us." Jason shivered, remembering it all. "How did it stop?"

"That was my fault," a voice behind him said. IAM appeared. "I had to knock you good."

Jason reached and felt a knot on the back of his head, contributing to his pain. "Thanks," he said. "I guess."

"Anytime," the scout said, grinning. "That's quite a power you have, but the back of my ax did the trick." He winked.

Teacher leaned close. "This is a delicate time for you, Jason. You haven't completed the Age of Wisdom. You need more time. You must resist bringing the two powers forth in tandem. You can summon the Pearl's confidence without harm. But you must resist merging it with the Stone unless it's truly needed. Understand?!"

"Understood," Jason responded. His shoulders slumped. "This is all happening a bit fast." He paused, whispering, "I think the first bit of confidence the Pearl provided wore off already. . . . I'm afraid again."

"I know," Teacher said as she continued to dab his brow with the damp cloth. "We must discuss your fear before we journey further." Teacher checked his wounded shoulder, noting signs of its healing. "Tell me about the evil."

Jason's face wrinkled. "The thought of destruction was in every corner of their minds. Nothing else. Only destruction . . . terrible and endless . . . " He trailed off for a moment. "When it attacked me in the chamber, I couldn't move. I was so afraid. If it wasn't for the Stone . . . "

"What did you feel when you moved to grab the Pearl?"

"I was still afraid . . . as afraid to move as I was afraid to stay where I was."

"That's right. The conscious mind is forever locked in one state or another . . . complacency, depression, joy, love, anxiety, fear, determination, and so forth. One state will remain in the mind until it is replaced with another. Complacency may give way to joy . . . joy to anxiety and the like. Great fear can only be displaced quickly by a mental state of equivalent or greater force, unless it dissolves naturally and over much time to a lesser state. In the chamber of the Tempest Spawn, you were as afraid to move as you were afraid to stay still. In a way, they canceled each other and allowed you to freely choose. Then in the passageway, a great fear of the beast was displaced by the greater confidence to destroy it."

Jason nodded. "To get rid of my fear, I have to replace it with an emotion as great."

"Exactly! When you are confronted by a paralyzing fear, you must displace it with a fear that isn't paralyzing, or with a great confidence to succeed, or a great joy. It won't come easy. It takes great practice, but you'll have a greater resource now."

"The Pearl," he said.

"Yes."

Teacher put a hand on his arm. "Experiment with the Pearl's confidence, Jason, but don't rely too heavily on it if you do not truly need it. Don't let it become a crutch. Deal with the lesser fears on your own by displacing them as I have described. You have a wonderful mind as it is."

Teacher dabbed his head with more water. "Tell me something else," she began gingerly. "Tell me about your brother."

Jason fidgeted. "You knew him. Theda was the best brother I could have had," he said earnestly. "He was a lot of things I wasn't."

"Like what?"

"He was stronger at my age than I was. And bigger. Got better grades in school . . . you know that. And no one pushed him around. He used to protect me. He used to teach me stuff."

"I seem to remember that you were with him when he died," Teacher said, probing.

"Yes . . . I was," Jason replied. He cinched his belt tighter. Teacher's eyes flashed.

"How did it happen?"

"We were gathering some berries . . . he got too close to Pike's Cliff . . . and he fell."

"How?

"I just told you . . . he fell." He cinched his belt again, tighter.

"Just curious," Teacher finished. "Perhaps we will discuss this again someday."

"What day is this?" Jason asked quickly.

"Beginning of day seven," Teacher said as she opened the locket about her neck and brought it close for him to see. A bead of light stood just halfway on its journey to the end.

"You slept through days five and six. Your bursts of stamina are improving, but they are also exhausting, as is your use of power. But there's still time for you to rest a few more hours."

Suddenly exhausted, the boy settled back, closed his eyes, and allowed his mind to begin to sink below its surface. His body jerked with restlessness. Jason thought of the Final Contest. His heart quickened. He suddenly remembered the evil he saw marching south toward Meadowtown. His heart quickened further. Jason's mind then wandered to Pike's Cliff. He saw himself and his brother years before. They looked so much alike. The two were gathering berries where the bushes meet the edge.

"Don't let them push you around," Theda said. "You're better than that. You're a Del."

"But they'll beat me up again," Jason shot back.

"You have to stand up to them. I love you, but I can't fight all your battles. No one can do it but you. You don't have to be afraid."

"I'm not chicken. *It's just always best not to fight.*"

"Farlo is what Farlo does."

"Don't call me that anymore!"

"Then don't shrivel away in the daylight! Farlo is what Farlo does!"

"Stop that . . . or I'll . . . "

"Farlo is what Farlo does."

"Nooo!" Jason shouted, waking up in a sweat, fear embracing him. He was in full panic, but he did not know why, could not remember why. A door within his mind suddenly blew opened, taking his breath away. An image rushed upward. It was spherical and brilliant in its splendor. Jason recognized it instantly as the icon of the Pearl of Anton.

"Use me!" it seemed to scream.

Remembering Teacher's warning, Jason kept it at a distance. But the Pearl was strong, enticing, and shrewd.

Maybe . . . just this time, thought Jason, shuddering.

A flash of light blasted from the Pearl's surface. Jason's mind reeled. The icon then vanished. With its passing, his panic was gone. He knew he would battle evil and win. He knew Meadowtown would survive. He knew his parents would be fine. Jason was restored and rejuvenated. He felt reborn. He recognized the sensation, shaped by a god for the benefit of a glorious, extinct Race of beings. And now, it was for him to command. Jason had the confidence of the Wallos!

But he was still uneasy. Though the fear was temporarily gone, there was something else within the darkness of his mind, something ugly. He could not identify it. But he did not pursue it either. It was a feeling that the confidence of the Wallos could neither eliminate nor illuminate.

It was guilt.

CHAPTER 13

A KING'S MADNESS

The hawk inclined its wings and was lifted high above Frantic Lake, its waters boiling in the late-morning twilight. From such a vantage point, the predator could see nearly all of Trinity: the majesty of the snow-capped Mountain High, the green forests of the vibrant west beyond, the sandy gray of the desolate east. It would see even farther if not for the darkening sun, which was growing dimmer with each passing day—a familiar sight this time of year, one the hawk had witnessed sixty times before. But even through the gray, the bird recognized every speck of its home, known well among its kind for almost as long as there were skies in which to fly.

Jason smiled from his own perch on a boulder at the edge of the lake. He had never touched the mind of a hawk before. It was shrewd, its thoughts simple and directed. Unlike humans, who were always swinging from one emotion to the next, the hawk's mind sorted all things it perceived into only two piles: those that would satisfy a need and those that would not. There was not even a sense of right and wrong, or good and evil, or bravery and cowardice. Hence, there was nothing to confuse its actions, nothing that would keep its mind in constant turmoil.

Abruptly, the hawk folded its wings and dove toward Jason. The boy could feel the hawk's essence grow stronger. It was intensely curious . . . of him. It instinctively knew something about him, he sensed. Within feet of Jason, the hawk spread its wings and diverted its plunge. It shot just above the Jason's head. He strained his mind to probe the thoughts of the creature.

More than human, it thought as it whistled by. The hawk pivoted its wings and soared straight upward to its home in the sky, slicing its way through the rolling clouds. It was gone.

More than human, Jason thought, confused. It must have sensed the Agate, he concluded. He put the thought away.

Teacher and IAM approached. It was time to go.

"To the Circle of Wisdom by way of Meadowtown, I hope?" asked Jason anxiously.

"Yes, but we can't go back the way we came," said Teacher, glancing at the Granite River that poured into Frantic Lake. "We now move east for a bit along Death Road and then south. It's the quickest route around Mountain High. And besides, we must also run an errand in the city of Zol."

IAM led the group east. The ground was flat and soft at first, the green brush abundant and the air a sticky warm. But it soon changed rapidly as the trio moved farther from the moist heat of Frantic Lake and into the beginnings of Death Road and the Desert of Zak. The route was hard on their feet and seemingly barren of life. Tightly compressed sand began to replace dirt, and sparse, thorny plants began to replace trees and brush. The sun was now at half its strength on day seven, leaving a chill that was probably far better, Jason thought, than the blazing heat of a full sun.

After a time, the sparse brush of this new environment made Jason a bit leery, for it provided little cover in which to hide if need be. And with his increasing apprehension, he could feel the remnants of the Pearl's conviction begin to fade in his mind, dissolving the confidence of the Wallos' touch. In a way, he was glad to be himself again. The Pearl's determination was false, and he felt as though he were cheating to use it. He felt the Pearl's touch fade even more.

"Are we safe from Bantogs?" he asked the warrior.

"Safe enough. Those critters prefer the moist parts of the west. We're not likely to find any of their kind out here."

Jason nodded, comforted. As they traveled, he became more aware of the life about them. Small reptiles scurried about, most finding their way to pleasant-looking watering holes along the road. Birds played above, darting on occasion to nearby trees to nestle in the shade. Small gophers were abundant also, popping their heads up from their holes, their whiskers twitching to sense whatever there was to sense. The more Jason looked for life, the more he found it.

"Why do they call this Death Road?" he asked the scout after a time.

"This passage was once called Zak Road, named after the Eastern Dwarf king," IAM began. "But that changed after the Second Race War.

The Eastern Dwarves are the ones your father held at the Eastern Pass so that my other forces could move into position. When the avalanche occurred, about two hundred Eastern Dwarves were killed instantly. After that came a snowstorm or two. Not being acquainted with ice and snow, the Eastern Dwarves had a rough go of it. In the end, only about half of King Zak's warriors returned alive to their desert home, and each carried a body of a companion lost in battle or the snow. I'm told that the procession along this road stretched for miles. The cries of family members could be heard for more than that as they ran up and down the line of death, tryin' to find their loved ones, and prayin' that their son or father or friend was carryin' another, rather than being carried. That's why it's called Death Road. It has left a scar on the Eastern Dwarves. And King Zak hasn't been heard from since. I'm told he still holds just about everyone responsible for that day . . . me, the Northern Dwarves, the Elves, but mostly your father."

"My father?" asked Jason gravely.

"Your father was in charge of the blockade. And worse . . . King Zak's son was killed at your father's hand during the battle."

Jason paused. "How do we move unseen through this region then?"

"We can't. These aren't Bantogs, boy. The Dwarves are the best of warriors and the best of sentries. They'll find us, all right, no matter how we try to elude them. So we wait until they decide to approach us. Then we will wait again to see how our case will be disposed."

"Our case?"

"It's against King Zak's law to trespass. It's even against the Triad Agreement, which called for separation. So any traveler found along this road must submit to trial." IAM shrugged. "That was one of my biggest blunders. I never should have consented to separation."

"But you ended the war!" Jason gasped. "Surely that was the most important thing!"

"There are worse things in the long run. The less the Races interact, the more difficult it is for them to resolve their hatred."

The conversation ended, leaving Jason pensive. The daylight was soon gone as twilight once again sat in control of Trinity. They made camp. Jason was surprised how rested he still felt after the long day's march. Teacher and IAM were still strengthening his endurance; he was sure of it. IAM set a fire and cooked a modest meal from the food he had gathered in the desert: mostly plant roots and berries. It was consumed quickly. Wisps of smoke and red cinders from the fire floated upward to mix with the bright stars as Jason ate the last of his meal: a Twilight Cake, still a golden brown on the outside and a moist, buttery yellow on the inside. He looked up and thought of Astar and the vision given to him in the room at the top of the stairs. A million stars and a million possibilities, he thought. IAM poked at the remains of the glowing wood, sending even more cinders to mix with the heavens, providing even more fuel to spark the boy's imagination. A sudden cold breeze interrupted Jason's thoughts.

"We're going to freeze out here," he said.

"Unlikely," Teacher replied. She warmed her hands over the fire pit.

"We won't be here much longer anyway," added IAM.

"We're heading out already?" asked Jason.

The Major rose slowly to his feet. "They're here, Sara," the Major said.

"Jason," Teacher whispered as she slowly stood. "Rise, but say nothing. Do nothing." Jason rose to his feet.

"So, the great Major T," a mocking voice called out through the air. Jason flinched. It could not have been more than a few feet away.

"My king has been waiting for a long, long time," it continued. "Let us honor him tonight."

Before the voice faded, it seemed that every bush and rock rushed toward them. In less than a heartbeat, the Dwarf warrior thrust a knife upward against Jason's chest, slicing through the leather. It stopped short of his skin. Two strong arms grabbed him from behind and brought him painfully to his knees.

Jason felt the warmth of his blood on his shoulder as his wound reopened. He began to tremble. The icon of the Pearl rose from the depths of his mind to give him aid, but he closed his eyes and redirected his thoughts. It vanished. He was happy that he controlled his fear, as small as it was. His Dwarf captor was covered with iron mail in the front. But his back was covered with a cloth that had a pattern of gravel embedded into its weave. It would make the wearer invisible when lying on the desert floor. The warrior must have spent hours, Jason thought, slowly and deliberately creeping toward their camp. It made the Bantog ambush outside of Torsen look childish in comparison. This one was engineered. The Dwarf before him had only two weapons: the knife at Jason's chest and a jewel-handled axe that swung from his thick leather belt.

Teacher was in the same predicament, upon her knees with one Dwarf before her and one behind her. But the Major still stood on his feet, six guards about him, their axes leveled. Another Dwarf stalked out of the desert night and into camp. He was a bit taller than the rest, much older, and wore no camouflage. Instead, he was dressed completely in mail with a bronze battle helmet on his head and a sword at his side. He moved to within a step of IAM. The Dwarf's eyes flashed with authority.

"I am Captain Bok," he growled, then spit. "I place you under the authority of King Zak."

The Captain waved his hand sharply, which set the warriors about Jason and Teacher into motion. They began searching the captives. The Dwarf before Jason worked his way downward, checking every flap and fold in his leather shirt. The boy's shoulder continued to ache. The Dwarf then grabbed the ancient chain and tugged the Agate from its dark, cozy home. The boy froze. He could not lose the Agate, he knew. It was the source of everything—everything! As his thoughts whirled, doors deep within Jason's mind blew open with an immense force that staggered the boy. Two familiar objects drove forward through his vast consciousness. Each spun wildly in his mind, just a moment away from merging the forces within. They would not tolerate the Dwarf's touch much longer—that was clear.

The Dwarf raised the chain and inspected the gray, unassuming object of power. "What's this?" he growled as one rocklike eyebrow rose sharply.

"A lucky piece," Jason responded calmly, attempting to allay his nerves.

"Stupid Man-beliefs," grunted the guard as he released the chain, allowing the Agate to dangle at Jason's side. The icons vanished. The Dwarf finished his inspection. Jason slowly retrieved the Agate and stuffed it into his pocket.

Teacher was similarly searched. Then one warrior was left to guard Teacher and Jason as the rest of the company descended upon Major T.

"Hands up!" came the Captain's order. IAM paused, his eyes darting about the nine Dwarves now surrounding him. The old warrior's hands reached calmly upward, but his congenial expression was not one of submission. Rather, it was one of gracious permission, Jason realized. The Manwarrior, though heavily guarded, was giving his permission for the Dwarves to search him. It gave Jason the strange feeling that Major T could prevent the search entirely if he so chose. Jason suspected that the Dwarves felt it also.

"Search him!" the Captain snapped in a low voice. A Dwarf approached IAM cautiously. He slowly removed the scout's visible weapons: sword, bow, quiver, and ax. He then reached inside IAM's leather shirt and removed three small hunting knives, followed by two small balls tied together with a three-foot cord. He found a club in the small of IAM's back and a thin rope lashed about his waist. He removed the Major's crossbow and arrow from one boot, and the Farlo branch from the other. The Dwarf collected the items and moved back as the other guards began to relax their positions.

"Wait!" said the Captain harshly, sending his warriors back to alert. The Captain walked to the Major and extended his two huge, rough hands. "Slowly lower your fists to mine," the Captain ordered, standing a good two feet shorter than the scout.

IAM did as he was told.

"Search these!" the Captain barked.

A Dwarf guard moved to the Major and carefully folded the Manwarrior's sleeves upward, revealing a Tork knife and leather strap bound loosely to each wrist. The guard looked at the Major and smiled briefly, respecting the warrior's trade, if not the Man. He unlatched the leather and removed the slender twin blades.

"It has been thirty years, Manwarrior," began the Dwarf Captain. "But we can't forget your many ways." He turned abruptly and marched west out of the camp. "Take them!" he ordered as he forged into the desert.

The Dwarf guards pushed the trio on through the night. After a few hours' pace they approached the rise of a large sand dune. Heavily guarded, Teacher and IAM were the first to trudge to the top. They disappeared beyond the ridge. Jason followed. To anyone watching from afar, it would have appeared as though the desert just swallowed them up. Which in a way, it did.

The company of Dwarves descended silver-lined steps for what seemed like hours to Jason. At the bottom of the tunnel, five passageways appeared. The company entered the middle one and traveled another good distance until it split into two. IAM and Jason were guided to the right, Teacher to the left. The Manwarrior and Jason traveled down their corridor until it ended at a small stone cell, its door constructed of ancient Tork bars. The lead Dwarf swung the well-oiled cell door open and motioned for Jason and IAM to enter. The door swung closed with a loud click of its massive lock. In a moment, the Dwarves were gone, leaving the captives in shadowy light, a Kevin Farlo some ten feet down the corridor. The cell was empty with the exception of one bench, cut from stone, on the wall opposite the cell bars. IAM and Jason stood for a moment and listened until the steps of their hosts could no longer be heard, then they reluctantly sat.

"We wait then . . . for trial?" asked Jason.

"Yep," IAM said as he leaned back against the granite wall and crossed his arms.

"It seems they are quite interested in the Major," Jason added.

"Sure are," IAM concluded as he closed his eyes to rest.

Jason began to pace. He stopped to test the cell bars against the lock and hinges. They held fast, without even so much as a rattle. Two small objects suddenly appeared at the edge of his mind. The icons began to rotate. And even though they remained distant, he knew that just one true and desperate thought, maybe even one not so desperate, would catapult one or both to the forefront of his mind. It was his to choose. The icons grew larger. He thought again of their power. Then he thought again of the cell door. Then he thought again of their power. The Agate at his side began to grow warm.

"Maybe I should use my power to get us out," Jason said aloud.

"How many tools did you see the Dwarves remove from me?" the Major asked without opening his eyes.

Jason thought it was interesting that the warrior would call his weapons "tools."

"Oh . . . about a dozen."

"I have at least that many on me now," the Major said plainly. "Some of which can move those doors. But we would solve nothin' by escapin' if it means we breed more distrust among the Dwarves . . . our cousins. If we can devote a few hours to help resolve our differences, it could last centuries."

The icons in Jason's mind vanished. "How do you know when it's okay?"

"Know what's okay?" IAM responded.

"When to use your *tools* . . . my *powers?*"

"The same as with any power, whether it be a fist, a knife, an arrow, a word. You use it only when it's absolutely necessary."

"And how do you know when that is?"

"Usually when a life is at stake and you've exhausted every other possibility. And I mean . . . every other possibility. But most of all, you know it inside yourself. If there's any doubt whatsoever, then the time has not yet arrived."

The Major paused. "It's the same advice I once gave my own son when he was just about your age."

"You have a son?!" Jason asked.

"*Had* one," IAM said dejectedly, his fallen tone cutting Jason in two. "He loved the backcountry . . . just like I do. Wanted to do everythin' I was doin', whenever I was doin' it. Even when I went off to the Second Race War, he wanted to be at my side. He wanted to help. I promised his mother I'd look after him—keep him well. He turned out to be one of my best scouts." The Major's voice soared just a bit, hinting of a pride long kept within, but hardly forgotten. But his next words fell once again.

"When Cyrus needed volunteers to blockade the Eastern Pass, Jerel was the first to step forward. Cyrus told him no. But when I saw my son lose pride in front of the company, I rescinded Cy's order and let Jerel go. And that was my greatest mistake. I didn't listen to my own best judgment. My son never came back . . . he died in that pass."

Jason reached out with his mind and touched IAM's. He felt the scout's agony, a painful void that could never be filled. It was the same grief that he had felt within the Major days before. But Jason detected another great sadness as well.

"And his mother?" he asked softly.

"We drifted apart . . . mostly my own doing. Jerel and his mother looked so much alike that when I gazed at her beauty, I saw only him . . . tall and strong . . . the blue eyes . . . the alabaster complexion . . . the snow-white hair."

"Teacher!" Jason gasped.

"I loved her very much! Still do. But I've spent most of the last thirty years away. Then she sent me an urgent message. And here we are."

IAM rose to his feet, walked to the Tork bars, and leaned against them as he hauntedly peered at the Farlo glowing down the corridor. "I pray every night that Jerel's soul was strong enough to make the passage to Anton."

"But he was more than a child," Jason comforted. "He surely made it."

"He was young by Ethan standards. And it's not necessarily the years that count anyway. It's the maturity of the mind. But I hope you're right, son . . . I hope you're right."

Click! The heavy Tork lock opened.

"Let's go!" barked the Dwarf Captain, a dozen well-armed guards behind him.

The Major and Jason followed the Dwarves down the glowing, shadowy stone passage. A moment later Teacher joined them, head held high. She approached Jason, her knowing eyes inspecting his. One look told her much.

"I'm sorry," he said.

Teacher smiled gently. "It's been a long time, dear. Don't let it disturb your own thoughts. Each of us must do what we must." Teacher then looked a second longer. Content with what she perceived, she took her place behind Jason.

They reached a large chamber with a huge stone door. Gruff voices echoed from within. They entered and saw hundreds of Dwarf warriors dressed in battle gear. Their weapons clanged against their own mail. Kevin Farlo lined the four walls. The light illuminated depictions of Dwarf history that stretched far too high for Jason to see. A raised throne inlaid with gold and silver sat in the middle of the hall, some ten feet above the floor. Upon it sat an old Dwarf king who wore an intense gaze under a troubled brow. His short, thick fingers rubbed impatiently at the throne's armrests.

"They are here, my king" called the guard. A hush fell over the hall as a multitude of angry eyes turned to meet the prisoners. They were led to the base of the king's perch.

"What brings you here?!" King Zak boomed.

"We are on our way to Zol," IAM began, "then to Meadowtown, then to the Circle of Wisdom. We offer no harm to the Dwarf children of . . . "

"Harm!" the king shouted, his voice vibrating with rage. He jumped to his feet. "You speak to me of harm," he continued as he stepped hurriedly down the steps that led to his throne. "Killing my son was harm enough for a lifetime." He spit in IAM's face. "My only regret is that your coward servant Del is not here."

Jason's eyes flashed. He reached out to touch the Dwarf king's mind, but instantly recoiled from the festering hate and pain.

"The war has tortured many of us," IAM said sadly.

"Silence!" commanded the Dwarf. "I sentence you to death for committing the greatest crime against Dwarfkind . . . killing of a Dwarf son. And too, for the breaking of the Triad Agreement. Yes . . . that's it . . . you will die to satisfy the law *you* enacted. It is my right!"

The hall swelled with cheers.

King Zak reached his hand to one side. A nearby guard slapped the handle of a Tork ax into his vengeful fist. The king nodded and four guards rushed to the Major and dragged him to the far wall opposite the throne. They tied his feet and arms to Tork bars that were embedded in the rock a couple of feet above the floor. A metal band was strapped about his head and bolted to the stone wall. The Major hung helpless.

It was too easy, Jason thought. The Major didn't even struggle. And even now, in the face of death, IAM seemed far too content. Jason suddenly realized that the Major had devised his own solution to the warring Races. He would sacrifice himself in a last attempt to put everything right.

"Let this douse the fire within you!" yelled the Major. "Let me be the last to die in the war that still consumes. Then let my friends go free."

The Dwarf king appeared not to hear the words. Jason could not believe what was happening. The Major was risking his own life—no— giving it away in hopes that the Dwarf king would be so satisfied with the taste of human blood that his hatred would subside for all time. Fifty guards lined the path between King Zak at the throne and IAM at the wall. Hundreds more watched.

"King Zak!" shouted Teacher as two Dwarves restrained her. "Do you believe that you are the only one who suffered? We lost our own son. You know that to be true!" Her words were strong.

"No matter!" shrieked the king as he tested the blade's edge against his finger, drawing a drop of blood.

"I need IAM," she screamed. "Anton is in need . . . the Final Contest is upon us!"

"Fairytales!" he snapped. "If Anton truly existed he would not have taken my son. There is no god but one's own might." The king threw back his arm and took aim. The ax glistened above him.

Jason's mind screamed as the icons burst forth, staggering the boy. They began to collide but he drove a wedge between them, not allowing the awesome powers to converge into one. IAM's words came sharply back. *Only when absolutely necessary,* he thought. He needed to buy time. But to do what, he did not know.

"It is me you want!" Jason yelled as he stepped forward, not even realizing that he had moved. "I am Jason Del, heir to the Royal House!"

Eyes turned. Silence reigned. The king held his swing. He snapped his eyes toward the boy.

"My father is Cyrus Del," Jason continued, defiantly. "If it is him you hold most responsible, then it is I who will pay the debt. Let it be a son for a son . . . what better trade to bring this all to an end!" Jason was surprised at his bold words. Was it the Age of Wisdom or stupidity?

"Done!" the king agreed with a crazed, exuberant smile. The monarch waved his hand. IAM was immediately released from the wall. Jason was immediately lashed to it. He peered down the corridor of Dwarf warriors to their king and saw the madness in his eyes, an all-consuming hatred that had grown over decades. Cyrus Del had killed the Dwarf king's son. And now, the king was positioned to collect on the debt.

Jason's mind ached at King Zak's madness. He was filled with hatred for him—for a boy he never met. The king raised his ax. The icons of the Pearl and the Stone grew in Jason's mind, waiting to be put into service, waiting to release their power. The Agate burned at his side.

"No!" Jason said aloud as he closed his eyes and pushed the icons back. They went. He wasn't prepared to wield their force . . . yet. The Pearl nudged its way back to the forefront, begging Jason to at least use its confidence. But he pushed it back again. He had to face the fear himself. Matthew Del, Tempest Slayer, had no Pearl to help him. His father did not have the Pearl. Theda would not have needed the Pearl, he thought. He suddenly had to prove to himself, and to his ancestors, that he was forged for the task that fell to him . . . by default. He was not chicken. He was not Farlo. He needed to earn a place in the Royal House, whatever the cost.

The king's arm stretched back to its farthest point as he took aim, revenge still flooding his mind. The Major could stand no more of it. He might have been prepared to die, but he could not allow Jason to do so. IAM hurled the two Dwarves that restrained him to the stone floor, one tumbling over the next. He lunged toward the Dwarf king. Four guards blocked his path, but the Major grabbed his collar and sent it flying. To everyone's dismay, the collar opened to form a net that caught the guards by surprise and tangled them tight, allowing the Major to leap easily over them.

The Dwarf king laughed mockingly at the sight.

Three more guards appeared, thrusting spears at the Major, but the warrior sidestepped one guard, picked him up, and threw him at the others. The Major was now within ten feet of the king. A long knife appeared in the warrior's hand seemingly from nowhere. Two axes launched toward IAM, but the warrior jumped and rolled to the ground, narrowly missing the blades. In one fluid motion, the Major sprang back to his feet at the base of the throne, just a few steps from the laughing Dwarf king. But before he could move another foot, ten Dwarf guards came crashing down upon IAM from behind. The Major tumbled upon the steps of the throne. Arms and legs flew. Two of the guards were hurled back, skidding to a stop. Four more jumped into the fray. A moment later, Major T lay struggling on the ground beneath nearly a ton of flesh and mail, helpless to render aid to Jason and just a few feet from the self-appointed assassin king.

In the corner of his mind, Jason could hear Teacher still attempting to reason with the monarch, her stern words falling on deaf ears. The king's arm began its lurch forward.

Choose me! the Pearl screeched as it overwhelmed Jason's mind, pleading to fulfill its duty to give him confidence.

"No!" Jason responded even as he burst with fear. Jason searched deep within himself, and he found a rage equal to the king's, a rage at the stupidity of the Races, at their blind and senseless emotions that consumed their happiness and forever led them down a pitiful, misdirected path. Jason's fear gave way fully to anger. Teacher's lesson had worked! The icon of the Pearl suddenly vanished, unneeded.

As the king's arm lurched forward, their eyes locked. Jason felt many emotions clashing within the Dwarf. The king needed to right a past wrong, had lived to do just that. But he was also haunted by the gruesome desire to kill a human child. It was the conflict that made him insane as the opposing forces fought each other for supremacy. It was so much like a Bantog, thought Jason, pulled between good and evil. But beneath it all, Jason sensed, the king was good. He had been a good father, a loving husband, a friend to the Races so long ago. And that haunted him most of all. He was not the Dwarf he once was.

Jason suddenly knew this pitiful Dwarf king better than the king knew himself. Then, somewhere deep in the king's soul, madness began to crack open to the emotion of remorse. Though it was only a small fissure, Jason could tell that it was not just a temporary break. It had permanence.

The ax left the monarch's fist and hurtled onward. The Hall of the Dwarf King fell silent as all ears anticipated the blunt sound of a Tork edge on flesh.

Choose me! the Wizard's Stone pleaded as it appeared once again, pulsating wildly in Jason's mind, waiting to be unleashed, yearning to merge with the Pearl. The Agate burned.

"Only when absolutely necessary!" Jason screamed to himself, gritting his teeth as he struggled to hold the power at bay. Jason prayed that he would not have to use the power against the Races. It seemed suddenly an evil thing to wield it at all. But to use it against the Races would be unforgivable—so much less than Pure Good, so much less than the virtues he was to represent. He could hear IAM in a rage, fighting unsuccessfully with the guards. A dozen Dwarves needed every ounce of strength to restrain the Manwarrior.

Jason followed the course of the ax as it drew closer. The air sliced and whistled before it. Jason hoped that what he had felt within the king was true. He hoped that the Dwarf's foundation of good was well beyond his capacity for evil. And then, as the ax slammed forward, just feet before Jason, it shifted slightly, not unlike the king himself. The Tork blade grazed his left cheek, sliced off his ear, and then smashed deep into the stone wall. Its echo boomed.

Jason hadn't so much as flinched. His eyes were still locked onto those of the Dwarf king even as blood trickled down his left cheek and disappeared into the collar of his leather shirt. The Dwarf warriors looked on in wonder. IAM, now unrestrained, rose slowly to his feet. Teacher was at his side.

"That Pearl is mighty powerful," whispered IAM.

"He didn't use the Pearl," she responded slowly. "The confidence was his."

The Major gazed at Jason and smiled. "So much like Jerel," he whispered.

The Dwarf king strode toward Jason. He still hung helplessly upon the stone wall. The king stopped a foot away and scrutinized him from head to toe. There was still a great and irrevocable pain in the king's heart, Jason knew, but the hatred had subsided. The king could not take one son for another. It was simply not within him, nor his Race. And now the king knew it better and perhaps himself as well.

"I'm told your father is made of similar stone," the monarch said sadly.

Jason uttered nothing, his own eyes filled with sadness for the king's loss. No words could ease his pain, Jason realized, nor could they repair a lifetime of hate. But to Dwarfkind, an act of bravery was different. It was a deed that survived even hate, even loss. King Zak turned abruptly and headed toward the huge door as warriors scurried out of his way. He passed the arch and continued along the corridor built of marble. His steps echoed behind him. As he turned to descend even deeper into Trinity, he shouted an order, which, like his footsteps, resounded throughout.

"Let them go!"

CHAPTER 14

AN UNEXPECTED TURN

The night had come and gone, as had the new morning twilight, before the trio began its travels once again. Jason was quiet as they moved south along the remainder of Death Road, a small bandage where his left ear had been serving as a reminder of his encounter with the Dwarf king in the monarch's buried halls of stone. As his head began to throb from the pace, Jason wondered if his actions had been foolish rather than wise, and if his desire to use his own confidence had been too risky. Nonetheless, he had reached deep within himself and obtained something that he wasn't sure was there, and it made him glad to find it.

This was the beginning of the eighth day and—as anticipated—the sun dimmed a bit more this day, making the desert cool, though still a bit warm by western standards. The land was barren as it had been in the north, and the ground was hard and cracked as they followed the route to Zol, city of the desert sun. Jason felt an odd pull of the land here, a sense of older times that lay hidden in the dry remains of an ancient riverbed or the hardness of petrified wood. This was not a region born to desert, he knew, but the remnants of a once great east that existed before the Beasts of Becus brought it to an end. He turned to Teacher.

"When do I learn to better use the powers?" he asked.

"In Zol we will seek the doors of Libra, the depository of all histories," she began. "You will learn more there."

"You mean I'm going to learn from books?" Jason asked, bewildered.

"You have something against books?"

"No . . . I just thought . . . well . . . that I would have to be shown . . . tutored. I don't know why exactly . . . I just *feel* it."

Teacher stopped. She peered into Jason's eyes, searching for something she had missed. IAM paused at her side. Though she gazed as far inward as her gift would allow, Teacher found nothing. But it didn't quite satisfy her curiosity. Jason's feelings were not to be overlooked at this stage. Still, there was nothing she could do about it at the moment. She shrugged then continued her stride.

"Well, as far as I know, it's books or nothing at all."

Jason followed, but the nagging feeling remained.

Just as a fading sun dipped below the western horizon to create a streaking red twilight, Zol appeared to the south. Its dome-shaped structures were constructed of compressed white sand that stood about eight feet tall, making the city appear as rolling hills upon the desert. The only sight that distinguished Zol from the desert, in fact, was a taller red building near the center of the town. Within the hour, the trio entered the city along a sand-swept road and found its Man-Race inhabitants hurrying about narrow, crowded streets. All wore the same garment: a loose-fitting white robe with an attached hood—perfect for the desert climate. Beneath the hoods were dark, dry complexions etched by the sun. The men sported closely trimmed black beards that seemed to have a pride of their own, while the women wore delicate, modest veils that revealed nothing but moist, brown eyes. All was festive as the inhabitants hurried about in a merry mood, haggling and laughing with street merchants along the way. Some of the merchants sold their goods from carts. Others opened their shop doors and allowed the goods to flow into the middle of the street. And all about, musicians blew strange flutes that entranced desert gophers to rear up and sway to the sound of the music.

Jason suddenly realized that the desert people were preparing for the Twilight Festival, unaware of the events that would unfold this year. He had almost forgotten that only a few in Trinity actually knew of the fate that awaited them all.

The leather-clad travelers meandered about the densely populated narrow streets, sidestepping the carts and the goods and the sea of white robes and dark skin. The people of Zol watched them keenly, their hushed voices uneasy wherever the trio passed. There wasn't one smile reserved for them, Jason noted, or a kind word or a gentle nod. Obviously, thought Jason, travelers were not all that common in the desert city—nor were they particularly welcomed.

The children, however, were different. When they saw the three strangers pass through the sandy road, they pointed and smiled and touched and waved. Soon, the children formed a procession that followed the trio everywhere, and it grew by the minute. Jason felt greatly welcomed by the children of Zol. But he could not help but think that their fate, and the fate of all unborn souls, now rested with him. The feeling significantly detracted from the dozens of smiles about him. So his mind sank deep within in order to cut himself off from the sight. And it worked. The less he thought about the children, the less the sadness reached him.

There was one little girl who watched with particular interest. She had black hair and green eyes. Her white robe was woven perfectly by someone who must have cared a great deal. Though her body was small for her seven years of age, her mind was different, speaking to her of things that she did not see or understand. The arrival of the travelers was one of these. Her mind first told her of their eventual coming many months ago. It had continued to speak of them since—in different ways and at different times. She watched as the three approached but she could see only the youngest one: his red hair, the green of his eyes, and the bandage on the left side of his head that she had foreseen in countless dreams. As he passed her in the street, she trembled. The time was almost at hand, she knew. It was the time when life or death would pass over them all. And it all depended upon the boy with the deep red hair. When the travelers passed out of sight, the girl ran toward home. She had an important duty to complete, a task she had also seen in countless dreams.

With the children still in tow, Teacher headed down one passage and then another until they reached a modest sand dome sitting off by itself. A sign hanging near its door read *Rooms Here.*

The Etha turned abruptly.

"Go home!" she scolded in a sudden, menacing voice that sent the children flying.

Jason felt oddly glad that the children were gone. A cloud seemed to lift from him. Teacher smiled. It obviously felt good for her to keep in practice, Jason realized.

"Lead on," she then said to the Major.

IAM entered the dwelling first, followed closely by Jason, and descended some ten steps to a large underground room. The air was much cooler, providing some comfort. A rather small and cheerful-looking Man sat behind a desk made of petrified wood, his feet propped up comfortably. He was reading a book that rested upon his plump belly.

"What can I do for you folks?" the Man asked with delight as he rose.

"Three rooms," IAM answered, returning the Man's smile.

"Staying the whole night?"

"Maybe, maybe not," IAM replied.

"Three Daca coins just the same," the Man said as he opened his hand wide.

"Three Daca coins!" Jason cried. "My father can work days for just one."

The Innkeeper laughed. "Then he should become the only Innkeeper in a desert. It pays better."

"It does seem a bit high, friend," the Major remarked. "But we have no choice . . . do we?"

The Major handed the coins to the Man.

"It may sound like a lot of money, friends, but since I only rent out about twenty rooms a year, I hardly make a living at all. Follow me." He hopped about his desk and stopped short, seeing Teacher for the first time. A glance of recognition passed between them. "Oh!" he said. "A repeat customer." He flipped one of the coins back to IAM.

Teacher nodded to the gentleman in appreciation. The Innkeeper led them down a short hallway to their rooms. While the Man merely pointed IAM and Jason toward their doors, he took the time to open Teacher's personally, ensuring that all the accommodations were to her liking. When he found that they were, the Innkeeper grinned, looking as though he had accomplished something rather special. Then as he began to leave, IAM held him back.

"How much for three desert robes?"

"Two Daca coins should do it," whispered the Man, smiling. "But . . . I know a place where I might convince the management to sell you all three for just one coin."

"And where might that place be?" IAM asked skeptically.

"Why, here, of course!" the Innkeeper laughed aloud.

IAM slipped the fellow a coin and then disappeared through his door.

Jason's room was small, but equipped. Just as he lowered his pack and began to loosen his soiled leather shirt, a gentle rap drew his attention to the dry, wooden door. He opened it hesitantly and found the Innkeeper holding a fresh cotton robe, identical to those worn above. He gladly accepted it and put it on without delay. It was cool and light compared to the leathers, though it was a bit large on his frame. He then fastened his rope belt in place so as to anchor his Agate, and then placed the jewel into one of the many internal pockets.

"Dinner ready!" the Innkeeper suddenly called from without. "Just one Daca coin!" A moment of silence passed before he repeated his call.

"All right, all right!" Jason heard their scout yell from across the hall. He smiled and then left to follow the Innkeeper to a welcomed meal.

After they ate, Teacher led IAM and Jason above ground and down several narrow passages, until the domes about them parted abruptly to reveal a building made of red brick, its design ancient compared to those about it. Though only two stories tall, it appeared much greater as it loomed over the younger sand dwellings. It was vacant by the looks of it, and half-swallowed by the desert, whose sand had poured into gaping holes in its walls. Tork letters above the structure's sun-cracked wooden doors said simply: *Libra.*

"Well, here it is," Teacher said, stopping before it.

Jason peered at the structure. There was something about Libra that didn't quite sit well with him, though he didn't know exactly what it was. It seemed imposing, bigger than it actually was, more vital, and perhaps even more dangerous. They entered Libra through the front doors that swung open and shut sporadically, banging to the current of the dry gale. Once inside, their feet rested in several inches of sand. IAM raised the Kevin Farlo. Its glow revealed that several interior walls had crumbled to the floor, exposing the rear wall. Wind whipped sand whistled through the gaps in the walls.

"Everything's gone," Jason said, covering his mouth to prevent sand from entering. "Follow me," Teacher said as she took the Farlo from IAM. She crossed the first room and stepped through one of the jagged openings in the next wall. Jason and IAM were close behind, reaching her at the top of a narrow brick stairway that sank deep into darkness. Jason followed Teacher and IAM down the stairs, touching the walls as he went to keep his balance on the sandy, loose steps. They reached an empty small room at the bottom. Teacher bent and brushed the sand away with her cupped hand.

"What are you looking for?" the warrior asked.

"A knob," she answered as she wiggled her fingers deep into the sand. "Got it." She pulled it. "Stand away!"

A portion of the floor began to rumble and fall slowly downward. The sand upon it poured onto brick steps that led to another room far below. Teacher moved to the hidden stairway and began her descent into pure darkness, the Farlo guiding her way. IAM and Jason followed closely and cautiously, their feet attempting to locate the brick steps beneath the fallen sand. The air in the underground chamber was stale and reeked of old parchment. Jason felt a foreboding. His mind was flooded with the intoxicating scent of a long-ago power—cold and exacting—that once filled this chamber. He trembled. The Pearl came to him, but he sent it back.

Just as the trio reached the bottom, the door above swung slowly back into place. As it closed, the entire ceiling of the underground chamber began to glow softly. Teacher gave the Farlo back to IAM, who put it away.

The room became visible. It was cavernous, with books lining each of its four walls from floor to ceiling. A huge oak table dominated the center. It had one dozen heavy, high-backed oak chairs sitting rigidly about it. Jason noted the back of the nearest chair. It had an intricately detailed carving of a fierce-looking old man, partly visible through the layers of dust. The figure wore a long robe, the grain of the wood highlighting the folds in the cloth. His eyes were a blazing red, inset with brightly colored jewels. Jason glided his hand gently across the carving. Chills rose along his fingertips. Although this was merely a work of art buried in dust, it seemed alive. Waves of ancient power seemed to flow from it—a power that he strangely recognized.

"Wizards!" he gasped as he approached the next chair, noting that while the craftsmanship was the same, the figure was slightly different from the last. He brushed the dust away to get a better look at the entire depiction. The Wizard's arms were stretched upward, and streaks of white power rose from his fingers to form a shield. Above the shield was a carved blast of red fire and black smoke that came from the heavens. Above that, another depiction was almost entirely buried in dust. Jason swept it away.

"Tempest!" Jason murmured. The beast looked fiercer than Jason had ever imagined. He suddenly thought of the great battles that had gone before. "Where are we exactly?"

"This is truly Libra," Teacher began. "Library of the Wizards. With the exception of one history entitled the Book of Endur, the rest of the history of Trinity is recorded here, mostly written by the Wizards themselves."

Teacher slowly climbed an ancient ladder to the top shelf. She reached behind several books and grabbed another. It had a velvet cover but no markings, title or otherwise. She clutched it to her chest and stepped down.

"Sit," Teacher said to her companions as she motioned to the chairs about the table. Teacher opened the velvet binder to the beginning of the book.

"Of Stone and Pearl," she began. "The following account is written for the Chosen One so as to learn the ways of true power."

Teacher paused and peered at Jason. His eyes were steady and sure, she noted. He was progressing well. She turned a page, her finger skimming across the lines.

"The instruction contained herein will be made known at the word of the Chosen One, a word to be found buried in the deepest cavern upon Trinity."

She finished, left the book open, and slid it across the table to Jason. Other than the words Teacher read, the rest of the pages were blank.

"So in the deepest cavern I will find a *word,*" he began, "that will make the words in this book appear."

Teacher nodded.

"Well," said IAM thoughtfully, "the deepest cavern I know of is down there in the Granite River. Looks like we're on our way back."

A moment of silence filled the room.

"That is not the deepest cavern," Jason said.

"Then what is?" asked the scout.

"My mind," he concluded.

Teacher smiled. "It is deep within yourself that the direction exists. Even I do not know how you will learn to fully master the Pearl and Stone. But I know the book will tell us once you find the *word.*"

"What do I do?" he asked, pushing the book to the center of the table.

"You must look deeper within your soul than ever before and find a *word* that lingers at the edge of a thought. It is that *word* that will make the rest of the book clear. It will help instruct you to use the power. Without it, the book remains empty to all of us."

"Well, the faster I start, the sooner it's over," Jason said. He grabbed the edge of the table to steady himself. After a deep breath, he closed his eyes and let his conscious mind sink slowly. His thoughts had form and dimension—more than ever now. Thoughts of Libra were at the surface, and of his companions huddled about him amidst the dust and smell of decay. Beneath that were thoughts of the plump Innkeeper and the long walk from the Desert of Zak. The Dwarf king was a stark recollection that did not fade so quickly, as were the Tempest Spawn that chilled even the warmer memories that flooded about them. The images were now fluid, moving through the corners of Jason's mind just as they had in life. He could almost reach out and talk to them, but they were too engaged in what had been. He plunged deeper. Some images loomed larger than others, particularly those of his parents, who grew younger as he descended into himself. He passed a memory of himself and Theda at Pike's Cliff. He hurried past it and plunged deeper into the senseless tears he shed as a child, the fears long forgotten, the excitement he felt at the prospect of discovery, and the joy of Twilight Festivals long gone. He was touching events that were not accessible from the surface of the mind alone—lost to all, except the one who bore the Pearl and Stone. He saw Teacher at the head of a younger class, and only now did he notice how intently she gazed at him as he prepared to recite a history lesson. But here, in the archives of his mind, no memories were lost, just buried below more recent events—sometimes buried so deep that they never made their way to the surface to be recollected.

He fell deeper. The images, which had started in a rush, began to thin out, coming at longer intervals: a birthday here and there, a first tooth loosened and pulled, a frightful first dream. He saw a brown wicker basket all about him. He felt the smoothness of a blanket. A delicately carved wooden animal was at his side. He sensed the first time he caught the smell of Twilight Cakes baking. Then there was no sight at all. He heard only the beating of a drum—his mother's heartbeat? And then, there wasn't even that.

Two specks of light appeared on a distant horizon. They intrigued his mind and pulled him deeper. Jason found himself in the resting place of the icons. The Pearl and Stone both glowed a gentle light as they rotated slowly, but apart, in the deepest reaches of his mind, placed there only so long as the Agate stayed snugly within his pocket in the physical world, he knew. They were magnificent: warm, strong, silently awaiting his command. It was interesting, he thought, that here in his mind they each had a continuous light of their own, whereas the Agate in the physical world reflected only gray. It was curious.

He pulled his consciousness from the light and continued his journey through an ever-deepening cavern of darkness. His mind reeled at the hollow, deafening emptiness of himself. But then, he saw the spark of an image. This was it, he thought, the clue for which he came. How long it had been there he did not know. Jason was intrigued as he drew near the beacon. It was hazy but oval. He moved close, inspecting it from all sides, but he could discern nothing. Without warning, the object crystallized. It grew to an enormous size. It was a cold red eye. It gripped Jason. He became anxious, and tried to pull away. But he could not. The eye looked into his soul. Again he tried to pull away, but again he could not. Jason panicked.

The Pearl of Anton hurtled through the blackness of Jason's mind to render aid. Its light flared up, driving a wedge between the boy's primordial soul and the heartless image. A roar blew through Jason's mind. When he recovered, the eye was gone. So was the Pearl.

"Jason! Jason!" IAM shouted as he shook the boy soundly.

Jason slowly opened his eyes, swollen and damp.

"You gave us quite a scare," IAM said. "You were out for close to two hours."

"What did you find?" Teacher asked. "Did you find the *word?*"

Jason thought of the cold, consuming eye. "Zorca!" he breathed.

The room trembled and the glow of the ceiling flickered dim. A fierce wind blasted the room, hurling the trio back in their chairs. It sucked the air from their lungs. The velvet book of Wizards spun rapidly within the wind's vortex, its pages flapping wildly. As abruptly as it started, the gale was gone.

Teacher slapped her hand on the book to stop its spinning. She drew it close and flipped to the previously blank pages. Her right eyebrow was cocked in surprise.

"This cannot be!" she said. Teacher slid the book to Jason.

With traces of sweat still lingering on his brow, he read. "And when the Stone was forged, their power therein transferred, two of the Wizards passed beyond Trinity to Anton, while the eldest, Zorca, lay in wait at the Lone Tower for the Chosen One."

Jason flipped hastily through the rest of the book. It repeated only two words: *Lone Tower.*

"What is it, Sara?" IAM asked.

Teacher looked at the Major starkly. "A Wizard lives," she said. "And we must travel to the Lone Tower to find it."

They reached the inn and were startled to find a little girl waiting for them in the hallway. She was asleep and at the foot of Jason's door. She held a bundle of cloth in her arms. As they approached, she awoke and began to quiver. Her green eyes flashed with fear.

"It's all right, dear," said Teacher, bending toward her. "My name is Sara."

"I know," she said with a wince, fighting back a tear. "My name is Jena, and I have been sent."

Teacher looked deep into her eyes. "Oh," she began. "She's gifted."

"How?" asked IAM.

"She can see things others cannot. It happens sometimes . . . falling at random." She turned back to the girl. "Where are your parents?"

"They died. Papa of fever. Mama of heartbreak. I live with others now. They're okay. But not like Papa and Mama."

"Why are you here?"

"I'm waiting for him," she said, motioning toward Jason. "If he wins," she sniffled, "then I will see my parents again someday."

Jason's heart burst. There it was again. Unless he defeated the evils in the Final Contest, her soul might *never* rise to Anton to be reunited with those of her parents. He felt a rush of shame. Earlier that day he had pushed the thoughts of the children from his mind to ease his burden. Jena's presence was not an act of chance, he suddenly knew. Anton had sent her as a flesh-and-blood reminder of why he must win. It was easier to ignore a million children he did not know than to avoid one he did. He joined her on the floor, placing his arm about her tiny frame.

"I will win," he promised, "and you will see your parents again."

She smiled, and then held up a present.

"What's this?" Jason asked.

"I made this for you," Jena said, smiling. "It's a robe."

Jason inspected his gift. It was well made, lighter than the one he now wore, but of a tighter and stronger knit. And within, there was only one small pocket, at belt level, a perfect size for the Agate.

"I hope you like it," she said, timidly. "I made it from what I saw in my mind."

"I will wear it always," Jason pledged.

"Good," said Jena. "Oh . . . and be careful of the Wizard," she continued as she suddenly remembered another dream. "It's not very nice."

CHAPTER 15

WIZARD

Cautious but steadfast, IAM led his companions from the dry heat of the desert to the humidity of the Misty Plains. They were in search of the Lone Tower, an edifice that stood in the western portion of the Great Swamp. Jason could sense the Major's apprehension. His mind now collected the mental vibrations of others whether he sent it forth or not. He couldn't stop it any more than his friends could stop breathing. Teacher was leery as well. Histories did not always speak kindly of the tower. Nor did they always speak well of its former inhabitants . . . Wizards.

This was day nine. The fog was so heavy near the swamp that the weakened sun could not penetrate its dark veil. The humidity taxed their strength. Sweat trickled freely down the companions' faces. They still wore the robes of the desert people, which provided little comfort in the new climate. The soil was soft and moist as the travelers drew near to the swamp. Before long, their feet began to splash through the water, which was surprisingly cold this far south, quite in contrast to the warm air that clung to their clothes and skin. Oddly shaped tree branches, twisted and stripped of leaves, reached at them through the mist. They made it difficult for the trio to keep a straight route. But Jason noted that the Major didn't seem to need one. An hour after entering the outlying areas, IAM paused.

"About a mile forward," he speculated as he peered through the fog. "Could be a mile and a half." The scout scooped some mud from the swamp bed. He placed a bit of it onto his tongue. "One mile," he confirmed.

Legends began to filter through Jason's mind of creatures born for the sole purpose of destroying the Beasts of Becus. The thoughts were far from comforting. Jason threw his mind cautiously forward, seeking the edges of another consciousness through the darkness. His mind cut through the gray warmth with nothing to restrict it, and nothing to show for the effort. But then, just as he was about to recall it, his mind suddenly tingled with the feel of something, a mind perhaps, buried beneath an impenetrable mound of shivering cold. Curious, he maneuvered his mind this way and that to gain a vantage point. But even as he did, Jason's thoughts bounced back rather abruptly. Whatever it was, it now knew that he was coming.

Each step toward the tower was colder than the last. Chunks of ice began to float lazily out of the mist, bobbing about and challenging their numbing steps. Jason felt a strong, tugging current at his feet. He paused. The water rippled at the surface. A moment later, the current was gone and the water smooth again. Jason sensed that a strange, foreign life lived beneath the waves. But it had moved on, and so did he.

A warm, northern wind began to blow at the travelers' backs. IAM abruptly stopped and glared into the gray haze before him. The mist slowly parted. A shadow rose. It was the Lone Tower, made of massive, gray stones that locked together tightly, rising to form a crooked but slender fortress. Beneath it was a solid-rock foundation that appeared to plummet to the core of Trinity itself. A shudder gripped Jason, a feeling colder than the water about him.

The companions continued their pace. The water began to fall beneath their knees as they approached a narrow rock shore. IAM stepped out of the water and drew his sword. The metal rang out. The warrior kept his eyes fixed upon the tower, which now stood just paces away. He slowly circled the mammoth structure as Teacher and Jason followed closely. It was a uniform cylinder. Rather than smooth, the rock blocks were coarse, as though their final contour was of little concern to the builders. As the warm air touched the frigid stone, it condensed just enough to create the perpetual fog that seemed to seethe from the stone itself. Some of the liquid turned to ice on the tower's stone, giving a glossy finish.

They found an arched passage on the western side. The doors creaked slowly open to acknowledge the trio's arrival. They entered. The tower's interior glowed with a cold dark blue. A rock stairway spiraled ominously upward into a mist that flowed through the tower. They began their ascent upon icy, narrow steps, the Major leading the way, his sword held high and reflecting blue. Jason went second. With each step the air grew colder still, freezing the moist tears that formed at the corners of his eyes. Fear began to steal its way into his mind. The Pearl came closer to the forefront.

The trio circled higher and higher through the mist. The floor below them was lost through the hazy, swirling clouds. A platform came into view. Its stone surface was slick with ice. They moved upon it cautiously. A solitary chamber, pulsating with a deep and frigid blue, lay just beyond the platform.

Teacher passed her companions and entered the room. The scout was close behind. Jason came last, his flesh crying out in pain, the cold stinging his skin. He clasped his hands together to generate heat, but it was no use. Between one painful inhalation and the next, Jason caught a glimpse of a crystalline blue stone slab rising three feet off the floor. The slab emitted the pulsating blue light that seemed to be the ultimate source of the cold. Upon the bed of ice lay a figure cloaked in a deep-green robe.

Wizard, Jason thought instantly.

Gray and wrinkled hands extended just beyond the sleeves of the robe and were folded rigidly across the figure's chest. Its bare feet were visible, with flesh hanging loosely from the bone. Between one breath and the next, Jason saw the figure's head, a mass of wrinkled and graying skin. White hair flowed downward from its balding crown, mingling gently with a beard that grew almost to its hands. Jason paused just before he reached the slab. The icy thought of untold power shot through his mind.

"Come," Teacher beckoned.

Jason stepped forward. His body trembled with cold and fear. He was surprised by his mentor's relative calm. IAM was near, his blade appearing as a bright icicle amidst a glacier. The warrior's thick eyebrows were covered with frost. Teacher raised her hand and gently touched the Wizard's neck, searching for a sign of life. The cold bit her flesh. She jerked her fingers away.

"The *word,*" she said to Jason. "Say the *word.*"

Jason looked down at the Wizard. The *word,* he knew, would awaken a creature that may best be left asleep, a creature that every Race regarded with caution and fear. He remembered the probing eye in Zol. He trembled. The Pearl lurched forward. Its light exploded.

"Zorca," Jason said as steam floated from his breath.

The slab began to vibrate. Sudden warmth poured from the slab. The Wizard's eyes began to quake, anticipating the rebirth of consciousness deep beneath the wrinkled flesh. Its face trembled in pain. Its fingers twitched slowly. Its arms then lifted forward, quivering in the light. Its hands grasped at the air as though searching for someone to return its reach.

Teacher grabbed Jason's wrists and plunged his hands into those of the Wizard's. They closed around Jason's fists and held him painfully tightly. It then pulled at Jason's hands, using his weight to tug its torso up from the slab. The Wizard rose slowly, trembling, until it was sitting upright. Its eyes were still shut, though a touch of pink now appeared at its cheeks. Its head turned slightly, facing Jason at nearly eye level. The Wizard's eyelids began to wiggle violently, battling their own muscles to follow the will of the unseen, ancient mind. With a snap, they shot open. Jason froze. The pupils were a piercing blood red, the same as the one he found within his own abyss. Jason's mind sought that of the Wizard's, hoping that knowledge of the creature would somehow ease his fear, a tactic that failed him in the lair of the Tempest Spawn. Yet the Wizard's mind was closed tightly. It was as though it waited behind an impenetrable wall. Jason pounded his mind onto the shield, but to no avail.

Suddenly, a passage opened to him, and Jason plunged into the Wizard's mind. He felt a collection of uncaring, all-powerful thoughts, organized and immovable. The Wizard's mind was without tenderness. Instead, there was only dedication so great that no room existed for anything other than the fulfillment of its purpose.

Jason's body lurched forward as the Wizard's thoughts gripped his own. The creature's mind sliced through Jason's consciousness and pulled one of Jason's memories—one of his father—rudely out of position. The creature examined it relentlessly and then pushed it back into whatever location was convenient. Jason's mind stung. The Wizard went back for another memory, then another, then another. Soon, Jason's mind was mixed and jumbled about in no discernable order: images out of context, people and places mingling in his mind that never had in life. The boy winced at the painful, perplexing incongruity. Then, individual thoughts were not enough for the Wizard. Whole sections of memories, years at a time, were yanked out of context and dissected. Jason threw back his head and cried out in pain. His legs buckled beneath him. Only the Wizard's gripping fingers kept him from falling to the cold, gray floor.

The Wizard found one particular memory that intrigued it, mostly because it appeared to have been intentionally hidden. It paused, examining the memory from all angles. A dry, crackling voice pierced Jason's mind, audible only to him.

"Memories are not to be hidden, boy. They're to be understood! Maybe Theda should be standing before me. And maybe you should have been the one to have died at the cliff."

The Wizard let go of the memory. But again it lashed out, searching for others. Jason's mind was emptied and recycled again and again. He called desperately for the icon of the Wizard's Stone, but it would not come to his aid. Jason heard a mocking laugh in his mind.

"The Wizard's power will not harm me," said the voice. *"It is me!"*

The Pearl injected Jason with confidence again and again. It served to keep him from going insane. Time stood still.

"It's well you use the Pearl, boy," the voice in his brain said. "Your *own will is too feeble, and I'm not a Dwarf ax you can just deflect with a mind trick."*

A *snap* then cut the air as though a taut rope had broken under the strain of a great weight. Jason fell straight backward onto the floor. He began to reassemble his thoughts, grouping those that belonged together. As he did, Jason suddenly understood the purpose of the Wizard. Ages ago, in a world now gone, the creator of the Races had conceived of a creature capable of defeating the Tempests . . . the beasts that could read the thoughts of others. The Wizard would have to match that power and more. There would be no room for emotions or caring or anything else that might impede its duty. As such, Anton created the Wizards to fight cold with cold. But because he was wise, Anton pulled them out of Trinity when their job was nearly done, knowing that they would be too dangerous to leave behind. But one Wizard was left for Jason to discover. Dizzy and confused, the boy questioned his own worth. What does Anton expect of me? he wondered. Does he expect that he, Jason Del, could somehow defeat two great evils when this already powerful Wizard could not? It didn't make sense.

Jason raised his head and opened his eyes. Through the haze, he saw IAM standing beside the Wizard. One of the scout's arms was locked about the creature's chest; the other held his sword against the Wizard's fleshy throat. Jason pursued the Major's thoughts and was shocked by what he found. The Major was filled with an all-consuming terror. IAM was afraid, and it was a foreign, plunging feeling for the Manwarrior. Yet there he stood, and when he spoke, his words were as strong as Tork.

"Harm the boy again and I will kill you . . . magic or no."

Jason marveled at his scout. This was bravery—not the kind that comes from eluding a Dwarf ax, knowing full well that you have the power to destroy it, but the kind that comes from not yielding to an overwhelming force, despite the terror.

The Wizard gazed at the Major with dead, cold eyes.

"Humans are still so pitiful. I see that nothing has changed in eons. Why my master picked the Chosen One from among your Race I'll never understand."

The Wizard began to sway as if it, too, was weakened by the encounter. Its body went limp, but its mind kept its consciousness.

"Lower your sword, Manwarrior," it coughed. "It is not I who will challenge your pup."

The Wizard's eyes, now weary and a pale red, peered intently upward as though searching for something far beyond the confines of the Lone Tower. It nodded slowly.

"The Contest grows near," it wheezed. "Very near." Its eyes narrowed. "The Champion of Cil is without merit . . . but the Champion of Becus is a Pure Evil that grows in power even now . . . already greater than the Tempest of my day."

The Wizard's words stabbed Jason. *Already greater than the Tempest of my day.*

"IAM, lower your sword," Teacher said.

The Major glanced at the Wizard and suddenly saw the creature as it truly was: immensely old, its eyes revealing strength long tapped, its flesh hanging limply. He lowered his blade. Jason felt relief wash over the Major.

The Wizard stretched its ancient arms. "My time is short and your need is great," Zorca began, looking down at Jason. "My mind is all that still functions. But that is all we need to train with." It turned to IAM. "Pick me up, as I'm too weak to walk."

The Major glanced at Teacher. She nodded. He carefully lifted the Wizard.

"Where to?" the Major asked.

"Through the door," Zorca replied, twitching a finger toward a solid stone wall. As the trio followed his gaze, the stone began to fade until a rounded opening formed to reveal a green and hilly countryside beyond. The sound of rushing water filtered through the crevice. The trio gazed in awe. It was a portal to a warm land that seemingly existed at the top of the frigid Lone Tower.

They stepped over the inviting threshold and left the freezing chamber behind them. Jason felt the warmth of his blood begin to circulate. He looked curiously about a grassy land surrounded by dark-green trees that swayed playfully beneath a light-green sky. While there was no sun in the heavens, there was ample light, the source of which could not be discovered with human eyes. Flowers dotted the meadow. A creek babbled in the distance, flowing around a bend and out of sight through the trees. The odd passage was still visible, revealing the cold chamber beyond.

"Where are we?" Jason asked Teacher.

"I don't know," she answered, captivated.

The Major placed the Wizard carefully down in the meadow. Upon touching the land, Zorca looked suddenly renewed. The Wizard's step was lively, its wrinkles less deep, and its eyes a sharper red. A large staff appeared in its hand. Jason was apprehensive of the Wizard's renewed vigor.

"Fear not," it said, sensing Jason's concern. "I am still old." It waved its hand about the countryside. "I trained in this meadow long ago. It should do for you also."

Jason's mind could not help but seek the Wizard's to see if the transformation was more than just bodily. He cautiously threw his mind forth and was washed over by the same wave of thoughts, cold and final, that he had experienced earlier.

"Your mind probe isn't very powerful," Zorca said. "But then, we didn't intend it should be." The Wizard moved quickly to the center of the meadow and leaned against its staff.

"Let's get started," it said. "First, you must learn to block out mind probes. We don't want evil to gain your thoughts. I'm going to search your mind softly. As I do, command the Pearl to expand until it covers the specific thoughts that I seek . . . simply imagine the Pearl stretching around it."

Jason felt the Wizard's mind delicately touch his own mind, searching his memories. While not as painful as the probe earlier, it was uncomfortable nonetheless. He concentrated on the Pearl and used his will to expand it. It did. He then brought the Pearl to the thoughts under scrutiny and used it to enclose them completely.

"Very good," said the Wizard. "Now prepare!"

Jason's mind reeled under a sudden attack. Memories and thoughts were once again jarred and pulled by the Wizard's full mind probe. Years collided. Jason fell to his knees and pressed his hands against his head in a feeble attempt to banish the agony. The Pearl was there, injecting him with confidence. But he had been taken off guard and wavered, almost forgetting what he had just learned. He reached out to the icon of the Pearl and shaped it, desperately pulling and folding it over thoughts new and old, piece by piece, fragment by fragment. Then, finally, every inch of his mind was covered. The pain stopped.

Jason opened his tearful eyes. He saw the Wizard bearing down. Its mind was bent upon gaining access to his thoughts. But while Jason could feel the probe trying relentlessly to enter, it could not. Jason's calm was restored. Zorca broke concentration, exhausted.

"Be careful of even the slightest probe," Zorca wheezed and coughed, the Wizard's true age showing itself. "Evil can learn much from just *one* thought." Zorca rose and looked at Jason accusingly. "And you have many thoughts you see fit to hide . . . about Theda, for instance . . . *don't you!*"

Jason ignored the comment. Teacher's eyes flashed.

"Bring both the Wizard's Stone and the Pearl forth," Zorca continued.

"But I haven't felt the Stone since entering the tower," Jason responded.

"It will be there now," Zorca declared. "Call it!"

Jason threw a short request into the abyss and, instantly, both Stone and Pearl were at the forefront of his mind, spinning silently and slowly, waiting to be commanded.

"At the passageway to the Tempest Spawn, your thoughts united the Stone and Pearl," said the Wizard. "We will do that again. But before you do, I want you to think of your arms as the pathway of power. The Agate at your side will use that pathway by channeling its power up your body and toward your fists. Once it's there, allow your mind to form a ball with the power and then hold it steady before you. Understand?"

"Yes."

"Then begin!"

Jason raised his arms to form the pathway while the icons moved closer in his mind. The Agate at his side grew warm and seemed almost to vibrate. Jason thought of the power he could not control in the chamber of the Tempest Spawn, the same awesome force that now waited for his command. But he did not hold back. The icons touched slightly. A white heat surged and inflamed Jason's body. He felt the force rise along his torso. Then, a blast of light engulfed Jason's arms. He was so stunned by its appearance that he inadvertently allowed the power to shoot from his fists and hurtle haphazardly into the forest. It exploded upon a tree in a blinding white flash, spewing smoke and ash in all directions. Jason trembled. The icons fell apart.

"Try it again," the Wizard said impatiently.

Jason took a deep breath. The power grew as before, rising up in a searing heat, and then bolted up his arms. But just as its force left his fingertips in a formless heap, his mind fashioned it into a ball. It hovered a few feet above the ground and waited, it appeared, for another command.

"Allow your mind to mold it into a net," Zorca said. "See its weave in your mind."

Jason imagined a net. The ball spread into an intricate, glistening, powerful web. It was a perfectly formed round, some five feet in diameter, with a weave loose enough to allow the human eye to see what lay beyond.

"Rotate it," Zorca commanded.

It immediately began to turn on a vertical axis. Its brilliance cast intermittent light across everyone's faces.

"Send it to the boulder at the edge of the meadow," the Wizard said, pointing.

The net moved silently across the meadow and stopped just above the large rock.

"Set the net all about it, but don't touch the stone itself or the ground upon which it sits."

Jason imagined it, and the force obeyed.

"Now, tighten the force about the rock."

Jason did so. The boulder exploded into a million pieces. The trio turned away. Jason swooned. The release of the Wizard's power depleted his strength.

"I need to rest a moment," Jason said.

"No!" yelled the Wizard. "A moment is all I have left."

The Major took a threatening pace forward. Teacher grabbed his arm and held him back.

"Form another power net," Zorca commanded.

Instantly it was there, perfectly formed and floating in midair. Jason was startled at how quickly the power now obeyed his thoughts.

"Keep the net there as if to protect you. Then command more power by overlapping the icons completely, forming a ball with the rest of the power created."

Jason hesitated. He remembered not being able to stop the power in the cave of the Tempest Spawn when the icons perfectly overlapped.

"Don't worry about that," Zorca snapped, understanding Jason's every twinge. "Now you know the icons better. They fall apart when you blank your thoughts . . . just think of nothing and they will separate."

Jason did as ordered. Heat coursed through his body. A moment later, a blinding ball of light bolted from his arms and hovered alongside the power net.

"Send the ball into the trees as before."

As fast as a thought, the ball raced toward the forest. But it dissipated too soon, weakening with every yard it traveled until, long before it made impact, it was gone.

"Release the net," the Wizard said irritably.

Jason diverted his thoughts. The icons fell easily apart in his mind. The net vanished.

"The powers are not infinite," Zorca began. "There's only so much you can tap. In order for you to extend the reach of the power ball, you must weaken the protection net. It's a terrible choice in battle. Now create another net, but smaller this time. Then produce a power ball with what remains."

Jason allowed the images in his mind to overlap only slightly. A net appeared but was considerably weaker, the fabric of light thinner and the weave larger. Then Jason overlapped the images completely once again and the power ball appeared, bigger this time. He sent it racing toward an unseen target amidst the trees.

Boom! Trees exploded and the ground rocked.

"Hmmm," said the Wizard. "Your magic is powerful, but not as powerful as we had hoped. You'll have to make do with what you've got." The Wizard then looked pensively into the light-green sky. "Though if the spawn of Becus becomes even a bit more powerful than it is today . . . "

The Wizard clutched its chest and bent over in agonizing pain, falling hard to the ground. Its flesh began to peel away. Body fluid oozed from its mouth.

"My task is complete," it wheezed in agony. "One more command . . . you must go to Spirit Lake before the Final Contest. A messenger waits. . . . "

Zorca began to convulse.

"Run!" Zorca cried. "Get out of the tower! Out of the swamp! Run!

The time is here!" The Wizard rolled to a ball and trembled violently, its ancient flesh falling off bone.

Jason hesitated. Teacher yanked him toward the passage.

"Run . . . fools . . . run!" the Wizard choked out as its dying fingers dug into the dirt.

IAM jumped through the portal and landed on the cold, icy floor in the chamber at the top of the Lone Tower. Teacher and Jason dashed through a moment later. The passageway slammed nearly shut.

"Run, fools!" shouted the Wizard. The tower suddenly lurched to one side. The companions fell hard against a stone wall.

"Run!"

The travelers staggered down the spiral stairs. The Lone Tower rolled and pitched. They slipped upon the icy steps. Stone crumbled high above and fell upon them. The tower suddenly lurched backward. Jason was thrown over the edge of the narrow steps and down into the spiral. He jerked to a stop when someone caught his hand. Jason dangled above the gray abyss as the tower continued to sway. Major T pulled him up. Jason cleared the specks of dust from his eyes.

Teacher was gone. They peered down into the spiral, but the mist shrouded what lay below. IAM jumped over the gap in the steps where Teacher had stood and raced downward into the darkness. Jason sent his mind into the spiral, seeking Teacher's thoughts. A shudder of relief passed through his mind as he touched a living being. But Teacher's mind was irrational and confused, buried deep within itself. Teacher was unconscious.

"She's alive!" Jason yelled as he followed IAM. "But hurt!"

As he approached the bottom of the stairs some minutes later, he saw the Major lift Teacher into his arms. Her body was limp, her head cocked back. She had a large gash on her forehead. Blood was spattered about her face. Her breath was shallow.

"Run!" the Wizard screamed. "I can't hold it much longer!" The tower jerked.

The Major sped out of the tower and plunged into the swamp with Teacher in his arms and Jason close behind. Jason heard massive stones tumble into the water about them. With each rock that fell, the water seemed colder and more restricting. They pivoted around the floating ice and maneuvered under the branches of dying, sunken trees. Minutes seemed like hours.

The foundation of the Lone Tower cracked and shattered, submerging the companions in the frigid water. IAM quickly recovered Teacher, lifting her over his left shoulder before pulling Jason to his feet. They turned and saw the spire collapse straight into the murk. As the tower's massive stones plunged through its own foundation, the water about the broken structure instantly became solid ice. But it did not stop there. The ice grew in circles, spreading out from the tower's grave.

"Onward!" shouted IAM.

The companions raced through three feet of water to a bank they could not yet see. Jason's legs burst forth, rising above the swamp to stretch his pace. The glacier approached. He knew it was only a few moments before the entire swamp would be encased in solid ice . . . and they with it. He also knew that the cold was not of this world. The freeze was created of magic itself . . . the magic of a Wizard dead. And worse, Jason instinctively knew that the ice was deadly to anyone caught within its embrace.

Jason's right leg was suddenly yanked from below. He whirled about and fell into the water. He twisted violently beneath the waves, attempting to tug his leg free of the grip that held him tightly, but he could not. His head barely broke the surface.

"IAM!" he screamed, gurgling. "Something's got me!"

The scout pivoted about. He drew his blade with his right hand while Teacher still lay draped over his left shoulder. He rushed toward Jason. The creature pulled the boy under. Jason felt a thick tentacle wrap around his chest. It squeezed with all its might. His lungs expelled his only air. He was pulled deeper. The water became colder. The ice drew closer. The icons raced toward him, urging him to use the power within, but all he could see was the black of the water, leaving him no clear target to strike. His leg felt the bottom of the swamp and he kicked upward, breaking the surface.

"Hold still!" the Major shouted. The Major's blade fell down hard, severing the restraining arm about Jason's chest, then plunging through the frigid water to slice through the grip that held him from below. Freed, Jason fell back with a heavy splash. The water exploded violently upward. A huge swamp beast broke the surface, towering above them. Its large head held a dozen vicious eyes. Its many arms reached for its prey. But they were no match for the warrior. Each arm that plunged forward was cut as short as the first. Then, with a short thrust of the blade, IAM pierced the head of the beast, spurting its thick black blood into the swamp. The creature's eyes went dark. It slid off the metal edge and slipped into the water with a heavy splash.

The ice was now just yards from the trio. IAM and Jason turned and bolted. Ice crystals began to form at the swamp's surface, slowing their step. The sound of freezing water was deafening.

"Merge!" Jason screamed, turning about and holding his ground firm. Power instantly drove into the freezing water behind them, melting the ice and turning the liquid to a boil. It bought time. IAM reached a dry mound upon the shore and placed Teacher safely upon it. But the ice began to rise against Jason's force.

"Run!" IAM called, waving him onward.

Jason released his power. He sped forward, still in two feet of water. The fluid about him turned frigid again. Ice crystals formed. Jason had little energy left. He heard the liquid hiss all around him. His legs were as numb as his mind. He staggered and ran and splashed and dashed.

Through the blur, he saw IAM stretch his arms wide open. Jason gathered every ounce of energy left and hurled himself into the air one last time. He seemed to be flying through the mist, suspended in the sultry haze of the swamp. The last thing he remembered was the fall into the Major's welcoming arms, then a plunge to the soft, comforting ground beneath their feet. Jason lost consciousness.

The Great Swamp turned to solid ice. And everything caught within its magical waters was dead.

CHAPTER 16

IT SHOULD HAVE BEEN THEDA!

Stone Forest was a gray, sterile rise of land in the south. It was marked by thousands of granite slabs that jutted out of the sun-bleached ground, some rising twenty feet into the blue Trinitian sky. Travelers who found themselves in the shadow of these magnificent ancient rocks were in awe of their size, reminding them of their own mortality in the presence of eternity, of their weakness in the presence of strength. There was perseverance here, and a feeling that the Races—and perhaps even Trinity itself—were but a fragment of a much bigger order. That feeling could be sensed most at the forest's summit, which was blessed with the city of Endur: home of the Etha.

The night's march to Endur was hard. But neither IAM nor Jason spoke of the pain that tugged constantly at their legs, or of the dizziness that made the level land appear to rise and fall. They weaved about the stone slabs on their approach to Endur. Jason mindlessly followed the scout as he jumped from boulder to boulder with Teacher cradled snugly in his arms. Soon, the stones were so numerous that the dirt disappeared completely.

When they were halfway to the summit, a distant and mournful bell rang out twice. Jason looked upward, seeing for the first time the huge stone fortress of Endur. As he did, a sliver of dull sunlight squeezed above the eastern horizon and stabbed the thirty-foot block walls. He saw two statuesque figures, their robes a forest green, their hair as white as snow. He felt a familiar sense of stability, strength, commitment, and endurance in the Race that stood upon the wall. One figure was old, but her thoughts were filled with a determination that rivaled—and perhaps even surpassed—Teacher's own. The other was considerably younger, her thoughts still embracing the fancies of youth. Both had been waiting for hours—days, in fact—in the event that travelers might arrive in need of assistance. The more he probed, the more he was sure they were waiting for Teacher. And beneath that, almost to their core, they were waiting for him.

Once at the summit, IAM passed quickly through huge iron gates and into a stone courtyard, his steps directed and sure. Jason followed closely. The structures were straight and uniform, he noted, and somehow mirrored the dozens of figures, cloaked in green, that lined the streets. The boy could feel their eyes scrutinizing him. They had come to catch a glimpse of the boy who would either save Trinity or plunge it into darkness forever. Sweaty and haggard, his robe filthy from the long journey, Jason realized that he was probably a disappointing sight. But then, he knew that the Etha were far above evaluating on appearances alone.

A wide marble plaza opened before them. IAM and Jason sped toward a palace built of granite, its turrets rising above the city's walls. They charged up two dozen stone steps and dove over the threshold of the palace, disappearing quickly within. A white stone stairway stood before them, stretching up to a landing where two women stood. Their features were so identical to Teacher's that, for a moment, Jason thought that he looked upon his own tutor. He knew instantly that these were the two he caught sight of earlier.

The Major shot to the top of the landing.

"That's far enough with you!" said the eldest, condescendingly. "You've done enough!" She took Teacher from his arms and disappeared behind a heavily curtained doorway. The younger Etha began to follow her, but stopped long enough to smile briefly at IAM. The Major took a deep breath and relaxed—for the first time since the encounter with the Wizard. Turning about, the scout began a slow descent down the stairs.

"Follow me," he said.

Jason followed the Manwarrior to a chamber at the far end of the entryway. The small room flickered with dozens of candles that lined the walls. It was filled with rows of books like those of Libra. Many large, green, velvet pillows lay scattered about the marble floor. The Major unbuckled his sword and dropped it at his feet. His bow and quiver followed.

"It will be a while," he said. "Let's get some sleep. Sara's in good hands."

Though thoughts of Teacher's peril still consumed them, they fell fast asleep. Even in slumber, Jason's mind was alert on levels that were hitherto unknown to him, levels that kept his heart beating and his mind dreaming. The Pearl stretched around his entire mind now, fulfilling a duty taught by wizardry. Somewhere in his shallow sleep, Jason sensed a small trembling in the cloudy sky far above. It was followed by a surge of energy that punched a hole in the heavens. A small seed dropped quietly to Trinity. It was very near—too near. Jason heard a voice call to him.

"Jason."

He thought he was dreaming. Then he realized that dreams were typically much deeper in his mind.

"Jason," it said again, softly.

"What?" he asked in his slumber.

"Let me in," it purred so gently that Jason wasn't sure he had heard it at all.

The Pearl flashed. Its aura blasted in all directions. The voice was gone. Jason thought a moment about the event and then dismissed it. I'm too tired, he thought. He then drifted deeper within himself to the place of dreams.

Jason was the first to stir, restored in body and mind. The welcomed aroma of hot breakfast and Farlo tea aroused his senses. A pleasant voice was humming a tune that drifted with the food's aroma. As Jason lay there, listening to the compelling voice, IAM stretched his arms upward and twisted them to their limit. His bones cracked.

"How long?" IAM asked.

"Don't know," Jason answered.

The two companions rose to their feet. An Etha glided into the room. She was the younger one who had greeted them earlier. Passing Jason with only a brief nod, she moved to IAM. Jason was entranced by her beauty—so like Teacher, he thought. She raised her arms gracefully to embrace IAM, her green robe following her reach. She hugged the Major's neck for a long moment and buried her face in his chest.

"It's been two years since you came last," she said sadly, her face still buried. "Have you been avoiding me or Grandmamma?"

"I'd never avoid you," the Major responded. He glanced at Jason. "But where are my manners," IAM said. "This is . . . "

"Jason Del," the Etha interrupted. "I know much of you." Her words were plain, but her slight curtsy pierced Jason. He blushed.

"My name," she began, "is IAM Beauty. But call me Bea."

Jason shot a surprised glance at the Major.

"This is our daughter," the Major confirmed proudly.

"Your name is fitting," Jason said. His cheeks grew red. He was suddenly glad to still have a bandage where his left ear had been. He felt disfigured and he did not want her to see it. After all he had been through, he thought, he was oddly vain. It was silly.

"You're too kind," she said as she curtsied low once again, lending her hand to Jason. He lingered on her smooth skin. She had a gentle disposition, and she did not care to hide it.

"How's your mother?" the Major asked.

"Well, but still weak," Bea said, turning. "She ate a small breakfast an hour ago."

"Then this is still the morning of day ten," Jason interjected.

"Day eleven," said Bea, well familiar with his plight. "You slept through day ten. Mother says you must all leave soon."

A chill rushed through Jason. He was that much closer to his destiny—just three more days—and it was not a comforting thought. He would never make it home before the Contest, particularly since the Wizard demanded that they go to Spirit Lake.

Bea spoke softly to her father. "It's been a long time since you and Mother have been together. I hope all is . . . well."

"As well as can be," IAM said with a twinge of guilt. He lifted her chin and stared deeply into his daughter's eyes. "But you know I've always loved her, as I do you."

Bea smiled. "I've prepared a full meal for each of you in the kitchen cove. Please help yourselves." She glanced at her father and added, "Grandmamma says you've never had difficulty with that request."

The Major's eyes flashed, but then he smiled.

"I'll call when Mother is ready to receive you," she said. With that, she bowed to Jason and flowed quickly through the door.

Jason swallowed hard. He had never felt like this before. Bea was so beautiful, so approachable. He found his heart racing with the thought of her. It was an odd thing, he realized, when compared to the Contest that grew near. How could he be so moved when so much else was at stake?

IAM knew his way about the palace quite well, finding first the bathing quarters and then the kitchen cove without one wrong turn.

"Grab two bowls . . . top left," IAM said as he pointed to a far wall that was lined with oak shelves groaning with cooking appliances. The meal was good and they ate heartily.

"Bea is beautiful," Jason said tentatively as he poked at a few remaining bits of food.

"As pretty as the day she was born," IAM declared. "She's Jerel's twin."

"Jerel!" Jason said. "But that would make her about . . . ah . . . "

"Let's just say she's over thirty years old," the Major said before putting a large spoonful of stew into his mouth.

Bea's image dashed from Jason's mind, her youthful demeanor losing ground to her absolute years. He looked back into his bowl.

"How old is Teacher?" Jason suddenly asked.

"Oh," the Major pondered, "I reckon she's nearly double my age."

Jason's eyes opened wide. "And her mother?"

An evil grin reached the warrior's lips. "As old as dirt."

Bea was not old at all, Jason realized. But he put it from his mind. It was a silly notion anyway, he thought, with the doom that approached.

"You don't get along well with Grandmamma," Jason said cautiously.

IAM paused. "There was a time when Mora and I were on good terms. But Jerel's death ended that. Now, she tolerates my periodic visits for Bea's sake."

The room became quiet.

"Come now," IAM said after a time, devouring the last of his meal. "Let me show you the palace."

They strolled down many long corridors and through an equal number of ancient, arched passages. The ages of Trinity floated before them, with artifacts from earlier days preserved and protected from the inexorable march of time: glass blown to delicate crystal, strange mechanisms that moved continuously without a touch, tapestries that revealed the work of artists long ago inspired. The palace was the final refuge of all that was once achieved by the Races. It was almost as sad as the home of the Wallos, Jason thought, almost as sad as Libra. There were so many precious things, now unknown to the Races. They stopped before a dimly lit chamber at the end of a long marble corridor. The room was empty except for a small table in the center. A thick leather binder, opened to thousands of yellowing pieces of parchment, dominated the table.

"Go look," said IAM, nodding toward the book.

Jason entered the room. He touched the ancient book's binding. The chamber was suddenly filled with images that passed like spirits through the night, arising from the book and then swirling, hauntingly, back into it. Only he could see it. Jason felt an ancient, unbroken line of blood rush through his being. Faces and deeds long forgotten by the world were suddenly etched upon his mind. He saw heroic acts. Suddenly, he realized that this book was his own, and of his ancestors. He lifted the book's huge front cover and peeked at the words that were burned into its thick leather.

"The Book of Endur," he read aloud, "an account of the Royal House of Del."

He paged through the fragile ages. Writings about Tempest Slayer were among the first. They quickly yielded to other ages as he turned the pages. He glanced at accounts of ancestors he had never known existed, written by different but steady hands over the countless years. Jason grabbed a bulk of parchment and pulled it over, allowing the book to fall toward the end. His eyes fell upon a recent entry, written in Teacher's own hand.

And in the hall of the Dwarf king Zak, the Chosen One confronted his fear, and in doing so, found a bit more of himself. . . .

He anxiously thumbed forward a few more pages.

. . . And then the Wizard showed him the use of power. . . .

Jason pulled his eyes from the page. He felt like an intruder in his own life. More importantly, he didn't feel he deserved to be in such a book. He hadn't achieved anything yet. How could he represent all that was good when he hadn't been perfectly good himself? Suddenly, a hideous memory began to push its way to the surface. Jason instinctively sent it away. He bolted out of the room.

"I need air," he said to IAM as he blew past him.

In a moment, the companions were upon a balcony that faced the eastern lands. Jason felt a slight, moist breeze rise off the Stone Forest below. It tousled his red hair. He took a deep breath and his calm was restored, his mind rising above the gloom—thanks to the Age of Wisdom.

"I thought I'd find you two here," Bea said with a smile as she approached. She turned to her father. "Mother is asking for you. She's in her . . . I mean . . . your room."

IAM departed. Bea and Jason silently looked toward the east for quite a while. Jason then saw a tall, green tree amidst the bleakness. He wondered how many times Trinity had plunged into danger while the mass of people, living out their lives, knew nothing of how close they had come to extinction. He thought of what he had become in just a few days. He thought of his lost youth. His heart soared one moment and then plummeted the next.

"Why do you smile and frown so?" Bea asked.

Her question pulled Jason back to the balcony.

"My youth is gone," he began, "and my future is in doubt."

Bea's left eyebrow shot upward. "You've just described us all."

Jason nodded. There was much within this Etha.

"Still," he said with a smile, "I'd give a pocketful of Dacas for just one more fight with Ben."

"Ben Wateri?" Bea asked coolly, suddenly so much like Teacher.

"Yes, that's right . . . do you know the name?" Jason inquired. He realized there was something Bea was not telling him. But his thoughts were interrupted by footsteps. Jason turned and saw Teacher in her flowing green robe, escorted by Major T.

"I was worried," he said, embracing his mentor.

Bea interjected, "Jason asked about Ben Wateri, Mother."

Teacher took a breath. "News from Meadowtown reached Endur. Ben is dead. So is David Grimm . . . both at the hands of Bantogs."

Jason gasped.

"Cil's creatures are massing around the town," she continued. "Endur sent supplies several days ago to help the town's defense. No word has been heard since."

A flood of thoughts cascaded down Jason's mind, images of friends and home mingled with anger and fear, determination and hope. And he suddenly felt sorrow for Ben and David. He nodded slowly.

"There was one more piece of news," Teacher began, her eyes shrewdly dazzling. "Perhaps you can discover its meaning better than I. They say that Meadowtown has placed the command of its entire defense into the hands of a mere shoemaker."

Jason smiled. His father was tied to the same events as he, and neither could do anything but follow their course.

The trio packed quickly to leave. IAM and Teacher donned clean leathers and soon arrived in the entryway of the palace. Jason was there to greet them, still dressed in his soiled robe, a rope belt, and a familiar chain. His companions paused when they saw him. His garment was not ideal for their journey back to the west.

"It just feels right," Jason said as he slung his pack over his shoulder. They were ready.

"Not yet!" a stern voice called out. Heads pivoted. Mora came slowly down the stairs followed by Bea. The elder's piercing blue eyes were locked upon Jason. He could feel her strength and pride. And now, with the closing of distance, he could see the evidence of age in her graying skin.

"I will test him," she said forcefully as she reached the floor.

"We haven't the time," Teacher responded coldly. Jason could feel both love and hate pass between the two.

"It is my right," the matriarch continued. "Or have you forgotten that I guided the Royal House for a hundred years before you were even born?"

Teacher took a step back, yielding.

The matriarch turned to Jason. He saw victory in Mora's eyes, having wrested control from her daughter. But it was a false control, he knew, for it relied upon his own yielding, his own willingness to be tested.

"Out of great respect for your family's commitment to mine, you may test what you will," Jason began. "But do so quickly, out of our need for swiftness."

The younger Jason Del would never have said those words to someone so forceful and grand. But this Jason Del would—without the slightest hesitation. He noticed a thin smile reach Teacher's lips. He realized that he had, just perhaps, passed the first test.

Mora stayed rigid. "Who is the creator of all things?" she shot at him.

"Of *all* things?" he began. "Nebus, yet not. Anton, yet not. The Wallos, yet not. Each of us, and yet none of us."

"Explain?" the matriarch insisted.

"That would take longer than we have," he replied. "Ask your next question."

Teacher faintly smiled.

Mora drew closer and extended her frail fingers to the boy's cheek, tilting his head slightly to one side and the other, inspecting something that went much deeper. She withdrew her hand.

"What is the Great Imbalance, and how will it be resolved?" she asked.

There was a great imbalance in Trinity, Jason knew. He felt it first in the Wallo caverns, their bounty rich but depleted. He felt it again in the Desert of Zak, its eastern terrain bitterly scarred by the ancient Beasts of Becus. The question that Mora posed had deeper meaning yet. She was making him aware of the heavy responsibility that would fall to him if he lived.

"West and east," he said. "That which flourishes and that which does not. Should I live, I am the one to resolve it, though no one knows when or where or how."

Mora accepted the answer, nodding. But she was not through.

"Lastly," she said with a deadly expression, "are you truly worthy to represent all that is good? There are some who think *it should have been Theda.*"

"No!" Teacher snapped. "Not yet!"

But it was too late. Jason's mind froze as a flood of conflicting thoughts raced through his consciousness. He was not altogether good. He still hated, still felt anger and a hundred other human emotions. How could he be completely good with all of those conflicts, all of those feelings . . . *and the hideous memory?* The question did what Mora had intended: it burned a hole through Jason's mind. Yet, he suddenly realized that he had to keep moving, passing from one thread of existence to the next. And more importantly, he realized that he could not let anyone know how truly perplexed he was. Not a moment had passed since the question was posed.

"Fate has selected me," he said calmly while his mind continued to whirl. "That is enough for us all to know." His eyes were confident and sure.

Mora began to relax. She was unable to detect his troubled thoughts, but not for long. Jason unconsciously grabbed his rope belt and cinched it tighter. Mora grabbed his hand and inspected it. She then peered into his eyes. Mora's expression turned grave.

"I cannot see it in your eyes," she began. "But there's guilt in your fingertips. We are doomed if you are not resolved."

"I don't know what you are talking about," Jason shot back, yanking his hand from hers.

"I know," said Mora. "That's what troubles me most."

Mora and Teacher shared a glance. Understanding passed between them.

"Go, Jason Del," Mora began. "It seems this is a lesson you must learn on your own. May a thousand ancestors go with you."

A bit shaken but committed not to reveal it, Jason bowed to Mora and then to Bea. He held the younger one's eyes for a moment, placing her image carefully in his mind, framed by the white stone staircase. He slipped out the door, his hands fixing his hood in place.

IAM embraced his daughter and held her tightly. He kissed her cheek and stroked her hair. His eyes spoke long and heavy for his heart. Then he turned and left.

Teacher approached her mother and kissed her. The matriarch stood

rigid, not returning her daughter's embrace. Teacher stepped back slowly, quietly, her eyes seeking a warmth within her mother that would not
come—could not come. As long as Sara could remember, her mother was
as such: serious and committed. It reminded her so much of herself and
what she had become . . . what she had been taught to be. Teacher
embraced Bea but would not allow a smile to reach her lips for fear that
Mora would think her weak. Where there was commitment to the Royal
House and to Anton, there could be no public display of frivolous emotions. She was Teacher, a title that was both a prize and a curse. So there
the three stood, nearly identical but not. And each knew that it wasn't
even age that separated them most; it was the layer of responsibility that
each carried. Teacher turned her gaze toward the objects of her home, the
treasures that she saw all too seldom. She turned and left it all behind.

Long after the companions had fallen beyond the horizon, two figures
still watched from the walls of Endur. Rain fell upon them.

"Your mother has taught him well," said Mora, a rare pride in her
voice.

"You could have told her that," snapped the younger one. Bea turned
and left.

But Mora continued to stand in the wet, facing the fertile west for
hours. She was one of the last of her kind, a near final link in an unbroken, weary chain of obligation. And she was the elder, the model for all
who would follow, which would be few. The responsibility she carried
was great, and what she was about to give to Trinity was greater still,
more than any mother could bear. And only she knew. Only she was supposed to know. It was all right to mourn, the Etha told herself, as long
as no one could perceive it.

"I love you, Sara," the older woman whispered, her lip quivering.

Far to the south, a shadow of a figure moved west to follow a path that
paralleled the one taken by the three travelers. The figure was quick and
cautious and silent as it floated easily about the rugged terrain, perfectly adapted for the world where it now found itself. Yet despite its perfection, it was still learning, insatiably, willingly, cruelly. And no one
who would look upon it could ever imagine the endless darkness within
its core, or the purpose for which it was created. It was a thing not of this
world, a thing created for one desire only: a champion born of Becus, an
embodiment of Pure Evil, an antilife.

It was the black seed of death. And it was following Jason Del, as it had since it descended to Trinity a couple of days before. If it could not get into his mind, it still had the shadows in which to hide and observe. For it needed to know Jason Del better. Such knowledge would make it stronger, more cunning, and more evil—if such a thing were possible. Its efforts had already paid off.

His mind is locked in conflict, it mused, recalling the interchange it witnessed between the elder Etha and Jason. *And the key to unlock the torment . . . to destroy him . . . just perhaps . . . has something to do with Theda.*

CHAPTER 17

A SPIRIT OF HOPE AND TRAGEDY

Near darkness hung above the land as the sun barely penetrated the twilight veil, making the Twilight Festival—and the Contest—closer still. It also made the afternoon of the twelfth day cold as the trio reached the rise of a tall hill. They looked down to see a shimmering blue lake that had healthy trees and abundant brush all around it. And just west of the lake, stretching along the horizon from north to south, was a magnificent line of shimmering green light against the gray twilight. Jason nodded. There was no mistaking the Farlo that hugged the distant Crystal River, or the sound of the water rushing, or the sweet smell of flowers that grew abundantly in the fertile meadows on either side of the river.

Jason was born to the west, and although he had always appreciated its offerings, he knew none other—until now. With the east at his back, every green leaf, every creature that fluttered above, even the moist soil at his feet seemed more vibrant. It takes knowledge of the one, he realized, to truly appreciate the other. It was the same with right and wrong, with good and evil, with young and old. He wished it weren't so, but it was.

As the travelers moved down into the west, a modest rain began to fall. The droplets danced on the surface of Spirit Lake. IAM led them cautiously onward. The scout's guarded approach reminded Jason that the threat of Bantogs was renewed. But the fear that once gripped the younger Jason Del was only a memory. Bantogs seemed insignificant now. Still, he followed IAM and Teacher and kept low to the ground. His mind more often went to the encounter with Mora, her words still ringing.

I cannot see it in your eyes . . . but there's guilt in your fingertips. He wondered what she meant.

Before long, IAM stopped amidst some brush. They were now within a stone's throw of the lake's waters. And for the first time since leaving Endur, they spoke.

"What now?" IAM asked.

"I'm not sure," Teacher replied, wiping droplets of water from her eyelids. She turned to Jason. "Do you feel anything?"

Jason threw his mind in all directions. "Nothing," he said after a while. "I sense nothing."

"Then we wait until providence finds us," Teacher counseled. The others nodded.

An hour passed, and then another as the travelers waited for whatever the Wizard foretold. Impatience began to build as the hours slipped away during a time when hours meant everything. The cold grew deeper. The rain began to pour.

"Sara," began IAM, "time's movin' on. Perhaps we should go around the lake. It could be that somethin's waitin' for us over there."

"If that were so," began Teacher, "the Wizard would have been more explicit, but it wasn't. Whatever will transpire here will be done with powers beyond ours. If something seeks us, it will surely . . . "

Jason's ears exploded with a sudden, dead silence. It filled the length and breadth of the lake. He jerked about and gazed at Teacher. She was frozen, her lips poised to deliver the rest of her sentence. IAM, too, was completely still as he knelt listening to her. Neither of them appeared to breathe. Jason cast his eyes about. He found the entire region as such; the trees were still, as was the breeze, and . . . and . . . even the rain! He blinked his eyes as he gazed upon raindrops that were suspended in the air before him, somehow prevented from taking their natural course downward. He reached out and touched one of the drops. It immediately fell to Trinity while all else remained fixed. He reached to touch Teacher, to shake her from her frozen sleep, but a sound caused him to retract his hand.

"Jason Del!" called a voice, masculine and strong. "Leave her to rest in the moment."

Jason looked up and followed the voice. His eyes darted through openings in the green brush. He suddenly saw a Man sitting near the shore of the lake, his back to him. The Pearl engulfed Jason's mind. The Wizard's Stone came to the forefront. The Agate began to vibrate warmly at his side. Jason reached into the droplets above him. The water globules instantly melted at his touch and slid down his head and shoulders.

He began to move toward the figure and then hesitated, glancing at his friends, fearful about leaving them unprotected.

"They will be fine," said the voice. "Nothing can harm them within the moment."

Jason felt comforted. He also felt a sense of familiarity with this voice, though he did not know why. He moved toward the bank while leaving a fragment of his mind near his friends should something go wrong. Jason cut a path through the rain in the shape of his sturdy physique. He wiped a flood of water from his eyes and then peered through the remaining droplets. The stranger rose sluggishly and turned about, revealing himself.

The nagging feeling of familiarity grew stronger. The Man was middle-aged, having a large build, thick flowing red hair—gray about the temples—and deep green, caring eyes. The grooves on his tired face revealed a lifetime of hardship and sorrow that was somehow matched by what he wore: an ancient and blackened tunic tied off with a leather strap, and tattered woolen trousers with leather leggings. Jason was stunned by the figure's uncanny resemblance to his own father. He sent his mind forth, but it passed through the Man and dissipated over the lake. The figure was not a mind embedded in a physical substance; Jason was sure of that. Yet, somehow, Jason felt a closeness to this Man that went far beyond appearance alone. The apparition then brought his hands up for Jason to view.

Jason winced. The Man's fists were hideously disfigured with scars and sagging flaps of skin. Patches of blackened flesh disappeared beneath his sleeves. Bone was visible here and there, piercing through the fingertips. The red of blood was imprinted in the flesh about the knuckles. The Man opened the palm of his charred right hand and there, at its center, was a normal circle of flesh, pink and healthy. It looked, Jason instantly thought, to be the size of the Wizard's Stone. Jason trembled and fell slowly to one knee.

"Tempest Slayer," Jason breathed.

"Then you know of me," said Matthew Del as he smiled wide. "Good, then come, rise and walk with your great-grandfather. I need to feel the land once more." The spirit walked north along the lake, its figure passing untouched through the rain.

Jason followed the vision, his eyes fixed on the hands blackened by Tempest fire. Even in death, Jason thought, Matthew Del carried the scars of his final, horrible conflict that rid the land forever of the most gruesome Beast of Becus. Some things, he realized, must transcend life itself.

"I've watched your progress and I'm proud," the spirit began as it glanced at Jason.

Jason blushed.

Matthew Del then sat on a boulder at the lake's northern edge. Jason joined him.

"It is I who will answer the question that lies deepest within you," declared the spirit. "Ask it."

"What question?" asked Jason, bewildered.

"It's a question that has forever intrigued you."

Jason thought a bit. "Am I worthy to represent all that is good?" he asked, his mind braced. He then added, "Should it have been Theda?" Jason began to cinch his belt, but then caught himself.

Matthew Del nodded warmly. "Those are interesting questions," the spirit began. "But they are recent ones. *Only you* can answer them. Search instead for the one question that you have pondered since you were a small child, the one that filled you with wonder."

Jason was disappointed. He had hoped to receive an easy answer, hoped to find out if he were truly worthy. But that would have to wait, he knew. He closed his eyes and searched his mind for all things unanswered. There were many questions: identity, the two great evils, what it means to be utterly good, the absolutes of right and wrong. But unlike memories of his younger years that revealed images as they had been in life, unanswered questions took on an entirely different appearance in his mind now. They had form, appearing as undulating, colored droplets. Fearful thoughts were dark and oozed slowly about the reaches of his mind, while good thoughts were bright and oval, dancing about with a will of their own. He descended further. Down beneath it all, there was one question that sat unanswered. It was a question of legends and of Tempest Slayer. Why it rested there he could not say, for it now seemed small compared to all the others. Still, it was there, in a place within his mind that it secured for itself, protected and in wait, floating upon an endless sea of nothing.

"Why did the Wizard's Stone, when in your possession, fade from a brilliant white to a dull gray when it repelled the last Tempest fire?"

Matthew Del smiled. "The answer has its roots near creation itself."

Jason's face brightened. Even though the Age of Wisdom was now fully upon him and the responsibilities that it demanded were great, parts of him remained a boy. He leaned forward as Matthew Del, Tempest Slayer, spoke.

"Ages ago the three last Wizards placed the remains of their power in the Stone for the Royal House to wield against the final Tempest. Then the Wizards went off, two to Anton and one to sleep. However, there's a history that has yet to be told. And it is this: the Wizards, in fact, could have destroyed the last Tempest before they left. Combined, their power was still great enough. But they did not destroy the beast, for Anton had yet another plan in mind . . . a plan that could not be made known to the histories. Our Lord decided that the power of the Wizards should become an integral part of the Races instead."

Jason's eyes flashed.

"The only flame strong enough to transfer the power from the Stone to the Races was Tempest fire."

Jason struggled to keep his raging thoughts in check.

"So my encounter with the last Tempest," Matthew continued, "had two objectives. As always, the first objective was to destroy the beast and end its deadly reign. The second objective, unknown to me or anyone, was to consummate the power. As the heat of the Tempest fire reached its greatest, the magic of the Stone joined with my flesh and became my own, though I never learned of it in life. And in the transference, the color of the Stone passed from white to a lifeless gray . . . for its power was gone. It became part of the Royal House."

The ancient one put his arms about his great-grandson.

"The Wizard's power is in you, and it has always been. And more. Within you now is the Pearl of Anton. The Agate at your side is nothing!"

Jason was motionless. The Wizard's Stone had always been within him, he thought, had always been a part of his flesh. Yet he never knew. And now the Pearl was there also. He searched his memory and recalled the searing white heat in the cavern of the Tempest Spawn as the Pearl's power rose upon touching the Stone, seemingly scorching his flesh before burning itself deep within his soul. That's when the Pearl had etched itself upon him, he knew. The icons had merged within his mind. He suddenly recalled his encounter with the hawk. *More than human,* it sensed from him. And it was right. It was true, he realized. He looked within himself. The powers were a part of him. The old belief—that the Agate held great powers—began to disintegrate in his mind even as he looked upon it. But suddenly, he stopped the process. The falsehood of the Agate reminded him of his youth. So he kept the lie within his mind as a memento. His mind pulled upward, leaving the thought intact. He looked into Tempest Slayer's eyes.

"Then my father has the Wizard's power?"

"Yes . . . but not having the confidence of the Pearl, he can only gain access to the magic when his life is in great danger and his fear explodes. He can't even see the Stone's icon, for it is buried too far within, as was yours before the Pearl. So he knows nothing of it."

"And Teacher?" he asked.

"She believes that the Agate is your source of power. That particular history was not for her to know. In all of Trinity, only you now know the true source of power . . . for you alone can protect your thoughts."

This was logical, Jason realized. The Races needed a champion and not a *Trinket.* They needed someone with great determination and compassion, not one that was as cold and heartless as a Wizard. They needed someone with genuine feeling for the land and the Races. And he, Jason Del, was selected, not to wield the Agate but to carry within himself the best of the Races and of the Wallos and of the Wizards. He was no longer who he was, but at least he now knew what he had become. He was the *Chosen One,* the coming together of all that was Anton. And it was best that he alone held the knowledge . . . the full knowledge.

Jason rose from the boulder. "Is there any other information you can share?"

"The Beast of Cil is strong but flawed. Pure Evil is still a shadow to our eyes, though Anton believes its power must be massive. More importantly, its seed has already dropped upon the land."

Jason flinched, remembering the voice that came to him in Endur. "Is it near?"

"Yes . . . and no. It is frozen within the moment so that it could not hear our words. But you must be vigilant at all times in what you say and what you do. It won't be ready to face you until the coming of the Contest, nor do I think it would care to."

"Is it more powerful than I?" Jason asked.

"It has great power in many ways, but not as much in others."

The spirit rose and rested its hand on Jason's shoulder. "This moment is coming to a close. I bring you one last piece of knowledge. Your father and mother are in great need of you, as are the children of Meadowtown. Even now a fierce battle breaks, and the town will flee south to the Circle of Wisdom, where it may be forced to make a final stand. There's a portal that will take you below to the Granite River. You will find the passage where Spirit Lake almost meets the Crystal River. Good luck, great-grandson. *A thousand ancestors go with you."*

The rain began to fall again.

". . . find us!" Teacher shrieked, finishing her sentence just as Jason vanished before her eyes.

"By the gods!" the Major roared, jumping up and unsheathing his sword with such force that the blade rang out for miles.

They flew to the shore of the lake, their eyes frantically darting about the wet, gray region to find their charge. They spotted Jason at the northern end of Spirit Lake and dashed toward him. Teacher looked deep into his eyes. She knew instantly that Jason had an experience beyond this world.

"We must go now," Jason said, his voice heavy with responsibility. "The children of Meadowtown will soon need us at the Circle." Without waiting for a reply, he dashed west through the rain.

Teacher and IAM glanced at each other and then raced to keep pace. Teacher realized that her teachings were coming to a close. She could feel it. Jason Del was all but complete, and it was now her duty to follow his lead. Major T was a bit more reticent. Their route was far too much in the open.

"Jason!" he called. "Go slower . . . near cover."

"No time!" Jason shouted.

The trio shot through a small clearing in the brush. The ground was soggy and a light rain continued to fall, obscuring their vision. The Major's instincts rebelled against the situation. What was the boy doing? he wondered. This was the perfect place for an ambush. Just then, amidst the smell of the falling rain, the sweet odor of death reached the Major's nostrils. Teacher noted it also.

"Jason!" they called in unison as the smell of Bantogs grew more intense.

But Jason continued his dash across the clearing. The Manwarrior pulled his bow forward, smoothly notching its string with an iron-tipped arrow. But in an instant, six Bantogs bolted out of the shadowy brush. Their twisted smiles and orange eyes gleamed. They loosened their deadly points, two destined toward each target. There was no time to seek cover, no time to drop. In that moment, IAM cursed himself. He had disobeyed all that he knew, all that had kept him alive for so long. He should have forced the boy to listen, he thought. And now, because he did not, all was lost. He had failed his friends just as he had failed Jerel so long ago. But he would not go alone. He let his own point fly. He watched as it whistled past the two that hurtled toward him.

Jason flicked his arm. *Boom!* A flash of light exploded in the clearing. Arrows burst into flames and vanished in a puff of smoke and glowing cinder. The Bantogs howled in fear and confusion and quickly scattered to distance themselves from the white magic. Jason passed through the smoke and ash that he had summoned. It was exactly what Anton would have wanted, he thought. He had ended a battle but kept everyone alive. It was clearly an act of goodness. Maybe he was truly worthy.

Teacher quickly shook off the event and raced behind him, smiling proudly. Jason's glory was as much her own. The Major was still leery. But he realized that Jason was no longer a boy but much, much more. He was more than the Races had ever seen, more than he had ever encountered. Teacher and IAM quickened their pace to follow rather than to lead.

The creatures of Cil regrouped and followed the travelers cautiously, waiting for a new opportunity to strike. They found it. The trio made its way over a small rise and through a circle of Farlo trees that stood where Spirit Lake almost touched the Crystal River. The Bantogs inched their way forward, circling the trees. They fitted their bows with new arrows. Yet, instead of their prey, they found only an odd, crescent-shaped pond that sat against a rise of solid granite. The creatures of Cil drew closer. A glittering blend of silver and red vapors rose from the water even as the rain dropped upon its surface. For a moment, it appeared to the Bantogs as though figures moved beneath the water's dazzling colors. They looked closer, curious, bending down until their faces were inches from the pond. But the strange vision was gone, probably just a reflection of the Farlo above, they reasoned.

The Bantogs called off their search. None among them truly wished to face the magic again. They turned about and began to make their way back through the trees, looking for cover from the rain. But they stopped, startled by a shadow passing among the branches above. They hid in the brush and took aim at the vision.

"Stops and comes outs," said the Bantog leader.

A noise sounded behind them. They pivoted to see a familiar figure, one that calmed their nerves and relaxed their bows. Safe, the Bantogs rose to greet the unexpected friend. Suddenly, a suffocating blackness engulfed them, blinding them, burning them. The Bantogs reached for their throats. Trees and grass withered about them. Birds dropped from nearby branches, fluttered, and went still. The Bantogs fell to the ground, dead.

The shadow rose up. It was so easy, it thought—easy to deceive them, easy to kill them. Then it wondered, Why hadn't the Champion of Anton done the same? Why had Jason Del spared the hearts and minds of these green, loathsome things? Perhaps, thought the creature, this was goodness. The beast's mind sparked with added knowledge. Goodness is a caring, a kindness, a mercy, it mused. It would rather save than destroy. The knowledge said so much. Goodness could be used against itself, it suddenly realized. It could be used to destroy the Champion of Anton utterly. That alone was worth the wait, worth the time it took to follow the boy. So the seed of Becus had a plan, so perfect in its design. Then the shapeless shadow glided over the bodies, over the stillness, over the absence of life, and toward the pond, to fall beneath its waters.

CHAPTER 18

ATTACK IN MEADOWTOWN

Back on day seven . . .

"Jason!" Cyrus yelled in a rush. He frantically searched the shores of a boiling lake. The gray air grew thick about him, reducing his visibility to just a few yards.

"Jason!" he repeated. "I can't see you. . . . Call again! Call again!" This place was familiar, he realized. It existed far to the north. But he did not know why he was suddenly there. All Cyrus knew was that his only remaining son had called to him in need of help.

"Jason!" he shrieked again, desperately running through the sultry mist. Suddenly, the gray parted. He caught sight of his son as he lay feverish upon the lake's shore. He dashed forward. Cyrus's heart pounded wildly with each step, his arms waving aside the mist that dared to obstruct his sight. He saw two familiar figures kneeling near his son.

"Father?!" Jason suddenly called, frantically, his body jerking upward in a soaking sweat. "Father?!"

With fury and hope mixing within, Cyrus bolted onward. But a column of steam suddenly blew strong and blotted out his sight.

"J-a-s-o-n!"

Cyrus thrust himself up violently from where he lay in his bed, perspiring in truth as he had in his dream.

"Cyrus!" Beth cried as she jolted awake. "It's all right," she said soothingly. "It's another dream. You're here . . . at home with me." Beth began to rub his neck and shoulders.

Cyrus took a long breath. "I heard Jason call for help," he said. "He was at a boiling lake. I think I've heard of that place before . . . it's beyond even Mountain High." The Man's eyes then sparked. "Beth," he said as he turned and looked deeply into his wife's sleepy eyes. "Jason is with the Major and Teacher both."

184

"The Major!" Beth blurted.

"Jason's all right," Cyrus said, comforted. He never discounted his dreams. "I know it now. He's with the Major!"

Bang, bang, bang! Someone was pounding on the front door.

"Captain!" shouted a youthful, concerned voice. "This is the sentry from the fifth squad. We heard somebody shout."

"We're fine!" Cyrus called back. "Return to your watch!"

"Yes sir!" came the snap response as footsteps quickly withdrew.

Renewed with hope, Cyrus dressed quickly. He forwent breakfast, despite Beth's urging, and hurried out into the dark, cold beginning of a new morning, his Sword buckled tight. His mind was more relieved than it had been for days. His son, Jason, was still alive.

"Sentry!" called Cyrus.

Dan Granger, an eager sixteen-year-old lad, bolted from his post and stopped before Cyrus. The boy's only weapon, a farming sickle, swung clumsily at his side.

The Captain smiled. "Smartly done," he said. "What have you to report?"

The boy straightened his shoulders. "Fifteen more farmers and their families . . . forty in all . . . entered Meadowtown last night. Most came from the northeast. They brought with them five swords, a sickle apiece, a half-dozen bows, about twenty hunting knives, and some assorted food and livestock."

More defenders of Meadowtown, thought Cyrus. Good. It had been six days since he rescued Squeki Joh from the Bantogs. Five days since he was unanimously installed as militia Captain. Seven days since his son had left with Teacher on a mission to find the Pearl of Anton. And much had happened since. Before the Bantog attack, the population within the town numbered five hundred and two. As Bantog sightings grew more numerous, the population swelled to over seven hundred. Healthy Men, age fifteen or older, numbered two hundred and twenty-seven. Women numbered about the same. Children numbered close to three hundred. And the families kept coming, bringing with them stories of mounting Bantog atrocities.

"Other news?" asked the Captain.

"Yes sir," the boy said. "We distributed all the supplies that came from Endur. Along with the supplies we had, they can support the entire population for two months if need be."

"Then back to your post . . . and good job."

The boy beamed and then bolted back to his position.

With his leg already beginning to ache in the early-morning chill, Cyrus moved staunchly north along the dark road, which days before sparkled with the joyful light of Farlo. But the branches were now removed because the light made the houses easy targets in the night. Within minutes, Cyrus entered the marketplace, sidestepped dozens of refugee tents that now dotted its ground, and made his way toward the town hall. The experienced refugees were beginning their task of acquainting the newest arrivals with the new routine of Meadowtown: the schedules, training, and battle plans. Several people pointed at Cyrus and spoke in whispers as he made his way through, his red hair and solid frame distinctive even in the dark. The Captain returned each glance with a friendly nod. Many of those scattered about had known him for years, or at least they thought they had known him. But he was someone different to them now: a Manwarrior from a distant time, a savior, a comfort.

"Morning, Cy . . . I mean, Captain," said Tome Joh as he stepped forward.

"Still Cy to you, Mayor," the eldest Del said with a grin. "How did the night go?"

"Fine. Just some new arrivals that came near midnight. In fact, they gave your squad formations more practice. The arrivals didn't know we were nearby until we were on top of them."

"Good," said Cyrus. "The squads need the practice."

Twenty-four squads circled the town, at Cyrus's orders. Each was comprised of four Men. Each Man was equipped with a bow, a quiver full of arrows, and a long knife. They were taught that if the enemy entered the squad's territory, the squad leader's job was to assess the situation and decide to fight or retreat. If the decision was to fight, the leader would identify the most accessible Bantog and order all the arrows to fly in its direction until it was silenced, while sending just enough arrows to the other Bantogs to keep them fixed. Then, when they were finished with the first Bantog, they would move to the next, then the next, always using the power of four to overcome one. In this way, one squad could attack as though it were four times its size. This particular formation would take the creatures off guard, Cyrus knew, for the beasts often attacked in many small, dispersed groups rather than in large united forces. He was counting on it.

Each squad was linked with two other squads, forming a triangle with each squad roughly seventy-five yards apart. The point squad faced farthest from Meadowtown, while the other two were on either side and behind it, closer to the town and out of sight. If the point squad encountered Bantogs, its goal was to pin them down, destroying as many as possible, one at a time, while the two squads in the rear moved to the enemy's flank, thereby putting them in a crossfire. This was the same tactic Major T had used thirty years earlier when he moved along the ridges of Mountain High during the Second Race War, capturing many Elf and Dwarf warriors in a moving wave.

Just beyond the squad defense were Farlo branches, laid ten feet wide, that encircled all of Meadowtown. They provided just enough light to reveal any intruders. The remaining Men, over one hundred in all, were used to relieve the squads and provide a barrier defense at each end of town and along rooftops.

Cyrus divided the squads into four regional groups—north, south, east, and west—and then chose men to command each sector. Mayor Tome Joh commanded the northern sector. Farmer Tod Tanner commanded the western sector. Craftsman Don Amunde was given the eastern sector. Council member John Grimm was given the southern sector. Cyrus was leery about his last choice because John's son, David, was killed by Bantogs. He wasn't sure whether he could trust him to ignore the desire for vengeance in the thick of battle. So Cyrus kept a keen eye on his friend. He knew that the loss of a son could not be so easily dismissed.

With each of his sector leaders in place and the squads set, Cyrus put himself in command of the internal defense. This included the rooftop defenders, the barricades at both ends of town, and the sentries posted along the road. For the moment, all was working as planned—better than even Cyrus had expected.

The doors to the town hall swung open and the three other sector leaders emerged to join Cyrus and Tome Joh.

"My squads snared some new arrivals last night," said Don Amunde.

"Let's see how well we fare when the new arrivals shoot back," said Cyrus.

"That will be the test, all right," agreed John Grimm, a cold gleam in his eye.

Tod Tanner nudged the Mayor.

"Oh," Tome said, turning to Cyrus. "There's one thing we would like to discuss."

"Yes?"

"It's about Beth," the Mayor began, his voice reluctant. "Well, we think she's doing a fine job at coordinating all the food preparation and rationing. And the help she's been to Healer Kantor has been great, too, particularly with him getting on in years. Why, even . . . "

"What is it, Tome?" Cyrus interrupted.

"Well . . . there are a lot of people in the town who feel she's gone a little too far by giving some of the women and children training in the bow and arrow. Most people don't think it will come to that and, well, the Men will be doing the fighting anyway. That's, of course, if there's any real fighting to be done."

Cyrus looked at them hard.

"Do you all feel this way?" he asked.

They all nodded.

"How about the women and children who go to Beth's classes—are they forced to go or do they want to go?"

"Well, they want to go. . . . " began Tod Tanner. "But . . ."

"No buts," interrupted Cyrus. "I'll deny no one who wishes to learn self-defense. I've seen what Bantogs can do. You've seen it for yourselves. The training will continue."

Hope faded from his Men's faces, but not another word was spoken. They were not about to argue with the Captain.

His words began to spread, from tent to tent, family to family, wife to wife. By the time Beth finished coordinating breakfast for the town and raced to her first bow class of the morning, her pupils had grown from twelve the day before to almost forty-five. Gasping, Beth stood there for a moment, still wearing her dirty apron, a large bow draped over her tiny shoulder.

"All right," she began. "Who brought some arrows?"

Forty-five hands shot into the air, each holding a crude, iron-tipped shaft.

As the day wore on, Cyrus felt anxious. It was far too quiet at the perimeter of the defense line. During his third training session of the day, a disturbance in the air reached his senses. He halted the Men who were engaged in flanking practice. They froze, seeing their Captain tilt his head one way, then the other. Cyrus broke into a choppy run toward the town hall. Many followed him.

"Watch!" he yelled to the bell tower. "What do you see in the northern sky?"

There was an uncomfortable silence below as the Man in the tower strained his eyes. He looked over the meadow, past the ancient oaks, and into the grayness beneath an expanse of low-flying clouds. A moment passed.

"Nothing!" he finally called back. The crowd below breathed a sigh of relief.

"Look again!" shouted the Captain.

The Man's eyes pierced the horizon once more. Another hard moment passed. "Wait . . . wait . . . there is something far north . . . I can see it through the trees now. . . . "

The crowd grew in the marketplace.

" . . . I see a slight haze . . . a faint glow . . . an orange glow on the northern horizon, I think."

The sector leaders arrived, racing to a stop before Cyrus.

"What do you make of it, Captain?" asked Don Amunde.

"The faint smell of fire is in the air," Cyrus said quietly, his eyes darting. "But it's not just wood that burns . . . I smell roof shakes, axle grease . . . and flesh."

Their jaws dropped.

Cyrus looked at his sector leaders. "Charity is gone."

Blood drained from the Men's faces.

"Alert the squads," said Cyrus, breaking the quiet. "We will be tested soon."

"Captain!" yelled a messenger as he ran into the marketplace.

"What is it?"

"A Man wandered into our northern squad. He's pretty shaken."

"Where is he?"

"Coming now," the messenger said. He pointed north along the road just as the crowd parted to let two militiamen through. A Man hung between them. His clothes were in tatters, burned in many places, soiled in others. The crowd grew thick around them.

"What is your name?" Cyrus asked.

The Man's eyes glazed over. Still held aloft, he sputtered, "In the night . . . burned . . . killed . . . in the night . . . burned . . . killed . . . "

Cyrus motioned to a sentry. "Get me a bucket of water." The recruit scooped up a pail, immediately plunged it into a trough, and ran to Cyrus.

"Pour it here," said Cyrus. The recruit dumped the water over the Man.

"What's your name?" asked Cyrus again.

"Pete . . . Pete Borson," he stammered, shivering.

"What happened?" Cyrus demanded.

"They came a day ago . . . in the early night . . . twenty dozen or so . . . slimy green things with orange eyes . . . a sickening sweet smell." The Man began to weep. "Be-before we knew it, they were on us . . . four here . . . four there . . . and then all around . . . captured most of us right off. Then . . . then . . . " His voice began to crack. "They started the killing . . . the Men . . . the women . . . the children . . . "

The Man shook and rolled into a ball at the Captain's feet. Onlookers gasped. Several townspeople dashed away.

"Then tell me," began Cyrus, shaking the Man, "did Charity have any defenses whatsoever?"

The Man didn't answer.

"Listen!" Cyrus shouted, shaking the Man hard. "Did Charity have any defenses?!"

"None!" the Man cried, sobbing uncontrollably.

Cyrus looked up and saw Healer Kantor. "He's yours."

The Captain patted the Man on the shoulder and then turned to his sector leaders. "Our enemy numbers over two hundred. As hoped, they attack in small groups of four. We have, at best, half a day before they could get here . . . maybe less. And more importantly, they won't expect our defenses." Cyrus looked to the north, his voice becoming sympathetic. "The people of Charity have helped us more than they will ever know."

Cyrus ascended the steps of the town hall. "Hear me!" he said to the crowd. "All women and children are ordered to attend bow practice, starting immediately. All who disobey will not be fed . . . any questions?"

No one so much as whispered.

"Good!" Cyrus said. He turned to his sector leaders. "Step up weapons practice for the militia. Reinforce the outer defenses by adding one Man to each squad, giving us five to the Bantogs' four. Relieve the squads less often. I want it quiet at the defense line. Then, I want you to make the town look normal. Have some children play in the center of town. Put some craftsmen back in the marketplace so it looks like a normal day of business. Push the blockades out of sight. We'll make them think we're as unprotected as Charity. Do you understand?"

The Men nodded.

"Then go," said Cyrus. They scattered.

Within the hour, Meadowtown looked normal to the unknowing eye. The sound of children playing and craftsmen haggling lifted on a light breeze and was carried far beyond the defense line. But to those who knew better, the town, both inside and out, was filled with silent and watchful townspeople, agonizing each minute as the time passed slowly by. As twilight began to turn to darkness, the glow of the Farlo branches that were spread outside the circle of defense grew brighter. It was comforting. But the comfort was short-lived. When the wind turned south, it brought the sweet smell of deadly creatures born to the darker shades. As the night lingered, the smell grew stronger and the town grew tense. Cyrus waited anxiously in the bell tower, scanning the cold, gray horizon outside the circle of flickering light.

"There," said the watch as he pointed to the northeast. "Something moved just beyond the light of the Farlo."

Cyrus jerked his head from the western horizon and followed the watch's line of sight. Suddenly, the sound of a screeching animal froze their blood. It was followed immediately by the distant cry of a northern point-squad leader.

"Third from the left . . . shoot! . . . again! . . . Now the middle, near the fallen tree . . . shoot! Let them fly, damn it . . . flank left . . . I need flank left now! Where's my flank left?!"

Shadows lunged to and fro across the line of Farlo, mingling and parting, jerking back and forth. Cyrus saw a Man fall hard, his body riddled with arrows that were visible even from a distance.

"Where's my flank?!" the squad leader continued to plead. But his words were quickly drowned out by sudden shouts all about the perimeter. Many squads were now engaged, their leaders barking commands, identifying targets, and frantically calling up flank squads to catch the enemy in crossfire. The town mobilized within. Men fortified the road and rooftops and women and children took posts in the weapons line or healer stations. Wooden blockades were pushed back into place. Cyrus paced in the bell tower, helpless as his Men waged battled in the shadows below. Sector leaders' voices started to rise above those of their Men. They shouted orders to a handful of squads at a time, shifting them to areas vacated by others. But shouts for reinforcements were not always answered.

Familiar voices cried out in the darkness. Some were brutally silenced. They were met by the cries of loved ones in the town. Cyrus gripped his Sword tightly, fighting the urge to draw it and run to the aid of his militia. He couldn't leave the internal defenses. A few Men ran frantically back toward the town. Two made it within the barrier, while three others fell to their deaths just feet from safety. Bone-chilling howls rose into the night. Men continued to scream; orders continued to be shouted and obeyed . . . and not. Then, with the exception of the northern sector, where the conflict had begun, all the fronts became silent, and all eyes now turned north.

"Regroup!" shouted Tome Joh in the thick of the battle. The sound of Men running and converging rose above the clamor of battle and death.

"Attack!" he roared. "Squad two, flank to the right! Squad seven, flank to the left! Hit them! Hit them!"

The battle went on for several more agonizing minutes. Silence then fell hard. It was more frightening than the sound of battle, Cyrus knew. It was a silence of ignorance . . . the not knowing if Men were alive or dead, whether they had won this initial engagement or lost. Some women became hysterical, running toward the blockades and screaming the names of husbands and sons. There was no response. Defenders on the rooftops became tense, their bows aiming this way and that to follow the slightest sight or sound from the darkness below.

Suddenly, out of the brush, three messengers, soiled and bloodied, ran forth through openings in the blockades. They pushed their way through the road and dashed to the base of the bell tower just as their Captain, who had seen their approach, hobbled onto the marketplace to greet them. As he met the Men, Cyrus saw the look of first battle in their faces . . . shock and fear igniting in the flow of adrenaline. They were in the fog of war. He knew them instantly to be the messengers from the east, west, and south sectors.

"Status?" Cyrus asked the western messenger.

"They hit us hard," he sputtered. "All of a sudden they were just there, several already beyond the light of the Farlo. . . . "

"Status!" the Captain shouted, but then softened. "Just status, son."

The frightened Man took a deep breath. "We counted sixteen Bantogs in all, Captain. Twelve are dead. Four retreated. Three of our Men were wounded and are on their way in." His voice shuddered. "And, well, we lost four Men . . . friends."

Cyrus placed a hand on his shoulder and turned to the next Man. "And to the south?"

"Lighter . . . we counted only seven, but all we counted are dead, caught by the flanks. We lost two Men. Five are wounded and coming in."

"The east?"

"Counted twenty. Killed ten. We lost three. No wounded."

The northern messenger came running to the tower, panting as he stopped before Cyrus. He carried three arrows in his hand, Bantog made.

"It was ugly," he began, coughing. "We counted sixty in all. We killed thirty but lost twelve of our own, including three point leaders. A dozen wounded." He handed the arrows to Cyrus. "The Mayor asked me to give you these."

The Captain took the arrows and inspected their points carefully.

"No poison," he concluded. "Our wounded may be safe." He turned toward the town hall. "Beth!" he called. His wife rushed outside.

"Yes!"

"Expect about twenty wounded."

"Kantor and I are ready, and we've got plenty of help . . . any poison?"

"Doesn't look like it."

"Good," she responded, and then disappeared through the doors.

Cyrus addressed the messengers. "We killed about sixty and lost twenty-one of our own. We did well for farmers and craftsmen. But there could be close to two hundred still about us if all who attacked Charity are here."

"Mayor Joh wishes your orders," said the northern messenger. "What do I tell him?"

Cyrus paused a moment. "Order the squads in . . . all of them."

"I can't speak for everybody," began the southern messenger, "but John Grimm will want to know why we're being called in when the squads work so well."

"The squads worked because the Bantogs didn't expect them," Cyrus explained. "Now they will compensate with bigger forces in smaller areas until they overrun the defense line. Call them in, now, while the Bantogs are stung and confused. Our troops will be reassigned to the internal defenses."

Cyrus grew pensive. The squads had bought them some valuable time. The next battle, he knew, would be much, much worse.

CHAPTER 19

FLEE OR DIE

Gloom fell over Meadowtown as the people burned their dead. The dark, choking ashes fluttered quietly south. This was not the way that the people desired it. It was customary to bury the dead beneath the gentle green hills and forests that encircled the town. But it could not be. There was no hope of burial with the town under siege.

The Bantogs were badly shaken by their first taste of squad play, Cyrus knew. The beasts remained silent for a whole day, hidden in the thick forest beyond. But no one ever doubted their presence. It took only a slight change of wind to detect the wretched creatures that smelled of sweet but stung of death. Captain Del increased the militia training sessions to six a day. Beth kept the women and children busy in the kitchens, in the town hall, where they cared for the wounded, or in bow practice. Routines were established and repeated.

On the ninth day, just after a weakened sunset glowed dimly upon the forest beyond, Cyrus walked toward the town hall. Along the way he gazed at dozens of his defenders on rooftops. These were not the hardened warriors he commanded years ago in the consuming blizzards of Mountain High. Instead, they were townspeople, known for their trade and not their daring. Yet Cyrus knew that what they lacked in a warrior's abilities, they made up for in their fanatical commitment to protect the families they loved. Their eyes burned with a common fire. They were fighting for their lives, and the Captain knew that such a quest made even the meekest among them a warrior.

Cyrus smiled proudly, and then entered the town hall to check on the wounded.

"How are they, Beth?" Cyrus called.

"Well, we're losing no one here," she said. She looked younger than her years, Cyrus noted. The care she gave others always seemed to do her wonders.

"If only the whole town could sleep here," Cyrus commented to his wife as she approached. "Perhaps you should be in charge of the defenses as well."

Beth smiled. "The sector leaders did come to me with that offer . . . but I turned it down. I have more important things to do."

"Come," began Cyrus, returning her smile, "I'll take you to your bow class."

The air was cold and the sun was only a faint glow to the west as the couple started their walk toward the southern end of town, where Beth's last bow class was scheduled that night.

"We haven't had ten minutes together in two days," she said.

"I know," Cyrus responded, putting a warm arm about her.

"How are you holding up?" Beth asked.

Cyrus smiled warmly. "Fine . . . I'm doing fine . . . and you?"

"All right, I guess," she responded.

But Cyrus knew better. "He's all right," he said.

"Are you sure?" she prodded, looking for comfort.

"The Bantogs wouldn't be giving us so much attention if they had already found him."

Cyrus knew that the more Meadowtown struggled against the Bantogs, the more the beasts would be convinced that the Sword and Stone and boy they sought were in the town. In an important way, Meadowtown was attracting the attention of the creatures of Cil. And that, no doubt, was aiding their son's cause . . . and the destiny of all of Trinity.

"Blessings come in all guises, I suppose," Beth said.

"Captain!" yelled Mayor Joh from the bell tower. "Better come up here!"

Without a word, Cyrus rushed to the bell tower and Beth hurried on to her class.

"What is it?" Cyrus asked, panting as he reached the tower's summit.

"Out there," Tome said, pointing at the Farlo that encircled the town.

The Captain strained his eyes. The Farlo circle was slowly thinning as the Bantogs pulled the branches deeper into the forest.

"Well," began Cyrus, "it was only a matter of time before they figured that out. Have the Men placed the remaining Farlo just outside the town's barrier?"

"Sentry!" called Tome to a militiaman at the bottom of the tower. "Distribute the remaining Farlo as planned."

Before long, the first circle of Farlo light vanished. Yet in its place, much closer to the town's structures, a new light began to glow as the last supply of Farlo was lifted up to the town's thatched roofs and thrown to the ground just outside the perimeter. The beasts gained precious ground in the dark.

"Here we go," Cyrus said to Tome as flickering dots of red suddenly ignited in a circle all about the wooded terrain. To the sound of an animal cry, fire arrows sped like comets high into the sky before arching down in a flaming race toward Meadowtown.

As rooftop defenders scattered to avoid the points, roofs were set ablaze. Fires rose quickly, creating a frightening glow all about the town. Even the oak roof of the town hall was on fire. Bantogs slowly advanced, waiting for the blaze to spread panic and consume the defenders' attention. Cyrus could see the creatures' orange eyes ignite in the darkness as the flames grew larger.

"Release the water bags!" Cyrus suddenly yelled.

Instantly, every other Man on the rooftops of Meadowtown drew a knife from his belt and cut furiously through knotted strings of leather sacks that lined the roofs. Almost as quickly, water rushed down to smother the consuming flames. Just as one water sack emptied, new sacks were handed up from ground crews that extended from the four water troughs that lined the town. Another volley of flaming arrows showered down. Men scattered once again. And so did the water: two sacks . . . ten sacks . . . thirty sacks . . . a hundred. Within minutes, two more volleys of flames rushed out of the darkness as the ground crews began to tire. Their pace slowed. The flames began to rise higher, as did the panic.

Suddenly, the children of Meadowtown were everywhere, rushing from their homes, where they had been ordered to stay. They helped their parents draw and carry water. With the children below, more people were able to take to the rooftops to pour water upon the flames. The fires caused by the latest volley were finally controlled. The flames died. The sector leaders sent the children back into their homes.

Cyrus then saw what he had hoped. The eagerness in the Bantogs' orange eyes was finally doused, along with the flames they created. The wretched beasts, angered and bewildered, turned and stalked back into the thicker brush. The town cheered, but all stayed watchful through the rest of the evening and early into the next morning. It was unusual that the Bantogs were so easily thwarted a second time, thought Cyrus. He was perplexed further as the gray lifted to reveal nearly two hundred Bantogs milling about in full view, without purpose, just beyond an arrow's reach. Then, Cyrus saw a beast more vicious than Bantog. It was a huge creature, cursed with a twisted and disfigured body.

"A Tog," Cyrus breathed. "I thought they were myth." He watched as the hideous beast patrolled the grounds. Bantogs raced from its path to escape an eager whip. And then, as the dimming sun rose higher in the sky, the Captain saw more Togs, six in all, slowly organizing the creatures of Cil. It went on for days as the Togs beat Bantogs into submission. But the Togs did not force the creatures to attack. While that comforted the townspeople, it made Cyrus anxious. The Togs were clearly waiting for something.

Then, on the chilly, overcast afternoon of the twelfth day, as the sun struggled once again to shed only a dismal light, the clouds parted to the north just enough to allow a few scant and desperate rays to reach Trinity. From the bell tower, Cyrus followed the brightened shadows to the northern horizon, his sight skimming the distant reaches. His gaze suddenly froze. His heart raced. He saw an undulating wave of black specks that swarmed south through the brush and under the trees. They came like ants over a hill. The moving shadow consumed more of the northern forest with each passing moment, signaling that some two thousand Bantogs were en route. Cyrus heard a distant animal cry from within the mass of creatures to the north, and before its sound melted from the sky, it was met by the Bantogs about the town as they rose to their feet, howling and peering anxiously north toward the wood, waiting as they had apparently for days . . . for reinforcements!

"Sector leaders!" yelled Cyrus down to the marketplace. "To the tower!"

Within minutes, the sector leaders were in the bell tower, their frightened gaze fixed onto the horde that drew close.

"How do we defend against that?" asked the Mayor, his breath racing.

Cyrus paused for a moment. He had considered this possibility, but he did not actually expect it to come. "We don't defend against it," he answered. "We must evacuate the town."

The Men pulled their eyes toward Cyrus, his words incredible to their ears.

"Their forces will overrun our defenses in one, maybe two pinpoint-ed attacks," Cyrus explained. "Then we're trapped here . . . unless we leave now."

As the Men considered his bold words, the Captain looked up toward a gray sun and a grayer sky. He alone knew that they stood just two days from the Final Contest. They had two days to stay alive before their fate was taken from their hands and placed into Jason's own. Their only hope was to run south as fast as they could, hopefully passing the Circle of Wisdom in a day's time. He was sure that the creatures would not go beyond the Circle's limit with the Contest so close. Cyrus drew a breath.

"Our only chance is to run south and keep ahead of them for two days. That's all we need . . . that's when the *real* battle begins." His words trailed off.

"What do you mean . . . what *real* battle?" asked the Mayor.

For the first time since he had taken command, Cyrus truly feared his next action. His sector leaders, he knew, would think that he was crazy if he told them the truth. Yet if he did not, he could never make them understand how important just two days could be. Without such knowl-edge, they would surely decide to stay within the seemingly protective limits of the town, to fight near the comfort of their homes, and be wretchedly, utterly destroyed. Cyrus put a hand on Tome Joh's shoulder. The Mayor was his only hope.

"The Bantogs are looking for Jason," Cyrus said. An awesome burden left him.

Tome's face dropped at the strange statement. He suddenly realized that he had not seen Jason for a while . . . for a long while . . . for too long of a while.

"Go on," the Mayor said, glancing at the swarm to the north.

"I don't understand it all myself, Tome. But days ago, Teacher took Jason north to uncover an ancient, powerful object. Once they obtain it, they're supposed to bring it back to the Circle of Wisdom to the south. That's where Jason will battle with two great evils . . . one of which, I imagine, controls the Bantogs. The battle begins as the fourteenth day reaches its summit . . . the summit of the Twilight Festival. Whoever wins that Contest will decide the fate of us all."

"This is gibberish," spat Tod Tanner.

"Why Jason?" asked the Mayor, his voice deeply troubled.

Cyrus paused for a moment, knowing that his response would be met with even greater skepticism. But he was too committed to stop.

"Jason carries my . . . his . . . Wizard's Stone," he said as he rubbed his belt where the chain left its eternal groove. "It has powers of its own."

The Mayor's eyes shot to the belt. He knew that chain well, as had nearly everyone in Meadowtown, though he never knew what anchored its links.

"Nonsense!" shouted John Grimm, his face crazed with hate for the Bantogs. "We must defend the town. We'll kill the Bantogs no matter how many of the creatures come against us."

"I vote for a town meeting," said Don Amunde, shaken and confused.

"Me too," agreed Tod Tanner.

Cyrus bit his lip, knowing that indecision was at hand, and with indecision came death.

The Mayor's eyes narrowed as he gazed at Cyrus. "The *Trinkets,*" he gasped. "They've been after the Wizard's Stone all along."

"And my Sword," Cyrus added as he patted the blade at his side. "I don't know why, but Anton needs both. They cannot fall in the hands of the Bantogs."

"More nonsense," objected John Grimm. Tod Tanner and Don Amunde nodded in agreement.

"Enough!" shouted Mayor Tome. He looked hard at the three other sector leaders. "We will evacuate the town."

"But . . . " Grimm began.

"No, my friend," said Mayor Joh. "Staying here will get us killed." Tome shifted his eyes slowly to each of the other sector leaders. They held their tongues. They were not about to challenge both Cyrus and the Mayor.

Joh turned to Cyrus, and the Mayor's eyes grew intense. "It seems I don't really know you at all, Cyrus Del," he said. "But what little I do know of you I trust completely. What are your orders, Captain?"

"Beth!" Cyrus called as he climbed down from the bell tower, the sector leaders in tow.

"Here!" his wife responded, moving quickly to her husband.

"How many are unable to march?" Cyrus whispered.

"There are five still in my care. Only one could march. Why?"

"Prepare them all. We'll carry who we have to."

"We're evacuating?" she asked, surprised.

"Yes. We've got to get everyone out of here . . . and fast."

As Cyrus limped down the road to make plans, Beth looked up. "Please, dear Anton," she prayed, "let my son find us." She wiped the tears from her eyes, pivoted about, and entered the town hall.

"All right!" she called. "Everybody listen up. . . . "

Cyrus's plan was simple but risky. It would rely on a small, token northern assault, followed by a quick departure of the mass of townspeople to the south.

"Captain!" called John Grimm, catching up to Cyrus as he moved to check the preparations. "Let me command the northern deception. I'll make those beasts run back into our trap."

"No," said Cyrus, leery of Grimm's impaired judgment. "I'll do it."

"You can't," Grimm said knowingly. "You're needed here at the defense line . . . and you can't run that fast. The Mayor is needed at the southern retreat. Don Amunde is busy rearranging the two wagon blockades. And Tod Tanner has the rooftop defense. I'm the most logical choice . . . even if you don't like it."

Cyrus stopped and faced John Grimm. He looked helplessly into eyes now filled with wisdom rather than hatred. The logic could not be ignored.

"All right," he said, "but don't take any chances. Just create the deception and then retreat back here. We'll do the rest!"

"Done," John responded calmly, then, turning about, he raced north to the Men who awaited his command.

Even as the first wave of Bantog reinforcements broke through the northern forest and began to intermingle with their own blood, Togs lashed at them. They attempted to create order and push them into battle formations. It was a chore. The new arrivals were tired from the race south. Yet the Togs gained control. Within the hour, they split the Bantogs into two groups. One thousand stayed north, while another thousand began to move just west of the town and south to reinforce the weak forces there.

"You know the plan!" shouted John Grimm on the northern steps of the old schoolhouse. He faced some thirty militiamen, young and old, skilled and not. Each carried a bow and a quiver full of arrows. But there were no swords, or anything else that might weigh them down.

"We move north and attack, then quickly retreat and lead the whole Bantog army right through here . . . any questions?"

No one responded.

"Does anyone wish to stay behind?"

John Grimm searched the eyes of the frightened decoys, giving each one an opportunity to speak up. His gaze suddenly rested on a small, unfamiliar recruit. The little Man's face turned abruptly away.

"You there . . . do you wish to stay behind?"

"No," said a cracking voice, the Man's features hidden behind a raised leather collar.

"Squeki?" asked John Grimm, surprised. "Is that you?"

Shoulders slumped as the boy revealed himself. "But I can help," Squeki insisted. "My leg is fine now. And I can fight as good as anyone. Beth Del showed me how."

"Go!" commanded Cyrus as he approached, having heard the boy's plea. But then the Captain remembered another youth—the Major's own son, Jerel—who sought to fight so long ago . . . and died for his efforts. "You're needed more to the south with your mother and father. Report to Beth once you get there. She'll put you to good use."

His pride shattered, Squeki broke and ran to join the group that awaited orders to push south.

"On the bell's signal," said Cyrus to John Grimm, "you will begin your deceptive attack to the north. The bulk of Meadowtown will begin its move to the south exactly two minutes afterward."

"Pull back the first wagon blockade," ordered Grimm, and it was done.

A messenger rushed to Cyrus. "Captain, Mayor Joh is ready."

Cyrus raised his hand in plain view of the watch in the bell tower farther to the south. The Man gripped the rope that led to the bell, holding his breath. Captain Del looked long and hard into the faces of the Men about him.

"May Anton be with you," he said. He thrust his fist downward. The bell rang out.

"Charge!" shouted John Grimm as he bolted through the opening in the blockade, flying far ahead of the thirty brave Men who chased his lead. They yelled as they went, almost hysterically, while loosening arrows. There was an odd silence as the one thousand creatures of Cil just north of town turned and watched the strange, unexpected sight. The thousand beasts that had just begun their way south also paused. Several of the Bantogs guarding the northern road suddenly clutched their throats and fell as iron-tipped points pierced their gullets. That was all that was needed. Two thousand beasts suddenly woke from their stupor.

Howling, the thousand creatures in the north were the first to rush toward the attack. Togs, suspicious of the human motives, lashed to keep them back. But they could not. Hungry Bantogs sought human blood . . . human meat. The thousand beasts on their way south suddenly raced toward the humans' flank, hoping to be the first to down the Men.

"Retreat!" shouted Grimm only a minute later, seeing that the plan had already begun to work. "Retreat!" His Men turned and raced back to Meadowtown. The sight of retreating humans drove the creatures to madness. The horde rushed on, their footsteps pounding the soil. Arrows flew after the human attackers, piercing two human hearts. Blood spilled. The Bantogs went completely mad, trampling over each other to be the first to taste the flesh of Men. They descended upon those who had fallen and instantly devoured them.

"Run!" Cyrus shouted from the blockade. Two more Men fell dead. The horde descended upon them.

Panting and spent, the remaining Men charged through the blockade.

"To your stations!" shouted Cyrus as they passed. He suddenly realized that John Grimm was not among those who had returned. He jerked his eyes about. He shuddered as he saw his friend still running north, sending arrows into the beasts.

"John!" Cyrus screamed. A moment later the Man was trampled under Bantog feet and devoured. Cyrus strangely knew that the Man had died as he had wished . . . punishing those who killed his son.

The Captain pulled away from the sight and moved into position just as the nearest Bantogs reached Meadowtown's northern blockade. The first two dozen of the creatures cried out as they pitched headlong into ditches fixed with razor-sharp Ethan spears. But the Bantogs behind them still drove mindlessly onward. They pushed forward until the ditch was dark green with the flesh of nearly fifty creatures, providing a bridge for others to traverse. They came by the hundreds, exploding through the first wagon blockade and running madly down the oddly vacant northern road of Meadowtown. As they pushed one hundred yards inward, dazed by the absence of Men, they were abruptly halted by a half-dozen more wagons that were pulled into place by human hands, thus blocking their menacing advance. Two dozen defenders suddenly appeared behind this second wagon blockade, shooting arrows point-blank into the stunned horde. Don Amunde and Cyrus Del led the attack.

The creatures began to cry and fall. But those behind reacted quickly, sending metal tips back into human flesh. Shafts of death suddenly showered down from the rooftops, guided by Tod Tanner's Men. Frenzy consumed the beasts. Many rushed forward. Others rushed sideways, attempting to find cover within the cottages and stores that lined the narrow road. But everything was boarded shut. Nearly two thousand beasts pushed from without, oblivious to what was happening within. Two Togs appeared within the turmoil, shouting orders. They beat the Bantogs into circles of defense in the street, crouching low behind the bodies of their fallen brothers. They let arrows fly.

Human voices began to cry out in agony. Wounded bodies rolled off roofs and onto the growing horde. Tanner kept the volley of arrows raining down. Cyrus and Amunde's men continued to trade arrows with the creatures that pushed toward the second blockade. Seven militiamen were instantly killed about them, slumping over the wagons where they had bravely fought. With the human forces weakening, the Bantogs began to rise to the wagons en masse.

Cyrus drew his Sword for the first time since the conflict began. It flashed in the dull sunlight. Bantog and Tog eyes fell hard upon it. This was one of the *Trinkets* for which they had been sent, the Sword of legends. And with it, they knew, the Wizard's Stone and the boy to wield them could not be far behind. Madness and rage mixed. The Togs pushed the Bantogs forward, convinced that the fulfillment of their quest was soon at hand.

They rushed the second blockade with renewed strength. Cyrus slashed at the creatures that jumped over the wagons. Four Bantogs soon lay dead at his feet, his Sword glistening green in the twilight. But he was losing his rooftop support. The militiamen began fighting hand to hand with Bantogs that had taken to the roofs. And then, a Tog found its own opportunity to strike. It jumped over a wagon and hurled itself through Don Amunde and into Cyrus before arrows or swords could cut it down. Amunde spun about and hit the ground hard. Cyrus and the Tog tumbled back and rolled just feet apart. The Captain tried to rise, but the creature gained its footing first and brought its sword down upon him. Cyrus rolled out of the way of the slicing blow. As the Tog raised its blade once more, towering above, Cyrus pivoted about and swung his own massive Sword. It cut deep through the Tog's abdomen. The beast came crashing to the ground in a bloody, lifeless heap.

Tome Joh came running up the road as the Captain recovered. Dazed, Don Amunde was suddenly there as well, letting arrows fly to protect them all.

"Let's go!" the Mayor shouted above the fury. "The militia is well under way to the south . . . the women and children behind them."

The weight of a renewed Bantog thrust shattered the blockade. Cyrus and the Mayor were thrown to the ground. Don Amunde and four of his Men were crushed under tumbling, wooden frames. Cyrus and the Mayor struggled to clear the dust from their eyes. Dozens of Bantogs rushed toward them. Cyrus brandished his Sword in an attempt to keep the creatures away, but he didn't know where to strike. The Mayor, on his hands and knees, searched for a bow that was now lost to him.

A strong voice suddenly cut the air.

"Ready!" it shouted. "Take aim! Fly!" Fifty arrows raced toward Bantog targets, finding their way deep into the creatures' flesh.

"Fly!" the voice came again as the next wave of creatures dropped to their deaths.

His eyes now partially clear, Cyrus looked up and saw Beth, standing firm in the late-afternoon twilight with twenty-five women archers on either side of her. They were already fitting their bows with fresh arrows. Bantogs began to retreat behind the wagons. Cyrus dashed toward Beth's final line of defense, staying low as arrows streaked through the air above him. Having found his bow, Tome began loosening points from a seated position. But he was unable to gain his feet in the rush, so he stayed within Bantog reach. As he grabbed for another shaft, he found his quiver empty. A Bantog raced toward him with a sword taken from a human dead. Tome froze as the creature raised its blade to strike, its orange eyes triumphant. But its body snapped backward as two arrows embedded themselves in its chest. Hands grabbed Tome and dragged him back to the line of archers.

"You all right?" asked Quen Joh as tears flowed down her cheeks, her son Squeki at her side. Both carried crudely crafted wooden bows.

"I am now!" Tome cried. "Let's get the hell out of here!"

"Retreat!" shouted Cyrus. Beth's line broke and ran south, followed by the few Men who were still near the remains of the blockade, followed by Tod Tanner and fifteen militiamen who dropped from the rooftops. Roughly fifty of their neighbors were dead in the road or beyond.

Bantogs began their pursuit. But two Togs, fearful of more traps, blocked their path. They sliced through the creatures that tried to move beyond them. Slowly, the Bantogs stopped and the frenzy ended. One Tog looked at the two hundred and fifty dead Bantogs piled thick in the streets of Meadowtown. It glanced at the Manmade structures about them.

"Fires," slurred the Tog. "Makes fires of Man-things."

"How did you know we needed the help?" Cyrus asked Beth as they ran past the last cottage south of Meadowtown.

"I didn't," she said. "But when Tome came back to get you, I decided to follow him with some of my class . . . in hopes of hurrying you along."

"How heavy is the fighting along the southern road?"

"There is *no* fighting!"

"*No* fighting! But I counted at least fifty Bantogs still guarding the south."

"I know . . . but they were already dead when we got there."

"Dead? How?"

"Don't know . . . but somebody helped us out."

CHAPTER 20

MEADOWTOWN'S LAST STAND

An orange blaze licked at the northern horizon. It brightened the gray rolling clouds that would have otherwise been invisible in the early night. Although the people of Meadowtown knew that time was of the essence, hundreds stood transfixed, dirty and worn, in a clearing just five miles south of the ominous glow. They watched intently through blood-shot eyes, knowing that the raging fire was fueled by their own homes and possessions: all that they had worked for, all that they had owned. As they gazed mindlessly upon the sight, they glanced periodically at those who stood near and saw the soiled, tearful faces of the ones who had miraculously survived. There was a comfort in those glances, for many were still level-headed enough to realize that it was the people, after all, who embodied the town, not the stone or wood or tar that went into its construction.

The stark silence was interrupted now and again by muffled cries of children, as the people anxiously waited for the last defenders to catch up with the main body. All braced themselves, knowing that many more must have fallen during the risky northern deception that allowed the rest to flee south. The last defenders reached them. Cries spread with the reports of the newly dead.

Cyrus and Beth were the last to break into the clearing. They saw the dazed townspeople gazing toward the glowing northern horizon. Cyrus winced at their pain. The battered, weary group then shifted their eyes down to their leader. One militiaman forced a smile. Others nodded in appreciation. A tearful child managed to wave. They had survived, Cyrus knew, and in so doing, they were still a town, a people unto themselves.

Their clothes reeking of sweat and battle, their limbs tired and spent, their minds swinging from hope to dread and back again, the people followed Cyrus south. The mass was surrounded by militiamen, their bows at the ready and their eyes jumping to every branch that moved unexpectedly. Stretchers carried the wounded, older townspeople leaned upon younger ones, and some children were fortunate enough to be cradled in the arms of their loving parents. Some children were without parents now, but no one was clear-headed enough to give immediate notice.

And so they went. The night became darker and colder and the wind came at them from the south. The greenery about them grew dense. Forest animals scurried from their path. Then, before the caravan of over six hundred moved far into the thickest of the brush, the point squad just before Cyrus darted for cover.

"Captain!" called Tome Joh.

Cyrus quickened his pace and reached Tome just as the Mayor bent over a thicket of greenberry bushes to expose what lay within: the lifeless remains of two Bantogs, their hands still gripping their bows, their placid expressions testimony to the quick fate that befell them.

"Just like the others," the Mayor whispered. "Never knew what hit them. What do you make of it, Cy?"

The Captain searched the bodies. He found a hole where a thin wooden shaft, smooth and deadly, must have penetrated the creatures' black hearts. But no arrow remained, having been carefully withdrawn after its use. Cyrus nodded, his eyes shining.

"Only one Race can kill this cleanly," Cyrus began. "But I never thought I'd see that day again."

"Captain!" called the point-squad leader, terror in his voice.

Cyrus pivoted and followed the cry, crouching low as he approached.

"What is it?" he asked of the point. The squad leader motioned through a sparse grove of oak trees to a mound that stood just seventy yards ahead. Cyrus followed the Man's line of sight. He saw a string of two dozen short, husky silhouettes against the night. The figures stood immobile and erect, like statues against the horizon. Cyrus then heard a faint grunt, followed by the rustling of leaves. Two dozen other silhouettes joined the first, though they were taller and slender in build.

"Who leads you?" called the tallest silhouette, his soft, noble voice carried gently—almost warmly—upon the cold wind.

Cyrus rose to his feet despite warnings from the point squad.

"These families lead themselves," he said as he took a few steps forward, breaking into a small clearing before the mound. "But I am responsible more than most. My name is Cyrus Del."

Silence fell upon the mound. The silhouettes conferred among each other in a strange tongue. Low, angry voices rang out from the shorter figures. They were met with calmer, gentler voices from the taller forms. Tempers flared. The stocky figures waved their fists to punctuate their arguments. But the taller shadows loomed over the smaller ones, their soft voices growing nobler, more reasonable, finally winning out over the gruff. The tallest of the figures took one step toward Cyrus.

"Modesty is a virtue from Anton, Cyrus Del," the soft voice said. "Come closer. My people talk of a Del in histories past. Is yours the name born of legends?"

"Some say so," Cyrus responded as he limped farther on.

The squads became anxious as their leader approached the foreign figures. Arrows filled bows and aim was carefully taken.

"Hold those arrows!" Beth shouted. She joined her husband.

An Elf bowed low to greet them. "I am Prince Alar of the Western Elves. This is Prince Dal of the Northern Dwarves. These are our warriors," he ended, gesturing to the Races behind them. Two dozen Elves bowed gracefully low, their fine leathers flowing with each movement. But the Dwarves stood rigid, holding up their proud heads, unwilling to acknowledge the Elf's introduction. Their battle gear seemed at home with their hostile expressions, and Cyrus knew that the Dwarves would just as soon war with the Races before them than with the Bantogs to the north.

"Why are you here?" Cyrus asked.

"We were ordered to the Circle of Wisdom to aid friends," said Prince Alar. "But when we passed by and saw your dilemma, we began to consider plans to help your cause. Instead, you provided the diversion first . . . a rather nice one. When we saw your larger group head south, we carved the way."

"Who ordered you to the Circle?" asked Cyrus.

"My father," spat Prince Dal, "King Tor of the Northern Dwarves."

This was not a task the Prince of Dwarves cared to take, Cyrus knew, as the years and prejudices still hung thick about the rigid warrior. Yet, he was here nonetheless, with Elves and humans both.

"And this is my wife . . . Beth. . . . " Cyrus began, suddenly realizing that she stood at his side.

"More Dels," the Dwarf prince interrupted. "Your name is not well remembered by my eastern cousins—nor should it be!"

"That's behind us now," interjected Prince Alar. "An ancient enemy is afoot . . . one that we must all attend to. We have our orders."

The Dwarf grunted.

Beth stepped forward, her pulse racing. "What friends are you seeking to aid at the Circle?"

The Elf smiled. "One you well know—Major T. And by the looks of it," he began, pausing as his eyes flickered from Cyrus to Beth, "your son, the Chosen One, whom we met some days ago."

Beth turned to Cyrus, gripping his shoulder. "Then it's true," she whispered, quivering. "Your dream was true . . . Jason is with the Major."

Cyrus met Prince Alar's gaze. "Was our son well when you saw him last?"

"Yes."

"And the Etha?"

"The strange one . . . yes . . . she was there, and also well."

Cyrus looked about, relieved. "How is it that Elf and Dwarf are together in this?"

The Dwarf prince turned angrily away as the prince of Elves spoke. "My hunting party came to your son's aid several days ago in the northern lands. Having broken the Triad during his rescue, I offered my life in return. But the Major absolved us of our transgression among humankind, and so we sought King Tor so as to make our transgressions known to him. When we told him of the Chosen One's search for the Pearl of Anton, it brought cooperation instead of death. That was his right."

Prince Dal turned about, grunting under his breath. "My father is old and foolish, believing in too many legends."

Alar ignored the comment and glanced instead toward the tattered militia, still half-hidden in the brush. "This is a story with many parts," said the prince of Elves. "But for now, we need to move south, as a wave of Bantogs is but an hour behind."

"Militia!" shouted Cyrus, concerned by the renewed threat of Bantogs. "Friends are before us . . . Bantogs are behind. Move out!"

The people of Meadowtown rose from the brush. They moved forward slowly, leery of the strange new arrivals that now took the point and rear positions. Few had ever seen the northern Races. The cautious humans found it difficult to peel their eyes away from their features. The Dwarves responded to the human curiosity with menacing stares. The Elves responded with noble smiles. Then, after a time, human fascination vanished as the townspeople started a mindless, grim march.

Hours passed but the self-absorbed agony continued. Few heard the muffled whimpers of solitary children. One mournful tune spilled from a blonde young girl of roughly seven years. Her clothes were torn and dirty and her head was hung low, hiding once-cheerful blue eyes. She was alone in the world, her parents tragically gone.

"There, there," said a soft voice as a nimble hands pulled her up into protective arms. The child relaxed onto strong shoulders. Prince Alar tenderly stroked the girl's hair as she sobbed. People were touched by the sight of a small human form within the gentle grasp of an Elf. The prince's warriors, one by one, sought the children that belonged to no one, seeing to it that none was on foot as long as each could find a resting place in the arms of Elves.

Many more hours passed and morning had come and gone. The sun was very dim on the thirteenth day when the point squad entered an immense clearing. Thick fog hugged the ground, shifting with the breeze that meandered north. And in the distance through the mist, a solid granite slab rose to form one of the most ancient of structures. It stood as a reminder of another time, its ten-foot slopes forming a perfect circle of stone one hundred paces wide. Light gray pillars, most of which were fallen and broken, dotted the Circle's summit. It had once served as an ancient center of the Races: a trading area, a meeting point, even a fortress. It was the Circle of Wisdom, a place created by the Races when the world was new, a place where a great evil was thwarted ages ago, and a place where a Final Contest would either rip the fabric of Trinity itself, or mend the tattered edges of a world that battled against itself.

Cyrus pushed his way through the growing crowd and looked upon the sight. He felt the Circle tug at him as though it recognized his blood. His Sword suddenly felt heavy, as though tingling with the same knowledge. Cyrus smelled the ageless dust, now mixed with dew.

"Quite a sight," gasped the Mayor as he approached. "Do we stop here?"

"No," said Cyrus, his eyes searching the Circle. He wondered how close his son might be to this very spot. "We continue south for another day. I don't believe that the Bantogs will pursue us that long or that far. This is where they will remain until the battle."

Prince Alar, near the rear guard, suddenly paused and turned, hearing something that remained hidden to all else. His slender Elfin features twitched noticeably. He gently handed his sleeping, parentless child to a passing family. The prince lowered himself to the ground and pressed his ear against the soil. He jumped to his feet.

"Bantogs!" he shouted, his words turning human blood to ice. The townspeople woke from their stupor and jerked about to see Prince Alar waving them onward. "Run!" he shouted again. "Bantogs within moments!"

The militia and townspeople bolted forward in a blind fury to escape death. Children began to scream. Flocks of birds scattered from trees.

"Where to?!" shrieked the point guard.

Cyrus jerked about and desperately scanned the horizon. He knew they had no choice. They could not outrun the hordes behind them. There was only one place they could turn. It would be both a blessing and a curse.

"To the Circle," he cried, "to the Circle!"

A mad dash ensued as the townspeople drove through the remains of the forest and into a clearing some two hundred paces from the slab. To the sound of a shrill whistle, the Elves unloaded their children into hurried human hands and then vanished from sight to a destination unknown. The two dozen Dwarf warriors, however, kept with the townspeople, running beyond them to reach the Circle first. The stocky warriors gazed upward, finding the Circle's pitch to be well over two times their height, angled steeply until the loose ground met the solid stone. Prince Dal looked back at the terror-stricken people stumbling forward. The Dwarf shook his head in disgust.

"Form a ladder!" he grunted. His warriors immediately fell upon the slope, one atop the other, until they formed steps made of flesh and blood.

The humans ran on, hundreds of them, trampling the soggy grass and soil. They ascended the Dwarf ladders. The first turned to help the hundreds who followed. Several people, crying and hurt, fell beneath the swarm and had to be plucked from under the pounding feet. Only the Dwarves, down underneath it all, seemed to bear the burden without faltering.

Cyrus reached the confusion and began to shout orders at the mass of panicked flesh. He succeeded to a point, but there were too many bodies and too few ladders. He ordered the militiamen to form other human ladders to hurry the process along. Just as half of the townspeople reached the top, terrifying animal shrieks of agony shot from the forest behind them. More panic ensued. People clawed and jumped and fought to reach the Circle. Then more voices, twisted in searing pain, rose from the forest beyond to pierce the cold dark air. More panic erupted. In what seemed an eternity, the last of the townspeople were finally hoisted up, as were the Dwarves and militiamen after them. They all lay scattered about the northern rim of stone, exhausted from the fear and the trek. The absent Elves sprang from the forest and sped toward the Circle. In what seemed only a moment, the slender Race gracefully bounced to the slab's summit, landing amidst the weary mass.

"What happened?" Captain Del asked of Prince Alar, the last to arrive.

"The creatures of Cil have been joined by even greater numbers, many huge Togs and Bantogs both. I'd say three thousand now stalk behind us. They were moving to take strategic positions on our flanks. We slowed their progress."

"How?" asked Cyrus.

"We killed twenty-four Togs, but five remain."

"Twenty-four Togs?!" questioned Cyrus in disbelief.

"Twenty-four arrows . . . twenty-four Togs," the prince explained calmly.

Cyrus marveled at the northern Races, still skilled in war, a forgotten trade among Men.

"Casualties?" asked Cyrus, looking about.

"None," Prince Alar answered.

Cyrus smiled. He turned to face the townspeople. Most were still on their knees, panting.

"Women and children to the center of the Circle!" he called. "Hide the children in the crevices where the pillars meet the stone. Militia . . . spread out along the outer edge of the entire Circle. Form two circular blockades with fallen pillars, one within the other some ten yards apart. Tome Joh and Tod Tanner, see to it!"

"Done!" called the Men as they flew.

Cyrus turned to Prince Alar. "I could use your warriors dispersed among my militia at the first blockade."

"My thoughts exactly," said the prince. The Elves shot into position.

Cyrus turned to Dwarf Prince Dal. "And you?"

The Dwarf rubbed his chin with his short, stubby fingers as though a decision much larger than the one requested was at hand. Cyrus could tell that he didn't like humans. He hated the Elves. And this was not his battle.

"My father ordered us to wait here to aid Major T when he arrives with the Chosen One. If it happens that Bantogs desire this spot also . . . then let them try to gain it from us."

Cyrus nodded. He knew that this was a big concession for the Dwarf. Their kind will not fight alongside just anyone.

"Then give your warriors their orders," the Captain said. The Dwarves dispersed around the Circle at the first line of defense, working along side Men and Elves.

Huge pillars, broken and jagged, were quickly lifted and moved to the edge of the entire Circle to provide a first line of defense. Behind that, lines of warriors and then more pillars were formed. The center of the Circle was crisscrossed with blankets that were stretched between broken columns, forming tents that gave the children beneath them greater protection from a shower of arrows. Beth placed her archers in a tight circle just beyond that. It would serve as a final line of hope for the children of Meadowtown.

When all was prepared, the silent, familiar wait began. The hazy forest all about the Circle was deathly quiet. The fog lifted from the ground and the sun, but a gray disk, was now past midday, peeking through low, lazy clouds.

Cyrus knew that the defense was not enough to thwart the evil that surrounded them. The positions were weak, the people too inexperienced, the northern Races too thinly dispersed, the Bantogs too many. He searched his mind for legends, hoping to find a fragment of a story that might unlock a secret of the Circle of Wisdom, allowing him to uncover a magic, a passageway—anything that might help. But the answers wouldn't come. He drew his Sword, gliding his hand along its blade in hopes of finding something written in its Tork.

"Tell me what you know . . . tell me how to use the power," he whispered, his knuckles white as he gripped the hilt.

There was only silence.

"Find anything?" asked Beth as she approached.

Cyrus sheathed his sword. "I'm afraid not," he lamented. "How are the children?"

"They are frightened, but safe for now."

"Beth . . . there's a legend that speaks of a child's soul . . . and whether the soul is strong enough to make the passage to Anton."

Beth shot a nervous glance across the Circle to its center, seeing the children huddled together under what little protection they had from the rain or the arrows.

"You mean if they die they may not go to the land beyond?!"

Cyrus nodded. "It's a legend . . . one of many . . . but if true . . . "

Without another word, Beth raced toward the children to double-check every precaution, every weakness, and every one of her archers who provided the final defense.

A light rain began to fall. Cyrus pulled his collar close, tying it off with leather strings. His leg began to grow stiff in the cold wet, restricting his movement among the debris as he once again rounded the edge of the Circle toward the east.

"Captain Del!" shouted Prince Alar. "They come!"

Bantogs began to step slowly from the forest into the northern clearing, about two hundred yards from the Circle. Men and women peeked above their defense lines to gain a look at the creatures. Jaws dropped as the horde piled in, spreading around the edge of the clearing, oozing into every available space while keeping outside an arrow's distance. For a half-hour the procession continued. Finally, the entire perimeter of the clearing was engulfed by the creatures of Cil, several rows deep, many more than even the Elves had counted. Humans spoke in frightened whispers. Elves counted numbers and discussed positions. Dwarves sharpened their axes against granite.

Then, the crack of whips cut the air. Bantogs feverishly parted, and five huge Togs entered the clearing about the Circle. The biggest Tog among them, entering from the northeast, lashed at the Bantogs to cut a path before it.

"Bukaaa!" it shouted. A Bantog sped from the trees and delivered a bundle to the Tog. The Tog slowly turned, laughing a low, gurgling taunt as it raised its deformed hand to reveal a small, wiggling form within its grasp.

"A trades!" shouted the Tog, amused. "A girls lifes fors *Trinkets* and the Chosen One."

Men and women, Elves and Dwarves bolted up to gain a better view. Within the Tog's squeezing grip was a child. The monster held her by the neck for all to see, her legs and arms dangling helplessly as she cried out in pain. Prince Alar recognized the parentless girl he had befriended. He suddenly realized that, in the rush, she had somehow been left behind by the adults he entrusted with her care. The prince was about to fly beyond the Circle, but Prince Dal tackled him, bringing him hard to the stone.

Cyrus was with them, his hand on the hilt of his Sword. In defiance of the Tog, he unsheathed his blade, stunning all those who had never before laid eyes upon it. Prince Alar, still not on his feet, was among them, recognizing for the first time the Sword of Legends. A hush fell over the land as the Tork edge glistened in the rain. The Tog was pleased.

"Then we trades?!" it asked, waiting.

Prince Alar looked at Cyrus. "There can be no trade," he said, confirming what the Captain already knew. "But," he began again, his Elfin eyes gleaming, "there can be justice!"

The prince rose to his feet. "Give us a moment to decide!" he called.

"I gives yous a humans minute!" the Tog gurgled as he shook the girl soundly by the neck. Over three thousand Bantogs laughed, finding joy in the girl's pain.

Prince Alar bent to one knee behind a pillar and removed all of the arrows from his quiver. He peered intently at each and rolled them between his fingers so as to choose the one most true. He found it.

The Elf looked at Cyrus. "When this hits its mark, it will be the beginning of the end for all of us."

The Captain shot a bewildered glance toward the Tog, the distance making it appear as a speck upon the dark horizon.

"Then let it be," he said, and turned. "Tome, send the word . . . prepare for battle."

As the Races scurried to make their final preparations, testing their nerves more than their weapons or positions, Prince Alar tested the arrow in the bow, drawing back the string to measure its force. He then relaxed its tautness. His eyes scanned both the clearing beyond and the strength of the rain that fell upon it. His eyes measured the distance to the target, compensating for the height of the Circle itself. He pulled back the string once more, aiming it into the darkening sky before pausing, waiting for the ideal moment to present itself. All who stood by the Elf were transfixed, watching his slender, yet strong fingers on the taut cord. They knew that few living could ever match the distance needed, let alone the accuracy and force. Men spoke in whispers. A light breeze rose above the Circle, and the prince relaxed his string, waiting. The wind stopped. He took a breath and held it. He pulled the string back.

Twang. The arrow immediately disappeared in the mist and rain above them. The Tog once again shook the whimpering child high in the air.

"What's yours answers?" shouted the Tog angrily.

"On its way!" the prince of Elves bellowed, freezing the beast with anticipation. Prince Alar counted his own heartbeats.

"One . . . "

Those about the northern ring exchanged glances.

"Two . . . "

The Tog pivoted to the right. Men's eyes widened, but it then pivoted back again.

"Three."

The Tog raised the girl high once more, its mouth opening to speak.

"Wells?" it asked, annoyed.

Prince Alar climbed atop a fallen pillar. "Four . . . five . . . *die!*"

An arrow rocketed downward through the rain. The Tog staggered. Its twitching hand opened wide and dropped the startled child to the ground. Its fingers reached to find the arrow embedded deep between its bloodied eyes. The Races about the northern end of the Circle frantically shifted their eyes from the Elf to the Tog and then back again, knowing that in all their lives they would never again see such a feat as this. Out of reflex rather than thought, the Tog pulled at the shaft. Its huge body plunged violently among the Bantogs, smashing the smaller beasts aside. It screeched, its wrenching voice sending chills through the onlookers. Then, with a tremendous yank, the beast jerked the wooden shaft from its skull. The Tog stood up and was still for a moment. It looked at the arrow. A residue of bloody brain tissue hung limply on the point. Grinning, growling triumphantly, and with ooze pouring from the gaping hole, the Tog waved the arrow high into the air. But its eyes suddenly rolled upward. The beast fell hard to the ground, convulsing and twisting and jerking. Then it was still.

Silence reigned in the clearing. Then a Tog at the western end raised a sword and rushed headlong to the Circle, screaming. And with it, the horde rushed forward in a blind rage, seeking blood. All those upon the Circle stood ready, trembling at the terrible sound. Cyrus climbed atop a fallen pillar and raised his Sword high.

"Militia!" he shouted above the approach of battle, his words echoing. "Hold your arrows. Elves . . . prepare for the first assault. Dwarves . . . prepare for the second."

Men waited in fear. Elves took deadly aim. Dwarves pulled leather slings from their belts and fitted them with stones. In the fearful moment that existed between anticipation and battle, Cyrus turned about, his eyes finding Beth positioned at the Circle's center. They shared a sad smile.

"Prince Alar!" Cyrus then shouted. "Tell me when the distance ensures absolute accuracy of the Elf bow."

"Now!" screamed Prince Alar instantly.

"Elves shoot!" the Captain shouted. Before the last of his words could leave his lips, over twenty Bantogs lay dead. Their falling carcasses tripped the creatures that rushed behind them. With another heartbeat, more fell. The volleys continued for many seconds, but still the Bantogs came, their distance closing to half.

"Dwarves shoot!" Cyrus commanded. Stones born of Dwarf slings rocketed into the mass of green flesh, crushing skulls and throwing lifeless bodies back into their kind. Both Elf and Dwarf were now firing at will. With the closing of distance, the creatures came within reach of human accuracy.

"Militia ready!" shouted the Captain. A moment passed. "Shoot!" he commanded, thus putting the final Race into action. Bantogs fell screeching to their deaths, but those that came behind merely jumped over those that had fallen. The numbers remained overwhelming. One row of Bantogs held back and formed a wide arch about the Circle of Wisdom, covered by their brethren that rush forward. The creatures sent a shower of arrows that fell indiscriminately upon the Races. The shafts kept many of the defenders low and out of battle as the horde approached. For the first time, screams rose from within the Circle as Men were stung with Bantog points. More took cover, reducing the number of arrows that were sent back against the creatures. The Elves and Dwarves rose frequently above their protective barricades to slay the enemy. But their bravery took its toll: six of the northern Race died quickly, brutally punctured with many points.

The first swarm of Bantogs reached the Circle's incline and began to climb. The Races met those that reached the top and sent them back with one swing of an ax or sword. Each death, however, provided better footing for those below. In just moments, the vile creatures were moving over the top with force, pushing the Races back and engaging in battle hand to hand. Metal clashed against metal. The Men at the second barricade continued to fly arrows into the mass of flesh, supporting the first line of defense. But the line before them was already failing against superior numbers.

Prince Alar continued to slash at the Bantogs and dodge their deadly points. Arrows whizzed from directly behind him, shot by Captain Del, who stood at the second defense line. The prince sidestepped a Bantog sword thrust and stumbled upon the rocks, falling to the stone. Cyrus shot his attacker. A Tog, dressed in bloodied mail, suddenly rose over the barricade and was upon the prince, drawing its broad sword. Cyrus fitted another arrow and sought to take aim, but the Elf, gaining his feet amidst the debris, blocked his view. The Captain then caught sight of the Tog's shoulder as it raised its sword. Cyrus freed the bowstring and sent the arrow exploding into the Tog's arm. The huge beast spun about and fell backward over the edge, but not before its sword slashed deep into Alar's chest. The Elf fell hard and the swarm came over him.

"Fall back!" Cyrus ordered, bringing the fractured, disoriented remains of the first line to the second blockade in a rush. Again the clash began. Hundreds of Bantogs were now on the Circle. The shower of arrows from above began to fall into Bantog flesh as well, but it didn't matter as their numbers were so great. The second line began to break almost at once, leaving the defenders dead and trampled in the creatures' wake.

"Shoot!" commanded Beth, directing about two hundred women archers to kill the beasts that already trespassed beyond the second ring. Bantogs fell to their deaths.

With a snap, the second barricade fell completely, allowing the beasts to move quickly within the Circle. One thousand of the beasts had breached the top. The Races that lived formed islands, fending off the Bantogs. Beth's archers began to fall. Bantog arrows pierced the tents that protected the children, but, as yet, they landed harmlessly within. The Circle rang with screams.

Cyrus was still at the eastern end, fighting back to back with Dwarf Prince Dal. The Captain's Sword flashed in the rain, reflecting the terror of those it slew. A Bantog thrust a blunt lance at Prince Dal. The Dwarf dodged it well, but the blow continued onward, hitting Cyrus in the back and bringing him to his knees, dazed. His right arm went numb and the tip of his Sword fell to the rubble. The Captain looked up. A Tog towered over him. Its sword was raised for a final, splitting blow. The rain ceased abruptly as though holding its breath.

Cyrus's eyes widened. There was no way out of the predicament, he knew—no place to go, no weapon to rely on. And in that terror, a fire ignited within him, rising from a power he thought was lost. His body trembled with the force of it. He knew this power, having felt it once long ago upon Mountain High. It was the magic of the Wizards. But how he managed to retain it, he did not know, nor did he care. It must be from the Sword, he reasoned. He welcomed the life it would give him. His blood boiled. The Tog's blade swept downward. Cyrus felt a blast of heat surge up from his chest.

An explosion ripped through the Circle of Wisdom. Every living thing fell to its knees. The Tog before Cyrus flew back and was gone from sight before its sword could fulfill its purpose. Pillars rolled over the edge, crushing Bantogs beneath them. A white light then blasted forth, briefly blinding all those with the gift of sight.

Cyrus lay frozen, exhausted, confused. The force did not come from him! His own power vanished when the explosion began, leaving him spent. As his numb mind whirled, another flash of light cut through the air on the western rim of the Circle, opposite Cyrus. The granite heaved and cracked with the devastating force. All eyes turned to meet the source of the disturbance.

And they found it. It came from a figure, cloaked in white, that stood atop a fallen pillar amidst a sea of Bantogs on the western rim of the Circle. The figure's hand was raised far aloft and was gloved by a brilliant ball of light. A bewildered hush fell over the battle. As silence reigned, words born of legend pierced the air. Only Cyrus knew their meaning—only he was supposed to know!

"Father!" yelled the voice from afar, ringing out with hope and urgency. "The Stone seeks the Sword . . . now!"

CHAPTER 21

FRIENDS DEPARTED

One day earlier . . .

With the Bantog scouting party close behind them at Spirit Lake and time slipping away, Jason raced on with Teacher and IAM in tow. They submerged themselves beneath the warm waters of the crescent-shaped pond that lay amongst the sparkling Farlo trees near the lake. They took a good many steps before they began to rise, gasping for air at the surface and then finding themselves in a small, dimly lit chamber. IAM and Teacher emerged drenched from head to toe. Jason, still cloaked in white, was completely dry. His friends looked upon him, startled, but said nothing. Jason saw it in their eyes. He was beyond them now, beyond nearly anything that had ever existed upon Trinity. And he was still growing.

Jason raced onward. The children of Meadowtown were in danger, he knew. He was responsible for them now. Jason alone was the power, a merging of Wallo and Wizard and the Races. He could not escape what he had become any more than Tempest Slayer could have prevented the Wizard's magic from merging with his own flesh. He was a pawn in a world created long ago, and the best he could achieve was to finish what the gods themselves had started.

He flew down into an abyss of shadowy tunnels and passages, knowing by instinct the way to go. His companions were nearly abandoned in his urgency. They descended a spiral stone staircase, perfectly carved and polished smooth. Warm, dry air rose from the tunnel of granite to meet the travelers. At the base of the stairwell, deep within the mantle of Trinity, they found the Granite River and boats, just as they had in the north. Farlo roots dangled above to within six feet of the river's sparkling surface. Familiar fire spouts were scattered about, glowing red, and touching the molten core of Trinity. Chambers were visible up and down the river's shore, their openings filled with the green treasures of life.

"Here," Jason called as he found a boat that could accommodate them all. IAM was beside him, helping him push the craft into the water. Jason suddenly paused. A wave of power vibrated through his mind from without. He wavered, dizzy, and then discerned its source. It emanated from the tunnel where they had emerged a moment ago. While the force was already gone, he studied the particles it had left behind. It was not so much a force, he realized, as an absence of all force—a black sheet that smothered. He sent his mind back through the tunnel and up to the pond. There was nothing, not a chill, or a breath, or a reflection. And that was most startling of all. Just minutes ago there had been Bantogs, trees, birds, insects, and even things that were far too small to discover with the eye. They were not gone. No, he realized, not gone, but dead . . . everything near the pond was dead.

"What is it?" Teacher asked, her eyes attempting to pierce the shadows behind them.

Jason looked at her, his expression surprisingly calm. "The Champion of Becus."

The Major drew his sword.

"Why so soon?" Teacher whispered. "The Contest is still more than a day away."

Jason wondered also. Perhaps it was learning, Jason suddenly thought—watching and learning about him. "Let's go," he said, redirecting his attention.

They pushed the boat silently—but quickly—into the water and moved slowly north through the ancient Wallo ruins. Chambers along the water's edge were empty, their treasures plundered or destroyed. The river became rough. Huge boulders had fallen from the broken ceiling and created a series of unexpected rapids. But IAM handled the rapids well.

Jason felt the lingering presence of Tempests long past, with their insatiable desire to destroy all that was Wallo. He was repulsed by their defect. His mind suddenly bore memories that he realized were not his, but the Pearl's. He saw it all: friends and creations, a glorious time and a hideous end. He knew that he was seeing through the eyes of the Wallos.

Many hours passed as they glided silently north. The battered canal gradually grew brighter, giving way to virgin beauty once more. And as it did, Jason broke his quiet.

"We're looking for an entrance," he began. "It's not as smooth as the Wallos usually made . . . though not rough like the tunnel to the Tempest Spawn. It's in between, as a Wizard would bore. It leads upward to the Circle of Wisdom."

Another hour passed. A tunnel finally appeared on the western shore, seemingly abandoned. Its entrance was dark, as no Farlo roots grew within it. The frame of the tunnel appeared smooth, not by the gentle and patient rub of a polishing hand, Jason saw, but by the melting heat of an immense force. IAM pulled on the tiller and guided the craft smoothly, effortlessly, toward a narrow bank, coming to a gentle halt upon the fine gravel.

The scout pulled the boat ashore as Jason and Teacher headed toward the tunnel. IAM joined them and used his Kevin Farlo. Its light revealed a steep, narrow stairway carved modestly from the stone. The Major moved past his companions and climbed cautiously up the dark, cool passageway. Teacher followed closely, pressing her hands against the wall to help guide her along the irregular steps. Jason came last. The climb was monotonous. Jason's desire to hear Teacher's voice was suddenly overwhelming.

"Tell me more about the Circle?" he asked.

"All right," she said as she momentarily turned about and smiled.

Jason suspected that she was pleased to still be *Teacher.*

"The history of the Circle is rather simple," she began. "When the Races came to Trinity, several Tempest Beasts still roamed upon the land. They wreaked destruction and battled the Wizards. To protect themselves, the Races built Fortress High to the far north. It served them well for ages. But as the Races multiplied and began to travel widely, they needed a safe haven in the south. So they constructed the Circle of Wisdom with its intricate passageways. In order to keep the beasts away during its construction, the Races lured them into the east, where many battles were fought, and many lost. That's why the eastern lands were the first to become barren. The Circle in the west was finally completed. The Wizards are said to have constructed many parts of the Circle, even parts like this tunnel apparently, that the Races may never have known. Your family distinguished itself very early in the Circle's history, not only in its construction, but also in the laws governing those who traded or lived here. That's one of the reasons why the Wizards chose your family. The Stone and Sword were also forged here in depths much greater than this, greater perhaps than the Granite River.

And as legend goes, the power of the *Trinkets* is greatest here, though no one knows why."

Teacher paused and carefully checked her footing in the receding glow. "In the early days, the surface of the Circle served as a marketplace and as a meeting site. The passageways below served to protect the Races when the Tempests drew near. . . . "

"But they didn't protect them enough," Jason interjected.

"Sadly . . . no," Teacher said. "This is also the place of a horrible incident, when many of your ancestors were devoured at once by the last Tempest."

"Dead end here!" called IAM, lifting his Farlo branch in order to inspect the dark corners of a rugged wall that rose before him. The air was stale.

"Let me see," Teacher said. She squeezed past him and ran her hand along the surface. It was pitted and sharp with no consistent grooves or corners.

"I think you are right," she said. "There's nothing here."

"Look!" said Jason, pointing. But then he realized that neither of them could see what was meant for him alone to detect. It was the mark of a wizard—*Z,* for Zorca—burned into the stone. Jason reached out and touched it. The letter suddenly glowed.

The rock before them began to quake. Rough, jagged contours began to recede and smooth, losing shape. The surface of the rock became transparent. Finally, it disappeared completely, revealing a tunnel. Fresh air brushed their faces. At the top of the long stone corridor, they reached a wide, level platform that separated into two tunnels. Each went in opposite directions. IAM thrust the Farlo into one opening, then the other.

"Any thoughts?" he asked, turning abruptly to Jason.

Jason inspected the openings. He felt a slight tug from the tunnel on his right. A smell, old and faint, swirled gently in his nostrils. He guided his mind cautiously forward. The cave was long and narrow, leading to a score of empty passages and chambers. His mind rounded a bend. He felt a sudden tingling sensation, alive with wonder. He took a step forward. He felt the presence of people, young and old, Men and women. Love and hope poured from them. And then he felt terror. Gasping, Jason suddenly realized that the thoughts had no bodies to contain them. They were without substance, yet they were real—hundreds of minds. They were waiting, patiently, in a mental prison of their own design. Jason backed up, attempting to understand. These were souls, he suddenly realized. Most had died old enough to have made the passage to Anton, he knew, but they did not. They were still here even though the flesh that once contained them had long ago eroded.

"There . . . " Jason choked as he pointed a finger into the dark opening. "My ancestors . . . died there . . . trapped and destroyed by the last Tempest ages ago."

Teacher put her arms around Jason as he continued.

"They were trapped here . . . hundreds of them . . . waiting one at a time to die."

Teacher whispered a familiar tale. "A thousand ancestors go with you. These must be them, though I cannot explain it."

Jason suddenly knew. "The souls of the parents," he cried, "refused to make the journey to Anton, knowing that their children would not survive the passage. So they have stayed here for many centuries, beneath this stone of sorrow . . . but at least they were together."

They were hushed by the incredible sacrifice. Then IAM stepped forward.

"What will become of them?" the scout asked.

"I don't know," Jason said with a sad smile. "Maybe they will be here for as long as there are tomorrows; maybe not."

A strange, fearful anticipation grabbed him. Jason's face turned expressionless and he withdrew from Teacher's embrace. Jason sent his mind up through the other tunnel. A moment passed. He winced. There was another tragedy calling him. It was not of the past, but of the present.

"Nooo!" Jason shrieked. He bolted up the stone steps and into the black. A light burst before his path, illuminating every speck of darkness, though the source of the power was undetectable to his startled companions, who raced to follow, losing ground behind him.

"Jason! Wait!" the Major shouted as he stumbled along the steps with Teacher.

But he did not slow down. He sped up, leaving his friends far behind. An hour later, Jason finally broke to the surface through a trap door. He was upon the western rim of the Circle of Wisdom. It was day thirteen. With the light came the sound of battle. He instantly recognized the people of Meadowtown as they desperately struggled behind two rows of fallen pillars. They battled to keep a menacing green horde from pushing forward. The first line of defense fell before his eyes as Men died. He saw the other Races also: Elves and Dwarves fighting and falling alongside Men. Those that lived scrambled back to the second blockade, just twenty yards from where he stood. This was a battle about to be lost. Jason jumped atop a fallen pillar. He was seemingly impervious to the arrows that whizzed past him. He saw frightened children huddled en masse beneath far too little protection. His eyes were suddenly drawn to thick, flowing red hair at the eastern end of the Circle. His father battled a Tog.

A force welled up within Jason, on the verge of exploding, but he held it at bay. He hadn't the power, he knew, to thwart the overwhelming swarm before him. His fists clenched as he saw his father fall to his knees, the Tog towering above. He could feel his father's own force begin to rise, hurling vibrations in all directions. Cyrus was close to death, Jason realized. But Jason also knew that the force would be uncontrollable, as Cyrus Del had not the will of the Wallo to command it. Many among the Races could die in a blinding flash of force. If only he could tap into his father's strength and wield it for him. The power of two would be enough, he was sure, to turn the tide. But how?

"The Sword," he breathed, " . . . of course!" It was a conduit of power, a metal edge that united father and son ages ago, and one that would serve again. Jason pulled the Agate from beneath his robe, knowing that its very presence would spin the creatures' heads and incite their cravings. As fast as a thought, light exploded from his fist. Everyone fell to their knees. A breath later, he sent another pulse of light flying in all directions, then another, leaving no doubt as to who sent the first. He wanted all the creatures of Cil to know that he was the *Chosen One,* so as to pull their attention toward him and away from the Races, *his Races.*

"Father!" screamed Jason, knowing that the beasts' initial shock was already subsiding. "The Stone seeks the Sword . . . now!" His words rang with hope and urgency.

The Tog towering over Cyrus had fallen from sight. Cyrus staggered to his feet and recovered his blade. He knew his son's words well. They came from the depths of legend, from the eternity of Tempest Slayer . . . the uniting of a Stone and Sword, the uniting of a father and a son. Cyrus raised his Sword high. It flashed in the twilight. The creatures of Cil awoke from their stupor. They flew toward the father and son. Militiamen were trampled. Chaos reigned.

Two figures suddenly appeared at Jason's side.

"Fall back to the Robe!" Major T roared, waving the Races at the western end toward Jason. His commanding voice was overpowering. Those at the western barrier scurried back and formed a wedge around

Jason. Teacher was there, brandishing a blade with a strength that rivaled a warrior's own. They battled the horde, hacking their way through the beasts that came for them. Two other islands formed, one about Cyrus to the east and the other about the children at the center.

Arrows launched at Jason. One pierced the flap in his robe. Suddenly, the air sizzled. A net of power shielded him, dissolving the instruments of death that tried to claim him. Jason sent a beam of light forward, seeking to unite with his father's inner power through the Sword of Tempest Slayer. But the beam dissipated before it reached the blade. Jason lessened his protection net in order to strengthen the power, but once again, it proved not strong enough.

Dwarf Prince Dal slashed his way toward Cyrus and took command of the Races about him. Cyrus felt a fire grow within, wanting to touch that of his son's. But he could do nothing but wait as friends died, struck by the arrows that continued to fall all about.

Jason relinquished his shield completely and willed his full power forth. The Bantogs surged when they saw Jason's protection net fall. The wedge began to fail. Major T rose to the blockade to protect Jason's back while militiamen protected his front, deflecting Bantog weapons. Jason's power blasted forth toward his father's Sword, cutting the twilight and burning the air. It went farther and farther, gaining yards, but it began to fade too soon. Cyrus saw it, too. He could feel the force that yearned to touch the Sword. But it was dissolving just feet ahead of him. He was unable to move toward it, as the fighting was fierce.

"Nooo!" Cyrus shouted. He tipped his blade forward and, with his last ounce of strength, pushed the Sword over the battle to catch the edge of light.

Boom!

Two immense forces merged into one. Thunder roared. The beam of power grew to twice its size. Cyrus shuddered. His head jerked back. His Sword glowed white hot.

Jason was in control of it now—all of it. The beam of light split down the middle and began to bow outward from its midpoint until a ring of light formed around the Circle, father and son anchoring opposite ends above the fury. The Wizardry then began to move downward, flowing from their arms to their waists until they were glowing, living torches.

An arrow sped toward Jason but the Major saw it in time. He lunged into the point to take the blow. The warrior spun about and fell headfirst into a Bantog. Jason's back was unprotected. Teacher rose to the blockade to protect it. She hacked at Bantogs who broke through the wedge.

The ring of light split once more, forming two.

The Bantogs to the west, having spent nearly all their arrows, began to throw swords and stones over the wedge at Jason, hoping to bring him down, to break his concentration. Teacher became bloodied as she protected Jason with her body, deflecting the instruments with her hands.

One ring of light began to move, sweeping outward, detaching itself from the Dels. The inner ring of power detached as well, but moved inward, becoming smaller as it converged on the center of the Circle. As the rings glided forth—one out and one in—they passed harmlessly through the pillars and the startled Races. But the creatures of Cil were not as fortunate. The light cut sharply through the beasts, slicing them in two. The creatures shrieked as they saw the light of death approach. Some tried to slip under the ring, but it lowered to meet them. The same fate was met by those who attempted to scale it. The beasts within the inner ring raced to the center of the Circle to postpone their doom. But they found Beth and her archers, feverishly loosing arrows to bring the Bantogs down. The creatures of Cil were caught between death by Wizardry or by Races. They fought desperately to prevent both, killing many of Beth's archers. Quen Joh fell back, an arrow piercing her shoulder. A Bantog came over the blockade toward her.

"Squeki!" shouted Quen. An arrow shot from the tent behind her and cut through the creature's throat. It coughed, its eyes bulging, then fell back. A moment later, Squeki was there, loosing more arrows to keep beasts from his mother. A sword rocketed over the barrier and grazed the boy, knocking him unconscious. Bantogs rose over the top, just feet from the children and feet behind the ring of death.

Jason saw it also. A heartbeat later, the inner power ring hurtled closed in a gale of force. It obliterated the creatures within it and then was gone. The outer ring of power blew outward beyond the Circle, leaving hundreds of the Bantogs dead and slicing through the remaining Togs. Then it dissipated and was gone. The few Bantogs that remained alive had already scattered into the forest.

Silence reigned.

The Races were unable to stir, their eyes locked on others that still stood above the piles of dead. Blood and flesh were everywhere. But there were no cries. No one could find the energy to utter one. No one could comprehend what had just transpired. There was only shock.

Cyrus was the first to move. He hobbled to the center of the Circle. His mind was on fire with worry. He quickly found what he had sought. Beth was alive, comforting the children of Meadowtown, all of whom had survived. Quen Joh was there also, blood oozing from her own shoulder as she cared for Squeki, the unconscious boy's head already bandaged. A moment later, Tome was there too. Over half of Beth's archers lay dead about them, their bodies intertwined with the creatures of Cil. Half of the militia was destroyed, as were over half of the northern Races. Cyrus and Beth embraced for a long moment, without words. Cyrus then took his wife's hand and both moved quickly west in search of their son. And as they did, others began to meander here and there, looking for signs of life beneath the carnage.

They found Jason on his knees. He was placing two lifeless arms across the chest of an Etha. Beside his former Teacher were the remains of a huge Manwarrior, nearly the last of his kind, barely recognizable through the wounds that he had suffered. Cyrus lowered himself beside Jason. Beth was behind her son, resting her hands on Jason's sagging shoulders. He stretched his head backward to see his mother's face, the memory that he had kept closest to him. He was not disappointed; he loved her so. Beth saw more than she expected. He was not the Jason who left two weeks ago. She couldn't even guess as to what caused the hint of gray to touch his red hair or the wrinkles to fill the corners of his eyes. A bandage that covered the left side of his head suddenly fell in tatters to the ground. Beth's eyes grew moist when she saw that his left ear was sheared off. She knew that her son had been through much. She smiled bravely, and so did Jason.

"He was my Major too," Cyrus said as he gazed wearily upon his friend's remains, then into Jason's moist eyes. "And she my Teacher." Cyrus reached for a small pouch at the Major's side. Opening it, he reached inside and removed a handful of *lupas*. Cyrus sprinkled the burial dust lightly over the couple as Jason looked on, his soul empty. When Cyrus finished, he clasped his hands before him and looked into the dark heavens.

"Anton," the eldest Del began, tearfully, "many husbands and wives seek your kingdom this day. You will recognize them easily. They are led by IAM and Sara, warrior and teacher, husband and wife. Find them all a place at your side. Each is deserving of the kingdom you've birthed, of the eternity you've made."

The battle of Meadowtown was over.

CHAPTER 22

THE FACE OF PURE EVIL

The natural laws that govern the mind of an Elf are the most different among the Races. The fair Race perceives only the extremes, unable to recognize all the shades that truly exist in the world. There is only good and evil, life and death, right and wrong, just and unjust, courage and cowardice. And nothing, to their senses, can live in between.

Jason could sense it all as he delved into the unconscious mind of Prince Alar, who was dying upon the Circle of Wisdom. As he drifted through the abyss in the Elf's minds, Jason realized that the prince would not allow himself to struggle to live. That would imply that he feared the next world, something he could not do. So the Elf waited bravely for the natural outcome of events. But Jason could not let so brave an Elf be free of this world when this world needed him so desperately. While the Elf may be ready to let fate consume his life, he may not be so ready to abandon another.

"She needs you," Jason whispered deep within the Elf's mind. Prince Alar was roused. Something was reaching out to him, he realized. Perhaps it was someone from the battle above. Alar opened his senses just a bit to capture a breath of it, but pain seeped in, causing him to wince. Recovering from the first wave of agony, the Elf realized that his forehead was being stroked by a small and fragile hand, dabbing on cool water, gingerly, nervously, before extending to the rest of his face and neck. The hand was gone, but for only a moment, returning soon with a fresh cloth soaked with water, cold and clean. It could not be an Elf, he thought, for the touch was too nervous. Nor could it be a Dwarf, for it was too comforting. It was a human's, perhaps?

"She needs you," Jason whispered again. Jason could feel a fire ignite within the Elf, burning the shrouds of death that sought to have him. He struggled to regain himself. The pain ripped at him, slicing its way through every sense. Prince Alar now fully knew the damage done to him. His legs stabbed with pain; his head throbbed. There was no sensation in one arm; the other ached. But nothing matched the searing pain within his chest. Every breath burned like fire, and he could now feel the sharp, splitting ribs that pierced his flesh. He could die, he knew, but he would not allow it to happen before he could render what little aid he could to the person above. He fought to rise to the surface.

Sensing his progress, Jason withdrew his mind and let the Elf break through. Prince Alar's eyes quaked, and then opened. Tiny lips kissed his cheeks. Golden locks of hair fell upon his brow. He found his head to be in the lap of a small girl, her long blonde hair wrapped about his face as she bent, kissing him. She cried upon seeing his eyes opened.

"Please don't leave me," she sobbed.

Prince Alar's eyes widened. This was the child he had befriended in the Oak Forest, the one held tight by the Tog. It was a miracle, but the Bantogs, in their lust for the Races' blood, forgot the parentless child that the Tog had dropped to the ground. She was alive.

"I will never leave you," he promised, his words squeezing breathlessly over dry lips. "What is your name?" he choked.

"Glenda," she cried, her face revealing sorrow and gladness both.

"Mine is Alar," said the prince, his voice ringing with nobility even through the pain. "And when the current shadow passes over us, you will be my daughter and will live with me in the Elf Kingdom of Roh as no human has ever before."

She clasped his shoulders and hugged him. The prince of Elves stroked her hair. "Today and for the rest of your life, little one," he coughed, "you have family among Elfkind."

Jason rose to his feet next to the girl. At least he was able to help these souls, he thought. There were so many others he could not. A battered Dwarf prince suddenly approached. He smiled when he saw that Prince Alar was alive.

"I will mend him," said the Dwarf as he reached into his pack for supplies, then added, "I'll mend him as though he were my own blood."

Jason beamed. He knew this was an immense concession for the Dwarf prince. The Races were coming together. He only wished the Major could have seen it. Jason then left to help what few others he could.

After many hours, those that had died were placed side by side, apart from Bantog flesh. The piles were set ablaze. The smoke, black and pungent, rose up to meet the twilight morning of the fourteenth day. The flames left nothing but ash among the ruins. Then, as though the sky wept for those fallen, it began to rain, and the water cleansed the ground of the tragedy, leaving the painful emptiness. As abruptly as the rain began, it ceased.

Wearily, Cyrus Del and Tome Joh began to organize the trek home. They were nearly alone in this, as Tod Tanner had been among the many that were consumed by the warfare. Dwarf Prince Dal proved himself indispensable, putting the northern Races to work building stretchers and splints and crutches. Squeki Joh took charge among the humans. Wherever his father could not be, he was there, carrying tools or food or orders. Beth and Quen spent all of their time with the wounded, giving comfort and aid. Numb, the children of Meadowtown huddled together in the wet clearing amidst some flickering Farlo, waiting for direction— any direction—that might end the nightmare.

Anguish invading his mind, Jason watched the preparations from afar. The sun was a deep-gray disk now, rising above the dark forest and fading higher into the gray sky. Stars shimmered faintly, attesting to the darkness beyond. The oaks above were still wet from the earlier rain, dropping water intermittently upon him when branches swayed in the wind. But Jason hardly noticed. He had killed many, and it weighed heavily upon him. He wondered if he had failed, wondered if there had been a way to win the battle but save the creatures. Was it absolutely necessary, he thought constantly, to have killed the way he did? Perhaps that made him just as evil as they, far less than the good he was supposed to represent. Why did humans have such imperfections?

The loss of IAM and Teacher was greater still. Jason had expected that his instructors would be there always, right to the Final Contest. Even with their ashes gone, he still felt oddly as though they would appear at any moment and order him to keep moving, to keep a grueling pace toward his inevitable fate. But they were dead, and nothing in Trinity could bring them back. And even after the Pearl of Anton merged with his flesh, and even after the apparition came to him at Spirit Lake, he still prayed that there was truly a heaven and an Anton, and that his friends were safely within his care. He hated to have doubt of the next world, but he could no more erase a trace of doubt from his mind than he could erase a trace of hope. They were always there, as they always would be.

The departure preparations complete, Cyrus found his son. Jason followed each painful step his father took. He knew him now to be a warrior. More, he possessed an inner strength he had never known existed.

"Time for Meadowtown to go," Cyrus said as he placed a hand on his son's shoulder. "The rain is gone, few Bantogs about, the people have rested . . . yep, time to go."

Their eyes met. They both knew that Cyrus wished to get the people far away from the Circle before the Final Contest.

"How much more time?" Cyrus asked.

Jason pulled a locket from around his neck and opened it to reveal a great many beads in uniform rows. The second to the last bead was lit, but fading, just as the last bead was beginning to glow faintly. It seemed so bright in the grayness beneath the trees.

"A couple of hours," Jason said. He then gently caressed the locket and felt a lingering trace of Ethan warmth. A long moment passed.

Cyrus put his arms around his son and held him close. Jason tried to cry, tried to release the pain within, but could not, for he was not what he used to be.

"I will stay with you," said Cyrus after a time. "Perhaps my Sword can be of value."

Jason smiled, comforted by his father's words. Those words said, too, that Cyrus still did not know the truth: that the power was not within the objects of legend, but within him. Jason's lips curved to form a word that would begin a long, unbelievable explanation that he had wanted to share with his father. But he paused instead, and fumbled with the chain that led to the lifeless Agate buried within his robe. Jason clutched his father's neck and kissed it. Suddenly, Cyrus wavered. He fell to his knees before Jason could catch him.

"I must still be weary from battle," he said.

Jason's skin tingled. The Pearl flashed in his mind. Vibrations gently stroked the air. Could it be a mind probe? Cyrus recovered. Jason helped him to his feet.

"I'm fine . . . I'm fine," he said.

"What did you feel?" asked Jason.

"Just dizziness . . . that's all."

"Did you remember anything while you were dizzy?"

Cyrus paused. "No . . . nothing . . . why?"

"Just wondering," said Jason. He suddenly wanted his father to stay close.

"I'm glad you will be with me," Jason said. "But in the Final Contest,

I must go it alone. Do not interfere." Though his father's force could double his own, Jason did not want his father involved for fear he would get hurt—and more. He strangely knew that the final battle would be fought on a different level altogether.

"Done," Cyrus said. "Then it's the two of us . . . you to battle . . . me to watch and to pray."

They embraced. Beth Del approached. Her dress was stained with blood, but it could not penetrate her spirit.

"Tell Tome he's in command," Cyrus said. "I'm going to stay with Jason."

"I already told him to expect that," Beth responded. They all smiled and embraced.

"Once you two are done with all this, I'll have dinner waiting," she said as she gave them one more squeeze. Beth turned abruptly and went.

The remains of Meadowtown moved slowly north along the muddy, dense path that they had cut a day before. A few dozen battered militiamen and a dozen Elves and Dwarves led the way. Packs and supplies clanked about. The warriors were fully armed and alert, though nothing would obstruct their path. Tome Joh and Prince Dal walked together, near the lead, conferring as they went. Jason and Cyrus saw Beth from afar, the last to leave, as she paused, raised her hand, and bid them farewell. They did the same, and a moment later she too was gone. In the seconds that followed, the thud of heavy, weary footsteps gradually ceased, opening a new silence in the shadowy but starlit Circle of Wisdom.

In another time, all the land would soon be celebrating the Twilight Festival. But all of Trinity was nearly silent this day. The ill news of Charity and Meadowtown had spread, and families far and wide remained inside. The silence traveled even as far as the northern reaches of the Desert of Zak, to a Dwarf king. He had recently thrown himself into the study of Dwarf legend, contemplating a boy whose courage seemed inexplicable, unless, he realized, the human had been touched by a god. Through his dissolving hate, King Zak wondered if the true Contest was upon the land as ancient stories had foretold. Prophecy, he recently discovered, even spoke of a crazed Dwarf king that would test the Chosen One for some small display of courage. The old Dwarf rose from his castle deep and, for the first time in decades, felt the filtered twilight rays upon his face. He sat upon his desert mountain and peered southwest toward the Circle of Wisdom. From such a distance, the monarch could see dark, ominous clouds begin to form all about the land, each beginning a lazy journey toward the Circle.

"Give him strength," he said.

He was not alone in his vigil. His cousin King Tor also waited far to the northwest, as did King Fali of the Elves, father to Prince Alar. All knew of legends. All studied the signs that had been mounting since festival preparations had begun: the renewed threat of Bantogs, the rumors of an Etha far to the north, the rumbling deep beneath Mountain High, and the quest for a fabled Pearl. But mostly, they listened to stories that had already begun to filter throughout the land about a boy, a descendant of Tempest Slayer some said. This could be the time, they knew, when the world would be reborn or perish. And there was nothing they could do but wait in their forest kingdoms and realms of stone. They knew that such evil is not overthrown by armies or weapons or strategy. Nothing in Trinity could stop the forces that would meet—must meet.

Even a little girl named Jena knew that. She waited in Zol, city of the desert sun. This was the day she knew that would decide her fate. If her champion won, her soul would someday make the journey to be reunited with the souls of her parents. If her champion lost, she would never see them again. Jena had prayed for Jason every night since he had left with his companions, but little did she know that she was in such royal company. As other children huddled with their parents, she stole away to Libra. She was comforted in the decaying structure. She huddled in a corner to protect herself from the dry, biting sand that forever blew through the broken walls. Jena closed her eyes tightly. She allowed her mind to drift with the clouds, moving faster and faster to a circle of stone and to a destiny that no one knew.

Jason felt it all. Thoughts and concerns from great distances were beginning to reach him. Some came from those he knew, some from those he did not. There were still some pockets of people in Trinity who knew nothing of the coming event, and their minds spoke of a glorious Twilight Festival that haunted all others. They were the fortunate ones, he thought. They were allowed to live happily to the end, never knowing of the gruesome fate that could grab them suddenly, snuffing out their lives before their minds could contemplate the end.

Jason looked inward. His senses were razor sharp, more than they had ever been before. His mind was clear, remembering his lessons well. The powers of Wizard and Wallo were there also, with stabbing clarity, ready to be put into whatever service he might demand of them. He was ready.

The wind blew strong, whistling through the oaks, twisting the lesser trees back and forth while hurling leaves and debris about the clearing. Dark clouds were swirling menacingly above, and more seemed to be converging even as Jason watched. And at its zenith, unwilling to be obstructed by the clouds, a gray sun glowed faintly. Jason took a deep breath and then checked his locket, finding the last bead brightly aglow, confirming what he already knew.

The time had come.

As he closed the locket and placed it down the neckline of his robe, a low, gurgling chant began to rise above the wind. Jason and his father rose to their feet. The larger Man fingered the hilt of his Sword. The disturbance came from a spot south of the clearing, hidden from view by the Circle of Wisdom. The chant grew louder, cutting through the swirling wind:

Jewel of Cil, come to mes. Take what's always yours to bes.
Jewel of Cil, come to mes. Take what's always yours to bes.
Jewel of Cil, come to mes. Take what's always yours to bes.

Jason and Cyrus moved carefully from the eastern edge of the clearing to the southern rim of trees to follow the chant, pivoting in and out of the dark, thick foliage. As they arrived at the southernmost point, they saw a circle of some thirty Bantogs, some of the few that had survived, sitting to the south, their spindly hands joined and their heads thrown back in honor of the gray clouds that swirled above them. Their orange eyes shone brightly. The creatures' song continued as the father and son peered from behind a massive oak.

"What do you make of it?" whispered Cyrus, his words just above the chant.

"They are calling their champion," Jason said quietly. "The one selected . . . or created . . . by Cil to fight me."

"Who is Cil?" Cyrus asked, never having heard the name.

Jason smiled at his own knowledge. "Cil and Becus and our Lord Anton are brothers," he began, not taking his eyes away from the Bantogs. "Each has a champion this day. I am Anton's. The Jewel of Cil, their champion, has much evil, but some traces of good. I'm told that my true concern, however, lies with the Champion of Becus, possessing only evil, pure and absolute."

The chant became louder. The ground vibrated as the Bantogs began to scream.

Jewel of Cil, come to mes! Take what's always yours to bes!

Light began to dance among the clouds above. A lightning bolt struck, starkly illuminating the circle of Bantogs. The creatures became hysterical.

Jewel of Cil, come to mes! Take what's always yours to bes!

A long beam of pulsating gray light blasted upon the chanting Bantog circle. The beasts' pupils began to pulsate in unison to the light. The wind became a gale. Cyrus and Jason held tightly to the tree. Lightning hit again, incinerating nearby brush. The air filled with the smell of sulfur. Then a massive explosion ripped downward from the clouds and blasted the ground, throwing dirt and rocks and burning embers in all directions. It torched the ground about the Bantogs. The ominous chant abruptly ended. The land eased its trembling. The wind died. When the dust and ash cleared, a huge and menacing creature stood within the circle of Bantogs.

The beast was nearly twice the size of a Tog. It stared evilly at the nervous Bantogs about it. It was naked, green, and bulky at the midsection, but with slender arms and legs. Its head was misshapen, with eyes that poured dark fluids. An oozing slime bubbled and smoked all about its festering body, smelling of sulfur, while faint flashes of light danced about its bony fingers. It raised its head, screeching.

The Bantogs scrambled to the safety of the forest.

Jason threw his mind outward and touched the beast. Evil filled his mind's reach, but Jason did not falter. He had felt far worse in the lair of the Tempest Spawn. Still, the evil was considerable, greater than that of the Togs, much more than that of the Bantogs. It was a progression of evil, Jason realized. Clearly, Lord Cil had grown more sinister over the eons, taking on more of the traits of Becus than of Anton, just as Teacher had suspected. The youngest god apparently felt that there was greater strength in evil than in good. Yet, still buried deep within the creature was a small but discernable nugget of virtue, wrapped in a dark and vile cavern of the beast's mind. Cil was not all consumed—but close.

The creature began to claw viciously at the air, searching for the mind that it felt touching its own. It gazed ferociously about. Jason snapped his mind back before the beast could discover from where it came. He then pulled his father behind the tree and out of view.

A chilly moment passed.

The beast moved cautiously, sluggishly, toward the Circle of Wisdom. Jason peered at its bulk as it went. Light continued to spark about its fingertips and smoldering sulfur continued to ooze over its festering flesh. The beast stopped when it arrived at the ten-foot slope of the Circle, which was at waist level. It looked about, scanning the trees and brush in all directions. Then, with one agile jump, the beast was upon the Circle itself, surprising the Dels with its inner grace. It stepped through the ruins at the southern rim of the Circle. The sky grew dark.

Jason waited only a couple of moments. Everything seemed right, he thought: the dark sky, the slight breeze, the champion before him, the quiet upon the land, and the calm within his soul. Yes. Everything was as it should be.

"It's time," he said as he brought his hood up to cover his thick red hair.

"What should I do?" Cyrus asked, placing a hand upon his Sword.

"Nothing. As I said . . . do nothing. I've prepared for this. You have not. It would be too dangerous for you to interfere, too dangerous for all of Trinity if you were to interfere."

A lump formed in Cyrus's throat. He knew that he must bow to his son's wishes, but he wondered if he had the strength to obey. He already lost one son.

"Then take care, my son," said Cyrus as he held Jason close. "A thousand ancestors go with you."

Jason knew that more than anyone. He nodded to the eldest Del, their eyes met, and then Jason was gone, leaving his father in the dark, moist green of the forest, the smell of moss and sulfur mingling as one. He made his way to the northeastern rim of the Circle, giving him distance from the beast. Almost instantly, the Champion of Cil saw his approach. Its nostrils flared with a hidden hunger; the flashes of light about its fists began to dart about its whole body, impatiently waiting to be released. Its head pivoted about to catch every detail of Anton's creature. The beast screeched as Jason moved so close to the Circle that he disappeared below its edge. But a moment later Jason was upon the stone, amidst the fallen pillars. The Champion of Cil looked hard upon Jason, its teeth grinding as dark-green, corrosive saliva dripped down its cheeks to the stone, where it sizzled.

Jason held firm. The icon of the Pearl still engulfed his mind, thus protecting it from the probe of another. The icon of the Wizard's Stone was there as well, waiting to be merged with the inner lining of the Pearl at any suggestion of danger. Jason thought about forming the protection net, but he held it back, for the moment of absolute necessity had yet to arrive . . . a lesson remembered. Besides, he thought, there was still one more champion to enter the Circle. Before the thought faded, he felt the approach of something else, a power perhaps, or an entity at least. The swirling clouds above began to separate, causing the white and gray and black to cling to similar colors, thus creating a hypnotic eddy far above. The Circle rumbled. Rock and debris shook beneath the champions' feet. They looked anxiously about. Then, near the western rim of the Circle, equidistant from the two champions, a slab of stone moved to one side, scraping and grinding the granite below it. Jason recognized that portal. It was the one that he had risen from many hours before. The evil had followed him, just as he had suspected, just as he had felt. And now, finally, he would see the face of Becus: the embodiment of Pure Evil.

A figure rose for all to see, draped in buckskin from his toes to his hooded face. Jason's eyes widened with stark recognition. His mind whirled. His pulse pounded. The Pearl injected raw determination. The Champion of Becus raised his two strong arms and threw back his leather shroud. Red hair fell to his shoulders. He smiled, comfortingly.

For all his training, Jason suddenly froze.

"Theda!" he gasped.

CHAPTER 23

THE FINAL CONTEST

Jason threw his mind forward. He was overwhelmed by the goodness that flowed through the figure's mind.

Could this really be Theda? he wondered. It must be a deception! He plunged deeper and deeper, yet he continued to find only peace and harmony. This was not like the Tempest of old, Jason thought. It was not even like the Tempest Spawn. Jason staggered. He couldn't believe what he beheld. It couldn't possibly be true. Appearance, he learned, often bore little resemblance to what lay within. That was his first lesson. But this was different. Even the thoughts within this creature were kind. Jason pulled his probe back.

"Who are you?!" Jason yelled.

"What . . . you don't recognize your own brother?" asked Theda.

"You can't be!"

"Why?"

"Because you died!" Jason screamed. "I was there . . . I know!" Jason grabbed his rope belt and cinched it hard. It took his breath away.

The Champion of Cil screeched. Anxious flashes of light shot from its fingertips.

"No," Theda said to Cil's beast. "That's not the way. I did not come here to fight. I came to make peace."

"I kills you first . . . then we make peace," said the Champion of Cil.

Boom! A flash shot from its fingers and hurtled toward Theda. But with a brush of a hand, Theda deflected it.

Jason's eyes flashed. Theda, or whoever he was, didn't kill. Perhaps he was good. How could it be?

"I have been sent by Lord Becus," Theda began. "He brought me back to life as proof that he has changed his ways. Anton and Cil are his brothers. He understands and appreciates that more than ever. And so he sent a brother to mend old wounds.

"Brothers," Theda began again. "Lord Becus wants you to know that enough blood has been spilt over the eons . . . Wallo, Tempest, Bantog, Races. It was all in vain; all for naught. We must, as inheritors of this precious land, put our differences aside and embrace Trinity in peace. It can be for us all."

The Champion of Cil swayed back and forth, confused and alarmed. Jason could feel its inner turmoil. The evil within it boiled. But the trace of good began to ease its way to the surface, wanting to believe that a truce was possible. The balance of evil within the creature would not have it.

"Garrr!" it shrieked. Out of frustration born of its own turmoil, the Champion of Cil drew upon its full power, raised its sizzling fingers, and sent a burst of gray light toward Theda. Jason flinched at the size of the force. It was far greater than anything he wielded. The Champion of Becus waved its arm once. The force dissipated harmlessly. Jason could not believe that Theda could ward off the blow so easily. The power was twice—no—three times more than Jason had ever wielded himself.

"Brothers," Theda began anew, untouched by the power of Cil. "We should not continue the senseless fighting. Right now Becus, Anton, and Cil are making amends. And they are watching to see if we are capable of doing the same."

His words pulled at Jason's will, diving deep to the place of doubt and hope. The real Theda was every bit as reasonable as this one. Is this really Theda?

The spawn of Cil trembled violently, shrieking in pain, as a morsel of goodness fought to free itself from the evil surrounding it. The fragment pushed to the top of the beast's consciousness, hurtling past the hate and the envy and the ugly side of its nature. The creature began to beat itself about the face, inflicting pain in an attempt to suppress the goodness. But it could not. When the ounce of virtue reached the surface, the Champion of Cil could suppress it no longer. The creature produced a long gurgling sigh of relief. Sweet contemplation spread over its grotesque visage. But it didn't last long.

"Garrr!" it shrieked as the evil within it took control again. Unable to destroy the Champion of Becus, it turned its attention to Jason. Instantly, power exploded from the Champion of Cil.

"Merge!" Jason screamed. His protection net blasted forth. But he never got a chance to use it.

A burst of insatiable black power exploded from Theda's hands. It was a mass of oozing darkness that blotted out all things it passed. The Circle buckled and cracked. The ground trembled. Everything within the power's grasp became nil. Jason could hardly believe his eyes. The shock wave threw Jason to the stone. The black power obliterated the Champion of Cil's blow before it hit Jason. Then with a clap of thunder it blasted the Champion of Cil. The beast splattered in all directions. Its blood fell like rain.

Jason struggled to regain his footing, wiping his eyes clean of the beast's green fluids. Cries rang out from the forest as Bantogs burst into flames and sizzled to an agonizing death. He shivered.

"I didn't want to kill it," said Theda. "But I couldn't let it hurt you. I guess I'm still fighting your battles!"

Jason swooned. He had narrowly escaped death. This was the Theda he remembered, the one who always fought his fights, always protected him.

"Theda?" Jason cried. "Is it really you?!"

Theda smiled. "Yes . . . and I've been given a chance at life by Lord Becus so that he can prove to you and Anton that he is reformed." Theda's smile became sad. "And I'm here to also let you know that *I forgive you!*"

Jason trembled. A memory, long buried, rocketed to the surface of his mind. He could suppress it no longer. Images of Pike's Cliff exploded within. He could see it vividly. He and Theda were gathering berries where the bushes met the edge. The voices rang in his mind's ear.

"Don't let them push you around," Theda said. *"You're better than that. You're a Del."*

"But they'll beat me up again," Jason shot back.

"You have to stand up to them. I love you, but I can't fight all your battles. No one can do it but you. You don't have to be afraid."

"I'm not chicken. It's just always best not to fight."

"Farlo is what Farlo does."

"Don't call me that anymore!"

"Then don't shrivel away in the daylight! Farlo is what Farlo does!"

"Stop that . . . or I'll . . . "

"Farlo is what Farlo does."

"Nooo!" Jason shouted as he pushed his brother. The boys fell and

rolled toward the cliff. Theda began to roll over the edge. He reached and grabbed the end of Jason's belt to anchor himself. Jason was dragged toward the cliff. Instinctively, he pulled his belt, yanking it from the tips of his older brother's fingers. The last memory Jason had was his brother disappearing over the edge.

Face in hands, Jason sobbed now as he did then. The memory exhausted him. It was one he had kept to himself for the past two years. He was emotionally spent.

"I'm sorry!" he cried to Theda. "I didn't mean to kill you!" He then turned his head, seeing his father amidst the trees to the south. Jason's mind sought his. Cyrus was equally moved, but not just by Theda's appearance. He was moved by his younger son's final release, and more. Jason found forgiveness in his father's heart. It had existed for some time. Cyrus Del already knew . . . already knew that Jason had a hand in his brother's death! Jason's tossing and turning at night, the shouts in the midst of nightmares, had not escaped his father's attention, Jason now realized.

Jason suddenly felt a tightening around his waist. He looked down. It was his belt, cinched far too tightly. He was surprised he hadn't noticed it before. He could barely breathe. Jason untied the knot and pulled the belt from around his waist. The release felt good. He suddenly remembered Mora's harsh words. *"There's guilt in your fingertips,"* she had said. Jason gazed at the belt. It was the very one he had pulled from Theda's fingers. It was the one that could have saved his brother's life. Jason unleashed the Agate's chain from around the belt and stuffed it in his pocket alongside the Agate. He then let the belt drop to the Circle, along with the guilt.

He looked at Theda. Perhaps Becus really did want peace. The god gave him his brother back. Theda smiled. Jason softened, yielding. He didn't want to kill. He was good. Theda was good, just as he remembered him. He loved him so. Jason finally knew he could relinquish the responsibilities placed upon him during the past two weeks. It should have been Theda all along. And in a way, it turned out to be. Jason smiled.

"No!" sobbed a voice from afar, shooting a dagger into Jason's mind. *"Don't give in . . . don't give in!"* it cried.

"Jena?" Jason breathed, recognizing the voice instantly. The robe he wore, the one she had made for him, seemed to vibrate with her words.

"Test him first!" she shouted. *"Test him!"*

Jason grew rigid. The children, he thought, think of the children, their souls, and their eternity. Jason's mind exploded with the responsibility that had come with the Age of Wisdom. He took a deep breath. Don't decide too fast, he thought. Don't believe too fast. Don't trust too fast.

"Jason," said Theda, smiling. "Why do you look at me like that? I'm your brother. Didn't I just prove it?"

Jason shot his mind toward Theda and examined his thoughts again. The same wave of goodness flowed over him. This time, he sought memories with his brother. He found them. Theda's mind was filled with recollections of many Del outings. He saw memories of the entire family, of Jason and his father, of his father and mother . . . and . . .

Wait! Jason thought. Something's wrong. He delved deeper. All the memories had one common link. Cyrus Del was in them all . . . *even when Theda was not.* These were not Theda's memories. They were his father's. The beast had used its mind probe to snatch them. But could he be sure?

"Tell me," Jason began, "what is my name . . . the name you called me . . . the name only you knew about?"

Theda frowned, thinking. "You must be mistaken," he said.

Jason felt a tingling around the periphery of his mind. Something was trying to gain gentle access. The Pearl denied it. Jason suddenly realized that if the creature before him was a beast, then he had to give it what it craved most: knowledge of himself; even a way to destroy him. It was a plan worthy of Tempest Slayer. Jason knew exactly which knowledge to give him. It was an old thought . . . a single idea that he no longer believed to be true. It would reinforce a thought that his father still owned. He knew that a beast would take interest in it and, just perhaps, be fooled by it. He would use deception to uncover deception.

Jason intentionally weakened the Pearl's wall in an area far smaller than a pinprick. He shoved the thought slightly through the hole, not wanting it to appear intentional. Instantly, the mind probe devoured it. He closed the Pearl behind it quickly, allowing the rest of his consciousness to remain protected. Satisfied with what it had captured, the mind probe was gone. Jason needed to complete the deception. From beneath his robe he pulled out the gray Agate. He raised it high above his head, holding it tightly within his right fist. The chain that was once tied to his belt dangled beneath it. A great white light burst from the Agate and cut through the air. It pounded into Theda. But it did no damage.

Theda flicked his wrist. A black wall of death swept across the Circle of Wisdom. The rock beneath them jolted. Pillars swayed. An ancient stone column crashed. Jason steadied himself for the blast. He formed a glistening white protection net. The blackness came on, swallowing up Jason's sight. Just as the power was upon him, it squeezed all of its deadly, blistering force into a ball no larger than a fist. It pierced Jason's shield of light, then smashed upon the Agate. It vibrated violently, and then exploded. Jason screamed in pain. His hand was gone. Blackened tissues throbbed and oozed a clear, thick fluid. But there was no blood. His skin was melted closed by the same heat that disfigured it. Shivering, Jason looked up. There was no bright shield to protect him now. Nor did the Pearl continue to cover his mind. He had sent the icons of Wizard and Wallo to a place so deep within himself that they would not be so easily discovered. Jason had done it all at the precise moment that the Agate had been destroyed.

This is not Theda, Jason now knew. His brother would never have taken advantage.

The beast smiled, and Jason knew instantly that his deception was complete. The creature now thought, as Jason had planned, that his power had lain in the Agate, just as the young man's thought had told him, just as he once believed. He thought of how close he had come to casting the thought away some days before. But he didn't. Instead, Jason had kept it to remind him of a time when he had deceived himself into believing the same. And now, the beast believed it also.

The beast's smile turned to ecstasy. Jason sparked with knowledge. This was the face of Pure Evil, he thought. It came as Pure Good, as a brother might: loving, trusting, and completely giving of itself. It had no scars to reflect its motive or true nature. Not even a violation of its soul was present. Jason was sure that the creature truly believed itself to be good. And in this way, it was a horror beyond belief, a demon that could seduce and destroy the most noble. This was what the god Becus had labored eons to achieve. It was evil perfected; a piece of craftsmanship that put even the work of the Wallos to shame.

Jason shuddered, terror gripping his soul. Pure Evil comes not only from without, he suddenly realized, but also from within. He now understood that his own thoughts and feelings can be his undoing every bit as much as those that tried to harm him. He thought of the guilt he carried since Theda's death, and the fear of confrontations he always suffered. Such thoughts lead to destruction. Jason now struggled with the terror before him, and the one inside. But he could not use the Pearl to gain confidence, for it would be detected. He drew upon his own strength, attempting to shatter the fear with great wisdom. Evil cannot be confronted, he told himself, until someone discovers bravery, the kind that Major T harnessed during the encounter with the Wizard. Evil cannot be destroyed, he thought, until someone devises a plan to outwit it. And Jason realized he had both the bravery and the plan. Inch by inch, wisdom smothered the fear. Jason grabbed control of himself as Teacher had taught. It worked. Jason prayed that the creature would not touch his mind and discover the truth: that the power was still his to wield.

If he only had a diversion, he thought. He needed a mere second of time to merge the ancient forces within. Maybe if he surprised the beast, he would have a chance to destroy it. But the creature's attention was immovable, drawn to him alone.

"We could have been brothers," said the Beast of Becus. Jason knew that the creature's awesome powers would soon be unleashed again. He also knew that he could muster no adequate defense against it. But there was hope, for the beast was still so euphoric and content over its destruction of the Agate that it did not bother to use its mind probe to discover the truth. Yet time was fleeting.

I need a diversion, Jason cried to himself. Dear Anton, I need a diversion.

It came, hurled forth in flesh and blood and courage and destiny and heritage and love.

"I carry the Sword of my fathers!" shouted Cyrus Del, standing alone where the Champion of Cil had been destroyed. "Take it if you can!"

The father had broken his promise. But it was not one he could keep. He could not watch his younger son die at the hands of an evil that looked so much like Theda. The minutes he had spent in the forest were like hours, eating at his flesh. Cyrus knew that Theda would never have moved against Jason, as this creature had done. He could bear it no longer.

The creature turned. Its eyes glistened when it saw the Sword of Tempest Slayer. The power of the blade, like the Agate, would be a splendid gift for Becus. Waves of satisfaction rippled across the Circle. A wall of black surged forth eagerly to claim its newest prize. A wall of white, emanating from Cyrus's very being, rose to meet it. The eldest Del was transfixed, unable to control the force that poured from him. He burned and ached with power. The Beast of Becus knew only what it thought it knew; that the power somehow came from the blade. The Sword exploded. Cyrus was thrown back beyond the edge of the Circle and was gone.

In that instant, Jason realized why he was not Purely Good. To be Purely Good meant to be defenseless. That's what happened to the Wallos. The poor creatures could never fight or deceive to gain the advantage. It was not in them to do so. They were *too good* to know how to defend against evil. So evil vanquished them completely. Jason suddenly realized that even if the Wallos had recovered the Pearl from the cave of the Tempest Spawn, they would have eventually fallen to the ancient Beasts of Becus anyway. So Anton, in his infinite wisdom, bequeathed a touch of evil to the Races. They were forever filled with specks of envy, anger, suspicion, and deception . . . especially suspicion and deception. The god gave his Races a touch of evil to allow them to recognize and fight against evils far greater than themselves. Jason had always suppressed such evil, and for good reason. But now he understood its purpose. And there was no better time to put it to use than now.

The icons of the Pearl and the Stone rushed upward from the depths of Jason's mind and merged. Awesome power was released. But there was more. Jason turned every ounce of past fear and anger into an unbreakable determination. A blast of raw energy exploded from his only fist. Only now did Jason realize that this destiny was his, not his brother's. *Jason had more to prove!*

"My name is Farlo!" Jason shouted as the power flew. His real brother used the pet name to teasingly nudge Jason to be more assertive. He understood that now. But the name suddenly had new meaning. He shouted at the top of his voice, *"And I shine in the darkness!"*

White power swept across the Circle. Though it was massive, Jason expected it to dissipate before it hit. But it grew. An immense force, almost forgotten, hurtled up through the stone. It was the strength of a thousand unnamed souls. Jason was stunned. He watched the wispy ghosts rise, their lifelike figures meshing with his power and increasing it tenfold. Another puzzle piece fell into place. A thousand ancestors did go with him. The phrase had meaning . . . prophecy. They were there to help him destroy the Beast of Becus. All things focused into one unbreakable purpose: the Wallos, the Wizards, the Races, his ancestors, himself. Power surged. White thunder crashed.

The beast turned, still euphoric over its destruction of the Sword. It felt Jason's force instantly. It countered with its own massive blackness, evil and pure, undulating as it came. A rupturing light flashed. A tremendous explosion split the Circle of Wisdom. Ancient and opposing forces collided. The universe trembled. The stars flickered above, there one moment and gone the next. Jason felt his heart skip every other beat. He was alive and then not. A decision was at hand, he knew, and every living thing felt its touch. Blackness roared against white, evil against good, nothingness against existence. Jason saw a brilliant light, then heard a deafening siren boom, then felt a blast of wind. He saw a thousand souls shoot skyward, using the power of the blast to rocket them all—children and adults—to Anton. Even that was part of a grand plan, he realized. The power that the children's souls lacked to reach Anton was being supplemented by this awesome force.

He was alive and then . . .

A giant ball of fire then exploded upward in view of all Trinity, testimony to the final struggle. Energy flew in all directions. But Jason sensed a higher purpose, a glorious purpose. As beams of power flew across the land, they found their marks in the bodies of all Trinity's children—their souls! A million children gasped at once. The raw energy supplemented their life force so that, should they die, their souls could make the passage to Anton no matter how young they might be, as could the souls of all future generations. Jason could not believe his senses. He could detect a sea of young souls spark with great energy. Anton used the immense clash of powers between good and evil to achieve something that Anton could not, by himself, accomplish. He twisted evil to do the work of good.

The Circle of Wisdom suddenly collapsed as the tunnels beneath it buckled and fell. A gale-force wind blew in all directions. The refugees on their approach to Meadowtown collapsed to the ground, dropping the stretchers that carried the wounded. The land buckled beneath Endur and the Stone Forest, toppling the stones that jutted above the land. The force rumbled through Mountain High, cracking the stone and disrupting the Granite River's flow deep within its core. King Zak rose to his feet just as the desert rolled beneath him. His eyes saw light one moment, then blackness the next. He was alive and then not. A decision was at hand, and the universe waited for the outcome. Then all went black, and all living things ceased to exist.

The land swayed to a stop. Slowly, the dark clouds dissipated. The gray sun, just past its zenith, grew brighter. Blue washed over the heavens. A warm breeze rose above the land. Every living thing began to wake and realize it was alive. Each tested its existence in its own way. Birds began to chirp. The Races began to rise to their feet. The insects along Mountain Marsh began to buzz. Kings rejoiced in the north. A cheer rose from the stone city of Endur. A tiny girl in Zol crawled from the collapsed remains of Libra, her body scarred only by a tentative smile. Ash began to fall everywhere, upon everything, a veil of wonder and mystery.

There was only silence in the depths of a huge, blackened crater where once sat the Circle of Wisdom. Choking ash and smoke rose from the deep pit. Trees smoldered in the distance. For many hours, there was no sign of life where the greatest of powers had clashed. And then, through the gray, where nothing could possibly survive, where only death could possibly exist, came the sound of struggle and footsteps as two figures emerged slowly from the wreckage and smoke. Their bodies were bloodied and broken. But they were alive, protected by a force that emanated from within, a force bestowed ages ago by an unseen god. It was a force that bound father to son.

CHAPTER 24

SCHOOL BEGINS ANEW

His parents' cot was uncomfortable this morning, just as it had been for the past two weeks. Jason felt every hard knot that protruded from the towels and blankets that comprised its mattress. He turned to ease the pressure upon his back, but it didn't help. Every position brought a dull pain from the bruises that still lined most of his broken body. He realized, though, that he was fortunate to have a bed at all, as most of the townspeople still did not. He was also lucky to have the remains of the stone cottage about him, as the wooden ones had been destroyed by Bantog torches.

Jason stretched his left hand above his head and flexed his fingers into a painful fist, testing his strength. It exhausted him to do so. He raised his right arm, but it did not match the height of the left. It ended abruptly in a blackened, painful stump. His arms appeared like faint shadows, for Jason was nearly blind—the penalty of having seen the radiant clash of immense powers. Weary, a pain throbbing behind his eyes, Jason relaxed his sight and lowered his tired limbs.

Only once during the past two weeks had Jason allowed himself to be prodded from the safety of his stone cottage. He had accompanied his mother to the town store at noonday, and regretted it from the very start. The town was busily under construction. Hammers pounded. Saws ground. Men and women working on new rooftops shouted orders to others below. Children played in the streets. But the noise fell to whispers as Jason and his mother passed. He was an oddity now, and he knew it. The people weren't malicious. But he could sense that, in a way, they were afraid of him . . . and of his power. On their return from the store, an island of silence still surrounding them, one woman backed into Jason by accident. She turned abruptly, startled.

"*The Robe,*" she gasped. It was a strange term, Jason thought. He barely remembered the Major using that reference when directing the townspeople to rally around him. But that's how people now referred to him. He wasn't a person as much as he was a thing.

That was his last trip into the world. It convinced Jason to stay within the comfort of his cottage for a little while longer. He had saved the world, and for that there was great joy. But it came at a high personal cost. The icons were still there. But Jason did not use them. They reminded him too much of what he had become at a time when he wished he could return to the boy he had lost.

After Jason's one and only visit to the store, he began to receive some company. Squeki Joh came on two occasions. On both, his young friend was outwardly nervous, uncomfortable in the presence of his former companion. Prince Alar, Prince Dal, and Tome Joh came next. Those meetings were more comfortable, Jason thought. They understood him better than most, and they were not afraid of him. Jason's strength during this difficult time came from his loving parents. Cyrus and Beth treated him no differently than they had in the past. They even expected him to continue many of his former chores. That was comforting, but still he resisted venturing out into the world.

Jason raised his arms high once again. He tested his sight. It was no better or worse than the moment before. He lowered his arms.

Knock, knock! A gentle fist rapped upon their new wooden door. His mother answered the knock. Beth let out a slight gasp, then recovered. Jason almost sent his mind outward, but he held it back, preferring to let the moment unravel naturally, humanly.

"You must be . . . " Beth began.

"Bea," the voice said.

Jason's mind reeled. He sat up. He straightened his hair, carefully placing some of it over the hole where his left ear had been. His heart fell.

"We've been expecting you," Beth replied. "But I didn't realize that you looked so much like your mother . . . so beautiful."

"Thank you. . . . Is Jason in?"

"Yes . . . of course. Please come in. Excuse the mess."

A few gentle footsteps drew close. Jason felt the cot depress beside him.

Jason saw the hazy outline of her figure. He looked within himself and saw the vivid memory of the girl he had met, allowing his mind to fill the void that his eyes could not. In that recollection, Jason suddenly felt the weight of guilt upon him. Her mother and father died to save him. Jason reached for her. He instantly felt her sweet embrace.

"I'm sorry . . . I'm so sorry," he said sadly.

"I know," Bea comforted. "But we must carry on . . . that's what my parents would want."

Jason felt a strength in her voice that she did not have weeks before in Endur. There was a kiss on his cheek and then Bea rose quickly.

"I must go. We'll speak later," she said. Four determined steps took her to the door.

"But . . . " he began, "you just got here."

"I know, but I'm late for work," she said.

"What work?" he lamented.

There was a heavy pause.

"School in Meadowtown is beginning anew," she finally began. "And I'm the new teacher."

The door opened and closed in a rush. She was gone.

The unbroken chain, Jason thought. Bea had inherited him. And with it came another veil of responsibility, a burden that was the heaviest of loads for the Etha, just as it was for all those that carry the name of Del. Jason suddenly felt a continuity of things. The Pearl of Anton suddenly rose up, spinning wildly in his mind. It, above all else, had waited for the boy to rise above himself and embrace the task before him. There was so much beauty trapped within the crust of the land, and it was Jason's responsibility to unleash it. He was the Chosen One, the protector, the guardian of all that was good, of all that was Wallo. And he had much to do, he realized. He also knew that it was Bea who would see that he did it.

Jason felt hungry, more than he had felt in some time. He rose, guided himself to the newly constructed family table, and sat as his mother poured tea. Just then, the thick oak door swung open again and his father entered, workmen's tools clanging about his belt. The Man's left arm was in a sling, mending a broken bone, but it hadn't kept him from doing his share of rebuilding the town.

"The town is really taking shape," he said.

"Wonderful," said Beth. She brought a loaf of fresh baked bread to the table.

"Mmm . . . smells good," complimented the big Man. "Don't you think, Jase?"

"Yes," Jason said with a smile, his first smile in weeks.

"I just wish we had enough fixings for Twilight Cakes," Beth complained as she began to slice the bread. "But everything was destroyed in the fire."

Jason grinned. He moved to his cot, guiding himself gingerly. He returned with the sack that had accompanied him on his travels. He quickly pulled out three Twilight Cakes—his last—and placed them on the table. They were crumbling. Their golden-brown color had faded. But they were still intact.

"These have been through as much as we have," Jason said.

"By the looks of them," laughed his father, "they've been through considerably more."

EPILOGUE:
DEATH AND REBIRTH

Assorted Histories from the Book of Endur,
Submitted during the Watch of Bea

One year after the Final Contest (1:FC), the full-twilight day did not come. The sun, instead, stayed the same as it had been all year long, never again to become increasingly gray during the winter months. But the festival remained, now called the Festival of the Rebirth.

• • •

In 7:FC, the Festival was graced with a grand wedding where the Circle of Wisdom had once been. Dwarves came. Etha came. Elves came. Men came. Prince Alar was accompanied by his ward, Princess Glenda. A young lady traveled from Zol. Her hair was raven black; her eyes were dazzling green; and her lips were ruby red. Her name was Jena. The two walked together, side by side, dressed in lace and silk, as bridesmaids do. Then, after vows of love and hope and commitment and strength, I, Bea of the Race of Etha, was married to Jason Del.

• • •

In the mist of the summer in 9:FC a baby was born in Endur. The event was described as miraculous, for in the history of the Etha, this was the first child that did not resemble the mother. Instead, the baby girl was born with a full head of red hair and sharp green eyes, identical to those of my husband, Jason Del. But my husband could not see her beauty, as

253

he was now completely blind. We named her Megani. Unfortunately, her grandparents—Beth, Cyrus, and Mora—could not rejoice in the news of her birth, as they had passed to Anton the previous spring. Megani grew strong and learned quickly over the years. So too did she learn of her powers. Whereas my husband forever felt uncomfortable with the powers within, our daughter found them to be a comfort. They were inherited at birth, and she knew none other. So the icons were her resources, like her eyes and ears.

• • •

In the year 10:FC miraculous events began to occur throughout the eastern lands. Water holes long dry became filled with soothing waters. Orchards long dead lived again. Tall, healthy grass grew where none had grown before. And with each tale came stories of a robed figure that traveled by night and slept by day, always in the company of an Etha and their child. But the great desert to the north and the swamps to the south still persisted. Then, in the year 12:FC, a nomadic innkeeper from Zol was escorted to the Great Hall of the Eastern Dwarf King. He carried a handwritten note that King Zak read silently.

"Years ago you tested my courage with the edge of your ax. My head still throbs at the memory. I learned much in your halls of stone . . . about courage, compassion, friendship and loss. I cannot repay all that is due to you and to your Race. But please accept this small gift in appreciation: tomorrow, when the sun reaches its highest point, the mighty river that once brought life to your kingdom will come again. Treat her well."

The Robe

The Dwarf king glanced up. His sight rested on a patch of stone at the far end of the hall. Buried deep within the granite was an ax with traces of blood and flesh still dotting its surface. He kept it as a reminder of how narrowly he escaped madness. The next day, a great river flowed from north to south in the desolate east. By spring, the desert to the north was in bloom and the swamps to the south had turned to fertile grasslands.

Trinity was restored.

• • •

In the year 70:FC, on a warm summer day, two robed figures stood along the northern shore of Spirit Lake. One figure was straight and tall and had all the signs of youth, though she was no longer a youth. The other was bent and wrinkled and slow, coughing as he walked, his lungs wheezing with age. She was my daughter, Megani, and he, my husband, Jason Del. The morning sun shone brightly. The blue lake sparkled. The sounds of life were all about the shore. Just past midmorning, a hush came over the lake. Jason knew instantly that what had happened once long ago was happening again. Our daughter was fixed, frozen in the moment. I alone was allowed to witness what came next.

"You have done well," said a voice.

"Who are you?" asked Jason Del.

"I am that which created the Races . . . the One that created you."

The aging Jason Del dropped to one knee. "How can I serve you?"

"Your service is done. Now, it is for me to honor your wishes."

"I cannot bring myself to ask for anything," Jason said, humbled.

"This is why you deserve it so," the voice said.

Jason winced with pain. He pressed his eyelids. He blinked wildly. Light exploded. Jason shielded his eyes against it. It was a light he had not witnessed in years.

"Behold your daughter!" the voice said.

The old man looked up, joyfully, his sight restored. His saw Megani for the first time. Tears flowed freely down the elder's face. He could see lines of wisdom on her forehead and an air of nobility about her chin. She bore all the traces of the Royal House of Del. Jason then looked over the lake. His eyes danced at the sight of the clear blue water, rimmed by vivid green foliage that met a blue morning sky. The yellow sun, now above the trees, cast crisp shadows upon the eastern shore. But there was no apparition, no spirit to give a body to the voice that spoke yet again.

"And a second wish is done!"

Jason lurched forward. Powers were plucked from his mind. The icons of Wizard and Wallo were gone. Great relief and great emptiness washed over his face. But it was a peaceful emptiness, a sense of responsibility gone. Jason took a deep, rattling breath and exhaled it slowly. His body still hurt, to be sure, but his mind was at ease for the first time in a long while.

"And another wish is done, Jason Del. Walk forward and feel younger soil beneath your feet!"

Jason Del took a few staggering steps forward and felt a renewed strength flow through him. Heat surged. Muscles flexed. His flesh grew supple. He raised his hands . . . *both* hands . . . and felt a younger man's skin, unwrinkled by the demands of great responsibilities. He felt his left ear, and it was restored. He was fifteen again. He turned about and saw his former, aging self fall to the ground in a heap of ashes. I wept.

"It is time we go," the voice boomed.

Jason gazed at his daughter and me.

"I came expecting to die, but now I don't know how to leave them."

"Both already know of your fate. But worry not. You will all meet again in a different place and in a different time . . . a time of my choosing."

A different voice suddenly called from over the lake. Jason Del jerked his head about frantically, his eyes widening in disbelief. It called again.

"Farlo!"

"Theda?!" Jason cried out, his eyes darting toward the center of the lake. "Theda . . . is that really you?!"

"Yeah . . . you made me proud. It should have been you all along. Always you, Jason. Always. But it's time to come home now. Mother has dinner almost ready. Then after we eat we're going see Ben Wateri and David Grimm. They've been waiting a long time to say they're sorry."

"Listen to your brother," said another voice, that of Beth Del. "And wash your hands. We have company tonight. You know how particular Sara and IAM can be. And they brought their son, Jerel, too. We all made the passage to Anton . . . and now it's your turn!"

Jason Del—the boy—knew his mother's voice like none other. He bolted over the lake, his feet skimming just above the water's surface. Every muscle flew. There was no hesitation, no doubt, no fear. He didn't even seem to notice the blue lake disappearing beneath him, giving way to the green of a meadow. He saw only a well-built stone cottage, Farlo wrapped about its trim, as a plume of smoke rose from its chimney to meet the bluest sky he had ever seen.

Jason Del was home.

Faithfully,
Bea